The Irish Prime Minister

Fergal is desperate to escape from his Provisional IRA past - having misguidedly attached himself to the terrorist organisation at a very young age - but there is too much in his background that prevents him making a clean break.

The Republican terrorist group have devised a strategy to achieve their goal of a united Irish nation by ingratiating one on their members within a British political organisation, ultimately rising to become British Prime Minister.

Escaping to America, Fergal has to avoid the clutches of the FBI, the British Secret Service, and his old terrorist allies – all of them want information from him, but most want him eliminated.

Also by the same author
THE DHOW

An Islamic terrorist, waiting in London for other cell members to arrive from the Arabian Gulf, is incandescent with fury when he discovers that his landlady/lover has disposed of one of his possessions; in a rage, he brutally murders her, the reclamation of his Dhow being the key to his mission's success.

Meanwhile, a small eclectic group of Londoners, friends and acquaintances, unwittingly become entangled with the Islamic terrorist's plans. An innocent transaction will bring the group into danger, the terrorist organisation relentlessly pursuing their possession across London, Ireland, then back to London, changing forever the lives of the Londoners.

A bloody trail of mayhem and destruction ensues, with a battle ensuing to prevent the fundamentalists carrying out a major atrocity in the heart of the City.

**THE IRISH
PRIME MINISTER**

DESMOND B. HARDING

Text copyright © 2016 Desmond B Harding
All Rights Reserved

ISBN-13: 978-1535423380
ISBN-10: 1535423382

For Gordon

Special thanks to my wife Juliette for her support, editing and her proof reading.

Also an acknowledgement to Kate Windley, (née Foottit), for her medicinal advice –
I hasten to add that the advice was gained prior to my daughter Laura also deciding to take up Pharmacy!

Finally, none of the characters or incidents portrayed in this story are based on people currently living or dead, nor on real events.

Chapter 1

Sweaty palms supporting his cheeks, elbows firmly pressed down on the windowsill, Fergal stared out of the window. The gathering rain clouds matched his mood, his expression altering from abject shock and surprise, to heart-breaking sorrow. The sky darkened, the heavens appearing to match his utter despair, the almost black clouds releasing the stored water in thunderous torrents. But as quickly as it had started, the torrent abated, the rain empathising with the boy's sorrow, the falling water softening from a heavy downpour to a more sympathetic trickle, raindrops tenderly caressing the glass. Tiny rivulets of water smeared softly downwards, tapping delicately against the cold glass of the window pane.

Tears formed in Fergal's eyes, welling over the rims, the salty liquid leaking downwards, spiralling over the young boy's cheeks, seeming to match and equal the droplets of rainwater. Through his tears and the heavy pounding of his breaking heart Fergal barely discerned an external sound, an annoying, repetitive siren-like noise, a sound that battered at the inner reaches of his own personal hell.

The disturbance was a voice, calling out his name, initially muted and then with increasing impatience and harshness, finally anger, due to the lack of response.

Fergal gulped, rubbed his eyes, sniffed loudly and swallowing the remains of tears and mucous that had gathered at the back of his throat, turned away from Mother Nature's attempt at providing him with soothing comfort. With red-rimmed eyes, runny nose and a lump in his throat that he felt, and indeed hoped, would choke him, he turned reluctantly to face the cause of the intrusion into his private moment of grief.

"Fergal," snapped the harsh, intruding voice, "Are you coming or not?" Without pausing for a reply his Grandmother barked, "Your father is waiting for you and he doesn't need this." She paused, adding with venom, "Dolores...your *mother*...is in the coffin and the undertaker is waiting to leave."

Little fists tightly clenched, Fergal wanted to reach out and thump this woman, this hard old bat, a woman whom his mother had never cared for anyway. God, he really hated his father's mother; it was such a tragedy that his mammy's mother had died two years previously. And now, his own mammy...dead; more tears began to well within and he desperately attempted to fight them away, keeping back the increasing tide of emotion that seemed sure to crush his little soul.

The Grandmother tugged him by the hand, pulling the grieving little boy through into the dining room.

Fergal's despairing eyes focused on the object that contained his mother, the coffin resting on the dining table, and unable to control himself he released a woeful sob. With tears cascading down his cheeks, he tore himself free from his Grandmother's grip, leaping forward to embrace the hard, cold, highly polished wood that now encased his beloved mammy.

But in his headlong rush he stumbled, thumping his head on one of the coffin's brass handles. Regardless, the boy reached forward, tiny hands desperately clasping at the ice cold wood, desperate for one more hug from his beloved Mammy.

Oblivious to the physical pain and of the lurid, purple bruise expanding on his forehead, he gripped the coffin as if it were still the living beating heart of his Mammy. Fergal was not prepared to let his Mother go.

But then he was roughly grasped by his Grandmother, her nails digging into his flesh, clawing away at his fierce grip on the wood. Unable to withstand the pressure, the old woman's talons sinking deeper into his flesh, he was dragged from the coffin, from the wooden box that contained the person that he'd loved above any other thing.

"Pull yourself together, boy," snarled the old woman, forcing the child backwards across the room.

Eyes sheathed in salty tears, Fergal glanced forlornly at his father, a father who was almost unrecognisable, the man's normal happy-go-lucky and cheerful demeanour now totally and utterly etched with grief. Fergal and his father needed each other as never before but each was unable to address the other's needs, to mutually console the hurt and pain inside, both immersed in their own private world of sorrow, anger, and utter hopelessness.

At that moment Fergal did his best to suppress the thought of cursing his hated stillborn sister, the sister whose birth had caused his mother's demise. Fergal's paternal Grandmother was the only person who, evidently, was not devastated, the facial expression of sorrow not matched by the immense joy shining in the woman's eyes.

It was not long before the funeral cortege wound its way slowly along the street, the mourners marching – if the slow pace could be described as marching – behind the black hearse that carried the coffin containing Fergal's mother and stillborn baby sister. He desperately wanted to see his mammy, to hold on to the rear of the hearse, to touch, or to be as close as possible to her but the four pallbearers, the paid undertaker's men with their ridiculously large hats, obscured his view. He quickened his pace, attempting to overtake the undertaker's men, but the firm hand of his Grandmother continued to pull him back.

The solemnity of the occasion was suddenly shattered by a loud beating of drums and stomping of feet; the drums pounding a seemingly monotonous rhythm, reverberating round the streets, resulting in a cacophony of unwelcome sounds that echoed off the walls of the houses.

The funeral procession was suddenly and surprisingly halted in its tracks by a group of advancing Orangemen - an Orange Band, the vanguard of an Orange day Parade. The marching men appeared as if spirited by magic, their numbers increasing tenfold as they turned the corner, marching brazenly down Fergal's street. The Protestant Orangemen had decided to deviate from their planned, approved route, intent on showing their superiority by parading through a predominately Catholic area.

The first Band was closely followed by another, then more in quick succession; each Orange Order Lodge keen to put out as many members as possible in the field, the objective to continue their 'right' of parading, but primarily to celebrate the victory in 1690 of William of Orange - known colloquially as 'King Billie' - over the Catholic majority of Ireland.

The marching men of the Orange Order, dressed in their finest regalia, their Sunday best, chests swelled with pride, bright orange sashes across their chests and over their shoulders, bowler hats perched on heads, strutted along the tarmac, their inalienable right to demonstrate their Protestant superiority - particularly in this predominately Catholic street - not to be denied.

Each parading Orange Lodge was led by a man carrying a banner proudly proclaiming the identity of that particular lodge, some of the marchers beating out a regular rhythm on the small drums supported on their hips. A select few carried huge 'Lambeg' drums, big monsters that only the very strong could cope with; the massive drums resting on their chests and supported by thick straps wound around the back of each drummer's neck. As the 'Lambeg' drummers, muscular arms rising and falling, seemingly huge hands clamped on the long drum sticks, beat the drum skins with powerful strokes, the sound pounded deep within Fergal's head, scouring his brain and accentuating his grief.

Fergal's family, loved ones, friends, the Priest and various other mourners, showing their love and respect to Fergal's mother, were taken completely by surprise, the initial mortified reaction of astonishment leaving the Priest's words of prayer frozen on his lips. However, the preliminary horror and shock quickly changed to a mood of intense anger, the Orange Men's lack of respect quickly turning the members of the Funeral party into a demonic howling mob, a mob of equal intolerance to the Orangemen.

The mourners, foregoing decorum, leaped at the advancing Orange Men who immersed in their own designs and importance, their right to march, were themselves caught by surprise when it dawned on them that they had inadvertently stumbled into a funeral cortege.

Too late to retreat, the Orange Men were set upon by the mourners, led by the raging, indignant, and no longer Christian, Catholic Priest, his fists flailing in any direction. Initially taken aback, the Orange Procession marchers quickly regained their composure, the two opposing groups tearing into each another with mutual hatred and loathing.

Hearing the resulting cacophony, the resident Catholic population from the surrounding streets quickly tumbled out from their homes, giving their support to the previously outnumbered mourners, the brawl between the two religious groups developing into a melee, and ultimately a full scale riot.

Separated from his Grandmother, Fergal attempted to reach the now stationary hearse and his beloved mammy. He ducked in and out between the legs of wildly fighting men and women but was knocked off his feet and sent skidding into a brick wall, thumping his already bruised head in the process.

Dimly he discerned the sound of police sirens, followed by army whistles and the distant, but distinctive sound of approaching military vehicles. The knock on his head took away any further immediate conscious memory, his eyes closing to the chaos and mayhem developing around him.

Coming round with a thumping pain in his head, an unknown hand pulled Fergal to his feet, the scene slowly unfolding to his waking consciousness leaving him static with shock. His Mammy's hearse was on fire, burning ferociously, his father desperately tugging at the rear door in a futile attempt to recover the flaming coffin.

The street resounded with a huge whoosh as the hearse's fuel tank suddenly erupted, engulfing Fergal's father in a fireball of flaming fuel, metal and wood.

Fergal watched, dumbfounded, his father's hair and clothes instantly immersed in flames, the remaining parent reeling round, calling out in agony, then floundering like a demented demon. Before any of the mourners or arriving security personnel could reach Fergal's father, the man's entire body was engulfed in the brightly burning flames. Fergal's father collapsed back towards the hearse, a human torch, sizzling furiously, re-joining his beloved wife in death, the sickening smell of burnt flesh and clothing melding together in the joint funeral pyre of Fergal's parents and unknown baby sister.

With legs no longer capable of supporting him, the boy sunk to the ground, his wails of anguish and disbelief ignored by the shell-shocked mourners, most particularly by his paternal Grandmother whose anger was directed at Dolores and that brat of a son of Dolores.

The Grandmother's mind was raging, furious, her thoughts racing, screaming; if the bitch Dolores hadn't married her boy then none of this would have happened, and her own son would still be alive. *That woman's* brat would pay in the years to come, oh yes, she would make sure of that! She would make sure that the woman's son suffered because she had had the audacity to marry and take away her own boy.

The Grandmother's twisted emotions would not allow her to love the fruit, the produce of her own boy, her own Grandson.
When night fell, Fergal cried himself to sleep, the word "Mammy" frozen on his lips. From that night his warmth, tenderness, kindness and all empathetic emotions died along with the death of his immediate family. The loving son that had been Fergal was to grow

up without experiencing any sentiments other than cold hatred. Good fruit was to be left to slowly rot on the vine, Fergal's soul handed over to the Devil's grip.

Chapter 2

Vernon Cole peered out through puffy, swollen eyelids and attempted to wipe away the blood that was trickling down from the nasty gash above his right eye. But, of course, he couldn't; his attempts to carry out any action were no longer in the realms of his control. His hands were tied, painfully tight, behind his back and he was roped very firmly to a heavy wooden hard back chair. He could barely move any part of his body, his muscles long ceasing to function effectively.

Vernon stared at the smiling face of his assailant. The man was not smiling to try and demonstrate his superior ability over a British soldier; no, he was smiling because he was genuinely pleased at the pain he was causing. His persecutor, a member of the Provisional Irish Republican Army, a terrorist organisation born out of the original IRA, was a master of torture and of inflicting pain and it was obvious to Vernon that this bully was revelling in every moment, jubilant with each tiny or major assault on the captured soldier's naked body.

Vernon had tried not to give the man too much pleasure, trying his utmost to stifle his screams, or gritting his teeth, his bound, nail-less hands clawing into each other as each fresh punishment had been administered.

The two separate bullets through both kneecaps had been one of the earliest incidences of his excruciating suffering, both to cause maximum pain and to forestall any attempt at escape.

His girlfriend, poor dead Fiona, had been made to watch his earlier periods of suffering. But the bastards - for there were three of them in this 'brave' little Provisional IRA cell - had had their fun with Fiona, before callously shooting her through the head. After that, Vernon no longer cared what happened to him; he had been frustrated and helpless as the thugs assaulted his woman, the anger within him, an apoplectic rage, almost causing him to have a heart attack.

Vernon's finger nails had been torn off, the Provo thug using a pair of rusty pliers. His big toes had been severed, the 'cell' leader using a pot of warm tar to stem the flow of blood that resulted. The soldier knew the names of his assailants - for some reason they had wanted him to know; he guessed because there was no way out for him, no escape. Although the man inflicting the pain, Colm, was not the leader - the cell leader being a man called Liam - the other two men merely stood by and smiled, enjoying the show. Seamus, the third IRA man, had been eager to join in in inflicting the punishment but Liam had held him back. For some reason, unknown to Vernon, this was to be Colm's kill.

Vernon's mind drifted, his brain trying its best to take him away from the current source of unending pain and torment. This had been his second tour of duty in Northern Ireland and the irony of it was that he should have left two days ago but chose to spend the first few days of his leave with Fiona's family in Donegal, the only County in Northern Ireland that was still part of the Republic of Ireland.

Huge mistake, a fatal error, not only for him but for Fiona as well. He hoped to God that these madmen's vengeance - against what Vernon didn't know - would end with his and Fiona's death, and that no further pain would be inflicted on her kinfolk.
Poor Fiona, a Catholic girl, seeking to improve her circumstances, had left her small village in Donegal and had headed to Londonderry where she had secured a job working as a secretary in the local Council. Unfortunately for her, she had met Vernon when he had been designated to deliver to some papers to the Council planning offices. They had hit it off almost instantly and became inseparable. But now, the few weeks of unbridled joy had been brought to such a horrific, painful, disastrous and bloody end.
"Oh shit, Fiona," he thought, "I'm so sorry I brought this on you; I wish to God I had never met you."

Vernon wondered if any of his family or Regiment would ever find out about his fate. He doubted it. He knew what his fate would be, where his body was to be buried, and how Colm would finally put him to death. The Provo man had enjoyed describing all the potential foul actions, all the anticipated torture and the infliction of pain, before carrying out the deeds; the bully enjoyed and revelled in his brutality.

The brave British soldier hoped that he would die before they cut his balls off, then his penis, which was to be used to finally choke him; all because the penis had sullied a good Catholic girl. "Absolute fucking hypocrites; the callous, deceitful, murdering bastards!" mentally raged Vernon, particularly after what they had done to his lovely Fiona. The way they had abused and used her; he tried to erase the memory from his tortured mind.

God! Vernon had never known such mental rage, anguish or frustration! They were cowardly men, bullies, hiding behind masks in public, with no respect for life, never prepared to meet their adversaries on a level playing field.

His immediate Officer in the Royal Engineers, Lieutenant Simon Spraggs, had often joked that because of his initials, Vernon was the only V.C. currently serving in the Regiment, but Vernon didn't feel that brave at the moment. He just wanted to die. What he actually wanted was to be cut free and then kill these evil fucking bastards for what they had done to Fiona, but he knew that wasn't possible. So, he just wanted it to be over, to die; for the pain to end.

Unfortunately, almost deadened by the excruciating pain, it was well over another hour before Vernon's weary, torn, worn out and bleeding body was allowed to escape to whatever existed after death.

Colm turned away from his broken victim's body and with eyes bright from killer lust, calmly cleaned his knife on the previously scattered clothing that had been torn from Fiona's body. The Soldier and Fiona were not permitted to be buried together. Oh no, Colm was not even going to allow them that pleasure in the next life. Fiona's abused body was to be disposed of in a peat bog in Donegal and something 'special', something different, was reserved for Vernon's corpse.

Chapter 3

Fergal didn't know the exact details of his mission. He had been allocated a stolen car and had been instructed to drive across the border from Ulster to Donegal. Tired and weary, he reached his destination, the rear car park of a small hotel in a Donegal village not too far over the border, and waited, fearful and alone, for the arrival of Colm and Seamus.

Fergal's stomach rumbled - he hadn't eaten since breakfast and now it was nearly nine thirty at night. He had forgone lunch, the attractions of an available and nubile young lady proving more alluring to a nineteen year old than the partaking of food. But now, more than anything, he needed a drink to steady his nerves. He waited and waited, sitting with increasing nervousness, hunching lower and lower in the driver's seat, desperate for Colm to turn up. Starving, tired and thirsty, his nervous restlessness gradually overcoming the instruction to remain invisible sitting in the darkness; he glanced furtively up and down, thoroughly scrutinising his surroundings. There were only two other cars and a pick-up truck in the car park but he was still very nervous at being noticed or approached even though he was not carrying anything incriminating on him and the car number plates had been swapped.

Finally throwing caution to the wind, Fergal exited his car, determined to grab at least a pint of beer before resuming his wait. Turning to lock his car he almost leapt out of his skin at the sudden heavy hand that thudded down on his shoulder; he almost screamed out, but the deep, gruff voice of Colm warned him to be quiet. Delighted at the arrival of company, he turned to face his colleague but the smile was instantly wiped from Fergal's face.

Colm was furious, almost apoplectic, admonishing Fergal for getting out of his car and for not being patient, not following implicit instructions. Discipline was paramount.

Fergal had tried to protest, explaining about his hunger, his thirst, but Colm was not prepared to listen to reason. He punched Fergal in the gut, making the teenager double up, the air expelling from youth's lungs in a frenzied gasp. With Fergal desperately trying to draw in air, Colm continued to berate the youngster, lecturing him about obeying instructions whilst threatening all kind of dire consequences if he didn't comply in future.

Suitably mollified and with the hunger still gnawing inside, Fergal had climbed back into his car and waited for his next instructions,

Colm having taken possession of the car keys. The teenager was aware of the car boot being opened and of a subsequent heavy thump when an object was deposited within the boot. The lid was then slammed, locked, and the car keys returned to the frightened and bemused teenager.

Colm had then instructed Fergal to return to Northern Ireland and meet up with a man called Brian who would be waiting at a known 'safe' house in Derry. Scared and worried as to what his cargo might be and still with a raging hunger and thirst, Fergal had followed instructions to the letter, his mission to hand both car and unknown contents to the man called Brian who would take over from there.

Crossing the border had been a nervous time but the British soldiers had paid scant attention to Fergal as he and his secret cargo had trundled through the check point. They obviously did not consider him to be a serious threat, only giving his vehicle a cursory check.

Fergal had never met Brian before and neither would ever meet up again. Unbeknown to Fergal, his cargo had been the deceased remains of Vernon Cole, wrapped in plastic, immersed in yellow building sand and all encased in a heavy canvas sheet. Vernon's brutalised and badly treated remains were subsequently 'buried' in the foundations of a new construction that was taking place at a Londonderry RUC police station. The Provisional IRA thought that that would be a 'nice touch'.

*   *   *

The man called Brian was killed two days later, a successful joint operation between the British Army and the RUC that flushed out Brian and two female colleagues who had been planning to plant a bomb in a favourite haunt of the British soldiers. Brian had not wanted to 'come quietly' and, stupidly attempting to shoot his way out of the trap, had died in a well-deserved hail of bullets.

Vernon's Cole's corpse had gained at least one moment of retribution.

Chapter 4

The eerie, silent calm of the night was disturbed by the distant sound of a cough; it was a hard and rasping vibration that grated on Fergal's nerves, a cough that could have escaped only from the lungs of a practised heavy smoker. He realised, much later, that he should have taken more notice of the harsh cough.

With the thick cloud cover making visibility quite poor, Fergal made his way carefully down the street. The air was very still, not oppressive but with a cold dampness evidenced by the hot vapour trails emanating and curling away from the mouths of the three people who were crouching within a deeply recessed shop doorway. Other than those three individuals the place appeared deserted, most of the inhabitants of the town having long since retired to their beds.

Fergal joined his colleagues, none of them speaking, a mere nod acknowledging his presence.

Through the large plate glass window of the shop he vaguely discerned faint images of bottles and cans, sweets and other confectionery. Above the shop doorway was a sign that Fergal remembered reading yesterday, the sign stating 'Dermot O'Brien - Licensed to sell beer, wine and spirits'. Another faint luminescent sign within the dimly lit murky shop interior revealed words that he could barely distinguish, indicating that 'Benson and Hedges', and presumably other cigarette brands, were available.

The clock of a nearby church struck one in the morning as Fergal, now crouching with his colleagues in the shop doorway, stuck out his head and scrutinised the road, straining his eyes, particularly trying to focus on the entrance of a British Army Post barely discernible at the far end of the road.

The approaches to the Army Post were protected by enormous, heavy concrete bollards positioned in the widened section of the road and set at angles to permit slow vehicular access, yet sufficiently spaced for the defenders to fire upon anything untoward or to prevent most potential attack machinery, whether it be the size of a three wheeler or an armoured car. A Union Flag flying from an observation post/watchtower identified the premises and its occupants.

The flag, gently ruffling in the moderate night breeze that had sprung up, was softly illuminated by a nearby dimly lit street lamp, (one of only three that were still operating in this street), the light reflecting off the lens of two forward pointing army arc lights positioned at the top of the wall, just behind a barbed wire fence, but currently switched off.

Fergal turned to face his companions, Colm, Bernie, and Seamus. Colm, the evident leader of this group of Republican rebels, was cradling a homemade mini-bazooka/rocket launcher and he grimaced in response to Fergal's glance. Seamus nervously swallowed, tightly gripping an automatic rifle in his right hand, his knuckles turning white as a result of the intense pressure of his grip.

Fergal licked his dry lips attempting to bring saliva to his mouth, his tongue merely sticking to the roof of his mouth. With a nod from Colm he left the sanctuary of the shop doorway and made his way, stealthily, in the opposite direction to the British Army Post. His task tonight was to be one of relative safety; all he had to do was watch the approaches from the RUC Police Station that was barely a mile distant. In his pocket was an old police whistle which Fergal was to blow if anything was amiss or if he became aware of any extra security activity.

Taking up his allotted position on the approach route from the Police Station, many streets away from the potential danger of his colleagues, Fergal skulked into the darkness, his body pressed flat against the end wall of a terraced house. Despite not being directly involved in the 'action' part of this terrorist operation, Fergal's heart was pounding furiously, the blood racing through his veins, the incessant throbbing resulting in a dull ache growing in his temples. Deciding that he was still partially visible, he crouched down, as low as he could, squatting so low that his arse was barely off the ground. It was difficult to peer into the inky blackness of the night but he forced his eyes to focus, the strain of trying to observe exaggerating the earlier effect of the throbbing blood, the dull ache growing into an intense, nervous headache.

An ominous foreboding began to envelope him and he shivered uncontrollably. He knew the path that he had inadvertently taken but didn't know how to break free from the terrorists' grip.

*   *   *

Having given Fergal sufficient time to get into place, the three remaining IRA terrorists prepared to set in motion their intended act of sabotage and murder, but Bernie was uneasy. "Sure, don't worry; we've run through this a thousand times; we'll be long gone before these 'ejiets' realise what's happening," reassured Colm, smiling affectionately.

Bernie grasped Colm's arm, looking up into his face, gazing searchingly into his eyes. Their eyes locked in magnetic contact, neither wishing to break the connection. Time seemed to stand still. Seamus shuffled his feet, his nervousness giving way to aggressive rudeness, "Come on; we have to move *now!*"

Bernie maintained her tight grip on Colm's sleeve, not wishing to let go; something was troubling her. Colm glanced from Seamus to the Army post, then back at Bernie. He frowned, anxious to press on but aware of Bernie's concern; his face broke into a sickly grin. "I have a bad feeling...a premonition," Bernie whispered almost inaudibly.

Colm hugged her, gently brushing the hair away from her face and gazed at her resolutely but with affection, staring deeply into her eyes. "Don't be daft, woman. We've done this many times. And we 'reckied' this place for three weeks – it can't go wrong; we have an hour before the next street patrol."

Seamus continued to shuffle his feet, his agitation evident; he fidgeted restlessly with his automatic weapon, an AK47, a gun named after its Russian inventor, Kalashnikov, the last two digits taken from the year of its most successful modification/specification update. This particular AK47 had begun life in a basement factory in Gdansk in Poland; had then been shipped out to Georgia - at that time still an integral part of the Soviet Empire – and had subsequently been sold to a terrorist organisation based in Libya. Ultimately, it had been donated as a 'charitable gift' to the IRA but the automatic rifle's cartridges had been paid for separately – a successful IRA drug trafficking operation providing the necessary funding.

Bernie was not to be fobbed off, her pleading persistent, something gnawing away at her very being. She tightened her grip on Colm's sleeve, "*Please Colm!*"

Her mood was beginning to unsettle Colm, making him increasingly agitated and uneasy, "For God's sake Bernie, will ya let go." The colour had drained from Bernie's face; something was very wrong, an unknown fear building inside her. A shiver ran down her spine, her grip on Colm's arm tightening to such an extent that she was now pinching his skin. "For God's sake woman, you're hurting me," protested Colm attempting to pull free.

"Listen," she paused, wiping a tear from her eye whilst gazing pleadingly into Colm's eyes, her own eyes reflecting only sorrow and despair, "Will you take care of our boy? Promise me you'll take care of him!"

Colm startled, was completely taken back by Bernie's intensity and by her words; opening his mouth he was unsure of how to retort, speech currently beyond him. Stunned and with a hint of anger, his eyes flickered in the direction of Seamus. Controlling the impulse to shout at Bernie, he mumbled, "Shush, Bernie, not now, not here, not in front of..."

Bernie was not in the mood to be patronised, aggressively interrupting, "Oh *sod* him; Seamus *knows*, everyone *knows* - even Jeannie, your bloody wife *knows!*"

Colm clutched Bernie's hand and pulled it free from his arm, his eyes burning with anger, "Shut up, will you, you're making enough noise to wake the devil and what the hell are you saying woman...be quiet!" He turned to Seamus, "I'm sorry Seamus, she doesn't know what she's saying." Agitated, he focused his attention on Bernie, searching her eyes, questioning with subdued ire. But the words spoken were directed at Seamus, "It's the fear, her mind is not working rationally."

Fresh tears formed in Bernie's eyes and she blinked, brushing away a falling tear, softly murmuring to the man behind Colm, "Seamus, will you tell him? Everyone knows, don't they?"

Shocked, ashen, Colm reeled round to look at Seamus, his eyes boring into his accomplice's pallid face. Seamus, under Colm's intense gaze, didn't know how to respond, awkwardly stuttering, "Ah, um, I don't..."

Bernie hissed, "Seamus!"

Seamus lowered his head, embarrassed and with resignation, softly mumbled, "Yes, we all know; Jeannie knows." Colm turned away from both of them, gently thumping his head against the shop door whilst moaning in despair, making Seamus think that his friend was ready to become an inmate of a mental institution, "What have we done?" Colm muttered over and over to himself.

Bernie pulled Colm towards her and lifted up his downcast head; holding his cheeks in her hands and staring into his eyes with a fierce, but deep love and affection, she gently pleaded, "Please

Colm, whatever happens, please watch over our boy Alistair. He's nearly nine years old now and you would be so very proud of him." She swallowed hard, holding back the tears welling within. "He has your eyes." Brusquely, she then wiped the tears from her eyes and with a voice raw with emotion, persisted, "My cousin Maggie and her prick of a husband, Robert, have formally adopted him. They have just moved to a big house in Edinburgh and will be able to give Alistair the home and security that he needs. Maggie loves him as if he was her own - that useless twat of a husband hasn't been able to give her, her own child!" She paused, gathering her thoughts, then continued, her voice hoarse with emotion, "If anything happens to me, keep in touch with Maggie and watch over Alistair; me mammy can give you the details."

Confused and bewildered, Colm didn't know what to say or how to respond. Not only was he astounded that everyone, particularly his wife Jeannie, appeared to know of his and Bernie's secret lovechild, but Bernie's apprehensive mood swept through him like a dose of diarrhoea. He dragged his hand across his forehead, the sweat sticking to the back of the hand, the bulging veins in his temples feeling if they were about to explode.

Absentmindedly wiping the back of his hand on his jacket, he stared out into the darkness, merely as if by saying nothing would make the whole unpleasant episode disappear. Bernie was insistent, "Colm, promise; promise me that you'll watch over our son!"

Still dazed and uncomfortable, Colm looked deeply into the moist eyes of Bernie, "Don't be silly woman. You're talking crazy; nothing's going to go wrong."

"Colm!" Bernie fixed him with a steely, unrelenting stare.

"Damn it woman, yes, all right," Colm resignedly retorted, "Now let's go, before we lose the opportunity to surprise those 'Brit' bastards."

Sweating profusely, Seamus peered out from the shop doorway but his nerves affected his guts and he farted, then distractedly re-checked his automatic weapon. Colm sniffed, screwing up his nose in disgust. "Phew Seamus, you stink, you dirty bastard. You'll give us away to anyone within a radius of a mile." Realising this was a good opportunity to change the subject and alleviate Bernie's concerns he stroked her face, grinned, and said, "Remind me to get Seamus a strong deodorant."

Bernie's tear-stained face melted into a warm smile and pulling

Colm towards her, she embraced him, fiercely planting a long and passionate kiss firmly on his lips. After what seemed like a lifetime to Seamus but was actually only a few seconds, Colm reluctantly broke his lips free. "God Bernie, you'll make me trip up over my third leg."

Getting increasingly nervous, Seamus fidgeted from one foot to the other, then removing a balaclava mask from his pocket, he put it on, almost getting his AK47 caught up with the mask. Colm and Bernie, observing Seamus out of the corner of their eyes, grinned affectionately at one other. He gently released himself from Bernie's hold, "Keep a watchful eye. We'll work our way through the back streets and come out the other side of the Army Post; if anything goes wrong we meet at Father O'Shea's, okay? Fergal will go straight to his place."

Reluctantly and with deep reservation, Bernie nodded meekly in response.

Colm put on his balaclava mask and with a quick glance out of the doorway, led Seamus out into the darkness. Glancing back, he lifted his mask above his lips and blew a kiss at Bernie. She smiled warmly in response but then involuntarily shuddered as Colm and Seamus slunk off along the street, the pair quickly becoming immersed in the inky blackness. Renewed tears sprang up in Bernie's eyes, one teardrop breaking free and slowly, gently, trickled down her cheek. A shudder ran through her body, quickly followed by an immense feeling of doom that totally engulfed her. Anyone watching would not have realised what a monster this seemingly gentle woman had been over the preceding years. But her immense feeling of trepidation, of impending doom, made her want to run away, to seek sanctuary. Something was wrong but she had no idea what. Her morose feeling of dread took her thoughts back in time to that night in Glasgow, a night of nine years ago, a black, stormy night. The memories of that night, full of pain, yet providing the most joyous thing in her life, flashed through her mind.

Chapter 5

The daylight hours had grown shorter, the weather stuttering in confusion, vying uncertainly between the rump end of autumn and the early stages of winter. The previous day's balmy weather had been replaced by cold, fierce swirling winds that howled along the damp pavements, buffeting against the dowdy tenement buildings of these Glasgow back streets, sweeping onward into the night.

The dark, jet black, oppressive night had been suddenly split asunder by a dramatic flash of lightening, hurriedly pursued by a booming peal of thunder. The lightening, rather than bringing relief to the menacing darkness, merely served to accentuate the heavy, repressive, and strangely eerie atmosphere. The single flash of fierce lightening had been quickly followed by further onslaughts of zigzagging lines of phosphoric light as each bolt of sizzling brightness arrowed its way downwards.

Not to be outdone, the thunder rumbled in tandem, each thunderclap in ever decreasing time gaps, desperately trying to keep tempo with the lightening; the night air had erupted into a maelstrom of piercing bolts of lightning accompanied by deafening peals of thunder. Previously invisible funereal black clouds had been instantly lit up in the night sky, the cloud cover hanging like a thick blanket, dark and heavy, spreading over the city. Taking their cue, signalled by both the lightning and thunder, the clouds had joined in heaven's wild party, the sinister rain clouds erupting like overflowing dams, spilling their contents, walls of water spewing forth, cascading downwards, the ensuing thunderstorm washing away every tiny creature and some of the larger ones that had not had the foresight to seek shelter before the storm broke.

A taxi entered this alien world, briefly interrupting the stormy night's proceedings, its presence unasked and unwelcome to the raging storm. The vehicle had sped along the sodden street that divided the rows of depressing tenement blocks, the beam of its headlights making a futile attempt to dissect the elements. The car swerved to avoid a flash of lightening, the zigzag arrow of pure white energy racing downwards in hot pursuit of the moving target; as the flash of white energy hurtled to its death on the tarmac, the taxi driver, soaked with beads of fearful sweat, pulled his vehicle into the kerb ignoring the stream of oaths and profanities that emanated from his back seat passenger.

Depositing his heavily pregnant passenger on to the pavement, he had dumped her small overnight bag by her side and without further thought or consideration jumped back into his taxi, accelerating away like a scalded cat, speeding away into the night. The rain had become even more of a deluge, smashing against the walls of the cheerless apartment buildings; orchestral crescendos of thunder and lightning hurtling against the brick and stone walls, threatening to lift the tiles from the buildings' roofs. The onslaught continued, gathering pace, rattling the windows, some of which appeared as if they would buckle under the fierce assault. The relentless wind, fighting its way through the storm, initially relieved at finding some small escape into crevices and spaces between the tenement blocks had nowhere else to go, and becoming compressed and contracted began to emit a woeful, low and despairing howl as it tried to free itself through the gaps sandwiched between the buildings, squeezing relentlessly onward .

Floods of invading liquid, rainwater mixed with earth and particles of assorted debris ran across the ground, desperately seeking passage into the rapidly overflowing metal grills of the City's drainage and sewer system.

Soaked to the skin, weary, and nine months pregnant, Bernie with great difficulty, had reached down and scooped up her overnight bag. With her last residue of energy she had fought her way through the storm, entering a grim and forbidding tenement building, a building only marginally favourable to the raging storm outside.

* * *

Robert Glen stood erect, and with mounting alarm, stared at the storm venting its anger against the windows of his guest bedroom, the weather adding to his feeling of nausea, the tenseness of the knotting muscles in the back of his neck beginning to agitate his mood even further.

Robert was a man who felt it necessary to carry the world on his shoulders and although only in his early thirties, was prematurely grey; his once jet-black hair having ignored the option of turning to a reasonably passable salt and pepper colour had changed, virtually overnight, into a white greyness that had aged him beyond his years. However, the upside to Robert's greyness was that it had given him a more distinguished appearance, a gravitas that was aiding him in his rapid advancement within the legal profession.

He frowned, looking up anxiously at the windows and shuddered involuntarily. In contrast to the outside elements, the bedroom was hot and humid, the windows steamed up, warm water droplets running down the panes, forming random damp patches on the windowsills. Robert glanced, reluctantly, in the direction of the bed and shuddered as his eyes fixed on the young woman who was the cause of his current deep concern, his mood not helped by the thundering attack of the outside elements.

Scarcely out of her teenage acne years, grossly pregnant and perspiring heavily, Bernie groaned pitifully, her delirious threshing making the small bed she was laying on creak and strain under her frantic movements. To Robert, Bernie did not look particularly attractive at that moment and his mind drifted, thinking of the unfortunate guy, poor deluded sod, who must have been really desperate to sow a few wild seeds with her. Maggie, Robert's wife, had continually boasted of her attractive cousin Bernadette, who apparently, had an army of male admirers, but to Robert she was just not his type; she certainly didn't match up to Maggie's hype. The unpleasant thought of Bernie copulating persisted in Robert's mind, his inner vision imagining Bernie still threshing frantically, not as she was at this moment, but rather laying under some guy, wriggling to a more pleasurable beat.

The storm brought him back to the present and disgruntled and disgusted by the images that were floating through his mind, he shook his head, trying to wipe clear the repulsive pictures from his newly created memory. Glancing back in the direction of the window he took a handkerchief from his pocket and wiped his brow; forehead furrowed, Robert's facial expressions quickly altered from worry, concern, to doubt and confusion.

The wonderful, efficient Maggie, standing by the bed, exuding efficiency, calmness and control, bent over Bernie, mopping the woman's forehead with a damp flannel. She glanced up at Robert and aware of his concern smiled comfortingly. Robert attempted to smile in response, the corner of his lip curving tentatively upward; nervously wringing his hands, unsure of what to do, he eventually allowed his mouth to form into a hesitant grin.

Relieved that Robert appeared to be bearing up to the situation and was not about to panic, Maggie returned to her primary attention, the pregnant Bernie.

A fierce contraction took hold of Bernie's body, the pain akin to a cheese grater being run along her nerve ends. She screeched in agony then released a deep and anguished moan followed by a stream of groans mingled with invective. "*Fucking* English condoms!" She cried out, once again emitting a long and anguished groan. Her contractions continued, taking control of her body, leaving her helpless, her emotions raw and at fever pitch; she sobbed in frustration and pain.

Bernie had always been strong, nothing had ever fazed her but this was different; she was annoyed at her apparent weakness, her perceived lack of strength. For God's sake, it was her own bloody body causing her this discomfort! Her body, the fucking useless English condom, everyone else, the whole damn world but not her beautiful, as yet unborn baby, were to blame. Even the father of her child received a mental lashing but not the baby, never the precious baby.

"It wasn't the English condoms doing the fucking," mumbled Robert wryly.

Maggie shot a warning glance at Robert, a look that spoke volumes, and taking the hint he decided to remain silent, merely turning his attention back to the storm raging outside. Better that than facing the far worse storm of his wife Maggie! A sharp flash of lightening, so close it made Robert jump, followed instantaneously by a clap of threatening thunder, rattled the window panes and shook the frames, making Robert to involuntarily take a step backwards. Feeling foolish he glanced at Maggie, muttering nervously, "The storm is threatening to shatter the glass." With growing alarm and deep concern evident on his face he stared at Maggie, waiting for some kind of reassurance from her and added, his voice registering genuine fear, "It's almost as if the Devil himself wants to welcome the new child."

"Will ya piss off Robert Glen; this brat may not be welcome by you but it's no child of the Devil!" snapped Bernie with pent up anger, the spasms of pain continuing to rack her body.

Maggie scowled at Robert, her eyes flashing a warning, her demeanour fierce. She fixed her poor husband with a look of intense anger. "He didn't mean it, Bernie; it's just Rob's way." Turning her attention back to Bernie she smiled with warmth and affection and mopped the perspiring young woman's sodden brow. "Anyway, when are you going to tell us?" She paused to allow

Maggie's response which was not forthcoming; then firmly demanded, "*Who is* the baby's father?"

Bernie panting, sucking in deep breaths, wheezed a slow, laborious reply, "I've told...you... before...I ...can't... I won't say."

Maggie wearily ran her hand across her mouth, "Oh God Bernie, the father must be a married man." Bernie writhed as another contraction travelled through her; she shook her head in response to Maggie's statement, just wishing to be left alone from these intolerable questions.

Relentless on the subject of the baby's father, Maggie gave vent to her emotions, "The bastard! It's someone who's had his bit of fun and then pissed off." She scowled at the unfortunate Robert, "Typical man!"

"Don't drag me into this," Robert sighed, annoyed at being the nearest target of blame for Bernie's pregnancy.

With a mix of pain and annoyance, Bernie screamed out at the top of her voice. Fortunately, the contractions then eased for a moment and she rested her limp body on the tousled sheet. With cold, hard staring eyes, she looked up at Maggie and softly whispered, "The baby's father is a good man, a good man to the Irish Republic. He's not a bastard." Bernie turned to face the wall, her eyes taking on a soft and dreamy expression and then they melted into a nebulous vagueness, giving an appearance as if they were staring into another, very distant, but much more pleasurable existence.

"Then who *is* it? Why won't you say?" asked Maggie, persistent as a dog with a bone.

Bernie faced Maggie, her expression hardening, the eyes hostile, but before she could respond, the contractions recommenced with a vengeance and she moaned with a deep weariness. Between the contractions that ripped through her body she spat words of deep emotion and aggression, "I've told you before, it's none of your fucking business!" The contractions became incessant, forming an almost unbroken chain of convulsions. "Ah, shit! Damn, damn, damn! Fucking hell!" She moaned, allowing her body to succumb to the pain, her venom against Maggie instantly forgotten.

Robert was becoming extremely agitated. "Come on, this is getting crazy, we have to get her to a hospital."

"Screw you Robert; I'm not going to the maternity hospital. I can't!" shrieked Bernie as she attempted to rise.

Maggie grasped Bernie, firmly holding her down by her shoulders, "There, there, take it easy, we wouldn't do that to you. It's only Robert showing his concern for you and the baby."

"Yea sure, that'll be right," retorted Bernie, "He can't abide me and hates what I stand for. He'd be happy for me to have the baby in some prison hospital."

"Don't be silly Bernie, Robert may have his principles and his viewpoints, but he would never betray family."

"I certainly don't approve, but my only concern at the moment is for the well-being of both you Bernadette and your unborn infant," replied Robert softly, his voice ringing with sincerity. Agitated, he pleaded to Maggie, "For the sake of both Bernadette and the baby we should get her to a maternity hospital."

"Oh Robert, we can't, the police..." Maggie beseeched, her sentence left unfinished but the connotation evident for Robert to comprehend.

Robert screwed up his face in frustration and retorted, "I can't believe we're doing this! For the sake of the baby we should do something. Housing a terrorist, cousin or no cousin, is not the issue; two lives are being risked. And of course, if either one dies, we'll all be in trouble. Thereafter, we'll all be in serious trouble for harbouring a terrorist, but if we took Bernadette to a maternity hospital, no-one here would know who she was. Surely that has to be the best option?"

Bernie, in mid contraction, stared with unbridled malice at Robert, whilst Maggie fixed her husband with one of her withering stares, but was immediately distracted by another of Bernie's involuntarily spasms. With eyes beginning to cloud in anger she spoke softly over her shoulder, "Rob, you know you don't mean what you're saying. We fight for what we believe in but we do it our way, through politics, whereas Bernie, through her beliefs, does it her way." She smiled at Bernie, "Blood is blood, Bernie; you know that Rob and I will always take care of you – whatever Rob may say in the heat of the moment."

Bernie dissolved into screams of pain, the perspiration leaking from her pores, the agony intense, "What's happening? No one told me that it would be this bad!" Her body was racked by convulsions and she cried out in despair, "I can't believe the fucking pain."

"Quick Rob, more hot water and clean sheets, the baby's

coming!" cried Maggie as she reached for a fresh towel.

Already in a state of flux and panic, Robert stepped forward towards the bed, almost fainting, the bile rising in his throat; he hesitated, paused with confusion, glanced round the bedroom and then hastened towards the door, departing the room with unseemly haste.

Intent on her patient, pleased at Robert's departure, Maggie sighed with immense relief; now she could get on with the matter in hand. She reached over to the table next to the bed, picked up a pair of heavy-duty scissors and then bent down over the pregnant woman. Bernie screamed out in renewed pain as Maggie cut her, allowing the stuck head of the unborn child to exit, the baby's protracted entry to the world almost costing it its potential life. If only...!

Bernie's screams of intense agony and pain increased as the baby was being introduced into the world, new life exiting the cosy darkness to a world of foreboding, eerie light. "It's a boy," cried Maggie wearily, yet triumphantly, as she grasped the bloodstained baby and cut the umbilical cord. The child, initially silent, drew a long breath, then wailed, announcing its presence with peeved anger.

Totally exhausted, shattered beyond her previous comprehension, racked by pain and soaked with sweat and blood, Bernie broke out into deep, heartfelt and uncontrolled sobbing.

Maggie silently, gently, wrapped the baby in a fresh towel, the last clean one remaining from her previous stack of pre-prepared towels. As she worked, cleaning mother and baby, she ignored the increasing tempo of the wind beating on the outside of the bedroom windows, the noise building to a full thunderous crescendo. Calmness personified, all her attention concentrated on the new life in her hands, Maggie placed the wrapped baby on Bernie's chest and allowed a brief contented smile to spread over her face, but only for a moment, for there was still much to do. She reached for a previously sterilised needle sitting in a cup of boiled water and picked up a roll of surgical thread. Occasionally glancing up at Bernie's face and at the new born baby she commenced to stitch Bernie, cleaning and dabbing with a flannel as she worked, her nimble fingers proceeding with a seemingly practised haste.

Vaguely, her mind was aware of the storm thrashing itself against the building but Maggie's only thoughts had been for the mother and new-born child. "Alistair," she mused, "That will be a lovely name for the boy. Whatever Bernie decides, I will call him Alistair." Suddenly and unexpectedly a horrendous snap of wood, followed instantly by shattering glass, harbingered the invasion of the raging and ferocious elements, the glass and frame of the bedroom window finally giving way, shattering, sending shards of broken and splintered glass flying into the room. The broken glass together with tiny slivers of wood flew deep into the room, hurried along by the wailing, howling and thunderous wind, chaperoned by the scything rain. The wind, enjoying its new found space, smashed the light against the ceiling, the bulb disintegrating, plunging the room into ominous, storm-filled darkness.

Terrified, Maggie screamed out, her voice rising above the bewailing, angry and aggressive wind. The hairs on the back of her neck were tingling, not from the effect of the wind but more through an unknown fear, a sad presentiment, an intuition of foreboding. But in spite of her shock and fear, her first thought was for the baby and she scooped it up from Bernie's chest and pressed it, face inward, firmly against her bosom. Bernie mercifully had slipped into unconsciousness, the mother's body no longer able to cope with the rigours of the world.

Chapter 6

Heart pounding furiously, mouth as dry as desert, Fergal wondered how his colleagues were progressing. He checked his watch, the faded luminous dial barely revealing the numbers. "God," he mused, the nervous concern eating through him, "I should have heard the explosion by now. What if something's gone wrong? What if they're captured or dead?" All manner of negative thoughts ran through his head and now he felt that he needed the toilet. "Oh shit, hurry up," he mumbled.

Fergal stood upright, loosening his stiffened limbs, shaking his legs, and hopped from one foot to the other. Remembering that he was not to draw any possible attention to himself by exaggerated movement, cognisant of the need to merge into the black background, he pressed back, keeping his body tight against the wall. He waited, nerves on edge, and his bladder seemingly ready to rupture.

*   *   *

With the growing feeling of dread sweeping through her, Bernie was oblivious to the fact that she was being watched through a pair of infra-red night vision binoculars, her every nuance being scrutinised as she nervously prowled at the front of the shop doorway. The binoculars watched her head poking out as she furtively glanced up and down the street, the head being quickly withdrawn as if pulled back by some kind of suction. For some unknown reason she shivered involuntarily, a shiver not from the cold bead of perspiration running down the centre of her back but one akin to the feeling that someone was walking over her grave.

Her watcher chuckled with evil menace.

Attired in the uniform of an Inspector in the Royal Ulster Constabulary, his uniform ironed and in pristine condition, Willie removed the binoculars from his eyes, wiped the slight perspiration from the lens and grinned wickedly; a malicious gleam lighting up his eyes. He turned away from the window of the ground floor room of this seemingly empty terraced house that was further along the street on the opposite side of the road to Bernie.

The empty derelict house had been targeted in the past by various youngsters out for a 'bit of fun' and thus it was that, other than the window currently occupied by Willie, the remaining windows of this uninhabited residence were boarded up. Willie's window, recently re-glazed, housed the building's only complete pane of glass.

Inside the boarded up window frames only broken shards of glass remained, the bare internal floors by each window having been carpeted by various shapes and sizes of broken glass kept company by the brick or stone that had been used to smash them. Used condoms, crumpled beer cans, empty food tins, a burnt-out fire in the sitting room fireplace and an old, well used, heavily stained mattress illustrated that the youths had made full use of the facilities. To complement the ensemble, a pair of dilapidated armchairs were positioned either side of the fireplace.

The Town Council in an attempt at 'reclaiming' its property had ordered their property maintenance department to board up the windows and nail the doors closed. Preparations were in hand for a complete redecoration until the Clerk of Works received new instructions from his superiors that the property was temporarily required by the Police for certain 'training needs', and thus it happened that this sitting room was presently under occupation as Willie's current centre of operations. Although two new hardback chairs had been added by the Constabulary they contributed nothing to the ascetic ambience.

Any movement within the room created swirls of dust that spiralled off into new, temporary resting places. The surroundings were of no concern to Willie, the Inspector oblivious to his current discomfort, his celebratory mood focusing purely and simply on the 'game' about to unfold. His face encapsulated a picture of triumph and malice.

In the dim gloom of the room he grinned wickedly at the two RUC Constables who had entered the room and were now standing in front of him. His eyes glowed brighter and his grin stretched into an evil smirk, "Well boys, we've got the Fenian bastards now. Give the signal."

"Shall we arrest the woman, Inspector?" asked the first RUC Constable, whilst the second Constable spoke quietly into a two-way radio.

"No! No, she's mine; I'll take care of her. You men go out the back and make your way towards the army base, and do it quietly, following the planned route, we don't want to give the game away," retorted Willie, his voice relaxed and his demeanour calmness itself. The two RUC officers left the room, Willie turning his attention back to the window, his eyes gleaming with untold intensity, a smile of pure malice spreading across his face. Raising the binoculars back to his eyes, he licked his lips in anticipation, muttering softly to himself, "Right you Republican tart, you're mine. You're about to experience a protestant rod of iron. I'll have you begging for more." Willie felt the throbbing hardness in his crotch and tingled with growing excitement.

Pulling up the lower half of the previously well-oiled sash window, gently easing it open, he deftly edged his way out into the street.

Hiding within the shop doorway, her head and upper body poking out as she peered out into the gloom, attention firmly focused in the direction of the distant British army post, Bernie was completely unaware of the figure creeping up from the opposite direction. Her feeling of certain dread, worry for her son Alistair and concern for her lover Colm had quelled her normal cautionary expertise, all her attention focused on Colm's progress.

Belatedly hearing a sound she attempted to turn round but was just too late, Willie pouncing, grabbing her from behind in a vice like grip and clasping his hand firmly over her mouth. Bernie tried to resist, to fight, but in vain, her efforts futile, Willie not only having the advantage of surprise but also the benefit of being considerably stronger. He pulled a handkerchief from his jacket pocket and forced it into her mouth, Bernie struggling fruitlessly and the choking gag in her mouth made her want to throw up. She desperately lashed out, kicking out behind her whilst bending forward in an attempt to release her pinioned arms from Willie's fierce grip.

"We can make this easy or we can make this difficult, you Catholic slut," he whispered into Bernie's ear. She lashed out again, attempting to kick Willie in the groin but he merely brought up his right leg and forced his knee into the back of her right knee, making it almost impossible for her to remain erect. Pulling her arms behind her back, he forced the defenceless woman down onto her knees, her head banging against the door frame before being pressurised downwards onto the ground with a thud. Bernie's head was grazed and a small cut appeared, a trickle of blood escaping from her broken skin. Willie exerted greater downward pressure, Bernie's eyes filling with tears of excruciating pain as she was close to passing out, the gag also restricting her breathing. Seizing his moment Willie reeled her round, looked into her face and gently stroked her face and hair.

"You and I are going to have some fun first," gloated Willie triumphantly.

Bernie's eyes opened wide in realisation and fear. She renewed her struggle, desperately shaking her head, attempting to cry out, "No!" But the handkerchief muffled her plea.

Willie smiled and contemptuous of Bernie's continued frantic but fruitless struggling, he took the handcuffs from his belt, calmly securing her arms behind her back. Standing in conquest over the prostrate Bernie and reaching down he pulled her roughly to her feet.

Bernie's frantic struggling had exhausted her energy, her strength no match for her foe and she became subdued, apparently subservient. Holding her firmly with his left arm, Willie grasped her chin with his right hand and pulled her face towards him; he licked her cheek, his tongue leaving a residue of saliva across her skin. Then he whispered into her ear, explaining in graphic detail the various perverted acts that he was going to carry out on her. Bernie shuddered with revulsion. Securely gripping her head under his arm and with her handcuffed arms firmly pinioned behind her, he forced the tottering Bernie in front of him. Pushing and shoving her along the street, he propelled her unwilling body in the direction of his allocated command post, the pavement softly resounding with the resistant scuffling of her shoes.

Reaching his window, he glanced over his shoulder allowing himself a smug smile. "Perfect," he muttered, and with a firm thrust shoved Bernie against the open window, attempting to push her into his command post. Bernie resisted as best she could, keeping her body upright and taut, stiffening every muscle that she could find.

"Right you slut, if that's how you want it!" Willie muttered aggressively and pinioning her with his shoulder, punched her in the abdomen with such force that the air was expelled from her body. As Bernie involuntarily bent double, her lungs screaming for oxygen, he took his opportunity to propel her, headfirst, into the room, badly grazing her elbows and thighs as she scraped them on the window frame, a sliver of her skin and blood remaining on the window sill. Glancing over his shoulder one final time, Willie paused and listened for a moment, smiled contentedly and then clambered onto the window frame, gently sliding into the room.

Dazed, bruised, grazed and bleeding from minor cuts Bernie desperately tried to clamber to her feet; groggily, she stood upright ready to run but Willie was too alert. Partially in the room, he stretched out his leg, connecting with Bernie's legs, pushing her left leg into the right and causing her to lose her balance, the woman toppling forward with a thump onto the floor. He leapt on her, pinioning her arms underneath her, pressing his right knee onto her chest, his heavy weight holding her firmly on the floor.

All Bernie could see through her hazy vision was a repulsive face, grinning, with saliva evident in the corners of a very cruel mouth. The grin broadened, revealing a set of misshapen and yellow teeth. A drop of saliva fell on Bernie's face making her feel nauseous and almost making her retch through her gag.

Slowly, calmly, Willie inspected the palms of his hands, turned them, studied the backs and once again, briefly, looked at the palms, clenching and unclenching his fists. He rubbed his hands together, grinning maniacally and then pleasurably and leisurely wrapped his clean hands around her neck, slowly choking her.

Bernie, frantic, eyes wide and almost popping out with the fear and the strain of trying to resist began to feel faint, her resistance waning; her eyes became unfocused as her body became limp and lifeless.

Grinning like a Cheshire cat, Willie unbuckled his belt, undid his trouser button, unzipped his flies and pulled down his trousers and underpants in a very neat and well-practised action. He lifted up her skirt and violently ripped off her knickers.

Unable to move under Willie's weight Bernie gasped in pain and fear, the realisation of what was about to occur causing a numbing shock to envelop her. She renewed her intense struggle, straining to free herself, but produced only a pathetic wriggle, the brute being far too powerful.

Almost frothing at the lips, he forced her legs open and with a brutality that only a pathetic bully could muster, violently raped her. Bernie's muffled whimpering were cruelly ignored, tears of rage and helplessness forming in her eyes. Her pathetic resistance only served to please the rapist further and he redoubled his pitiless efforts, drops of spittle falling from his mouth onto Bernie's face.

When Willie had joined the force many years earlier he had been an upright and decent man, intent on serving justice, defending the rights of both Catholics and Protestants, protecting the innocent. But the years of malice, cruelty, irrational and malicious behaviour from the terrorists had worn him down, eradicating any goodness and decency in him, finally handing him over to the same emotions of those who were his enemies; he had changed sides, no longer fighting for decency, only interested in his own aims, debauchery taking over honour and goodness.

Bernie was desperately hurting, violated, angry, yet powerless, but realised that this maniac on top of her was enjoying her struggling; the more she tried to resist the more he hurt her. She switched off, deciding not to resist any further in the hope that he would relax his aggressive pressure on her, her body becoming limp, unresisting. Resigned, wanting this violation to be over, desperately trying not to be sick, she tried to fix her thoughts on something that would comfort her mind, her son Alistair.

Chapter 7

Colm peered out from a corner of the alleyway close to the British Army base, his eyes focused on a rubbish skip parked outside a partially demolished building. The derelict building was directly opposite the army base, the contract to demolish the building, an old warehouse, having been obtained by a demolition company loyal to the IRA Council. Everything had been planned, worked out to a finite detail.

Gripping a remote controlled timing device, Colm whispered to Seamus, "Those Brit bastards are about to get a real headache, we're going to shove their heads right up their arses! The explosives planted in the skip will not only blow the gate in but should be enough to incinerate some of the bastards in the first accommodation barracks." He turned to Seamus, ordering, "Get down."

Both of them dropped to the ground, Seamus gently lowering his weapon to the floor as he did so. With a heart as evil and black as Willie's heart, Colm peered out through cold, hard eyes. His eyes glowed, not with love but with intense hatred and malicious intent; the eyes were not capable of true spiritual love. There was no kindness there, no softness and no mitigating humanity. The ugly weal on his cheek resonated with a red-purplish hue, the weal a result of a previous punishment that had gone awry; his skin stretched tightly on either side of the puckered weal adding to the macabre evil that was deeply engraved into the man's features.

Although the intended victim had managed to snatch the knife from Colm's hand, cutting the Provisional IRA man's face in the process, Colm had quickly regained control, his massive paw-like hands and bear like strength being no match for his victim. But because his face had been cut in the fight he had made sure that the punishment was not a simple case of inflicting a facial scar; oh no, his victim had been made to suffer. Colm had removed, one by one, all the fingers and thumbs from his victim's hands; the pain and loss of blood had been too great and the victim's heart had given out, the man dying in excruciating pain and absolute terror, the torment and distress forever etched on the dead man's face.

Colm was a terrorist thug, long since moulded into a tool of untold evil and malice, who would not think twice of killing women or children, young or old, if they did not follow the doctrine that he strictly adhered to and which was dictated by 'The Executive' or by the seven member volunteer 'Army Council'. He pursed his lips, a cold, malignant, thoughtless anger sweeping up through his body; here indeed was a blood brother of Lucifer.

With icy calm in contrast to his inner angry malice, Colm pressed the button on his remote device, "Well, here goes; bye boys!" His cruel, hard eyes lit up in evil anticipation.

A large blast cleaved through the air, the night exploding from silent stillness to a noisy frenzy, brightly burning flames shooting up into the night sky. Pieces of burning debris flew upwards, scattering across the road, the explosion, flames, and flying debris causing ear-splitting panic, all hell seeming to break loose.

Instant and rapid gunfire erupted in response and the Army arc-searchlights glowed into action, the beams searching for the adversaries. The gunfire melded with myriad other sounds, screams from homes further up the street, barked orders, cries, and general yells of mayhem all giving rise to a surreal scenario.

But no-one was hurt, the explosion terrifying, yet muted? It wasn't what Colm had expected. The explosion had been... contained...like a controlled firework display...spectacular...but without real punch. Realisation that something had gone wrong spread quickly through Colm's evil, cruel, calloused, yet intensely cunning thoughts. His mind began to race.

"Something's wrong," whispered Colm, "That explosion was controlled, it wasn't the device that we originally planted!"

*   *   *

Deceived by Bernie's apparent passiveness, confused that she no longer appeared to object to the rough sexual intercourse - he'd never done it any other way than taking his partner violently - Willie relaxed his hold. Perhaps this slut was enjoying his attentions, his manhood. Wow. He grinned in deluded self-satisfaction.

Seizing her moment, taking advantage of Willie being off-guard, Bernie summoned all her remaining strength and arched her body, twisting sharply to the side, resulting in Willie slipping to the floor. Rolling fully away, she almost broke free, almost scrambled to her feet, almost tasted the euphoria of freedom, but Willie reached out, grasped her leg and hauled her back, Bernie tumbling unceremoniously back downwards, a shower of dust swirling around her.

He pounced on her and now violently angry, renewed his efforts with intense aggression. Bernie, almost gagging and unable to breath, used her tongue to push the now loosened gag from her mouth; drawing breath, she garnered her inner strength one more time. With a mouth full of saliva and dust she spat into his face.

"You dirty slut," whinged Willie, slapping her forcefully across her cheek, causing a large purplish bruise to form on the battered woman's already cut face; he paused, his petulant expression forming into a grin and slowly rose from Bernie's body, the woman emitting a audible sigh of relief.

Willie smiled down at her, his cruel eyes gleaming brighter as a fresh thought travelled through his twisted, tangled, evil mind.

Momentarily relieved by the removal of this oaf from her body, Bernie frowned; oh dear God, it was not over, this evil bastard had something else on his mind, something else planned, "Please," she croaked in desperation, "Let me go."

Willie reached down and helped Bernie on to her feet. "Perhaps it is over," she thought, "Perhaps this fucking oaf realises that he's a policeman and has come to his senses."

Suddenly, Willie twisted Bernie round and forced her face down over the arm of one of the armchairs.

Bernie screamed, her initial relief rapidly turning to abject fear. It was then that the noise of the explosion reverberated in the street, quickly followed by the sound of gunfire interspersed with a cacophony of voices calling out; amidst this mayhem was the resonating echo of running feet, soldiers' boots scuffing on the tarmac and pounding across the pavement. Total bedlam and utter chaos was now the dominant force.

Heedless to the outside activity and grinning inanely, Willie held Bernie face down firmly over the arm of the chair and brutally sodomised her. In pain, tears rolling down her face, she could only emit cries of anguish to match Willie's grunts of pleasure and exertion. Their mutual sounds increased in volume until Bernie pitifully cried out, then instantly became silent, her body succumbing to the relief of unconsciousness. Regardless, Willie continued until he was spent.

Rising, smiling smugly, he looked with disgust at his victim's exposed body, "Repulsive slut!" he muttered as he pulled her skirt down to cover the sight that was now offensive to him. Calmly and methodically he pulled up his underpants and trousers, buckled his belt, brushed down his clothes with his hands, paused, listening for any sounds and then stepped serenely towards the window. Satisfied that he had restored himself and his uniform to his demanded pristine condition, Willie gloated inwardly, looking forward to the undoubted capture of Colm; after all, he had *so* much to tell his adversary.

*   *   *

Having failed to get his key into the lock of his front door - the eight pints of bitter he had consumed clouding his vision and coherent ability - and giving up on his futile attempts to enter his abode, Trevor Mahoney had collapsed in a drunken heap in his tiny front garden. Stretching out over the small patch of grass that barely encompassed his six foot frame he had quickly succumbed into a deep, beer sodden sleep.

Unfortunately he chose that moment to dazedly waken from his drunken stupor, the sudden explosion and disturbing noise bringing him to a semi-conscious state. Groggily, Trevor scrambled to his feet, utilising his small brick front wall to pull himself erect. Big, big mistake!

The RUC Policemen supported by a platoon of British soldiers were naturally and instantly alerted by the sudden movement and diverted their primary attention to the incoherent, bemused Trevor Mahoney.

Trevor suddenly found himself the target of advancing firing soldiers, his descent back to the grass of his front garden quicker than his rise. He had also, inadvertently, discovered the best hangover cure that he had ever had, that is, if he could survive this episode. "What did I do?" He wondered.

*   *   *

A rattle of automatic rifle fire broke out, bullets zipping in their direction, crunching into the wall behind. "God, Colm, it's a fucking trap," shrieked Seamus fearfully, "They were expecting us!"

A Police Land Rover that had been hurtling in the direction of Colm and Seamus screeched to a halt, distracted by the furore surrounding Trevor, its wheels squealing in protest on the tarmac road.

Colm reached into his bag, the strap pulling down on his shoulder and muttered to Seamus, "We need a diversion; I have just the thing." And quickly pulling out a crude rocket grenade from his bag, he snatched up the homemade bazooka/rocket launcher.

Peering round the corner of the alley, smiling grimly, he fired a rocket at the stationary Land Rover, the Policemen disgorging just before the rocket hit. The Land Rover, its fuel tanks full, exploded in a sea of fire and sparks, adding another dimension to the cacophony of sound and mayhem, the night now lit by the blazing vehicle and a nearby burning building. The hungry fire quickly spread to the rubbish skip resulting in a plethora of aggressive flames and burning embers of paper shooting into the air. Discarded tyres in the skip began to burn, adding their part to the chaos, producing a nauseating, pungent smell that together with thick choking smoke clogged up the nostrils.

Seamus standing, watching as Colm fired his rocket launcher was simultaneously hit and mortally wounded by Army fire; the soldiers' bullets also hitting the AK47 and knocking it clean out of his hands where it clattered onto the pavement. Seamus crumpled to the ground, groaning in pain.

Startled, Colm turned, suddenly aware of the blood springing from his friend's head and chest; he dropped his home made rocket launcher, took hold of the surprised and shocked Seamus and cradled him in his arms. A second shot found its target, hitting Colm, but luckily the bullet passed straight through his upper arm, causing limited damage. Aware only of a sudden sharp pain, Colm initially assumed that he had banged his arm on his accomplice's head as he helped his wounded fellow murderer to his feet.

*   *   *

The unexpected explosion of the Land Rover had disorientated the small group of RUC Officers, some of whom were blown to the ground, others merely diving for cover. Only the driver had been killed, the remainder lucky to be alive.

Police Constable 769, Angus McBride, cowering flat on the pavement, shivering with fear, whispered almost inaudibly, "Shite! I'm really scared; this is madness." He tentatively moved his leg, "I've been hit; I can't feel my legs...and they're bleeding."

A Police Sergeant crawled to his colleague and crouching over the 'wounded' Constable, scoffed, "You great soft bastard, you're not bleeding, you've just shit yourself! God, Angus, you stink, you dirty bastard." He held his nose in an attempt to ward off the stench. Pausing momentarily, the Sergeant looked skywards, despairingly moaning, "Why do they give me sodding boys to do men's work!"

"Thank you Sarge, we're not all like Angus," protested another of his Constables."

I know, I know," wearily replied the Sergeant getting to his feet, gun now in his hand, "Let's get after those murdering Provo scum; come on, now!" He led his men in the direction of where the rocket had been launched.

* * *

"I think its bad Colm," wheezed Seamus, blood trickling from his mouth, "And it fucking hurts!"

Colm helped Seamus unsteadily to his feet, "Come on, we'll get you to Father O'Shea's; Doc Flynn can sort you out there." Suddenly conscious of a tickling sensation along his left arm Colm glanced downwards and groaned inwardly as he became aware of the blood trickling from his sleeve. Dripping onto the pavement the crimson blood left a trail of tiny droplets that formed neat little circles on the alley pavement. "Shit, must have been hit myself," he muttered, the earlier numb feeling in his arm now beginning to throb, "And I can start to feel the pain. Shit, shit, shit!"

"What?" faintly responded Seamus, his voice feeble, his body becoming weaker.

"It doesn't matter".

With Seamus slumped against him, Colm struggled out from the alley and into the next street, the trail of blood now forming irregular smears along the concrete pavement. Resting the tiring Seamus against a wall, Colm ripped material from the tail of his shirt and wrapped it around the wrist of his wounded arm forming a temporary tourniquet to prevent more blood dripping onto the ground. Attempting to aid his friend Seamus and to stem the give-away trail of blood he ripped the lining from his jacket, making an impromptu bandage for the large wound on his friend's chest; hurriedly working, he tore the sleeve from his colleague's shirt, wrapping the piece of shirt round Seamus' scalp, the blue material quickly becoming blood sodden, forming a scarlet band that circled Seamus' scalp. Satisfied with his temporary medical care Colm lifted Seamus and struggling under the dying man's weight, they staggered across the road, edging into the darkness at the far side.

"Just leave me Colm; I really am hit quite badly." He looked plaintively up at his friend, the blood oozing from his wounds, and continued self pityingly, "Or just finish me off now."

"No! I'll not fucking leave you. We'll get you to Father O'Shea's." Without another word Colm half dragged and half supported the weakening Seamus as they made their way along the alley. In the chaos of the acrid, blinding smoke and the burning buildings, the noise and bedlam of Police and Army personnel getting in each other's way, Colm helped the mortally wounded Seamus as they scrambled away, escaping into the night.

*   *   *

"This has been an almighty cock up," bellowed the army Captain, inches from the Police Sergeant's face, as they simultaneously reached the spot that Colm and Seamus had recently vacated. The army Captain's voice, heavy with frustration and anger, roared his displeasure at the bemused, unfortunate Policeman, "If you had left us to deal with the situation then we would have caught the bastards! We should never have agreed to your Inspector's request to make this a dual operation; fucking amateurs!"

The enraged and irate Captain stalked off, yelling to his men, "Regroup, regroup, we'll organise a house to house search.

Chapter 8

Willie stared out from his command post window. A fire was raging outside the Army barracks, with flashes of lesser fires lighting up other areas of the street. "That sounded more than just our controlled explosion," he thought absentmindedly, "At least the bloody fools drowned out the slut's screams with their gunfire." He glanced back at Bernie's prostrate body, muttering with self-satisfaction, "Ah, that was sweet."

Returning to the comatose woman, he noticed her discarded torn knickers and picking them up he put them in his pocket. Walking to the window Willie realised that traces of the woman were on the window frame. Hastily using a rag he calmly wiped the frame in an attempt to remove any traces of Bernie from the window. Satisfied, the Inspector stepped back to Bernie's body and looking down at her prostrate form, gently caressed her neck, then grimly tightened his hands around her throat.

Smiling maliciously, he gradually drained the life from her. Bernie's unseeing eyes flickered open, her body involuntarily gasping for an un-given breath, then she died in a final shudder, the spasm of death enveloping and sweeping through her body. Continuing to squeeze her neck Willie listened for any signs of life and then contemptuously and disdainfully released his grip. "One less Republican to worry about," he chuckled.

Searching his mind for inspiration, he made a sudden decision; removing a pair of rubber gloves from his pocket and hurriedly put them on, he lifted the deceased Bernie over his shoulder and carried her from the room. Stepping through the kitchen he reached the back door and quietly opening the door, peered out into the gloom. Satisfied that the coast was clear, struggling with a limp Bernie across his shoulder, he walked to an outhouse that contained the home's former toilet and bath. Opening the outhouse door, the Inspector unceremoniously dumped Bernie's body beside the bath.

"Where's the damn plug?" he murmured, his eyes searching the room. "Bollocks, there isn't one - bloody kids!" Willie complained, exiting the outhouse. His frenzied searching around the floor area around the building having proved futile, his eyes lit up, "Of course, stupid, there's a plug in the kitchen!"

Hastening back to the kitchen, slinging open the door, he wrenched the plug and chain from the large Butler's kitchen sink socket, then rushed back to the outhouse. Placing the plug in the drain-hole, he found it be almost a perfect fit, and then tried to turn on the tap. "I don't bloody believe this," Willie cried out in frustration, "The fucking taps jammed; bollocks!"

Frustrated, he aimed a kick at one of the spindles on the tap but losing his balance, he almost fell into the bath. Making a renewed attempt, this time holding onto the wall as he let rip with his heel, a thrusting jerk applied to the tap, the tap spindle turned and a drop of cold water trickled from the tap spout. Kicking out once more, he succeeded in making the tap spindle turn a couple of revolutions, the drops of water growing from a trickle to a healthy flow. Triumphantly, Willie turned the tap to maximum flow, the bath beginning to fill with water.

Sweating profusely, he left the outhouse and ran out of the garden towards his unmarked Police car parked outside the back gate. He extracted four plastic bottles, each containing a litre of very strong bleach, from the car boot. "Glad I always keep a couple of these handy," he muttered as he returned to the outhouse.

Pouring the contents of the four bottles into the bath he carefully plopped Bernie's body into the bath, ensuring that she was fully immersed. Pleased with his efforts, Willie turned off the tap, cleared up all traces of his existence in that place and exited, closing the door behind him. Pausing for reflection, he re-opened the door, reached inside for the key from the inside, retrieved it, and locked the door, putting the key in his coat pocket.

Whistling cheerfully and patting the key from the outside of his pocket, the immaculately Uniformed Inspector strolled down the garden, departing the premises, closing the gate meticulously behind him.

Chapter 9

Administering to Seamus' bleeding chest wound, Father O'Shea immersed a cotton face flannel into a bowl of warm, blood-stained water.

Watching the priest, his face drawn and concerned, Colm removed his torn jacket, slinging it haphazardly over the back of the bedroom chair; he leant against a dresser, thirstily slurping beer from a beer can, drops of the light brown liquid dribbling down his chin.

The Priest wrung out his flannel, the water in the bowl changing to a deeper shade of crimson, and once more tended to Seamus who lay very still on the bed having succumbed to unconsciousness, the under-blanket on his bed now soaked with blood. Father O'Shea spoke over his shoulder to Colm, "If Dr Flynn doesn't get here soon, well, I don't hold out much hope." Looking closer at the seriously wounded man he raised one of Seamus' eyelids, peering into an unseeing eye; then with his ear against Seamus' mouth he paused, listening.

The room became deathly silent.

Father O'Shea rose, shaking his head woefully, "I'm going to have to give him the last rites."

Colm nervously dragged the back of his hand across his mouth, "God, father, you're joking; Seamus will be fine when Dr Flynn gets here. He'll sort him out - he always has."

Father O'Shea dropped his flannel into the water bowl, turned from Seamus, wiped his hands on his cassock, and looked with sadness at Colm, "It's too late for that I'm afraid. I must be quick with his last confession."

Colm suddenly sentient to an emptiness, alert yet fearfully hesitant, became agitated, a growing unease that there was a void, another thing that had gone wrong. Something had definitely gone awry with their plan and...but...someone was missing? Abruptly, a feeling of deep bewilderment swept over him; he glanced around the room expecting to see another presence, another being. Father O'Shea had told Fergal to go straight home after their mission but Bernie was missing - where was she?

"Where's Bernie?" he demanded.

"Eh; what?" retorted the Priest distractedly.

Colm strode to Father O'Shea, grasping the Priest by his cassock, aggressively demanding, "*Where's Bernie?*"

Father O'Shea stared into Colm's eyes, quietly responding, "Bernie's not here - she never arrived." The Priest, unflinching, calmly removed Colm's gripping hands from his cassock. "I assumed that she went straight to her home."

Colm raised a clenched fist to his forehead, his anguished voice exclaiming, "No, don't be stupid, she should have been here; she was to come here, that was the plan. Oh God, she's been caught, or worse, she may be lying somewhere, hurt." Thumping his beer can on the table, the contents splashing over onto the doily, he snatched up his jacket from the back of the chair and stepped towards the door.

"Don't be a damn fool. You can't go out there – they'll be watching out for you," snapped Father O'Shea as he grasped Colm's arm.

Colm tried to pull his arm away in a futile attempt to get free but Father O'Shea retained his intense grip, only relaxing his grasp when he was sure that he had Colm's undivided attention. Looking firmly into Colm's eyes he softly continued, "Look, it's too late now. Bernie is either safe or in their custody. Nothing you do can make any difference now. Seamus is in more need of our current help - he needs the last rites!"

Father O'Shea tightened his grip on Colm's arm, the Priest's eyes now registering a cold thoroughness, an icy control. "Seamus needs our *immediate* attention."

Eyes clouded, registering anxiety and concern, Colm bowed his head and reluctantly threw his jacket on the chair.

Father O'Shea hurried to a corner cabinet and opening it, pulled out a small chalice. Taking a prayer book, he commenced to bless a wafer of holy bread and some Communion wine that he had poured into the Chalice, quickly returning to Seamus' bedside. Leaning over Seamus he futilely attempted to obtain the dying man's last confession then commenced to administer the Last Rites.

In a terminal spasm as death took hold of him Seamus' body jerked in brief and frenzied alarm and opening his eyes he stared sightlessly ahead, a final wheezing gasp of repulsive air expunging from his body as he died.

Ignoring the man's obvious death, Father O'Shea persisted in reading aloud from his prayer book whilst Colm, anguished and with growing concern, wrung his hands together, continuously glancing in the direction of his discarded jacket. Eventually the situation got the better of him and Colm resolved to find Bernie. He quickly rose from his kneeling position, getting to his feet, but taking a step towards his jacket, the sudden movement coupled with his injury and earlier exhaustive exertions in carrying Seamus back finally took their toll, and he collapsed, his weary, weakened body fainting with a thud onto the bedroom rug.

Father O'Shea glanced dismissively at Colm, shrugged obliviously, and continued with his toneless monologue of the Last Rites, apparently sending Seamus forward into God's forgiving kingdom.

*   *   *

Colm tossed and turned, gradually wakening from a troubled sleep, the dull ache of the wound on his arm causing him momentary confusion; why did his arm ache so much? His eyes resisted opening, the brain still confused as to why his arm ached and where the hell was he? His sleep had been restless but so necessary and welcoming.

The morning light was streaming through the thin cotton of the curtained windows and he reluctantly opened his eyes still not sure of where he was. Slowly the eyes began to focus and he became aware of Father O'Shea getting up from a chair near the bed.

Father O'Shea's face registered a mixture of regret, sorrow, and pity.

Colm raised his torso, scanned the room then returned his gaze to Father O'Shea, the facial expression reflecting back at him being one of great sadness.

The ache in Colm's arm was suddenly replaced by a huge knot in his stomach, a gripping cramp of worry and anguish, the biting concern accelerated as his mind recalled the events of last night. "Bernie...?" he croaked questioningly, eyes wide with foreboding and dubious expectation as they fixed on the man with the dog collar.

Father O'Shea's face exuded concern and anguish, his eyes becoming deeply saddened, the eyelids drooping at the corners, a despondent and pitiful expression sweeping over his face. The Priest proffered a very slight negative shake of the head, "No trace, disappeared. No one knows. The police didn't arrest her and they don't know where she is; they knew she was there but she seems to have escaped. She hasn't turned up anywhere. Just vanished; apparently they are hunting high and low for her."

Colm covered his eyes with his hand in an ineffectual attempt at blocking out the world. "Oh dear God, Bernie, no, no, no!" he wailed in despair and grief.

Staring pathetically at Father O'Shea he despairingly muttered, "She knew, Father, she damn well knew that something was going to go wrong." Colm broke out into wretched sobbing, the sound both unsettling and disturbing to Father O'Shea because he had never seen this hard, brutal man show any softness or loving emotion; it was the only time that Father O'Shea would ever witness this different, apparently softer, side of the callous terrorist thug.

Colm looked heavenwards, cursing with venom, "I hate you God!"

Although fleetingly taken aback by the man's blasphemy, Father O'Shea hastened forward to comfort the emotional, deeply sobbing Colm.

Chapter 10

The car slowed, turning into a small street of terraced houses in Armagh. It was early evening and although not quite dark the twilight had reduced the visibility to a shadowy haze.

Fergal, sitting in the rear seat, scrutinised the numbers on plaques by the side of some of the front doors. "Bloody lazy bastards, you'd think that they would take care in keeping up their house numbers; some of them are missing and some are so bloody dirty that you can't make them out. How the hell is the postman supposed to find where to deliver the letters?"

Mick, the car driver, a lieutenant in Colm's cell, glanced at Colm, grinning, "Since when has Fergal given a shit about postmen – or any government servants?"

"Well," grumbled Fergal, "It just makes our job more difficult." He suddenly pointed, "Thirty-three! That's the one."

"Pull up outside thirty-seven," instructed Colm.

Mick guided the car towards the kerb, pulled in, and switched off the engine.

His attention somehow focused on a three hundred and sixty degree radius, Colm softly uttered, "It seems to be clear. Masks on boys; time for some action," his eyes hardening to pinpricks of venom, "Time for a little vengeance!"

Colm and Mick slipped on their balaclava masks with practised ease whilst Fergal sat quietly in the back of the car, wringing his hands nervously together, desperately wanting to go to the toilet but didn't dare ask because this was the third time in the last hour that his bladder felt as it was about to explode. Trying to keep control of his bladder, he fumbled, struggling to put on his balaclava.

Mick, glancing in the rear view mirror, was about to let loose with a string of vituperate swear words until a calming hand from Colm was softly laid on his arm. Eventually satisfied that Fergal was now correctly attired, the three masked men exited the vehicle, Mick firmly grasping hold of a sledgehammer in his stodgy and callused hands.

Striding purposely to number thirty-three he raised the sledgehammer and with two mighty blows shattered the front door, splitting it asunder, creating an opening almost as wide as the door itself.

Gun in hand, Colm pushed past Mick, kicked away the remaining shards of wood and crouching through the smashed door entered the house, closely followed by his two accomplices.

A young mother, Rosie, rushing out from her sitting room, paused in shock and fright, then screamed in fear at the sight of the three masked men standing in her hallway, men whose appearance caused her heart to almost stop. Momentarily frozen, her limbs instantly became alive and gathering her wits she turned to flee from these three obviously violent and evil men.

Before she could escape and barely a footfall further Colm stretched out and pulled Rosie back, hard, by her hair; she squealed in pain, tears of anguish forming in her eyes. Colm callously drew the woman towards him, pulling out some of her hair in the process and then threw her to Mick standing directly behind, who then manhandled the terrified woman, holding her in a half-nelson style lock, clamping his hand over her protesting mouth.

The pent up fury and malignant evil evident in his eyes, akin to a hungry hyena about to feed on its prey, Colm sprang into the sitting room just as Danny, the householder, was trying to climb out of a rear window.

Danny and Rosie's two young children, having yet to reach their eight and tenth birthdays respectively, burst into tears, retreated and cowered, absolutely terrified, behind a sofa.

Virtually leaping through the air, Colm dived at the departing Danny, grabbing his target's leg and roughly hauling him back into the sitting room.

With cold calmness, Mick dragged the terrified wide-eyed Rosie into the sitting room, the smell of her and her children's fear adding an unpleasant aroma to an already unpleasant situation.

Fergal went to the sofa, gently pulling the two hysterically screaming and sobbing children to their feet; he put his finger to his upper lip, the mouth hole in the mask having ridden up over his bottom lip, and futilely attempted to quieten them down.

"If you don't shut those kids up," Mick bawled at Fergal, "I'll cut their fucking worthless throats."

Rosie struggled fearfully and frantically tried to break free from Mick's iron grip; they were *her* children and the thought of anything bad happening to them was almost driving her crazy;- no one was going to lay a finger on her kids if she had anything to do with it. She lashed out, kicking Mick hard on the shins and broke free, scrambling in the direction of her children, but quickly recovering, Mick lunged forward, grabbing her, wrapping his arm around her neck whilst he knocked the back of her leg ensuring that Rosie stumbled and fell. Almost choking, she collapsed onto the floor, Mick on top of her, his arm around her throat, restricting her breathing.

The children screamed hysterically. Not only was their father in some kind of trouble but their mother was also being attacked and would probably be killed.

Mick raised his upper body and bringing his hand sharply down, chopped the back of Rosie's neck with the heel of his hand, instantly knocking her out cold, her unconscious body crumpling flat out on the floor. The Provo enforcer got up and viciously kicked the woman in the ribs for good measure. The sound of a rib being cracked, coupled with Mick's ferocious eyes glaring at the children through the fearful slit eyeholes of his mask, reduced their sobbing screams to terrified whimpers.

"Fucking bitch!" Mick hissed, turning his attention to Danny who was being firmly held by Colm.

The two children continued to whimper in abject fear, terrified beyond reason.

Wide-eyed with terror, Danny wet himself and trembling, attempted rational conversation and appeasement, "Colm, I know it's you behind that mask. For God's sake, what's this all about?"

"You know damn well; you betrayed us to the RUC!" retorted Colm almost growling, his tone deep and menacing.

Danny shivered uncontrollably and tried to edge towards the window, tears of fear rolling down his cheeks. He wailed "Please Colm, it's not true, I did no such thing."

"No one else knew about last Tuesday's operation, the information could only have come from you," growled Colm.

Mick stared with disgust at Danny, "Look at the state of him, he's peed himself. Let's just take him out; let's finish him now." Taking a revolver from his trouser pocket, Mick took a pace closer to Colm and Danny, his gun aimed at Danny's head.

Colm pushed him away. "Lower your gun, I'm not ready yet Mick. I want to know who Danny informed about our target. I want the name of his police or army contact."

"But I swear Colm I didn't tell anyone. I didn't know what target you were after, where you were going to attack, what you were going to do," whined Danny, pleading, his legs almost buckling with fear and trepidation.

"Lying piece of shit; it had to be you." Colm clouted the hapless man about the head, the force hitting Danny like a concrete fist on a punch bag.

With stone cold iciness and menace Colm unsheathed a knife from a scabbard strapped to his lower leg. He grabbed at Danny's shirtfront, gathering a fistful of material as he pulled his victim closer. "Now, you're going to pay for your betrayal...and for Bernie's death."

Danny desperately attempted to ward off the expected knife thrust, his arm reaching out in a feeble attempt at protection whilst using his other hand to grasp hold of the wrist of Colm's knife wielding arm, "Swear to God Colm I wouldn't be so stupid."

"I don't believe you and I'm going to enjoy making you really suffer." Colm wrestled his arm free from Danny's pathetic grip and forced the terrified victim onto his knees.

"Please Colm; not here, not in front of the kids," snivelled Danny, but realising that there was nothing he could say or do that would prevent this evil madman from carrying out some kind of retribution regardless of his innocence he made an effort to compose himself. Although he didn't want his family to experience his surely guaranteed bloody and violent death he certainly did not wish for them to be spectators to his evident abject fear and terror.

Oblivious to Danny's protestations of innocence, Colm coldly pronounced, "It's too late for niceties, you turncoat scum." And without further thought or compassion, the brutal Colm took a firm grip on his knife and slashed Danny's face, cutting it open from ear to ear.

Arms thrashing, Danny desperately and vainly tried to defend himself, his scream of sheer pain and agony cut short as his lips were severed, his scream turning to a gurgle of purple blood and spittle.

Now crazed with bloodlust Colm repeatedly slashed at Danny, slicing through the man's throat, but not satisfied, repetitively stabbed random parts of his victim's body in a fit of savage frenzy. Danny's blood spurting from his throat, spraying Colm, Mick and the surrounding carpet, being of absolutely no distraction to the murderous thug.

Their victim's terrified children, in abject fear and horror, both vomited, sick to the pit of their retching stomachs.

Rosie slowly regaining consciousness glanced up horror-struck, wailing in terror.

Mick having missed his opportunity to bully and maim, decided to grab Rosie and dragging her along, he threw her down onto the blood stained carpet next to her writhing husband's body, where she screamed in utter fear, and wailing pitifully, clawed at the carpet fibres, pleadingly beseechingly, "My children. Please God, don't kill me, my children need their mother!"

Mick responded with another kick to her ribs. "That's for good measure, you wife of a police snout; traitorous whore!"

"You murdering bastards, you got it wrong!" Rosie whimpered, "Danny has been in bed with the flu for the last few days; he would never have had the chance to betray you." Rosie scrambled to her feet and with a sudden release of pent up anger furiously clawed at Colm's face. "If I'm going to die I'll bloody mark you first; people will then know you for the cowardly woman killer that you are," she ranted at him, her maternal fury superseding any other feeling or emotion.

Colm contemptuously pushed her away, clutching the back of her neck and forcing her back down onto the floor; he glanced at Mick, indicating Rosie by a nod of his head.

Pleased at the opportunity of causing pain and revelling in his bullying control, Mick stepped forward, taking hold of the now subdued Rosie, the woman quickly realising that her anger and fury were of no match against these brutal, savage men. Although afraid for her children Rosie now accepted the inevitability of her fate; for when these brutes had done their deed and left, Rosie was sure that the neighbours would rally round and take care of her children. She just hoped that, one day, the trauma and anguish of this situation could be blocked from her darlings' thoughts. Her mind searched frantically, wondering which one of her relatives would prove to be better parents for her soon to be orphaned children.

"Use your gun," dictated Colm, nonchalantly cleaning the dead man's blood and gore from the blade of his knife, wiping it on the sofa, leaving a residue of large unpleasant smears and stains over the previously attractive rose patterned material. Satisfied, he replaced the knife in its scabbard.

Beaming with malicious anticipation and pleasure, evidenced only by the piercing evil of his eyes visible through the eye socket holes in his mask, Mick leant heavily with his left forearm on the back of Rosie's neck. In order to maximise the poor woman's fear he delayed pressing the trigger, lingering over his bullying triumph. Interminable seconds ticked by, the room seeming to stand still.

Rosie's two children, already traumatised for life, simpered, waiting for the expected brutal death of their mother. The younger child pressed his palms firmly against his ears and squeezed his eyes as tightly shut as possible. Having seen his father perish in such a horrific manner there was no way that he wanted to witness the termination of his mammy.

The elder child, Rosie's daughter, ashen, drawn face washed with tears, began to recite a prayer, 'Hail Mary, full of grace...''

Mick chuckled and placing the cushion against Rosie's leg fired the revolver almost at the same time, the bullet penetrating the woman's skin and travelling through her kneecap, exiting with a jagged tear of broken bone and flesh.

Rosie, despite her intentions of staying controlled for the sake of her children, unavoidably howled at the excruciating pain.

Mick's eyes gleamed with wicked satisfaction.

"Let that be a lesson; any trouble from you or the authorities and we'll be back...for the kids!" warned Colm.

Rather than being relieved at still being alive and despite the unbearable and excruciating pain, Rosie's dander was up and boy was she angry as hell. "You fucking, vile monstrous bastards ...you fucking bastards! Don't you go near my kids! Women, children and defenceless people are just about your level. You're not heroes; you're just cowards and bullies."

"Oh shut up woman," barked Mick as he aimed a kick at Rosie's mouth, lashing out with unfettered venom. Rosie's mouth gashed red, her lips split, her jaw broken, three broken teeth spilling out onto the carpet.

Colm turned his attention to the simpering, traumatised children, "You've seen nothing and you know nothing; understand?"

The two children looked back at Colm with incomprehension; shaking with fear, tears rolling down their cheeks, holding each other tightly, they stared blankly at this fiend in front of them. Reason, sanity and logic had long since left their world.

"Do you fucking understand?" snarled Colm.

The two terrified children, frozen in terror and trauma, nodded woefully in response but without any comprehension of the question or any understanding of its preceding events.

Colm, satisfied, assuming that he had achieved some sort of vengeance, glanced contemptuously at Rosie and then departed the room.

Mick raised the lower part of his balaclava, worked saliva into his mouth and spat down onto Rosie, the spittle landing on her hair, with specs trickling onto her face. Turning in the direction of the children, he fully removed his balaclava mask, glaring at the children with a demeanour of such evil and threatening menace that the youngsters were filled with increased dread and foreboding. He raised his revolver, pointing the gun in their direction, "Remember, Brats, you've seen nothing!" Pleased with himself, he replaced his balaclava and followed after Colm.

Fergal wearily removed his mask, revealing a dismayed and wan face, his eyes soft and full of sorrow and remorse. Being young and fairly new to the concept of being a Republican 'hero', the violent and bullying behaviour he'd witnessed had been totally unexpected. This was not what liberating Ireland should be about. Feeling the bile rising in his throat, he threw up, inadvertently once again setting off the two children in following his example. Fergal retched, emptying his stomach; wiping his mouth with his jacket sleeve he looked up to see the two pairs of young eyes just staring at him blankly, without understanding, just void, empty sockets.

Hesitantly, he walked forward towards the whimpering Rosie. "I'm so very sorry," he apologised, and with an outstretched helping hand he bent over to help Rosie, "I had no idea. I didn't know that it would..."

Mick re-entered the room, commanding, "Leave the bitch."

"But..."

"Do you want some of the same?" Mick's eyes narrowed threateningly. "If you do, just disobey me!"

"I was merely trying to help."

Mick took am intimidating step towards Fergal, who quickly came to his senses.

"It doesn't matter," muttered Fergal, his eyes haunted. He glanced back at the sobbing Rosie, then at the sullen, darkly aggressive, now mask-free Mick and shook his head. Fergal, head bowed, reluctantly departed, stepping past the menacing figure of Mick who favoured him with a look of intense scrutiny, the eyes seeming to bore into the back of Fergal's head and deep into his bemused and tortured brain.

Fergal was already beginning to regret the road that he has chosen, the romantic notion of 'liberating' Ireland being quickly overtaken by the reality of the unreasoning and unrelenting brutality practised by people who claimed to be representing freedom and decency. Now, unable to break free, he only stayed because the apprehensive fear of quitting caused his stomach to knot; a fierce, angry pain that shot through him, setting his guts on fire.

He just wanted to die.

Chapter 11

Edinburgh, Scotland.

Colm and Bernie's illegitimate son Alistair, now a young man of twenty-two, attired in tennis shorts, polo-shirt, and expensive, fashionable tennis shoes, prepared to swing at an approaching tennis ball. Beads of perspiration trickled down his face, a look of intense effort and concentration furrowing his brow. He ran diagonally across his side of the court and swung his racket at the speeding ball approaching just to his right. Aiming at the ball, he smashed his racket at it, grunting like an enraged bull; but at that moment his racket disintegrated, the impact of the hurtling tennis ball being the final straw in its years of faithful service.

"Shit!" bawled Alistair as he glared with dismay at his broken racket and at the tennis ball rolling away across the ground on his side of the court. "I had that covered, you lucky bastard."

"Yea, sure," retorted Jamie, a young man of identical age but three inches taller than Alistair. "I had you well beaten."

Alistair turned his attention to the two attractive young blonde females, each attired in the briefest of tennis whites, who were sitting on a bench just inside the court, gossiping for all they were worth and previously oblivious to the two preening males desperately vying for their attention. "Um," the nearest female hesitated as she looked to her friend and gossip partner for an inspirational answer.

The second girl frowned, "I wasn't watching." But she hastily reconsidered her reply when she noticed the deep disappointment flying across Alistair's face. "Um, I mean I didn't see, sorry."

"Well thanks Monica, thanks for your support," Alistair replied with merriment but the disappointment was evident in his eyes.

Jamie grinned, "See, I *did* have you beaten! They just don't want to admit it to you."

"Huh," retorted Alistair, "Anyway, I'll get another racket; I'm sure that Mother has a spare one then we'll see who the better player is."

"I'll be ready for you," Jamie chortled.

Monica rose luxuriously from the bench, stretched, ensuring that Alistair had a good eyeful of her sexy tennis knickers, then smiled alluringly, sweetly demanding, "Oh come on boys, we've had enough of the tennis."

"And your constant competing with each other," interjected Miriam, her equally blonde companion.

"Yes, and of your constant competing," echoed Monica. "Can't we call it a day? I'm dying of thirst. Can't we stop now and go down to the pub; did you know that the 'George and Dragon' is offering a free glass of wine with lunch today?"

"Okay, okay, I'll just get a new racket and finish off this set." Opening the wire-net door of the tennis court, Alistair paused and yelled across to Jamie, "That okay with you? The winner of this set is the overall champion?"

Monica petulantly regained her place on the bench, slumping down on her bottom, "Oh Alistair, for goodness sake, we're starving!"

"That's fine by me," hollered Jamie, "I am winning 4-2."

"Not for long," rebuffed Alistair over his shoulder as he exited the tennis court and hastened up a wide and ornamental flight of twelve garden steps surrounded by herbaceous borders containing a myriad of multi-coloured flowers each of which threw off a beautiful scent.

Ducking under the trailing leaves of wisteria and honeysuckle that dangled from an arched trellis he followed the gravel path that dissected a wide, meticulously mown lawn; every blade of glass appearing as if it has been finely manicured by a discerning army of gardeners each equipped with a pair of nail scissors. Bounding up the path, Alistair approached a large suburban mock Georgian house and climbing a final set of four garden steps, reached and crossed a patio heavily laden with a mixture of elm and oak garden furniture. He stepped towards an open pair of large French-windows.

Alistair vigorously wiped his feet on a patterned coconut mat that extended the width of the open French-windows, ensuring that the soles of his tennis shoes were thoroughly clean. Entering the house, he stepped onto a highly polished parquet floor. The hallway was of sufficient size that it could fit the entire house size of some of the new homes currently being built in towns and cities around the country. The tastefully painted walls were 'decorated' by the occasional framed picture, spaced at seemingly irregular intervals along the walls but, of course, each painting's subject and location had been carefully planned. If the room itself did not speak of money and wealth then the paintings certainly shouted out that this was a residence of extreme fortune and privilege.

The years had certainly been extremely generous to Robert and Maggie since their early difficult days in a Glasgow tenement; the law is more often than not a very generous paymaster. Robert had progressed up the legal ladder to such an extent that he and Maggie were now the proud, mortgage free, owners of this seven-bedroom house located in the salubrious suburbs of Edinburgh.

Alistair quickly traversed the large hall, heading for a door at the far end, impatiently called out in mid stride, "Mum? Mum, where's the spare tennis racket? I've just broken mine."

From another room a voice faintly and distractedly replied, "I don't know Alistair; try one of the hall cupboards."

Alistair turned on his heels and crossed back to the wall opposite the garden entrance, striding to a row of four oak cupboards built into the wall; each of the cupboard doors extended from floor to ceiling.

He pulled open the door of the first cupboard, ferreted inside, but after a moment withdrew, disappointed. Pulling open the door of the next cupboard, he extracted assorted bric-a-brac, depositing some of the unwanted items gently down by his feet, but also inadvertently allowing some papers and files to fall carelessly onto the floor behind him. The disturbed pile of papers included a large foolscap envelope, carelessly discarded onto the parquet floor, its end splitting open, the contents spilling out, scattering various papers and leaflets onto the polished wood. Alistair, oblivious and impatient, reached deeper into the cupboard. "Ah-ha; got it!"
He withdrew his hand, triumphantly holding the sought after tennis racket and removing the cover, examined the racket. "God, this is so *old*, strung with goodness knows what but I suppose it will do," he muttered. Turning, he became aware of the mess created by his carelessness and impatience.

Bending down, his eyes caught sight of the loose papers and leaflets and in particular a leaflet referring to the 'Irish Republican Army', including an unpublished booklet detailing "A brief history of Irish persecution by the English." Intrigued, incredulous, he softly uttered, "What's this?"

Alistair squatted down, placing the forgotten tennis racket on the floor, and rifled through the papers; he whistled involuntarily. Pausing, he raised his head, calling out, "What's all this stuff, mum?

It seems to be a lot of bullshit about the Irish troubles... and various Irish Republican organisations?"

Examining the leaflet in his hand, he added in amazement, "This is a bit subversive, isn't it? Why are you keeping it?"

Maggie, drawn face paler than the white lines of their tennis court, entered the hallway, staring wide-eyed at Alistair. Nervously and with a tinge of uncertainty, she hesitantly responded, "You...you shouldn't be going through those," and continuing under Alistair's inquisitive stare, "They're private."

Alistair's face creased into wry amusement, "Private, mum, from me?" He looked down at the leaflet in his hand, rose from his squatting position and waved the papers at his mother, "Anyway, how come you're keeping all this anti-British material, and where the hell did you get it from in the first place?"

Maggie stared at her son, searching into his inner being, her mind racing; she looked down at the material in his hands then glanced in the direction of the open windows. Nervously, she dried her damp palms on the sides of her skirt. "Um, it's a rather long story, darling."

"Well go on then, out with it?"

Maggie once again glanced in the direction of the French-windows and was startled by the sudden sound of jovial female laughter, which although distantly emanating from the direction of the garden, was indicative of approaching people. Perspiration breaking out on her brow, she cleared her throat and having inwardly been on the cusp of revealing innermost secrets to Alistair, she hastily changed her mind. "It is a long story, darling, but it really isn't important. It doesn't matter."

Unperturbed, Alistair was persistent; he gathered up some of the other spilled notes and gently waved the offending literature in front of his mother's face, "But this stuff is advocating violence and mayhem against us, the British."

Maggie her voice quiet, but firm, gently replied, "No, not against us, Alistair, not against us."

Alistair was momentarily confused, "Eh? What do you mean, "Not against us"? I'm British; we're British, well, Scottish anyway."

Tremulously quivering, Maggie shook her head, glancing once more in the direction of the garden, and continued softly, "We are more Irish than British. Anyway, you'd better give me those." She stepped forward reaching out for the papers in Alistair's hands.

"With your father being an Advocate and his imminent transfer to London, and you destined for a career in law, I don't think we should keep such material anymore."

"What do you mean '*more Irish*'; I'm Scottish, and so are you."

"Not now Alistair, your friends are coming up from the garden."

"Tell me mum, come on, what *are* you talking about?"

"We'll talk about it later but you know my side of the family is originally from Ireland and there was a long history of anti-English feeling in the past."

Alistair chuckled affectionately, "Ah-ha, so you were sympathetic to the Irish Republican movement once!"

Glancing over her shoulder, she made an attempt to snatch the papers from Alistair's grasp, but he refused to relinquish his grip, and holding the papers behind his back, he ensured that they were out of his Mother's reach, whilst an amused smile played on his lips.

Maggie gazed firmly into Alistair's eyes, "Yes Alistair; yes, I was sympathetic to the various Irish Independence movements, but that was a long time ago. A lot of water has passed under the bridge and we have to live and let live."

"But if you felt so strongly, why did you give up your beliefs and why have you, with Dad, become pillars of the British community?"

"Needs must, darling; I fell in love with your father but his feelings for Ireland weren't the same as mine. Then you came along and my priorities changed. Nothing seemed as important any more as my life grew with you and your father."

Eyes imploring, Maggie reached out her hand for the papers, virtually snatching them from Alistair's relaxed hand; she hastily screwed up the offending literature into a tight ball and scurrying forward two paces, bent down, picking up the torn foolscap envelope, before scooping up the additional spilled literature. "I'll burn all these papers."

Jamie called out from just outside the room, "Ali, are you coming out to finish this game, or have you chickened out?" Entering the hall, his eyes lit up at the sight of Alistair's Mother. "Hello Mrs Glen," he smiled broadly, "How are you?"

Nervously, Maggie held the offending literature behind her back, "I'm fine thank you Jamie. I see that you're well; how are you parents?"

"Fine, as usual, thanks."

Alistair put his arm round his mother and whispered into her ear, "Wow mum, I never knew; I had no idea." He removed his arm, stepped back and winked, smiling with filial admiration.

Maggie embarrassed, began to feel awkward, "Of course you didn't know. You were never meant to know."

"Know what?" Jamie inquisitively demanded.

"Oh nothing, it's not important; a private thing," responded Alistair nonchalantly, once again favouring his mother with a conspiratorial wink.

Although pleased at her son's initial response, Maggie was wary of the literature in her hands and chased the boys away, "You'd better go and finish your game."

Alistair, facing his mother, chuckled and silently mouthed, "My mum was a rebel! What a laugh." Grinning, he turned to Jamie, "Come on then, time for you to get a lesson in how tennis should be played."

"That would be nice, but it will never happen from you," riposted Jamie.

"Will you boys and whoever else is with you, want some lunch?" Maggie demanded of their departing backs.

"No, it's alright thanks Mum, we're going down to the 'George and Dragon'; they've got free booze going with lunch. You know how Monica loves her wine."

"Is she here? Tell her to come in and see me." Instantly remembering the offending literature in her hands Maggie hastily changed her mind, "Tell her to see me later actually; I have to pop into the kitchen to sort out the menu with Mrs McCloud for your Father's important dinner this evening."

Jamie stopped in his tracks and turned to face Maggie, "Oh, I almost forgot Mrs Glen; Monica and Miriam were wondering if you had any squash? They're currently sunning themselves on the patio; seems they've got thirsty watching two superb tennis players on the courts."

"And who would these superb tennis players be?" Maggie riposted; her previous concern replaced with an amused expression.

"Why, Alistair and me, of course!" replied Jamie with feigned hurt.

Maggie gently laughed with a mixture of relief and amusement, "No problem, I'll get Mrs McCloud to bring out some fresh lemon barley."

"You're a gem Mrs Glen." He paused, "Hey; that almost rhymes!"

"Oh shut up, you moron," Alistair gently, playfully, struck his tennis racket on the back of Jamie's head.

"Ouch!" Jamie responded with mock hurt.

"Get out, both of you," chortled Maggie, but just as the boys were about to leave the hall she called out, "Alistair?" Both boys turned to face her. "Alistair, may I have a quick word?"

Alistair looked at Jamie, despairingly shook his head in mock annoyance, saying to his friend, "You go on, tell the girls that life-saving liquid is on its way, and I'll be out in a second."

"Delaying tactics, that what it is," grumbled Jamie, "You're just trying to wear me down but it won't work; I'll be ready." He departed into the garden, calling out, "Don't worry girls, your dream man is back."

Female groans wafted back in response.

Alistair, questioningly, waited for his mother to speak.

"Please Alistair; promise me, not a word to your Father about this matter. He'd kill me if he knew I hadn't destroyed this literature."

Alistair grinned affectionately, "Don't worry Mum; your 'rebel' secret is safe with me."

Maggie's frown evaporated and she grinned, her eyes reflecting love and warmth. "Don't push your luck. Now, you'd better join your friends. I'll get rid of this literature and then bring out the lemon barley myself." Cheerfully, she added, "I do like that Monica; such a lovely girl. She'd make a great daughter-in-law."

"Mum, she's just a girlfriend; that is a female friend. I don't intend to tie myself down for years yet."

With a twinkle in her eye, Maggie persisted, "But she's such a beautiful girl; she would make you a lovely wife."

"Mum, forget it." They exchanged grins.

Whistling cheerfully, nonchalantly swinging his racket, Alistair exited into the garden.

Maggie's grin evaporated, her eyes clouding over, a deep frown furrowing her brow; speaking softly to herself, she muttered, "Silly woman; why on earth didn't you destroy this stuff years ago?" Looking up to where Alistair had just departed, she mused, "Perhaps subconsciously you wanted him to know, to find out?"

Chapter 12

Teeth grinding together with nervous energy, Fergal gnawed on an imaginary piece of chewing gum. The eyes that stared out into the gloom were those of a frustrated and sad man. The perspiration stuck to his brow, his body sweating, but the cold wind cooled the perspiration into tiny beads of drying moisture as soon as they formed.

His emotions were racing, vying between a mixture of reluctance and determination; determined not to let his peers down and to fulfil the necessary task, and yet reluctance, a great reluctance and sadness almost overwhelming him at the impending pain and sorrow that he was about to cause to others.

He clenched and unclenched his fist, reassuring himself by patting the bulge in his coat pocket. Gingerly he reached into the coat pocket and extracted a loaded pistol, ensuring that the safety catch was on. Rubbing the weapon between his palms, the cold metal only served to send shivers up his spine. Fergal shook his head, clearing the negative thoughts that were beginning to take hold and steeled himself for the impending action.

Squatting down, he slowly, very slowly, partially rose, peering intently over the bonnet of the parked pickup truck. Satisfied that the coast was clear he stood to his full height and using the shadows, skirted the building, gently making his way towards the target.

Fergal almost leapt into the air in surprised fear when he encountered another form, a moving shadow, approaching from across the street. The air expelled from his lungs with immense relief when he realised that the approaching shape was actually Colm; even in the blackness of the night he was convinced that Colm had winked at him.

Silently, without a word being exchanged, the pair proceeded onward into the night. Approaching the targeted house, Fergal's stomach muscles knotted even tighter; this would be yet another day, or in this case, night, when a harsh punishment would be meted out.

As a small consolation to tonight's task, the victim – or transgressor as the 'Army Council' named him – would be permitted to live, the powers to be deciding that a severe calf wound, a bullet fired through the back of the victim's calf, would be sufficient punishment. It didn't matter to the terrorist council that the intended victim, a highly acclaimed member of a local sports club, had a promising future as an Olympic athlete; the track records that the young man had been scorching through the race meetings of the Province would be a thing of the past.

Whilst Colm took up his position, pressed tightly against the wall, Fergal reached up and gently knocked on the intended victim's front door.

Another bleak episode was to be etched into the increasing unwilling mind of the disillusioned Fergal, wondering how on earth he could escape from the folly of his carelessly chosen path; this was no longer an organisation that he had read about, started with honourable aims, of sons and fathers fighting for independence, but was now a political body that had been taken over by self-serving terrorist bigots.

The door was innocently opened by a young, happy, ambitious, and trusting future sports star, a man who would soon learn of the folly of crossing these self-important bigoted morons. His error had been to publicly decry a known IRA member who was scheduled to be released from the Maze prison. Unfortunately, the subject of the young sportsman's conversation was a close friend and lover of the local Republican cell's female leader, who also happened to retain a reasonably high position on the committee of the sportsman's local Athletic Club. His fate had been sealed.

Wanting to hide, to be sick, to faint, the blood rushing through his temples, his head pounding and with stomach-numbing regret, all Fergal wanted to do was to run away, to disappear, to fade from this sickening world. But he was also a captive in his own way, yet another victim of the wicked and evil deed that was about to be carried out.

Swallowing the rising tide of bile accumulating in his throat and grateful that his bowels had been emptied earlier, conscious of the pair of evil eyes - Colm's eyes - driving him forward, he leapt at the poor, unfortunate athlete.

* * *

With the deed done, Fergal finally released the bile from his throat, his stomach pumping up a thin viscous liquid of vomit that spewed from his mouth, spurting into the gutter.

Colm pulled Fergal away, dragging him from the whimpering athlete; the sportsman's left leg spilling copious amounts of fiery red fluid. The victim's dazed, shocked face staring up incomprehensively at the terrorist thugs, the image lingering in Fergal's mind. Feeling faint, Fergal's legs were barely able to support him, Colm helping him to walk, but unlike the athlete, his limbs would soon recover, the blood pumping safely inside the veins, the legs able to support him as he and his cowardly mentor hastened off into the night.

A few curtains twitched but no one interfered, no one dared; they all knew the price to pay if they crossed this evil band of bullies and murderers. There were also, of course, a small echelon of misguided and ignorant people who actively approved and supported the terrorists and their tactics; the possible worst of the people were those who offered taciturn support, turning their faces, yet still praying to their Gods.

Chapter 13

Humming a repetitive tune, Alistair sat behind the wheel of a two-year-old Ford Estate car that was travelling through the Irish countryside, heading for a small town in Monaghan, southern Ireland. It was a warm, balmy day, the fields covered with crops shortly scheduled for harvesting.

A wheat field was soon overtaken by a mustard rape seed field, then a field of potatoes, each separated by sickly looking hawthorn hedge bushes. The fields were empty of life, one forlorn scarecrow dressed in an old Irish rugby union shirt and accompanied by three crows happily perched on its arms and head, being the only visible interruption.

The crop fields were immediately followed by a large storage barn currently empty of produce and in a serious state of disrepair; there were holes in its roof rafters, boards fallen from its supposedly closed-in side, and a decrepit piece of farm machinery, an old potato plough, lying in a corner. The barn, although initially giving the appearance of almost falling down, was obviously still very much in demand by the farmer. This was evidenced by the three hard working individuals, one of whom was painting the walls, the other two at the top of ladders, furiously banging nails into loose beams of wood.

Alistair blinked, almost missing a very small farmyard cluttered full of derelict machinery; but his eyes took in the next property, a well maintained farmhouse surrounded by fields of burgeoning rape seed, gleaming bright yellow, the sun reflecting off the crop almost dazzling him; the contrast between the two properties was quite evident, the latter being funded by the recent intake of European Economic Community contributions.

Directly after the farm, a sign indicated that the countryside had now ended and that the town began. A speed limit sign reinforced this fact, the town's buildings quickly taking shape in Alistair's windscreen.

However, the first few buildings appeared to be in the same condition as the previous older farm, with long forgotten mechanical equipment, scrapped cars and an assortment of derelict machinery filling up the yards and driveways of these homes.

Alistair turned to the middle-aged woman sitting in the front passenger seat and grinning, asking, "Don't these people ever get rid of their rubbish; all that old machinery. Why on earth don't they dispose of it?"

"Oh Alistair, we never throw anything away round here," jovially replied Naimh, genuine warmth and affection reflecting in her eyes. "We're sure that someone, some day, may want to buy an old relic, or maybe they'll want a particular spare for a long obsolete piece of equipment which can then be obtained and dismantled from machinery that only these people have kept; if a use can't be found, it will eventually and ultimately be sold for scrap."

"You've got to be kidding. All that stuff is already total crap, if you excuse my language; in fact, I honestly believe that none of what I've seen has any value, scrap or otherwise. They should dump it."

"Where?"

"I don't know, there must be some kind of refuse tip that you could use."

"Dear Alistair," Naimh chuckled. "That's the problem. We don't have a tip; we have *nowhere* to dump the stuff."

Alistair drove deeper into the town, turning into an industrial estate where he pulled into a builder's merchant's yard. He parked the Ford, exited, and walking to the passenger side, assisting Naimh from the car. Without bothering to lock the vehicle they both went towards the trade counter doorway.

Approaching the trade counter they were greeted by a young man who looked up, smiled, and waited patiently until Naimh had reached the counter. "Hello Mrs Hanratty; how are you today?" He nodded in greeting to Alistair.

Naimh responded warmly, "Just fine Joe, just fine. Is Colm in?"

"Of course I'm in," yelled a voice from the back of the warehouse. "I recognise those dulcet tones and wouldn't miss the chance of a pleasant conversation with Naimh Hanratty, now would I?"

Colm, smiling, appeared from behind the racking. Stepping towards the service counter he noticed Alistair and paused, his eyes clouding over. Quickly overcoming his hesitation he rushed forward, his face alive and beaming with pleasure. "Alistair! How are you, boy?" Colm looked him up and down and continued before giving an embarrassed Alistair a chance to reply, "Well, you're looking well. University has done you good."

"He's finished at Oxford University now; got a first," proudly interjected Naimh; then, glancing at Alistair, added, "Made his mother's aunt very proud, didn't you?"

Colm's eyes misted over, a hazy expression taking the place of the earlier brightness, "I didn't expect anything less; he's a smart boy."

"Not a boy any more, Mr O'Driscoll," retorted Alistair with good humour.

"No you're not, I can see that. Besides, call me Colm, Mr O'Driscoll seems strange and too formal; we've had you visiting nearly every summer now, you're almost blood kin." Turning to Naimh, momentarily forgetting himself, he beamed with pride, "He grows more like Bernie every day."

Naimh cleared her throat in warning, Colm quickly regaining his composure, "Um, how's your Mother?" he stumbled on the word, 'Mother', "Is...Maggie well?"

Naimh gently interceded, "Maggie's fine Colm; she sends her love."

"Thanks; that's very much appreciated," responded Colm, his voice husky. Gathering his composure he added, "So Naimh, what brings you here today, social, or more likely, necessity?"

Naimh bantered, a twinkle of merriment in her eye, "Why Colm, why wouldn't it be social?"

"Because we don't see you that often anymore unless, of course, there is a problem on your farm."

"Ah well, that's where you're wrong," merrily lilted the older woman enjoying her moment. "Maggie thought that it would do Alistair good to spend some time fishing. I know that you like to go fishing near Derry and wondered if Alistair could spend a weekend with you?"

Alistair enthusiastically interrupted, "Yes please, Mr O'Driscoll." Becoming aware of the exasperated expression on Colm's face, he instantly corrected himself, "I mean, Colm; I'd love the chance to do some proper fishing."

"That would be no problem Alistair; in fact, I'd be more than delighted." Turning to Naimh, he said with sincerity, "Do thank Maggie; I really appreciate this. It'll be a great chance to bond."

Baffled and not a little confused, Alistair glanced from Colm to Naimh, a frown forming a crease on his forehead, his eyes questioning. "I don't follow; what are you talking about?"

Covering up very quickly Naimh interjected, laughingly explaining, "Oh, Colm loves the opportunity of teaching the youngsters how to fish properly. He feels that today's youth only want to listen to 'pop' music. You're his chance to fight back and reclaim fishing for the future generation."

His frown still evident, Alistair glanced doubtfully from Naimh to Colm.

Colm smiled, relieved at Naimh's quick recovery to his careless words and hastily nodded in agreement, "Yes, that's right; it'll be a pleasure to have another young man learning the arts from an expert angler."

Remaining slightly dubious and confused Alistair shrugged nonchalantly, deciding that his questioning mind was reading incorrectly and seeing something that didn't exist.

"Friday evening then?" Naimh blurted, determined to keep the conversation flowing without the possibility of any further questions from Alistair.

"Sure; I'll pick him up on Friday at four," replied Colm becoming efficient. Turning to Alistair he instructed, "You'll need 'wellies', waterproofs, and a thick jumper; it can be windy and cold where we are going."

Naimh interjected, "I'll organise those; I'm sure there must be a few spare bits and pieces around the farm."

Colm smiling broadly, recklessly added another demand, "And don't forget a hip flask. A warm tot will do you the world of good Alistair."

"Thank you Colm O'Driscoll, but he won't be touching the booze," Naimh snapped primly but with a trace of merriment.

"But, Naimh, come on, the lad will need…"

"Alistair will be fine with proper warming food not booze, Colm. At least not your doubles and trebles, the boy's liver is not ready for your treatment." Naimh smiling warmly, subject resolved, concluded the arrangements, "Right that's all settled then, we'll see you on Friday – without the whiskey!" She grinned affectionately and made for the exit.

Colm winked at Alistair and pointing to his chest he raised a pretend glass to his lips, indicating to Alistair that Colm would provide the booze.

Quickly comprehending, Alistair enthusiastically smiled in response, "Thanks; see you Friday." Turning smartly on his heels he caught up with the departing Naimh.

Colm's broadly smiling countenance immediately altered to one of pathetic dejection as he watched, sad eyed, as Alistair departed. He often wondered what life would have been like if he had chosen a different path. But then his thoughts drifted to Bernie and his heart froze, the evil blood re-filling his veins, the cold callousness overtaking his softer emotions.

Chapter 14

It was Sunday evening, the roads of the village on the outskirts of Derry, Northern Ireland, almost deserted. The religious people who were so inclined had duly paid their respects to their God, having performed their Christian duty in attending their local church or chapel, listening to their priest's or vicar's sermon, cleansed their souls and feeling like born again Christians, had long since retired to their respective abodes, supposedly recharged and reinvigorated. The problem evident to an outsider was that there appeared to be some confusion as to whether God was a roman catholic or a protestant. Even the priesthood seemed to be confused on this point.

However, the only current evident movement and sound in the village was that of two young boys banging a football against a garage wall. Occasionally a car could be heard speeding up, changing gear, then accelerating into the distance. Good honest folk had, apparently, settled down in front of their television sets or were still entrapped within the weekly gathering of relatives; mothers, fathers, grandparents, brothers and sisters, all equally bored but none having the heart to discontinue the routine 'duty' of this special religious day. Sometimes the only way to escape the routine was for the younger members of a family to move away from the area, usually to the imagined brighter lights of Liverpool, London, or Glasgow. The very lucky ones made it to America.

The village boasted a small group of shops covering nearly all the needs of the locals, the exceptions being the former butcher's shop and the village bakery, both of which had long since been forced to close as a result of the opening of a massive supermarket on the outskirts of Derry. The surviving shops were conveniently positioned at the major crossroads junction in the village. Opposite the grocery/general provision's store, on the corner of the main village road, was the 'Fisherman's Hook' public house. Some wise arse had had a brain wave and thought that the appellation would be the most appropriate name to attract tired fishermen, weary after a day 'labouring' under the experience of fishing from the bank of the lake, or wading in the shallows, or - for some of the more adventurous or wealthy - actually hiring a rowing boat and fishing in the deeper waters, but all of them subsequently needing to replenish their 'energy' levels in the 'Hook'.

The 'Fisherman's Hook' was also a good place to exchange

fishing yarns, claims of record catches, huge fish, the length and size of which beggared reality, were constantly being expounded. In addition to the pub serving as a fisherman's haunt it was also warm, friendly and welcoming, particularly after cold days spent suffering under wind, rain, or snow. Inside, frills would be hard to find, the interior being basic with a bare wooden unpolished floor and solid, hard backed chairs. The wall running diagonally from the bar counter housed a large fireplace in which a warming log fire was burning merrily. Surrounding the fireplace, for obvious reasons, was the only area of the floor that was properly protected by a bank of fire-tiles. However, no one sat close to the fireplace because the flames were just a little too hot close up, not to mention having to avoid the occasional red-hot cinder that shot out from the fireplace, landing on the fire-tiled floor before fiercely burning itself out.

Just inside the entrance door was a large coat-stand full of damp and dripping overcoats. On the floor around the coat-stand were two large fishermen's wicker baskets and three sets of fishing rods. Colm, Mick, and Alistair were seated around a table, each of them savouring their partly consumed pints. Attired in heavy boots, thick woollen jumpers and corduroy trousers, they were slowly beginning to thaw out.

The pub was relatively empty except for the landlord, a barmaid who appeared to spend most of her time watching a television set in a room off the bar, and a group of four men sitting at a table closer to the bar counter.

Mick slurped, swigging his beer, contentedly smacked his lips and then replaced his glass on the table. Contented, he questioned their guest, "So Alistair, did you enjoy the fishing?"

"Yes, it was great, thanks. That was my first time," replied Alistair agreeably.

Mick was amazed, "Is that the first time you've ever been fishing? I can't believe it; don't they have lakes and rivers in England?"

Colm gently interrupted, "Scotland, not England; Alistair lives in Scotland."

"Of course they do," laughed Alistair. "It's just that I never thought of going fishing before now. No one I know ever goes fishing; we're not a very sporting family. We have a tennis court and my parents occasionally join the local Hunt, but that's the extent of our sporting activity. Actually the Hunt for us is more of a social occasion than sport."

"Not even your dad?" Colm hated to say the word, his voice raising an octave. "Has he never taken you fishing?"

Alistair shook his head negatively, "Always been too busy I guess, working his way up the legal ladder. He's a top Advocate now, you know; it's the equivalent of a Barrister in England."

One of the men in the group of four at the table near the bar looked up, a flash of recognition shooting across his features as he stared at Colm. Tapping one of his colleagues on the arm, he indicated Colm's presence with an inclination of his head.

Willie, in mid conversation, his back to Colm's table, glanced over his shoulder, immediately stiffening. His face clouded with black anger.

Oblivious to their having being noticed by others in the pub and with the alcohol beginning to affect his brain cells, making him slightly aggressive, Mick scathingly uttered, "Pah; I hate lawyers. I can't be doing with all that legal mumbo jumbo. Anyway, all British police and lawyers are corrupt."

Colm shot a cautionary glance at the belligerent Mick, but Alistair was taken aback by Mick's indirect attack on his father. "That's a bit steep, and unfair on people such as my father. He is an honourable and just man, a very good person."

Willie and his colleague, unnoticed by Colm's group, approached their table. Eyes as cold as ice, Willie spoke in a low, threatening voice, "Hello, hello, what kind of scum do we have here?"

Colm startled, looked up, convulsed, and emitted a deep groan.

Mick's shackles were up and he spilt some his beer replacing his glass on the table with a thump, his face turning scarlet; he leapt to his feet ready to take on the whole world and especially this interloper.

Initially shocked, Colm quickly regained his composure and calmly, firmly, he placed a restraining hand on the bristling Mick's arm; Mick reluctantly drawing himself back from striking Willie, a look of intense hatred and animosity registering on his face. Disappointed and angry at his inability to take action Mick was unable to resist ranting, "One of these days we'll get you, especially when you are without your support."

Supremely confident in his authority, coupled with the knowledge that he was being backed up by three additional RUC Officers, Willie effused an aura of power, becoming the epitome of a controlling and domineering bully. He revelled in the obvious control that he could hold over other people and almost swaggered with self-important pride. With hands planted on hips he fixed Mick with a cold, cruel and baleful stare, "Just do, scum, please do have a go. I'll enjoy smashing your head into that wall."

Although afraid, Alistair was nevertheless angry and he started to rise from his chair, his trembling hand on the table to help him up. With words spilling out in a tremulous, high voice, he protested, "What's going on? Who are you? We can get the police you know."

Colm butted in, "Don't worry Alistair; the police won't be needed. These *gentlemen* are 'the police'; they're off-duty RUC garbage."

Willie slowly turned his gaze from Mick, leisurely scrutinising Colm, his eyes gleaming, a cruel smile spreading over his lips. "I'm *never* off duty." Almost instantly he diverted his attention to Alistair, the cold, cruel eyes boring deeply into the trembling young man's skull. "More to the point, *boy*, who the hell are you?"

Colm calmly, but with an underlying warning resonant in his voice cautioned, "Leave him be Inspector, he's a just a visitor."

"There's no such thing as 'just a visitor' with scum like you Colm, or with the people who keep company with you," rasped Willie. Eyes burning fiercely, he glared at Alistair demanding with practised authority, "Your name *boy*, what's your name?"

Alistair feeling intimidated, yet annoyed, regained his seat and with his hand shaking quite badly he picked up his pint. With his voice still tremulous and an octave too high, he petulantly retorted, "That's none of your business." Desperately needing a drink to soothe his dry throat, adrenaline quickly altering the body's relaxed functions in preparation of flight or fight, and to camouflage his obvious fear he quickly raised the glass to his lips; the haste was particularly necessary in order to ensure that his visibly shaking hand did not spill the beer over himself or the table. The glass reached his lips, liquid beginning to enter his partially opened mouth.

One of the RUC Constables took a pace forward and before the first flow of beer could reach Alistair's throat the man slapped the glass out of the young man's hand. The glass wobbled momentarily as if caught on a piece of string suspended from the ceiling, then tumbled, spilling beer over Alistair and continuing on its inevitable route, smashing onto the bare wooden floor boards, the residual spilt beer forming a pool of frothy brown liquid next to Alistair's feet. The beer glass disintegrated, shattering into seemingly myriad pieces, one or two of the larger glass shards travelling across the floor as if fired from a catapult. Tiny slivers of glass floated in the pool of beer, reflecting back the light from the fireplace, making an almost attractive pattern on the dull wood.

Unfortunately, no one had time to notice the beautiful reflections as Colm leapt from his seat, sending his chair flying onto the floor behind him. He literally sprung at the Constable, fists flailing, but in his anger he didn't make contact, the off-duty policeman calmly taking a backward step.

Instantly, Willie took an intervening pace forward and with great impetus, summoning all his forceful strength, he swung out, connecting, landing a ferocious punch on Colm's temple. The impact sent the already unbalanced Colm flying over the next table, knocking the table over and snapping one of its legs in the process.

His blood at boiling point and happy to get involved in what he did best, Mick leapt up, grabbing Willie from behind in a stranglehold. Without further prompting the other two off-duty RUC men rushed over to join in the fracas, a major brawl ensuing.

Dumbfounded by the dramatic turn of events Alistair barely had time to get to his feet before a punch from one of the RUC men knocked him to the floor. Dazed and afraid, he remained prone, a small trickle of blood forming on his freshly cut lip.

Alistair's assailant assisted the other RUC men, all three turning their full attention on the fiery, furiously battling Mick, dragging him off Willie and repeatedly hitting the Republican terrorist, punching the living daylights out of him. Eventually one of the men smashed a chair over the savagely battling Mick's head. Gradually the punches and blows took their toll, subduing their victim and the pounding, wreaking havoc on the man's hitherto rhino skin was turning the body's resistance to jelly. With his ox-like frame weakened under the relentless assault, Mick's face became a bloody mess and he collapsed onto the floor like a sack of potatoes, the fight fully knocked out of his system, a final blow knocking him out cold.

Meanwhile Colm, disadvantaged from Willie's earlier blow had no time to recover, Willie laying into him like a whirling dervish, pummelling him into an almost senseless heap. Defeated, Colm curled up his body and lay in a protective ball on the floor, his arms vainly attempting to afford a protective shield for his head; this position, although restricting the potential of a fatal blow being struck, did not prevent him receiving further punishment, Willie continually punching and kicking, the more powerful and vengeful police Inspector intent on causing maximum damage to the terrorist thug.

Perturbed at the violence being enacted within his Pub, sickened by the brutal beating being administered by the Police Inspector, the pub landlord tentatively exited from behind the bar counter; nervously he addressed Willie, the fear and respect evident in his tone, "I think they've had enough, Sir."

Willie hoisting up an almost comatose Colm by the man's shirt front, with his right fist poised over Colm's nose, looked up at the reluctantly brave landlord and growled, "Just keep out of this; it's none of your business."

"Any more, and you'll kill him," persisted the fearful yet brave landlord, nervously wringing a tea towel in his hands, "Surely even RUC officers must be subject to the law?"

Willie glanced from the landlord to Colm and snarled in response, "I've seen the evil that scum like these do. Unfortunately the law never seems to touch garbage such as Colm and Mick." He paused, wiping away the angry spittle dribbling from his mouth. "But of course you're right; I can't throw away my career for shit like Colm." Willie aimed a last, but vicious, kick into Colm's abdomen, drawing a faint gasp of pain from his victim. "Just remember, landlord, they started this." He stared threateningly at the publican, "Didn't they?"

The landlord, his tone weary, afraid and resigned, responded, "Yes, of course, whatever you say Inspector." He had long since realised that this particular RUC Inspector was an exceptionally cruel and vicious bully; the word on the street was that Willie Davidson was not a person to be messed with or crossed in any way.

Reluctantly and regretfully Willie relinquished his grip on Colm, throwing him down, Colm's body hitting the floor with a thump, the man's head banging hard against the solid wood. Severely beaten and bruised from head to toe, the bang on the head actually served to bring Colm momentarily release because it knocked him out cold, his brain temporarily relieved at the cessation of further pain. Willie not entirely satisfied, tipped the remains of Colm's drink over the head and body of the unconscious figure.

Alistair, shaken, bemused, terrified, yet retaining a vast amount of anger, was being firmly pinioned on the floor by the boot of one the RUC men. Frustrated, he yelled, "You bloody bastards. Wait until my father hears of this. You'll be thrown out of the police!"

Distracted from his gloating over the unconscious Colm, Willie turned his attention to Alistair. Amused, he demanded, "Oh yes? Who *is* your father, boy?" The grinning RUC man removed his boot from Alistair's chest, allowing the fuming Alistair to hastily scramble to his feet.

Upset and warily eyeing Willie whilst backing away to a safe distance, Alistair effusively retorted, "Robert Glen, a top Advocate in Scotland; he has connections. He'll probably complain directly to the Chief Constable of Ulster."

Feigning fear, pretending to nervously bite his finger nails, his voice mocking, Willie lamented to his off-duty colleagues, "Oh dear, lads, seems that we're in trouble. Oh, oh. The boy's hot-shot dad is someone well connected." Contemptuous of Alistair, his voice heavy with sarcasm, he continued derisively, "We're done for, ruined." The RUC officers laughed in response, more from fear of Willie rather than appreciation or amusement at the Inspector's humour. Willie's false apparently concerned demeanour changed to one of bullying malice and he took a pace towards Alistair, straddling the prone Colm, ensuring that one of his feet actually landed on Colm's chest.

Stretching forward, he grabbed the fearfully backtracking Alistair. With a handful of Alistair's jumper, and his face inches from Alistair's face, he smirked repulsively.

Alistair revolted, recoiled. "God, you stink!" He instinctively put his fingers in front of his nostrils. "Your breath, it's vile."

Peeved, Willie tightened his grip on Alistair's jumper, screwing a handful of the material into a tight ball. In doing so, he grabbed a fistful of the young man's flesh, pinching his skin.

"Ouch, you're hurting me," whined Alistair in protest, his eyes moist with an unshed tear.

Ignoring Alistair's whining complaint, his face millimetres from Alistair's face, their noses almost touching, Willie barked, "I don't know who you are boy, or who your dad is, but I *will* find out." His face white with anger, eyes blazing, spittle leaving tiny droplets on Alistair's face, he snarled, "If I find that you, or any of your kinfolk are involved with Colm or any of the Republican illegal organisations, then you'll not get a day's peace from me. I'll hunt you down and put you in your grave."

Pausing, he glared meaningfully and with deep menace into Alistair's eyes, "Do you understand boy?"

Ashen, more afraid than ever before, Alistair nodded hastily in affirmation, replying in a very weak and fearful voice, "Yes."

Willie persisted in glaring at Alistair for what seemed an eternity but in actual fact was only a few seconds, finally releasing his hold on the young man's jumper. Almost simultaneously Alistair's legs gave out and he crumpled to the floor, the fear having overtaken any control that he might have had on his leg muscles.

Willie turned his attention to the publican, firmly stating, "We'll settle our bill landlord; how much do we owe?" Pausing reflectively, he pointed instead to the unconscious figures of Colm and Mick, "No, hang on, they caused this problem, they'll pay for our drinks and the damage to your property."

The Inspector exited accompanied by his three colleagues.

Chapter 15

The Ford Mondeo car crawled along, its two occupants discreetly following Naimh's Toyota Corolla car as it travelled through the High Street of a small town in Monaghan in the Irish Republic.

A 'Gard' patrol car driving towards the Mondeo from the opposite side of the street, caused alarm to the two occupants in the trailing Ford Mondeo, the Irish police vehicle making them nervy and anxious. The policeman in the 'Gard' car stared attentively into Naimh's vehicle and recognising Naimh, smiled at the elderly lady, at the same time exchanging a friendly wave.

The two men in the Mondeo held their breath in unison, turning their heads away when the patrol car drew level, attempting to act nonchalantly by glancing in the direction of a shop window. To reinforce the supposed casualness the passenger pointed at something in the shop, apparently indicating a particular piece of garish furniture that had yet to make its way into the current IKEA catalogue. His driver friend feigned a laugh whilst nodding sagely in response.

Unable to scrutinise the faces of the Mondeo's occupants the affable Irish policeman merely gave a cursory glance in their direction and continued on his travels.

"Even more stupid than the British Police," scathingly muttered the Mondeo's driver whilst peering into the rear view mirror watching the 'Gard' vehicle disappearing from view.

Naimh and the pursuing Mondeo went past the town library, the large clock housed in the library tower indicating that it was now one o'clock in the afternoon. Naimh decreased her speed, changed down into third gear and looking up into her rear view mirror stared at the Ford Mondeo following closely behind. Grinning, she slowed almost to a stop, changed down into second gear and flicking on her indicator only at the last possible second, turned right into a Pub car park.

The Mondeo driver, caught off guard, rammed his foot on the brakes, just managing to stop his car from hitting Naimh's vehicle. "Fucking stupid women drivers!" he swore as he hastily changed gear, swerving into the Pub car park just in front of an oncoming pickup truck. The driver of the pickup truck jammed on his brakes, a mad squeal of burning rubber evidence of how close the Mondeo had avoided being hit. Relieved, yet angry, the pickup driver loudly pressed his truck horn, the raucous sound abetting the heavy squealing of his ferociously protesting and smoking tyres.

Rather than the pickup driver receiving an apology, the passenger in the Mondeo turned to look at the pickup driver, grimaced and raising his arm, merely showed a two-finger salute at the offended pickup truck driver.

*   *   *

Oblivious to the near miss in the street outside, Colm, Mick, and Alistair were participating in a reflective drink in the back room of the Public House, the three men deeply immersed in a muted and subdued conversation. Colm's left arm was encased in plaster, a sling over his shoulder adding support to the protected broken arm. Colm and Mick's faces were scoured with cuts and bruises, Colm's face having an additional line of yellow/mauve unsightly skin centred with a row of heavy stitches stretching from the side of his left eyebrow to the edge of his mouth. He would soon have another scar to compliment his already malignant features.

The two men who had been following Naimh entered the room, each carrying a pint of Guinness.

Colm and Mick immediately tensed, conversation between the three seated men instantly ceasing, the room now being bathed in a venerated silence; they stared up at the new arrivals with a mixture of total respect, apprehension, awe, and palpable fear.

Alistair, picking up on the sudden mood change and aware of the fear emanating from his two companions had a dread that a new episode of fighting was about to occur. "Oh God, not another barroom brawl," he mentally sighed.

"Hello boys," said Eamon, the Mondeo's driver, "I see you've been in a spot of bother." He thoroughly scrutinised Alistair, giving the young man a meticulous up and down inspection. "Is this him?"

Alistair quailed, ready to leap up and run for all his worth.

"Yes, that's Colm's boy!" hastily blurted Mick, nervously licking his suddenly dry lips.

"Colm's boy?" Alistair's eyebrows shot up enquiringly, questioning surprise replacing his earlier fear.

"Thanks Mick," softly interjected Colm, "I haven't told him anything yet."

Alistair nonplussed, glanced inquisitively from Colm to Mick. "Told him anything? What the hell are you both talking about?"

Eamon sighed, turning to his Mondeo passenger, Liam, "These

clods will be the death of me, so they will." Dispassionately, he sat down at Colm's table and proffered his hand to Alistair. "Hello, I'm Eamon and this here," indicating Liam, "Is Liam."

Alistair dubiously extended his arm, Eamon firmly and warmly shaking him by the hand. Liam nodded in greeting, his expression non-committal as he took the chair next to Eamon; he neither proffered his hand nor smiled in greeting, all the while his eyes never leaving Alistair's face, staring silently and fixedly at the young man. Alistair felt uneasy and uncomfortable under the hard man's gaze, the hairs tingling on the back of his neck. Unable or unwilling to match Liam's stare he averted his eyes, his thoughts temporarily distracted from Mick's earlier statement.

Eamon relaxed, partaking in a slow, delicious sip of his Guinness, smacking his lips in satisfaction. Elated with the taste he devoured a large proportion of the drink, looked with admiration at the Guinness and pronounced with approval, "This is a really nice drop of the black stuff. So often it's not kept well. This is really worth the journey." Satisfied and content, he placed his pint glass on the table and fixed his piercing green eyes on Alistair. "I've recently heard a lot about you Alistair and of your unpleasant experiences with the police in the North."

Alistair eyes lit up and he became animated, eagerly responding, "Yes, they were bloody bullying bastards! They really laid into Colm and Mick, punching and kicking, behaving like wild animals."

Eamon grinned, "I think these boys have seen it all before; they'll live to take part in many more good fights yet." He looked over at Colm, his eyes gleaming with malicious humour, "Isn't that right, Colm."

Colm nodded and smiled in response, the tenseness easing from his body.

Animated with his subject, Alistair blurted, "It wasn't fair. I'm going to follow this up with my Father when I get home."

Eamon gently put his hand on Alistair's arm, "Not *your* Father." He stared with deep penetration into Alistair's eyes and smoothly changed the subject of conversation. "I hear you have sympathies with the Irish cause?"

Alistair not immediately registering the first statement, nodded eagerly at the second, so Eamon feeling encouraged, continued, "Well, we have more important work for you." Pausing, he sipped his drink, never once taking his eyes from Alistair's eyes, "That is, if you are genuinely interested in our just Irish cause and if you can keep your own council. You will have to keep secret whatever you hear in this room and anything you commit to thereafter. Of course if you do decide to join with our cause, and if you subsequently betray us, well, I don't think I need to explain what will happen. But it won't be pleasant, will it boys?" Eamon, green eyes cold as ice, looked to Colm and Mick for confirmation of his statement.

Colm and Mick, the latter now nervously sweating, both nodded in affirmation. But Alistair was unperturbed by the threat because at this juncture he was unaware of the dangerous cruelty and unbridled brutality of the man speaking to him, and gushed enthusiastically. "Of course I'll be committed to the Irish cause and yes, I can keep secrets. I'd love to help and to get my own back on that bastard RUC Inspector!" He paused, frowning, his face adopting a confused expression, "But I don't follow? I don't understand...what do you mean, not my Father?"

Eamon softly called out, "Naimh, you'd better get in here."

"What! What's Mum's Aunt doing here?" Alistair's frown deepened. He politely rose from his seat as Naimh, slowly and with heavy feet, entered the room, her eyes moist and her cheeks stained with recently cried tears.

Naimh paused, staring momentarily with a tinge of sadness and regret at Eamon, then her eyes focused on Alistair; she spoke hesitantly but with deep affection, "Alistair dear, it's time you knew about your real parents."

Alistair, astounded, his legs becoming limp, slumped back down onto his chair, "My...my real parents? What on earth are you talking about?"

Her eyes burning with profound love and affection, Naimh approached Alistair, putting her arms around his shoulders; speaking with a lump in her throat, she blurted, "It's time you knew; you have to be told. Your *real* mother was my daughter, Bernadette."

Alistair was astonished and knocked for six, nothing could have prepared him for Naimh's blurted statement; gobsmacked, he angrily refuted, "But that's not possible. My mother and father are both in Scotland, Robert and Maggie Glen are *my* parents!" His mind racing, thought processes aghast, a sudden horrific though taking hold of his befuddled brain, he stared forlornly at Naimh, "Oh

God, you don't mean that my father had an affair with his wife's cousin?"

Colm reached across and affectionately grasped Alistair's sleeve, "Shush son, let your Granny finish."

Traumatised and annoyed, Alistair pulled his arm away from Colm, almost knocking Naimh's face in the process. "My *Granny*? No! No, this is crazy; she's my mum's aunt."

Naimh held tightly onto Alistair and pleaded with intense solemnity, "Listen please Alistair, I know that this is difficult for you but it is time that you learnt the truth." She paused for breath then hastily continued, "Neither your father nor your mother are your real parents. Robert and Maggie adopted you only after Bernadette died; before that they were only taking care of you until one day Bernadette could," she paused, a lump in her throat, "Marry and settle down." With tear-filled eyes and her voice becoming hoarse making it difficult for her to continue, she mumbled, "But Bernadette died, was killed, God bless her." She made a sign of the cross.

Alistair, mortified by this totally unexpected revelation, frenziedly rubbed his brow in consternation, "Oh my God, it can't be true!" He stared wildly around the room, his eyes unseeing. Dazed and confused, he didn't know what to say or do, and shoving his hands into his pockets he searched for something that didn't exist. Then, eyes fixing on his drink, he decided to hide behind the glass, picking it up and devouring a large gulp of beer.

All eyes were fixed firmly on him, each waiting for his next reaction, particularly Eamon who had formulated plans for this young man and desperately needed Alistair's one hundred percent loyalty.

Tears rolled down Naimh's cheeks, her heart aching for herself, for Bernadette, and for her grandson.

Alistair replaced his glass not knowing what to do, except realising that all he really wanted was to run from this room and from these lying people, yet subconsciously, he knew that there must be a grain of truth in what they had told him; they couldn't all be lying. And *who* the hell were these two strange men, so obviously held in awe by Colm and Mick. His wild eyes began to re-focus and he balefully and woefully demanded, "Naimh, if this is true then why didn't Mum and Dad tell me?" Anguished, he wretchedly added, "All these years not telling me. It has all have been a lie; my entire life a lie!"

Taking a tissue from her pocket, Naimh wiped her tears and then with the same sodden tissue, blew her nose. Speaking lovingly and gently she softly muttered, "Not a lie Alistair, it was never a lie. They loved you deeply, as their own, you were never to know."

"Of course it was a lie, a bloody lie!"

"As I said, as much as I wanted to claim you as my true grandson, I respected Bernie's pact with Maggie, but after your trip to the North, things changed," She glanced unhappily over at Eamon, "Other people had other ideas."

Eamon, bored, interjected with authority, "Naimh."

Turning her red rimmed and tear-stained eyes from Alistair, Naimh stared despondently at Eamon, before nodding with resignation, a deep sadness growing within her eyes. With no more tissues available, she used her fingers to wipe away a newly formed tear before once again turning her attention to her real and beloved grandson.

Alistair appalled and dazed, began to recover his thoughts. His mind raced, "Could it be true? Could his life have been a lie? What if these people were right? His mother's cousin's mother, or second cousin's mother, or whatever? For God's sake...or was she really his grandmother?" His head began to pound and he rubbed his temple with a tightly clenched fist. Out loud, he involuntarily uttered, "Oh my God; oh, my God! This can't be true!"

Naimh ignoring Alistair's outburst, continued, "And this clod," She glanced despairingly at Colm, "Is your biological father."

His head thumping, Alistair pushed Naimh away, jumped to his feet and brushed past Liam's futile attempt at restraining him. "This is all fucking lies! I don't believe any of it!"

Colm pushed his chair back, hastily rising, "Please Alistair, listen, please...son."

Alistair clamped his hands over his ears, "No, no, no! This is just all total nonsense; I'm not your bloody son."

Feeling faint and beginning to weaken Naimh wearily sunk onto Alistair's vacated chair; her tears flowed, her downcast eyes staring vacantly down at the table.

Colm persisted, "But Alistair, please...please listen; we have proof."

Alistair not wanting to hear any more of these imagined lies shook his head, rushing from the room. Colm was about to follow in pursuit but Eamon placed a restraining hand on him.

His voice firm but with an underlying softness, Eamon ordered, "Leave him be Colm; it's a lot for him to take in. He'll need time but he'll be fine. Naimh has told us that he's already an active socialist, having become quite enthusiastic and energetic in socialist organisations during his time at his University. As I understand it, he's joined the Scottish Labour Party and is actively campaigning on their behalf, and he wants to be a Member of the British Parliament one day. Plus, he also has very strong leanings for a united Ireland." Eamon looked to Naimh for confirmation before continuing, "Isn't that right?"

Disheartened, miserable and afraid for the future of her grandson, she tearfully nodded in agreement.

Enthused, Eamon resumed, revealing his thoughts and wishes for Alistair's future. "Well, he will make a fine politician – for us. We'll give him every support necessary through all our contacts and connections!" Green eyes gleaming, his face erupted into a huge smile; taking a large and triumphant gulp of his drink, Eamon enthusiastically continued, "Besides, our cause and objectives are of far greater importance than his current confusion of identity. By hook or by crook we'll have an Irish Prime Minister in charge of England, and then we'll slowly rip the bastards apart. By working from within their system we'll not only achieve our aim of one united Ireland, but also we can destroy everything that they stand for. Bit by bit we'll cause divisions and split the British Union." Smugly, he gently swirled the remaining liquid in his glass, "Cheers boys, and Naimh." Raising his glass, he toasted, "And here's to the future Irish Prime Minister of Britain, and the end of English dominance!"

They raised their glasses responding to Eamon's toast, the exception being Naimh who continued to stare abjectly at the table surface, desperately scrambling in her pockets for a reasonably dry tissue where none existed.

Indulging in a large satisfying swig, Eamon finished off the remaining Guinness, "Boy, that was really good. I think I'll have another; Liam?"

"Yes, of course," Liam jumped unquestioningly and obediently to his feet.

Chapter 16

Loins emptied, his sexual needs sated, Fergal rolled off the woman lying beneath him.

Maeve scowled with displeasure, her tousled auburn hair spreading above her on the pillow; slowly, she lowered her left leg from the missionary position. "Is that it?" she demanded, "You have your fun and sod me; what about my needs? I haven't been satisfied yet."

Now on his back and staring contentedly up at the ceiling, his breathing still laboured, he grinned sheepishly, "Sorry Maeve, I just couldn't hold out any longer. I'm so bloody tired, fucked," he added with a jovial afterthought.

Maeve was not amused. She had escaped from a potentially boring evening with her husband and had been expecting a lot more action from this younger man. "Well bollocks to you Fergal Mulroney, all you men are the same, just selfish bastards! So long as you get your needs filled, then sod us women." Maeve swung her arm, thumping her forearm onto Fergal's chest, making his already laboured breathing more difficult. She dangled her legs over the side of the bed, scooped her clothes from the discarded pile on the floor and not bothering to cover herself with any of the garments, stormed from Fergal's bedroom.

"But Maeve," protested Fergal hearing the rustling of Maeve dressing in the hallway, "I really am knackered' it's been one hell of a long day and I've had to drive for miles." His protests were oblivious to Maeve, the frustrated woman thundering from the house, slamming the front door behind her.

Fergal sighed wearily, his tiredness sweeping through him like a raging fire; he had reached the end of a grim day, his experiences working as part of a terrorist punishment squad leaving his mind and body with an overwhelming feeling of exhaustion and self-disgust. Fergal's eyelids became heavy, drooping and finally closed, his body desperately keen to sink into a balmy deep sleep. His body lay still, overly exhausted, desperately seeking the salve of slumber but his raw and shredded emotions kept resurfacing, preventing his mind's escape. He tossed and turned, his mind seeking sanctuary, seeking rest, even the fitful sleep of exhaustion and anguish would be welcome.

Fergal's thought's drifted back to the time of his 'introduction' into the terrorist organisation, recruited almost by accident into the dark, nefarious machinations of an organisation that had become corrupted by evil men and women.

Then, as a pimply faced, naïve teenager, still a virgin, yet to experience any relationships with a member of the fairer sex, he had inadvertently taken a mighty leap in a new direction. It had all started out very simply. Fergal and some of his teenage mates had got tangled up in a Catholic protest against the ruling Protestants and their perceived British Army lapdogs. Little did he know what a profound effect that day would have on the rest of his life!

Fergal and his friends had been playing street football, kicking a stuffed pillowcase 'borrowed' from the pram of the annoying younger sister of one of his friends. Despite the girl's howls of protest, the boys had kicked the pillow along the street until they suddenly became aware of a rumbling noise, sounds of chaos and mayhem springing from a few streets away. As they sought out the cause of this disturbance their attention was quickly drawn away from the now dirty and torn pillow 'football'. The annoying little girl, tears staining her dirty face, picked up her soiled pillow, threatening her departing brother with all manner of retribution when the episode was relayed to their Mammy.

Indifferent to the girl's threats Fergal and his mates hurried through the streets, the clamour of shouting, swearing, and stomping of feet, plus other sounds with which they were vaguely familiar, drew them closer to the cause of their interest. They knew that some kind of protest was taking place and their pace quickened as the wind carried the hullabaloo which promised something much more exciting than kicking a pretend football along the street. Fergal exchanged grins with his mates as they broke into a trot, rushing round a corner and running slap bang into a crowd of baying Catholics being driven backwards by baton wielding, Perspex shielded, British troops.

The area was in chaos, the road littered with upturned and burning cars and a destroyed bus. An RUC Land Rover has been upended and set alight, the three policemen previously inside, scuttling to safety behind a British Army armoured car. Some people were laughing, a crazy maniacal sound that was surreal within the context of the mayhem and burning vehicles, flames leaping higher and thick smoke beginning to climb into the sky.

Five shots rang out, the whistling of the bullets whining through the already busy and noisy carnage. The advancing British soldiers, attired in army issue gas masks, halted in two lines, the gunfire a warning that this riot was turning ugly. An order was fiercely barked and the second rank of soldiers opened fire, aiming over the heads of the troopers in front of them. Almost at the same instant, a thump, thump, thump noise was heard from the rear of the Army positions and Tear Gas canisters whizzed through the air landing with a thud onto the street below, two of the canisters actually connecting with scurrying people. Before the baying crowd could comprehend what was happening many of them collapsed screaming to the ground, complaining bitterly of being shot, but in fact, although severely bruised, their 'wounds' were as a result of being painfully hit by rubber bullets. The next instant their mouths and lungs were assailed by the released Tear Gas, the Gas fumes rising into the air, penetrating noses and entering open mouths, filling lungs with a noxious gas, causing eyes to stream; raucous coughs and unpleasant splutters added to the already deafening noise, bedlam and pandemonium.

Fergal felt as if he had suddenly gone down with a flu-like virus, his lungs wheezing, his nostrils flared and sore as the pungent, acrid gas seared his very insides, stinging every molecule as the gas worked its way inward; but the eyes, his eyes stung and the more he rubbed them, the worse it became, streams of fluid filling his eye sockets and running down the outside of his nose and across his cheeks. He hastily tied a handkerchief over his nostrils and mouth. Suddenly more shots sounds were heard, the bullets hurtling out into the maelstrom, causing Fergal to dive to the ground. Two or three women in the mob cried out, "They're firing real bullets; the bastard British are shooting at us!"

"Mother of God," howled a woman, her piercing shriek somehow rising above the general sounds of mayhem, "Mother of God, they're shooting at women and children."

Barely able to see out of his raw rimmed, fluid filled eyes, Fergal lanced up just in time to see the advancing British troopers, batons raised, pummelling the head and bodies of the mob members who had recklessly stood their ground. A woman rushed towards one of the British soldiers who had momentarily been left behind by his comrades, her hand wielding a broken chair leg; the advancing Army man, himself no more than a confused boy, looked to his erstwhile comrades for advice on how to handle the situation. But he was suddenly alone, his fellow soldiers separated in the swirling mists of Tear Gas. He ducked as the woman flew at him, her arms flailing, her eyes wild and her voice baying like a demented demon. The bemused boy soldier attempted to hold the terrifying woman at arm's length but she was determined beyond reason and began to rain blows, pummelling his head. Reluctantly, the young Soldier swung the butt of his rifle at the woman, knocking the woman's head sideways and sending her sprawling against a wall.

"Why you fucking bully," Fergal cried, scrambling to his feet, ready to lunge at the afraid and confused Army man. "What kind of men hit women and fire at unarmed people including women and children!" He clenched his youthful fists into tight balls.

"We didn't start the shooting, you people did," plaintively retorted the soldier, his voice meek. He was caught out of place and time and really didn't want to be there.

"Lying bastard!" Yelled a woman barely visible inside an open doorway.

Fergal's attention was immediately drawn to this woman; unknowingly, his first introduction to a member of the terrorist organisation that was to take over his life. The woman's skirt was raised displaying a pair of flaming red knickers and the smoothest thighs that Fergal had ever seen. His thoughts were instantly drawn from those of a violent nature to one of total lust.

The woman's dress dropped down and Fergal was visibly disappointed when a man stepped out from behind her, fixing Fergal with a searing look of cold-hearted ruthlessness. The woman shuffled uncomfortably, a hot revolver, its cartridges spent, burning her flesh, having only just been tucked by Colm under her dress and secured into the reinforced elastic at the back of her knickers.

The young soldier hastily moved onward, re-joining the sanctuary of his platoon colleagues.

"Did you see that," demanded Colm earnestly to Fergal, "Those Brit bastards were shooting to kill and yet none of us were armed."

His fists re-clenched, turning his attention in the direction of the departed British soldier, Fergal missed Colm's lazy wink, Bernadette smiling back in response to her terrorist lover and colleague. "Fucking shites," protested Fergal moving in the direction of the Soldiers, "I'd like to kill the murdering bastards."

Colm placed a restraining hand on Fergal's shoulder. "Not now son; if you really would like to get your own back then there will be plenty of time in the future."

His expression quizzical, Fergal turned to look at Colm. The eyes that met his were no longer full of malice but never-the-less retained a menace that caused Fergal to involuntarily shiver; he demanded cantankerously, "How?"

Colm smiled. "We know people, son; we know people." Colm paused, searching into Fergal's eyes, "Interested?"

Fergal had nodded enthusiastically.

If only he had known then!

Chapter 17

The years quickly flew by, Alistair's rise within the British political system being meteoric; his ascending star was such that as well as having the ear of the leader of the Socialist Party, he had also gathered the confidence and support of many of the Party's rank and file members. Indeed, a large proportion of the younger Members of Parliament looked up to Alistair as a person of growing influence and status within the Party's Parliamentary organisation. Furthermore, there was a great feeling, a sway of optimism for, although currently in opposition, the Party appeared to have every chance of winning the next General Election, subsequently forming a new, and many people considered well overdue, left wing Government. Yes, times were changing and Alistair with the backing and resources of his secretive terrorist supporters had engineered himself to the forefront of the people who would see through the change.

* * *

Having temporarily slipped away from his office in the House of Commons and away from his Parliamentary colleagues, Alistair was now ensconced in a sitting room of a terraced house in Highgate, North London.

His journey to this location had been via a very circuitous route to ensure that no one had followed. The chosen meeting point was in the vicinity of an area heavily populated by an Irish community, evidenced not only by the Irish accents and Irish Clubs but also by the names over the shop doorways, McCartheys, O'Connells, O'Reilly's, O'Briens, Finnegans, being just some of the names in verification. The Roman Catholic Church, although in decline in many areas of England, still had a very healthy customer base in this district. Although abortion and divorce had reached their Congregation, the Catholic Priests still exercised their power of forgiveness in the confessionals and maintained their control through the power of apportioned penances. However, many of the younger women from their congregations were also discovering a new kind of rhythm method that had nothing to do with birth control but more to do with music and song. The old avoidance of procreation rhythm method had been replaced by a combination of condoms and the birth pill.

The occasional collection box made its way through the assorted clubs and pubs with the intended objective of helping the 'cause' back home; the 'cause' was left vague but its aims and intentions were well known to all its contributors, many of whom did not wish to give up the price of pint but were self-consciously aware of the reverberations in not doing so. 'Green' was very much in evidence in the Clubs, particularly illustrated in some establishments where the very young girls were seen rubbing sore and aching limbs caused as a result of the repetitive practising of Irish dancing, which subsequent to musicals such as 'Lord of the Dance', had now made something of an unwanted revival.

Colm, Eamon, Liam, and Mary had joined Alistair in the sitting room of the terraced house, its bland décor making it inconspicuous with the others surrounding it. Reclining on a comfortable sofa and armchairs, they sipped tea whilst looking out through the glass of the sliding French-style windows onto a compact garden with a neat and tidy lawn. Eamon, relaxed, puffed away, smoking contentedly, drawing up the tobacco fumes from his lighted pipe.

Mary broke the reflective silence, "It's going to take far too long before Alistair gets the chance to become Prime Minister."

"I don't see why?" responded Colm, "Brenda Lawson may be the current leader of the Labour Party and although the Unions want Denis White to succeed her, Brenda favours our Alistair as her eventual successor." He turned to Alistair, "Doesn't she, Alistair?"

Alistair, in sombre mood, merely nodded in affirmation.

Mary impatiently continued, "Look, the Conservative Party is in a mess and they're sure to call a General Election within the year." Pausing for effect, she glanced at Eamon, "Which means that Brenda Lawson will become the next Prime Minister and will hold office for at least five years."

"Yes," responded Colm eagerly, "But then we can engineer Alistair to succeed her."

Mary becoming agitated, heatedly snapped in response, "But that's what worries me; we've all worked very hard to get Alistair into a very strong position, but anything can happen over the next five years. Denis White, as the current Deputy Labour Party Leader, could become stronger, or indeed some other bright young star might suddenly come forward."

Colm countered in a dismissively intolerant tone, "Yes, yes, I know, but..."

Glaring, focusing his piercing, authoritative, cold green-eyed

stare, Eamon silently ordered Colm to clam up, to keep his own council. Everyone knew the penalties or retributions in crossing Eamon, no one prepared to disobey or argue with him.
Satisfied that he was now master of the conversation, Eamon declared, "You're right Mary. We've come too far for it all to go wrong." Turning to Alistair, he enquired, "How is Brenda Lawson's health?"

Staring down at his highly polished expensive shoes, Alistair lazily replied, "Oh, she'll go on forever."

Liam animatedly entered the conversation, "But I thought that she had severe asthmatic problems and that she was close to jacking it in a couple of years ago."

Glancing at Liam, Alistair responded with indifference, "I would forget about hoping that she dies or retires. Her Doctors have got her stabilised; she's well under control, and she's just been given a full medical with satisfactory results. There's no chance of her suddenly dying."

Irked at Alistair's laid-back attitude, Eamon scowled, rose from his armchair and grimaced contemptuously in the direction of the, once again, non-attentive Alistair who was using a finger to wipe a speck of dust from one of his highly polished shoes. Striding to the French windows, he slid open the door and exited into the garden. Walking across a tiny paved patio area Eamon knocked his pipe against the rear wall of the kitchen extension, proceeding to empty the contents onto the grass, all the while his attention far distant in deep and reflective thought.

The others remained seating, waiting, staring at his back, waiting in anticipation for Eamon's wisdom to be imparted and obviously each too afraid to interrupt. After a few moments Eamon turned round, retraced his steps across the patio and re-entered the room, a beaming smile now lighting up his face, his eyes gleaming with malicious brightness. Gleefully he advised his colleagues, "That's it, sudden death!"

Alistair vigorously interjected, "But I just said that Brenda had been given a clean bill of health; she won't die suddenly!" Aware of Eamon's contemptuous scowl and cold stare Alistair immediately regretted his impertinence, "Sorry, go on."

Eamon permitted his scowl to soften; he smiled, "That was yesterday, her clean bill of health was yesterday. Tomorrow is another day." His cold eyes were gleaming maliciously, the implication obvious.

Liam responded dubiously, "Of course, but how? I suppose that we could arrange for an accident, or the wrong drugs, or something like that?"

Eamon raised his eyebrow in exasperation and turned to Mary, sternly demanding, "Mary, this is when your nursing experience should give us a solution?"

"Um," Mary hastily pondered the possibilities. Nervously she bit her lip, Eamon's green eyes piercing though to her soul. Inspiration suddenly arrived; it was amazing what fear could do! "I know, a Beta-Blocker! Brenda has two 'Puffers'."

Eamon stared at her with total incomprehension, "Puffers?"

"Puffers, inhalers; Brenda is severely asthmatic and uses two inhalers and a nebuliser." Mary shook her head in response to Eamon's questioningly raised eyebrow, "Don't ask! Anyway, if we substitute Beta-Blockers for her sleeping pills she'll end up with a Bronchiospasm."

"A what?"

"A Bronchiospasm." reiterated Mary. "Never mind," she continued in response to Eamon's questioning look, "All you need to know is that it should kill her and is virtually unlikely to be detected. They'll think that she died from a massive asthmatic attack."

Eamon triumphantly smacked his left palm with his right fist, "Perfect! I knew I could rely on you, Mary."

Alistair shot to his feet, protesting, "But you can't! We'll never get away with it. Brenda's Doctors would suspect foul play."

Mary coldly retorted, "It'll work. I can make it happen and no-one should suspect anything; it's not a problem."

Eamon terminated the discussion, squashing any potential debate by quietly but firmly stating, "That's settled then."

Alistair was stunned by the proposal; it couldn't be that simple, surely? Remaining standing, he demanded, "And what about Denis White? I can't see him relegating his position for me. He's very popular in the Party and his background in the coal industry makes him a hero figure to many of our voters."

Eamon sighed, favouring Alistair with a long hard stare akin to that of a headmaster to a junior teacher who should know better. He softened his stance, and stepped towards the doubting Alistair, putting his arm around his protégé, cajoling, "Alistair, oh Alistair, you worry too much. Denis White has already been taken care of."

Alistair recoiled, horrified, his brow instantly furrowing, "Oh, my God! You haven't killed him, have you? There was nothing on the news."

"Don't be ridiculous," snapped Eamon, becoming vexed. "No, of course we haven't killed Denis White, but we've done better than that. We've got pictures of him with a whole series of rent boys!" He waved his left arm in the direction of Mary, "All arranged by Mary here."

Mary glowed with a sense of achievement, proudly declaring, "It took some doing. Some of those boys couldn't figure out why I was enticing them until too late, others needed a shed full of drugs to perform. Setting up Denis, knowing his predilections, was the easy bit."

Eamon added with triumph, "So, you see, getting Denis to step aside for you shouldn't prove too difficult. We can also tell him that he'll be the next person to take over when you resign." Eamon chuckled in self-satisfaction, "But, by the time we finish with our plans and objectives there won't be much left worth taking over."

Alistair was still not convinced, "But what happens if he sticks to his principles and resigns, throwing me...us...to the wolves."

"He won't be given the chance," Liam menacingly muttered.

A shiver ran down Alistair's spine.

With the subject matter resolved Eamon gleefully turned his attention to the smiling Colm, "I think it's time for a celebration. By this time next week Brenda Lawson will be dead, Denis White will have stepped aside, and your boy, your boy, Colm, will be the leader of his Party. And if the stupid Brits don't change their minds by deciding to keep the Conservatives, he will be the next Prime Minister of Britain!"

Smiling broadly, Colm strode to Alistair, embracing his son in a huge, affectionate bear hug. Mary joined them, locking her arms round both Colm and Alistair, the three of them remaining locked in a triumphal embrace.

Not being of an affectionate nature and not given to affectionate displays Liam gruffly announced, "I need something stronger than tea; time for the pub and for a true Irish celebration."

Eamon readily agreed, "A drink wouldn't go amiss but I can't abide the local Guinness. Remember though, no loose tongues, we are so near to our goals we mustn't screw it up now by being careless."

In jovial mood they all headed for the door but a sudden thought hit Eamon causing him to pause in mid step, "What the hell am I thinking of? We can't allow Colm and Alistair to be seen together. Colm's got a police record, not to mention his time in the 'Maze' Prison."

"Ah, come on," pleaded the flabbergasted and perturbed Colm, "No one will know me here; I have to celebrate with my boy."

"Out of the question," Eamon angrily snapped. He took two twenty pound notes from his wallet. "Here Liam, nip out to the off-licence, we'll just have to make our celebration here."

Wordlessly, Liam took the money and departed.

Colm's face visibly dropped with disappointment, the remaining quartet trudging back to their seats, Eamon deep in thought, his brain racing with new thoughts of problems and their potential solutions; the previous mood of joyful anticipation quickly turning to one of quiet reflection.

Looking at his biological father's disappointed face Alistair then glanced in the direction of Eamon, quickly scrutinising and comprehending the thoughts that were obviously flying through the man's brain, then he returned his gaze to his disenchanted but uncomprehending parent. The son shuddered involuntarily, a sixth sense warning him of Eamon's current thinking and the possible future repercussions.

Chapter 18

Ubiquitous pipe in his hands, Eamon knocked the bowl against the glass ashtray, removing the remnants of burnt tobacco. His eyes glanced heavenwards, a frown spreading across his forehead as he stared through the smoke filled room. Liam sat passively, waiting for a response; Mary staying patiently still.

Outside, the distant sounds of a police siren reverberated, disturbing the peaceful serenity currently residing over this area of west Belfast. Distracted, Eamon turned his attention away from the subject matter, muttering, "Hope the bloody Ulster Constabulary bastards crash their car – that'll be a few less to remove when the times comes!"

"I'd rather kill them myself," Mary interrupted eager to demonstrate her fervour but merely received a scowl in response.

Eamon fixed his hard eyes on Liam, returning to the subject matter, "For God's sake Liam, I've explained this to you many times." He sighed, exasperated, "If you weren't so good at what you do – enforcing – then I think I'd have to get rid of you."

Glancing at Mary, a wry smile on his face, Eamon added with amusement, "Perhaps I'll let Mary kill you!"

Liam bristled with indignation but Eamon ignored the man's discomfort, continuing regardless, "You're just so bloody damn thick at times." Before Liam could protest, Eamon, his tolerance ended, barked, "Just shut it and listen. As I've explained countless times before, once we get Alistair into position as Prime Minister of England..."

"Of Britain," interjected Mary, instantly regretting her interruption as she recoiled under Eamon's harsh answering stare.

"When we get Alistair established as Prime Minister we will get him to use the various British systems to destabilise the country. We can utilise their so-called system of British fair play and justice. There are enough lawyers, whether driven by monetary considerations or left wing idealism, to tie-up their Law Courts for years. The Courts and legal professions can be overstretched in fighting human rights issues and illegal immigration cases, the floodgates could be breached wide open. If anybody dared to protest then they could be labelled as fascists or racists. It really is a no-lose, win-win situation for us. Furthermore, when Alistair's Government network and media agents are fully established he can ensure that only those of the correct political persuasion can be promoted, whether Chief Justice, Law Lords, Chief Constables, media, and so on; the possibilities are endless.

The English...British...Universities are full of young idealists who, when armed with their degrees and not having any real experience of practical work, or having carried out a hard day's work in their lives, can be put in positions of administration or authority, diverting resources from where they are really needed and end up producing reams of humbug, unnecessary statistics and figures; all of them will genuinely believe in the good they are doing but without any practical application."

Warming to his subject, Eamon articulated, "In addition, quite a few of the people representing Alistair's Party are from other British origins, so ultimately, they wouldn't care too much what happens south of the border."

Almost close to a rant, he verbalised, "The Police could be persuaded to concentrate on political correctness and enforcing profitable revenue laws against the English middle classes. We would demoralise and destroy the heart of England, the English middle class power base."

"What about your suggestion on education?" Mary intervened, "Denis White would never agree to students having to pay for University education. You know his feelings on an egalitarian society where all can afford to receive equal education."

Eamon scowled and utilising a partially burnt match, cleaned out the remains of his pipe. "Um, that could be a problem," he mused. "Kill the fucker," exhorted Liam.

Before Eamon could reply with a venomous, scorching retort, eyes bright with zealous fervour, Mary almost screeched in delight, "That may not be a problem," Pausing briefly for dramatic effect, she continued, "With the idea of devolution, you know, separate parliaments for Wales and Scotland and subsequently, parliaments, or regional assemblies for England, we can persuade Denis to push the proposed Scottish Parliament to pass an act providing free university education for Scottish students."

"Oh, yea, sure," Liam snapped bitterly, peeved at the growing rapport between Eamon and Mary, "And how will the Scottish students explain their free education to their fellow English students. Your human rights lawyers would have a field day with cases of racism."

Eager to push forward her suggestion, Mary hastily retorted, "Well then, it could be done so that the Scottish Parliament, in theory using their own money but subsidised through the national Tax system, could agree to fund only Scottish students using Scottish based Universities!"

"Brilliant," beamed Eamon, "Bloody brilliant!"

"Won't work," muttered Liam, sulking and glaring daggers at Mary.

Eamon ignored him. "That really is brilliant Mary and once we get all that in place we can make University too expensive for the important subjects such as medicine and science. Not only can we deal a mortal blow to the long-standing pedigree of some of England's finest Universities we can also sow the seeds of destroying their health service and future science and chemical industries – doctors, nurses, scientists, all will become a rarity!"

"What about the poorer people, many of them vote Labour?" Liam interrupted sharply.

Disgruntled, Eamon glared at Liam but then instantly smiled, an idea rushing into his head. "That's an easy one; the lower income people will get free education, but then many of them won't be able to afford the on-going costs of studying for their degrees. Alistair will also make so many nonsense courses available, spreading the concept of having a degree for each individual, that it will not only make the government financed education system untenable, it will downgrade the English degrees to virtually a worthless piece of paper – a third world education certificate which every single person will own." He chuckled mirthlessly and with self-satisfaction, reached for his tobacco pouch.

Chapter 19

Downing Street, London.

It was a beautiful spring day, the weather relatively warm and sunny, clear blue skies interspersed by the very occasional cloud. The climate matched the mood of the gathered crowd, the atmosphere being one of happiness and joviality, a general air of bonhomie.

The large police presence benevolently controlled the gathered huge crowds, some of whom were pressing firmly against the Downing Street gates. The police, arms linked forming a human impenetrable chain, were preventing any members of the public from entering Downing Street and were also preventing the public from blocking the approach road.

The gathered crowd cheered, wildly waving their Union Flags, many of the throng jumping up and down in gleeful excitement whilst others waited in silent reverence, their hopes and expectations welling up gently within.

Within the confines of Downing Street was a myriad of reporters, cameramen and television crews, many of whom had travelled from far-flung locations with a brief to report on the meteoric rise of the newly elected British Prime Minister and the successful General Election campaign of his Party. The languages spoken reflected the interest of many different nationalities in the outcome of this British General Election. Spanish jostled with French, with Arabic, with German, Dutch, the Scandinavian languages, Hindu, Urdu, Portuguese, and many other tongues. Camera crew instructions were yelled by directors, producers, and by the more senior reporters, all of them adding to the general cacophony of sound.

Those at the 'front line', microphones poised, waiting excitedly for the Prime Minister's arrival, speaking in English as well as their own native languages, all adding to a babble of sound that reverberated off the walls of the buildings.

The police fervently restrained some members of the Media who tried to step over the designated area clearly cordoned off within a line of rope, each Media crew trying their best to obtain the optimum position. A bank of microphones had also been set up in front of a partially raised dais, each microphone clearly stamped with the logo of its host television or radio station.

The assembled crowd erupted into a noisier cheer, applauding thunderously, ensuring that the accolade would reach the ears of the new Prime Minister and his wife who were approaching Downing Street in the official governmental car. The incoming Prime Minister's cavalcade was preceded by two police cars, the police officers armed and alert for any trouble. The Prime Minister's limousine, a Rover with bullet proof windows, was surrounded by police motor cycle outriders, two further police cars bringing up the rear. As the Prime Minister's limousine drove past the ecstatic assembled throng, who were now being physically, strenuously and forcefully restrained by the police, its occupants smiled and waved through the thickened, bullet-proof windows.

A cry of 'For He's a jolly good fellow' rang out, many taking up the refrain, joining in.

As Alistair and Serena, his wife, were driven into Downing Street, he could not resist hungrily taking in his surroundings, broadly smiling at Serena. "We made it, sweetheart, we made it!"

Serena smiled warmly, cradling his hand, and lovingly planted a kiss on the palm. "I never doubted that you would, darling," she breathlessly replied, the excitement of the moment welling up inside.

Alistair winked, "Of course you didn't sweetheart and there were times when I thought that the Polls were going against us and that the fickle British people were going to change their minds and vote the Conservatives back into power."

The car slowed to a halt outside number Ten Downing Street, the waiting Police Sergeant standing outside the Prime Minister's residence hastily stepping towards Alistair's side of the vehicle. Immediately upon stopping, the car door was opened by the Sergeant and a visibly beaming Alistair exited, his smile spreading from ear to ear. A second Police Sergeant appeared as if from nowhere and opened his wife's door, Serena rushing to take her place by her husband's side.

Alistair and Serena, holding hands, had barely exited the official vehicle before it was driven away. Hastening between the police outriders who had not been given the chance to move out of the way, they rushed back to the now closed Downing Street gates, their appointed Special Branch Officers desperately trying to keep pace with them. Alistair released Serena's hand and shook the hands of as many as possible of the gathered members of the public and Party supporters as he could. His Special Branch

Protection Officers, unnerved by this lack of security, made futile attempts to steer the new Prime Minister back towards Number Ten.

Espying a marvellous photo opportunity and being the consummate politician that he was, Alistair approached a young mother cradling a baby girl, and with eyes twinkling and face beaming, he almost drooled over the mother and child, declaring in a voice as smooth as silk, "Hello, thank you so much for voting me in as Prime Minister." He leant into the gate bars kissing the proffered baby on the forehead. "Our 'new caring, sharing policies' will secure such a bright future for you and your baby."

"Thank you Prime Minister," responded the fawning woman as the surrounding crowd erupted into reinvigorated cheering.

Alistair, turning from the adoring woman, smiled deeply into the camera of the cameraman who was dogging his footsteps, the camera almost in Alistair's face.

Pleased, satisfied, contented, he re-joined his wife and once again together, they almost bounced with glee back towards the assembled banks of microphones and reporters.

When Alistair returned to the waiting press throng, the cameraman focused his camera on the political reporter from the BBC. The female reporter, slightly out of breath having fought her way through the melee of journalists, breathlessly and enthusiastically pronounced into her microphone whilst staring earnestly into her camera, "Well, now the nation has seen it, too. We have elected a caring, sharing Prime Minister. Britain is about to step into a new age of State concern, compassion, and meritocracy. We have finally got the Prime Minister that we truly deserve."

Chapter 20

The late evening was gradually subsiding into the early night as a stolen BMW 3i car pulled up to the kerbside in a street in Armagh, Northern Ireland. Mick, in the driver's seat, and Fergal, his front seat passenger, were wearing dark clothes underneath their hooded coats, the hoods pulled tightly around their heads.

Mick switched off the engine but left the keys in the ignition. It was very quiet and still, virtually no sound disturbing the peace; he extracted a cigarette from the packet in his shirt pocket, putting the filtered end to his lips.

Fergal glanced at Mick, frowning, but his fear of the man sitting next to him, despite the thought of Mick lighting a cigarette bringing attention and possibly putting them both in danger, ensured that he didn't utter a word in protest.

Sharply aware of Fergal's glance and subsequent frown Mick was annoyed with himself, particularly because this little prick had obviously picked up on something that he should have realised before attempting to have a quick smoke. Fergal's frown had been sufficient to bring him to his senses and cleansing the thought of smoking from his head he removed the cigarette, replaced in the packet, tossing the rejected packet into the rear of the car.

They both sat quietly, neither interested in each other nor wishing to take part in any small talk, and waited patiently as the dusk turned speedily into a relatively dark night only occasionally lit up by the lights of infrequent cars that sped by.

Fergal, distracted, watched a Spider forming a web from the visor above him and backed away, pushing himself hard into the seat upright. He watched, fascinated, as the spider occasionally tumbled downwards only for it to pull itself back up by re-climbing its sticky thread.

Bored and fed up with Fergal's attention on the spider Mick lazily stretched across, grabbed the spider and crushed it firmly within his fist. He wiped the resulting mess on the side of the car seat.

Although having a fear and phobic hatred of spiders Fergal was irked. "What did you do that for? It wasn't doing any harm?"

"Yes, it was!" barked Mick, "It was spoiling your concentration."

Nervous, piqued, Fergal fidgeted restlessly, then discovering a morsel of food in his teeth, he picked at it until the offending particle was dislodged. Fed up with the silence, he demanded, "Anyway, who's the target? He's one of ours, isn't he? Someone stepped out of line with the Council, have they?"

"You'll find out in good time," gruffly snapped Mick, "This one is going to be very dangerous. There'll be a back-up team ready in case we fail."

Fergal alarmed, demanded, "Who? Who's backing us up? What the hell is this all about? I don't like not knowing."

"Don't be stupid boy; the least that you or I know as to the reasons for a target in these situations, then the better for both of us."

"But I'm really nervous," he persisted, "I don't really like doing these jobs."

"They all serve the ultimate cause."

"I know, but it doesn't make it any easier," Fergal grumbled.

Mick was beginning to lose his patience, "Shut the fuck up, will you!" Turning his attention from staring out of the window he snarled at Fergal, "Just be careful tonight. If you fail, you'll have me to answer to... on the spot! The order for this one has come from the very top."

Fergal nervously cleared his throat, his killer accomplice returning his attention back to watching the road ahead. "It doesn't matter who the target is," Mick stressed, "But when I say 'now', you let them have it. *Clear?*"

Fergal nodded in the darkness.

"Answer me you prick!" growled Mick, his eyes fiercely focused on his companion.

Fergal replied defensively, "I did; I nodded."

"Sure, and I can see that in the dark. Saints preserve us." Mick jerked head in amazement, "Why do they give me such complete pricks to work with!"

"Cheers," responded Fergal petulantly, "I told you that I didn't like these kinds of jobs."

Senses alert and sharpened, Mick suddenly tensed, his eyes peering out through the windscreen, staring along the darkening street in front of him, "The target's coming now, prepare your weapon, but don't do anything until I say."

Fergal grasped hold of a semi-automatic pistol previously placed in the foot-well.

Quickly pulling a pair of gloves from his pocket Mick hurriedly put them on and reaching behind, stretched to the back seat, grabbing a parcelled sack. Undoing the sack with a deft movement, he held a sawn-off shotgun snugly in his gloved hands; hastily loading the gun with familiar ease, experiencing no trouble despite the darkness, the years of practice and training making it second nature to him, he stroked the stock with reverence..

Oblivious to his impending danger, whistling whilst strolling contentedly along the pavement, not an apparent care in the world, Colm abruptly stiffened, his sixth-sense kicking in, suddenly becoming aware of the two figures in the parked car. The hairs on the back of his neck rose, his throat drying up and the adrenalin starting to rush, past experiences of previous familiar activity warning him of the impending potential threat. He hesitated and thinking furiously, perused the options available up and down the street, trying to determine his potential avenues of escape.

Mick exited the car whilst placing his loaded shotgun out of sight on the seat; he left the door open.

Colm grinned, sighing with immense relief, "Christ, you had me worried there Mick. I thought it was a 'UDF' hit squad. I was figuring out how many of the bastards I could take with me."

Fergal remaining in the car, muttered to himself, "Oh, dear God, no! It's Colm. It can't be Colm!"

Mick bent down and reached back inside the car.

Colm, alarm bells ringing once again, cried out, "Mick? What's up? What the fuck's going on?"

Mick did not respond, merely glancing at Fergal ordering, "Now Fergal, now!"

Temporarily overcome and immobilised with a combination of shock, dismay, fear and panic, Colm was surprised at the grip that this unexpected situation had put him in. He was experiencing newly discovered emotions of being on the wrong side of one-sided conflicts. The fright and the unexpected seriousness of the situation had a taken a fierce hold on his heart. For God's sake, these were *his* people. He never expected this! This couldn't be happening! He was a staunch Republican! But now for the first time in his life he was experiencing what it felt like to be defenceless, at the wrong end of a gun, with the added knowledge of his inevitable fate. Finding his voice he pleaded, "For Christ's sake Mick, what's going on? We're mates, we're in this together!"

Mick wordlessly raised his shotgun whilst Fergal slowly and reluctantly exited the car.

Glancing desperately around, making a hasty and final appraisal of his situation and seeing no possible opportunity of hiding or taking cover, Colm belatedly turned to run.

Mick fired, releasing both barrels of his shotgun. The first cartridge missed but the second hit Colm on the leg causing him to crumple to the pavement. Not giving up, Colm pulled himself to his feet and half limped, half crawled away as best he could, a pool of blood smearing across the ground.

Mick turned angrily to Fergal, "Shoot him you prick, shoot him, *now!*"

Tears in his eyes, Fergal opened fire. "Sorry Colm; so sorry."

Colm was shot three times, in the chest and abdomen. Mortally wounded and bleeding profusely he collapsed, prone on the pavement.

Calmly reloading his shotgun, Mick hastened to the recumbent Colm and without any feelings of compassion or remorse he stood over his victim, eyes staring down with contempt.

Sadness and sorrow replacing his previous anger and with breath rasping, Colm hoarsely asked, "Why Mick, why? And why you? We worked so well together, taking care of each other."

Feeling angry, ashamed, and impotent, Fergal slung his pistol into the car, aiming a kick at the door. "Shit, shit, shit!"

Mick remained standing over Colm, no pity evident in his eyes, his loaded shotgun poised over Colm's face, "It's just a job, like all the others. You mean nothing to me; it's the objective that matters."

Barely audible through the blood trickling from his mouth, Colm demanded, "But why? What did I do?"

Mercilessly and indifferently, Mick retorted, "I don't know; don't want to know. The Council said that because of who you were, you were now a danger to the cause."

Sudden realisation hit Colm. "Of course...to protect my son! I am expendable because of the threat to Alistair!" He smiled sardonically. "Dear Alistair, I hope it works."

Mick depressed the trigger, firing his shotgun at point blank range into Colm's head. Blood, bone and body tissue sprayed everywhere in a gory mess, Mick showing total disdain for the slime and blood mottling over his clothes and face whilst also demonstrating absolutely no benevolent compassion regarding the demise of his former friend and colleague. Dismissively, he threw the shotgun down by the body and returned to Fergal and their car. "Get in the car. This one will go down as another sectarian killing, a 'UDF' revenge assassination; the shotgun was taken from one of their guys we killed last month."

Distraught and disconsolate, Fergal clambered into the vehicle, slamming the door behind him, the frustrated anger making him want to smash Mick's face to a pulp but knowing within himself that he was not powerful enough to take on this cruel, unfeeling man.

Mick calmly shut his door, fired up the engine, and abruptly they roared off into the night.

Across the road a curtain twitched but was immediately closed. The earlier undisturbed silent stillness resumed.

Mick steered the car round the corner into the next street. A rocket fired from a mortar smashed into the front radiator, the BMW 3i skidding across the road and bursting into flames. Fortunately not wearing his seatbelt, Fergal was thrown clear, the car rolling over on its side. The burning BMW came to a halt smashing against a lamppost, bending the lamppost in two so that the upper half of the post twisted and collapsed onto the road, a shower of sparks dancing along the tarmac, the light filament briefly flickering in joy and then abruptly dying. A strong smell of petrol began to seep from the wreckage, swarming up into the night; almost instantaneously the car exploded, sending a shower of flames and debris into the night sky, scattering the remains of metal, glass, and rubber, mixed with human flesh and bones, onto the road and pavement.

Two men swathed in dark clothing and barely visible in the shadows emerged from an alleyway and watched the burning car spewing its remnants across the road and pavement. They exchanged glances, the first one shrugging as the second shuddered with a mixture of disbelief and sorrow. The first man, tightly holding a shortened mortar, stepped into the road and dropped the weapon down a previously opened manhole; as soon as a splash was heard the second man replaced the manhole cover. The mortar operative grinned in the darkness, his blackened face discernible only as a result of highly polished teeth visible from his grin. As he turned to his accomplice, a flash of firelight reflected off his glasses, the teeth and two glinting points of light from the lens giving the eerie appearance of a ghoulish apparition. In spite of being fully aware who his colleague was, the second man was unable to control the shiver that ran down his back.

The ghoulish man actually broke into a throaty chuckle but aware of the expression on his accomplice's grimaced face, now clearly visible in the glow of the vehicle fire, he muttered, "I wonder what those three poor buggers did, especially Colm and Mick; they'll be hard to replace."

The second man stared with sadness, muttering, "They must have crossed someone in the Council." Involuntarily he shivered again, a cold bead of sweat running down the small of his back, "Come on; let's disappear before the police get here."

The two men turned and scampered back towards the alley, the same alley from where they had appeared a few moments previously. Climbing across two garden walls they clambered into an adjoining street and quickly ran off into the enveloping darkness of the night.

Cowering undetected in a nearby doorway where he had rolled when flung from the vehicle Fergal waited until the two shadowy men had disappeared. "Bastards, fucking bastards!" he muttered having heard the men's conversation.

Hearing the sound of approaching sirens and the unmistakable noise of a British Army armoured car, he legged it as quickly as he was able but in a different direction to Colm's corpse and to that of the two terrorist hit men.

Chapter 21

A general feeling of contented well-being, together with a 'selfish', I want something for nothing' ethos was beginning to pervade society within the Western world. Britain and the United States of America, having two charismatic leaders with apparent socialist inclinations, seeming to work in unison, each well practised in the art of pleasing the public, both leaders equally and fully aware of how to play their respective media. The two leaders were very popular, almost Teflon-coated, their mutual aims appearing to be working well. The American President and the British Prime Minister had the luxury of strong economies and reasonably controlled rates of inflation, as indeed did most of Western Europe; most Western European Nations evidently in a very healthy position.

Of course, countries in Eastern Europe and other countries around the Globe were not so healthy and looked on enviously as the stronger capitalist economies continued to grow.

*   *

Shannon O'Rourke, delighted with her own current burgeoning financial status, exited from her recently acquired red Ford Mustang sports car having parked it in one of the allocated visitor's parking spaces in this car park clearly the property of the Federal Bureau of Investigation in Boston, Massachusetts, United States of America.

Locking the car door, she contentedly patted the vehicle and humming to herself, swinging her handbag strap over her left shoulder, she walked towards the Federal Bureau Building. "Life is getting better all the time," she thought to herself, "Pay rise to go with my recent promotion and now I've finally got my hands on the car I wanted. It may not be new but at least it's all mine, and it's paid for."

Pleased as punch, she strolled briskly into the Federal Building, flashing her badge at the security guard positioned just inside the entrance door. Waving cheerfully at the male receptionist who responded with a warm friendly smile, she proceeded to the elevator, pressing the button to ascend. Almost immediately the elevator appeared, the doors swishing open to reveal an inner emptiness that pleased Shannon. Entering, she pressed the button for the twelfth floor. The security man turned to discreetly watch her as the doors closed. Noticing him, she smiled broadly, but embarrassed at being caught ogling, he coloured slightly, the lift doors closing cutting out any further possibility of voyeurism.

Smilingly, Shannon checked her image reflected on the clear Perspex covering the elevator wall. Her auburn hair was swept back, the face with dominant powder-blue eyes virtually clear of make-up other than minimal coverage of lipstick and some eye shadow. She straightened her knee length skirt and made sure that her blouse buttons were securely fastened. Although Shannon wanted to look sexy, no she corrected herself, attractive not sexy, she didn't wish to be mistaken for a tramp or for someone who had to 'sell' sex to get to the top.

Having recently celebrated her twenty-eighth birthday the world seemed to be at her feet. She loved her work in the Bureau and was ambitious to rise to the summit, but purely on merit; Shannon would love to become the first female Director of the FBI. "If only," she muttered to herself lost in her thoughts.

The elevator made its way quietly and efficiently to the twelfth floor without interruption, where Shannon hastily re-checked that her hair was neat and in place before the doors opened, and she nervously swallowed to clear her throat. The doors slid open and she stepped boldly out onto the twelfth floor, the executive floor.

Entering into a wide, brightly lit foyer, immediately facing her was a set of heavy duty clear glass doors encased in a wall of bullet proof glass. Seated behind a desk on the other side of the wall was a middle-aged woman of dowdy appearance with the exception of the woman's hair which had recently been under the keen attention of a professional hairdresser, the hairdresser obviously suggesting highlights in an attempt to camouflage the increasing spread of grey strands; unfortunately the lighter 'tone highlights' only served to accentuate and exaggerate the woman's greyness.

The Receptionist looked up, smiled, and indicated that Shannon should use her FBI pass in the security lock.

Shannon nodded in agreement and reaching for the handbag strapped from her shoulder, extracted the pass from a pocket in the handbag. Swiping her card through the security lock, the door clicked and she pushed it open, walking through to the inner sanctum.

"Good morning Agent O'Rourke," smiled the middle-aged woman, "You are expected. Go straight down the corridor," indicating left down the corridor by extending her arm, "And take the door right at the end."

Shannon cheerfully thanked the receptionist and almost skipped along the corridor with animated anticipation, tingling with excitement. She was actually about to meet the District Bureau Chief - things were certainly getting better and better.

"Come in," a voice bellowed from behind the door responding to Shannon's firm knock.

Opening the door and entering a lavish and opulent office equipped with the very latest in luxurious furniture, she was greeted by the stonily staring faces of two men, neither of whom stood up to welcome her.

Behind a huge and expensive looking mahogany desk sat a stern featured man with obvious authority, thick-set and in his late forties, with cruel eyes and a hard mouth. On the wall behind him was a United States map with an assortment of markers highlighting various State locations. A plaque on his desk denoted him as Daniel Hogan, Director, FBI Divisional Office Massachusetts. Seated in front of the desk, on a dark brown opulent leather chair, was a bespectacled, middle-aged man, wearing a rather old fashioned suit, giving him the appearance of being a dowdy geek; he had an open briefcase on his lap. Next to the bespectacled man's chair was a second leather chair which was where Daniel Hogan sternly indicated that she should sit. Shannon noticed that the office walls were adorned with framed awards and certificates, all apparently in praise of Mr Hogan, obviously a very vain man!

Treading through a deep, shag-pile carpet, her feet almost sinking with each step, Shannon sat, all the while Daniel relentlessly fixing her with his cruel eyes, staring deeply at her but not saying a word.

When the man in front of the desk commenced to remove some papers from his briefcase Daniel's eyes flickered in the Geek's direction, his face registering annoyance. The Geek paused in mid action, quickly replacing the papers back into the briefcase. Daniel re-focused his unblinking attention back into scrutinising Shannon's face.

Becoming extremely nervous and suddenly feeling unsure of herself, Shannon blurted, "Sir, can you tell me what this about? I'm in the middle of investigating an alleged Iraqi terrorist funding operation, and..."

Daniel stopped her, interrupting in an authoritative and supercilious tone, "I *know* what case you are involved in. I know *everything;* nobody even breathes around here without me knowing about it."

Shannon was becoming twitchy, "Have I committed an error? Done something wrong?" She paused as she hastily ran through recent events in her memory. "Ah, is this something to do with that pervert Antonio? I did nothing wrong, sir. He was interfering with the illegal female immigrants so I merely stepped in to save the Bureau from any future problems."

The Geek in front of the desk gulped, nervously shuffling his feet.

"What?" demanded Daniel, "Antonio? I didn't know that it was *you* who almost ruined that operation!"

Shannon taken aback, mortified and colouring, exclaimed, "You didn't know? But I thought you said that you knew everything?"

The Geek sitting next to Shannon hastily made a warning noise, his Adam's apple rising quickly up his throat.

Glancing at the man, Shannon took heed of his warning, continuing in a conciliatory tone, "Besides sir, I didn't ruin the operation; I just tipped off the local Police Chief to keep an eye on Antonio."

"And blew his cover," dryly replied Daniel.

Shannon was irked, defiantly retorting, "But not the operation, it's still ongoing, and legal."

"No thanks to you."

"But, sir."

"Shut up Agent O'Rourke," ordered Daniel. He finally removed his eyes from Shannon, fixing his attention on his colleague, "Are you sure you've done your homework effectively? Errors here could cost lives in the future; very important lives!"

The man sitting next to Shannon nervously gulped, staring fixedly at the wall behind Daniel. "All the information is in the file, Daniel; it's been checked and re-checked."

"Oh, by the way", continued Daniel, eyes once again focused on Shannon, a poor imitation of a smile playing on his lips, "This is Jim Nulty; Jim is my right hand." Shannon smiled at Jim but received only a cursory nod in response.

Without further explanation, Daniel's matter of fact introduction was replaced by his trademark hard mouth and cruel eyes, "Well, that's the pleasantries over with. Your parents; first generation

American, yes? Emigrated from Donegal, Ireland, in the early sixties?"

Shannon replied dubiously, "Yes Sir, it's all in my records."
"Ah, but did you know that your father was once involved with the IRA in Ireland?" pronounced Daniel triumphantly.

Shannon was visibly shaken, "No! That's not possible. He - both my parents - love Ireland but neither of them could be described as supporting terrorism!"

Daniel ignored her response. "How do you feel about Ireland?" Rapidly adding, "About its division by the British?"

Shannon, confused, reflected for an instant, "Me sir, why? I've not really thought about it."

"Think quick, girl," he snapped, "You must have an opinion, particularly bearing in mind your background, your roots." Taking his eyes from her face, he quickly scanned through the file open in front of him on the desk, then looked up, his eyes cold and penetrative. "Your records show that you and your family have been heavily involved in Irish American Societies and activities; your family has a strong leaning to anything remotely associated with the Emerald Isle and your parents are regular contributors to '*Noraid*'."

"But that doesn't mean that they are terrorists, my family or me," snapped Shannon suddenly feeling the need to be defensive. "Yes, we love our Irish roots and background but we are Americans, and proud of it. With the '*Noraid*' thing, my parents specify that the little amount of money that they donate is for good causes only, for housing, schools, industry, and so on."

Again ignoring her response, Daniel peremptorily demanded, "Have you ever visited Ireland?"

"No sir, never." She was feeling increasingly defensive.

"Are you seriously telling me that your parents, with their strong beliefs, have never persuaded you to visit their ancestral homeland? What about relatives? Haven't they asked you over? Or have they ever visited you?"

"Of course; my mother's family have been over many times, my father's family only once. My parents had a holiday in Ireland a few years ago but I couldn't go with them. As it happens, I was tied up on a case at the time."

"So," lazily drawled Daniel, glancing at the very still and quiet Jim but immediately riveting his eyes back on Shannon, "You've never been to Ireland, have no real wish to, and have never made contact with any of the Irish terrorist organisations? In fact, you have no opinion on the Irish situation whatsoever, is that correct?"

Shannon glanced nervously from Daniel to Jim, her thoughts racing as to what possible information was in her file to cause these people to think that she could be a terrorist sympathiser, or worse, actually supporting an organisation such as those born out of the original IRA! A bead of perspiration formed on her brow. What on earth could be in that file on Daniel's desk?

"Well!" sternly re-iterated Daniel, his voice emanating from somewhere deep below a pair of voracious eagle eyes, or that is what it seemed like to the perspiring Shannon, her body temperature going into overdrive.

Shannon hesitantly answered, "Well I, um, that is, actually, I did promise myself that I would visit one day, both to Ireland and to visit my parents relatives." Daniel's eyes seemed to tear into her eyeballs, travelling into her brain. The room was getting hotter, time standing still, Daniel's eyes like two pin pricks searing through her head. Shannon fidgeted, growing increasingly unhappy and uncomfortable but then her awareness of injustice kicked in. Enough is enough she thought, I've got nothing to be afraid of, nothing to incriminate me; balls to it! Firmly, she announced, "Sir, what is all this driving towards? Do you suspect me of involvement with the Irish terrorists?"

"No," coldly snorted Daniel, "Why? Should we suspect you?"

"Of course not," snapped Shannon, "But what is this all about; why all the questions?"

Daniel turned to Jim, his face softening into a smile but almost instantly reverting to his previous hard-nosed and cruel expression. "Jim here has recommended you for an operation that I'm running. Although he's thoroughly checked your background and your service record I had to make sure of your pedigree."

Almost visibly exhaling with relief Shannon gushed, "So, you want me to go undercover to assist the British authorities against the terrorists?"

Daniel grinned, shuffling the papers in his hands, "Yes...and no."

Shannon was perplexed, "I don't understand? What the hell is this all about?"

"Oh do shut up and be patient, Agent O'Rourke," he ordered, finally taking his eyes off Shannon, demanding of Jim, "Are you sure that she's right for what we need?" Glancing back at Shannon, his eyes rolled heavenwards, "She seems too damned argumentative and feisty for my liking."

Jim coughed to clear his throat. Removing his glasses and taking a handkerchief from his pocket he distractedly and comfortingly cleaned the lenses. Whilst doing so, he quietly stated, "That's why we chose her and because of her Irish roots, Daniel; that's why she was selected, for her very independence."

Shannon glanced from one man to the other, "Selected me for *what?*"

"All in good time Agent O'Rourke." Daniel was exasperated, "All in good time."

Extremely peeved, Shannon stared down at her feet, then feeling angry, reached for her handbag strap, keyed up in preparation to depart. "Sir, I am an agent with the FBI, with a responsible and proven track record. It's not necessary to treat me like some little girlie; if you can't tell me what is going on then I request permission to leave, to resume my Iraqi terrorist funding investigation."

Daniel finally allowed himself to break into a broad smile, "I think you'll do, Agent O'Rourke." He allowed Jim the benefit of a rare smile, "I think Miss O'Rourke has the qualities that we are looking for."

Jim's visible relief was profoundly evident, the justification of his choice appearing to be vindicated.

Daniel returned his attention to Shannon, his face muscles softening but his eyes could still have frozen a hot oven. "I need you for an important mission. Jim here will be your contact point for an operation that has been ongoing for some time but which now needs some critical tuning."

Jim now feeling relaxed, rose from his seat, grinned at Shannon and extended his hand in formal greeting; Shannon stretched forward, her and Jim exchanging a handshake, Shannon smiling warmly in response to Jim's cordial grin.

Whatever the mission was going to be Shannon felt that she was now 'in', her tenseness melting as she snuggled into the comfort of her luxurious leather chair.

"So, in response to your earlier question," Daniel explained, "Yes, we are going to help the British Government," He grunted, "Or some of it, anyway."

Brow furrowed, Shannon glanced at Jim for clarification but her attention was immediately drawn back to Daniel who continued with his explanation, "The current British Government want an end to what the 'Brits' call the Irish problem. Their objective is to hand the North back to the Irish Government."

Shannon was astonished, "But the Protestants in the North would never agree to that!"

Daniel gleefully chuckled, "I know, but they won't know until it's done. Steps are already in motion to break down the channels that have supported Northern Ireland as being a part of the British United Kingdom." He sourly repeated the word "'United Kingdom', that's a laugh!" Earnestly adding, "However, we have set up a task force to assist the British Government. As you must be aware, here in America we have various ex Irish Republican personnel, some legal, some illegal, and we have done our best to keep a trace on these people. When the current British Prime Minister took up his office he persuaded our President to run a '*peace operation*' and this operation has now been functioning for almost three years, under my sole control." Pausing, his chest expanding like a proud peacock, he boasted, "And it has proved very successful."

Daniel looked at Jim, seeking his subordinate's glowing look of admiration and approval; Jim hastily smiled, vigorously nodding his head in confirmation.

With smug conceit, Daniel continued with his subject, "Together with the support of a clandestine British Secret Service operation, our objective has been to work with some of these ex Irish Republican 'soldiers', with the ultimate intention of destroying any resistance to the British Prime Minister's aim of offloading Northern Ireland."

Shannon flabbergasted, blurted, "My God, are you saying that we are actively going to work with, and support, terrorists? I can't believe it!"

"Ex terrorists."

Unappeased, Shannon persisted, "But surely our Government would not countenance such a proposal?"

"This has come directly from the President himself," sternly retorted Daniel. "Highly classified; from this point on you are part of the team and will be on twenty-four hour surveillance."

"Me? Being watched?" Horrified and perturbed, she rose from her leather chair, "I don't like it; I don't like the sound of any of this. Has the Defence Committee in Congress been informed?"

Daniel's cold eyes almost froze, "That's classified. This entire operation is highly classified, on a firm need-to-know basis. The end results are too important to be revealed or bandied about with any Tom, Dick, or Harry in Congress."

"They are not just any Tom, Dick, or Harry," heatedly retorted Shannon, "They are our elected representatives!"

"Sit down, *now*, Agent O'Rourke!" Daniel's face was apoplectic.

Jim, gently and warmly, stared pleadingly up at the white-faced Shannon, "Shannon, I'm afraid that you can't walk away. You won't be allowed to. Sorry, but whether you like it or not, you're in it now – committed - until the bitter end."

Shannon was indignant, "I joined the FBI to serve my Country, not to support other countries' terrorist operations."

"What we are doing is for the greater good," coldly responded Daniel, adding with threat, "If you don't sit down and compose yourself then I'll have no option but to terminate your role not only with my Department but also have you labelled as a traitor."

Astounded and mortified, Shannon implored, "No one would believe it. Too many people know that I'm not like that; I love America too much."

Realising that the situation had the potential to get out of control, Jim softly interceded, "Please sit down Shannon; we need you. Believe me; the ultimate aim is for a relatively peaceful transfer of the Northern Irish Government. For reasons of security only the President and a handful of his closest advisors are aware of the plans. For Congress to know, and for the majority of British Politicians to know, would make the whole thing a lame duck from the outset." Tenderly, he touched her arm, "Wouldn't your parents be proud if they knew that you were involved in the peaceful unification of Ireland?"

Shannon, partially mollified, yet confused, dubiously regained her chair; browbeaten, dazed, she muttered, "How...how long has this operation been active?"

Jim opening his mouth to reply was interrupted by Daniel, "As I said earlier, a little under three years."

"Then, why do you need me now?" she questioned.

Jim hesitating, glanced questioningly at Daniel, awaiting Daniel's nod of affirmation, then commenced his explanation, "Things were working well and our mutual objectives were taking shape but now we have a few loose cannons. It was decided that a fresh face was needed, someone not known to our British colleagues or to the various Irish Republican sympathisers operating in this area. Particularly, we need to investigate a certain individual." He removed his glasses, fiddling with them in his hands whilst continuing his narration, "We accidentally found out that there was a certain British Intelligence Officer here in Boston who seems very keen to track down a 'retired' Provisional IRA terrorist. We need to know why."

"I thought you said you were working with British intelligence?"

"We said we were working with unofficial lines of British intelligence, the official sources are unaware of this operation." Daniel's facial expression was bordering on aggressive belligerence, his impatience growing. His eyes snapped over to Jim, the voice and tone menacingly authoritative, "Continue."

"Anyway," Jim cleaned his glasses once more, "This particular British Intelligence Officer, known as Willie Davidson, was originally a Chief Inspector in the Northern Ireland Police force, the Royal Ulster Constabulary or RUC as it is known. He overstepped his brief."

Daniel eagerly interrupted, "It won't be known as the Royal Ulster Constabulary for much longer! Besides, there were rumours that Davidson was involved in illegal killings, plus intimidation and abuse of women."

Jim cleared his throat, "Ah-hem, though there was strong evidence against this man, Alistair Glen, who as you know is the British Prime Minister, persuaded his security services that Willie was too valuable to let go."

"Much to the annoyance of Willie's senior officers in the police force, who felt that they should throw the book at him," Daniel growled.

Jim glancing at Daniel, paused, eyebrow raised, then satisfied that Daniel had finished his intervention, persevered, "So, Willie Davidson was transferred from the Northern Ireland Police Force to British Intelligence."

Daniel enthusiastically intervened once more, "Where, as hoped for by Alistair Glen, Davidson is causing chaos plus immense resentment from the Northern Irish Catholic community."

Jim stared softly at Daniel, Daniel meeting his gaze, his cold eyes questioning. They both paused, each waiting for the other to continue the tale. Eventually Daniel snapped, "Well?"

Jim responded with the slightest hint of sarcasm, (he certainly would not dare to be overt with a sarcastic comment). "I thought that you were going to continue the story, sir."

Daniel glared sternly at Jim, "Hmmm." Deciding that it was his baby anyway he almost became ecstatic, continuing with the explanation to Shannon, "Well, it seems that Willie has discovered something that has got him 'hot and bothered'. He arrived in the States last week and is very keen to track down an escaped Provo terrorist, Fergal Mulroney. We need to know why."

"Is this Fergal Mulroney character part of your operation?"

"Good God, no!" Daniel snorted, "As far as we know he's retired. He escaped from the Maze Prison in Northern Ireland, made his way to America and through various Irish support organisations, is now working towards obtaining his green card."

"Latest reports we have is that he's just an old 'soak', a 'has been'. He'll probably drink himself to death before too long," interposed Jim.

"So why does this Willie Davidson want to find him so desperately?"

Daniel's almost friendly face immediately adopted a callous expression, "That's where you come in; it's what we want to know. No, I'll put it stronger; it's what we *have* to know."

"Then why haven't you pulled Fergal in?"

Daniel exasperated, impatiently snapped, "Of course we've pulled him in, quite a few times. Sober or drunk, there has been nothing interesting coming out of him. It's a complete mystery."

"Then, where do I start?" Shannon was eager to start the new operation and eager to escape from the stifling atmosphere pervading Daniels office, "Where are these Fergal and Willie characters and how do I meet them?"

Jim declared with triumph, "They are right here in Boston." Daniel broke in, "Yes the bum, Fergal, has given us the uninvited *pleasure* of his company, residing here in Boston. We need you to get 'close' to him."

"When you say get 'close', sir, how close does that mean?"

Daniel adopted a lewd expression, his cold eyes almost undressing Shannon, a lecherous smile spreading across his lips. "As close as necessary, an intimate relationship would be preferred.

We have to unravel his secret." His tone hardened, "Before Davidson finds him!"

Her new mission explained Shannon shuddered involuntarily as she departed from Daniel's office; she was not sure if it was because of the look from that slimy man across the desk from her or if it was because of the thought of an intimate relationship with some unwashed, ex-terrorist drunken bum. All she wanted to do now was to jump into a hot bath and wash away both possibilities. Her new life was no longer looking quite so rosy.

Chapter 22

Despite three days of patient work trailing Fergal, dogging his footsteps and becoming his virtual but, unseen shadow, Shannon had got absolutely nowhere with her given objectives. She hadn't been able to fabricate an innocent contact or ascertain any activities or actions that would determine if Fergal was some kind of threat to the American or British Governments. To her, he really did appear as a down and out slob, a no-good drunk, on the verge of being an alcoholic, if he wasn't one already.

"What a waste of time and effort", thought Shannon, "I really have an important case to work on and they stick me on this washed-up loser."

She kicked out at a litter bin in frustration before entering O'Reilly's Bar, located in a commuter thoroughfare some way off Boston City centre. This area of the city was jam-packed with brownstone buildings, the air heavy with the poverty of the predominant immigrant population that had settled here.

O'Reilly's was relatively empty except for a few hardened male drinkers and one young couple standing at the far end of the bar counter, wrapped up in their own little world and having eyes only for each other.

It was an 'in-between' time in O'Reilly's, too early for the evening social drinkers who were still enjoying their food within the bosom of their families, but was subsequent to the rush-hour, early evening clientele. Most of the early evening drinkers, mainly office workers who had stopped by on their way home from work to quench their thirst, had either resumed their journeys home to their loving families or secured a green light for the next stage of their office romance and moved on to the fulfilment of their illicit relationships. One couple, not having the patience, their ardour having overtaken all other emotions, succumbed to the opportunity of a drink fuelled fumble at the back of adjacent alleyway.

Shannon was dismissive of the unnecessary activity, her focus purely on Fergal. She spotted him straight away, his unshaven and dishevelled appearance immediately making him stand out. Fergal was well on the way into his customary inebriated state, slumped on a chair, slouched across his table, a half empty whisky bottle and partially full tumbler of whisky on the table in front of him. Even if the Bar had been full Shannon suspected that no-one would wish to share Fergal's table or the man's company.

She approached the bar, ordering an orange and tonic-water and a club sandwich. The young Bartender looking up, smiled, and winked in a salacious manner. Shannon had visited his Bar quite a few times in the last few days and he suspected that she was looking for a virile young man, perhaps someone like himself, to be her lover, her 'booty' call.

"You know what these sad late twenties women are like," he thought smugly.

Shannon scowled in response to his wink, fixing him with an unwelcome stare, making the Barman hastily put aside his obscene thoughts. Pouring her drink, he instantly became the epitome of a professional Barman without any further suggestive behaviour.

Taking her drink, she sat at a table close to Fergal, positioning herself so that she had a clear vision of the drunken slob, the Bar entrance, and the Bar counter. An hour passed without anything untoward happening. Shannon had eaten, or more truthfully, picked at her food; she was sure that there was definitely fresher food in her dustbin, and had downed two further soft drinks. The young lovers had left the Bar to be replaced by three business executives partaking in a late evening meeting whilst enjoying a congenial atmosphere.

Fergal's bottle of whisky was now empty, his tumbler housing only an infinitesimal drop of drink.

Bored out of her skull, Shannon sipped her third drink, a tomato juice, trying her utmost to ignore the lecherous glances and smiles of the three admiring businessmen and one or two other males in the room, all the while keeping a discreet eye on Fergal. "I don't know why it is," she murmured, "But all men seem to think that any woman drinking alone in a Bar is either looking to be picked up or is some kind of tart."

His eyes glazed, deep in some dark inner thought running round in his head, Fergal ran his finger along the rim of his glass tumbler; shaking his head to clear the memory, he picked up his tumbler, raised the glass to his lips and consumed the remaining drops of drink in one gulp. Picking up the bottle, he held it over his tumbler, but it was empty. Refusing to accept the inevitable, he kept the empty bottle poised over the glass tumbler, waiting as the remaining droplet trickled into his glass. Frustrated, he slammed the bottle down on to the table and rising unsteadily to his feet, and staggered awkwardly in the direction of the bar counter.

Shannon instantly alert, sprung from her seat, scooping up her drink at the same time. With a full glass of drink in her hand she hastened towards the bar seemingly unaware of Fergal heading in the same direction but ensuring that she cut in front of his path.

Oblivious to his surroundings, Fergal stumbled into Shannon, almost falling down in the process. She seized her moment, stretching her leg out, discreetly managing to trip Fergal so that they both tumbled to the floor. In falling, she skilfully and deftly contrived to throw her drink over her clothes. They tumbled together in a heap, rolling on to the floor, Shannon surreptitiously removing Fergal's wallet from his back pocket and sliding it, in one graceful movement, under her dress into a prepared pocket in her underwear.

Two of the businessmen ran forward to assist and the Bartender, throwing down his bar towel, rushed from behind his bar counter. But by the time the businessmen reached Shannon she had already got to her knees and was straightening her dress ensuring that nothing was visible - but not from a modesty point of view.
The first businessman, grinning madly, extended a helping hand, helping Shannon to her feet.

The solicitous Bartender, afraid of a potential lawsuit, rushed forward on the heels of the businessman; anxious and apologetic, he grovelled, "Sorry Lady; you okay?" Looking down with repugnance and disgust at Fergal, he remonstrated, "Drunken old sot. Get up! And get out! You're barred!"

Fergal, drunk, confused, bewildered, mumbled incoherently, "What...what happened?"

"You *happened*," yelled the Bartender, "You silly drunken slob. You *happened* to drink too much whisky in my bar!"

Bemused and utterly confused, Fergal attempted to rise but only ended up flat on the floor, his co-ordination not sufficient to allow him to get to his feet. With drunken naivety he protested his innocence, "But, but, I didn't do anything."

The Bartender was livid, and unceremoniously yanked Fergal to his feet. He berated, his voice rising in angry contempt, "I've been watching you for days; always in here, always getting drunk. Well, that's it. Pay up and get out. We don't want you in here anymore."

Shannon was still being 'supported' by the firm grip of the over eager businessman, and she gently pulled herself free, her over-amorous 'knight' reluctantly giving way, his face registering immense disappointment. With exaggerated movements she smoothed down her dress, brushing away imaginary dirt, then suddenly made a great show of pretending to 'discover' the spilt drink on her clothes, gasping in mock disbelief. "I can't believe that he walked into me! The man's completely drunk, and he made me spill my drink on my clothes! Who's going to pay the cleaning bill? This is an expensive dress. I spent nearly a month's salary cheque on this! This is my special interview outfit, my only luxurious purchase!"

The Bartender crowed, "Oh, he'll pay, lady, he'll pay." Firmly gripping the bewildered Fergal by his collar, he demanded, "Won't you pal? But first, you have to settle your bar tab!"

Fergal's unfocused, red-stained eyes look blearily from the Bartender to Shannon and he tried to clear his head in an attempt to bring sanity. All he received in response was a vigorous shake, backwards and forwards, from the Bartender, the movement doing nothing to help him overcome his drunken and nauseous state. His legs almost gave way but the Bartender's grip was strong enough to keep Fergal, unsteadily, on his feet.

Still aggressively shaking Fergal like a rag doll, the Bartender persisted with his demand, "You will pay, won't you friend? It's not a question, it's a statement. Get your wallet out pal."

Fergal belligerently tried to pull free but in doing so almost crumpled to the floor. For his pains he was then firmly and unceremoniously hoisted up by the Bartender and shoved aggressively against the bar counter.

"*Wallet! Now!*" ordered the huge, physically strong Bartender who would make Arnold Schwarzenegger look like a wimp.

Desperately trying to regain his wits, some sanity, and trying to focus effectively, Fergal reluctantly reached towards his back pocket, fumbled ineffectively, frowned, and then stared with blurred vision in the direction of his recently vacated table. Vaguely and uncomprehendingly he looked down to where he had first stumbled onto the floor. "What the hell; where's my wallet?" He exploded with drunken indignation, "Someone's taken my wallet!"

"Sure Pal," responded the Bartender with extreme sarcasm, "Sure Buddy, we've heard that one before. The 'I've lost my wallet' cry is one of the oldest ploys in the book; it's been tried before by better men than you will ever be. Now stop messing about and get your money out, that is, if you don't want me to take you out the back."

Fergal became defensive, "No, seriously, I have lost my wallet." He scratched his head desperately trying to think, "Or someone's taken it."

The Bartender's patience was close to snapping, his face turning red, blood pressure starting to climb, the hairs on the nape of his neck beginning to rise. He was ready to punch the lights out on this pathetic drunk. With threatening menace, the burly Bartender demanded, "I'll count to three pal; if you don't pay up, then I'll..." Pressing Fergal against the bar counter with his left hand, he raised his right fist in preparation of the promised punch.

Shannon stepped between Fergal and the Bartender's raised right arm. "But what about my dress if you beat him up; who's going to pay for that?"

"Lady, join the queue," The aggressive Bartender was not going to be distracted by Shannon's statement and question; Shannon's needs had now been relegated and were of little consequence compared to the potential loss of wages if the Bartender could not recover the money owed from this drunken bum. Ignoring Shannon, the Bartender commenced to drag Fergal towards the rear service door of the Bar.

Shannon was hot on his tail, "Now hold on a minute. You can't just leave me without recompense." She quickly scrutinised the few customers desperately hoping for some assistance, "Does anyone know where this joker lives?"

With belated deference the Bartender paused and stared questioningly at his customers. No one proffered a suggestion or uttered any words whatsoever, one or two of the customers even turning away, not wanting to get involved becoming the more common thought in these sad days of litigation and fat cat lawyers. "I guess they don't, lady," he dryly uttered, continuing with his task of dragging Fergal towards the back.

Nervously and a little unsure, a solitary male customer at a table tucked in near the front window recess quietly spoke up, "I think he lives near Mother Clancy's Deli."

Shannon eyes lit up and she smiled with relief at the customer, calling out, "Thank you." Striding to her original table, taking her handbag, she walked back to the static Bartender. "Right, I'll get a cab, take him back to his place and get my money, or anything that will cover the cost of this dress." She reached for Fergal but the Bartender pulled him back.

"And what about his drinks, who pays for those?" queried the very sober and angry Bartender.

"I'll bring the money back," Shannon smiled sweetly.

"Sure you will, lady, and I'm the magic fairy."

Shannon not liking being foiled, lost her patience, "Godammit, I said I would bring the money back, and I will!"

The Bartender still angry at Fergal, remained cool with Shannon, "It's no good getting 'arsey' with me, lady. I ain't letting him go without some recompense."

"Oh, for goodness sake," Shannon snarled, "How much does he owe, a few dollars?" She opened her bag, inserting her hand.

The Bartender erupted into laughter, "A few dollars? Lady, you're kidding. His tab was up to fifty-three Dollars!" Chuckling, he recommenced his journey, dragging Fergal behind him.

Shannon desperate, whistled to draw the Bartender's attention back on to her and as the man turned, uttered with resignation, "Okay, I'll settle his bill; it's the only chance I have to get my money and my dress cleaned or replaced."

The Bartender, in mid step, seeing a way out of his dilemma, shrugged and allowed Fergal to flop ungraciously onto a chair.

Shannon sighed in gratification, knowing that she had won this particular little battle, her thoughts quickly skipping forward to justifying the costs on her expense report. Taking her wallet from her handbag, she quickly counted out the specified amount of dollars, handing the money to the Bartender, "Here's fifty-five Dollars. I need a receipt." Then adding, voice heavy with sarcasm, "Keep the change."

The Bartender, his blood pressure instantly dropping, thanking God that he wouldn't have to make up the money after all, gratefully reached for the proffered cash. However after counting it, he glanced slyly at Shannon. "And, er, don't forget your own tab of seventeen dollars!"

Shannon, not pleased, extremely pissed off to be more accurate, extracted a twenty-dollar bill from her wallet, passing it reluctantly to the Bartender, "Bloody mercenary!"

The Bartender grinning, gratefully took the tendered money,

"Thank you, ma'am."

Shannon irked, acerbically inquired, "You gonna call me a cab or will that cost extra?"

The Bartender, extremely relieved and grinning broadly, made his way back behind the bar, cash tightly gripped in his hand, retorted light heartedly over his shoulder at Shannon, "No, lady, you can have that for free!"

Chapter 23

Shannon helped Fergal exit the taxicab, the vehicle having pulled alongside the kerb outside a very run down brownstone building. The derelict area reeked of poverty and decay, the affluent having long since moved elsewhere.

Even in this late evening dusk Shannon was only too aware of the abject deprivation of the district, which now appeared only to house those unfortunate enough to be either unemployed or work-shy, and the drug dealers and petty criminals, all combining to drag down the neighbourhood. The knock on effect was that people no longer seemed to care about their local surroundings. The adjacent alleys were littered with an assortment of refuse that also included discarded cans with jagged metal edges exposed, rotting discarded food that even the local cats seemed reluctant to tackle, and empty, broken bottles, most of which still contained the stench of alcohol within the various coloured exteriors.

Many of the people who passed by seemed as if they were carrying the weight of the world of their shoulders, particularly the younger adults who still had the hope, vision, inclination and desperation to climb out of this ghetto environment.

A rather old and excessively powdered prostitute, the make-up in thick layers, but with a sad and desperate demeanour, leaned against a lamp post a few yards from a public bar, obviously waiting for any desperate punter exiting after having imbibed a few drinks and hopefully having his 'beer goggles' on. The days had long since expired when a sober man would find this particular hooker's wares of any attraction. However old Mel, the prostitute in question, just managed to eke out a living and having experienced the utter shock of needing false teeth, unbelievably rather than putting off certain punters had seemed to have the opposite effect by increasing her business. But she was still waiting, forlornly, for someone like Hugh Grant to pass by. Mel regularly thanked God for the gift of alcohol and men's wallets and for certain 'men's bits' which needed her occasional maintenance.

Spotting a couple of inebriated men staggering out from the nearby run down bar, Mel hoisted her suede mini skirt a notch higher and stretched out her leg revealing stockings and suspenders. Smiling seductively, she waited expectantly with hands on hips.

Glancing over at the prostitute, Shannon shook her head in dismay. "What a way to have to make a living," she muttered more in sorrow than contempt.

Partially lifting, half dragging, the inebriated and almost comatose Fergal, Shannon clambered up seven steps and entered through the main door of Fergal's building. The youths sitting on the steps paid scant attention to the new arrivals, the familiar sight of some of the locals coming home in such a drunken state not warranting much attention. It was a recognizable pattern, a way of escaping the depressing routine of life, but in doing so only served to increase the permanent cycle of poverty.

There were also a few 'ladies' who journeyed up these steps, each trying to make a few extra dollars by taking men up to their rooms. Fleetingly, one of the youths thought that Shannon was a little bit more special than the usual 'talent' seen in the area but he was quickly distracted by his colleague passing him a lighted joint. Drugs were another imagined escape route from the hell hole known as Sixth Street.

Passing through the disgustingly dusty hallway and quickly ascertaining that there wasn't an elevator, Shannon staggered under Fergal's cumbersome weight, mounting a broad flight of stairs to the first floor. "Thank God his apartment is on the first floor," she mumbled breathlessly. Having tailed him for a few days she knew exactly where he lived; she probably knew more about his current habits then he did.

Panting and almost totally out of breath she quickly checked out the apartment numbers. "104; that's yours, isn't it?" she queried rhetorically. With one final effort she hauled Fergal forward and, with the use of her hip, supported him against the wall next to his apartment door. "Right 'friend', key; where's your key?"

Fergal barely able to stand, slurred in response, "No key." His eyes rolling heavenwards he did his utmost to focus, "Wh...what...who are you?"

Shannon changed her position, using both her hip and shoulder to hold Fergal against the door whilst she fumbled through his pockets. "Um, s'that's nice," slurred Fergal.

"Oh shut up, you piss head."

"Hey, 'doesnt talk to me like s'that'," he protested, trying to resist, attempting vainly to push her away; but unbalanced and inebriated, his legs crumpled under him.

Sighing with deep disgust, Shannon quickly pulled her hand from his pocket but too late to prevent Fergal sliding down the wall and onto the floor, his back resting against the doorframe. Fergal blacked out.

Shannon stood over Fergal, a look of contemptuous disgust on her face, "Terrific! What a pathetic, drunken slob." She hastily ferreted through his pockets. "Uh-ha, got them," triumphantly pulling out a key ring with three keys.

"Well, here goes," she muttered, hurriedly inserting the first key. The door unlocked. "Hey, that was lucky." Pushing the door open, Shannon poked her head into the room, quickly scanning the insides of this dirty, dingy place. Appalled at the state of the Fergal's domestic abode she pulled her head back. "How can anyone live like this? Even rats would have a cleaner place!"

Disgusted, but shrugging her shoulders, she emitted a heartfelt sigh. "Oh well, here goes; I will need a long hot bath after this." Taking hold of Fergal's legs she dragged him forward; unfortunately as she pulled, his upper body slid down and the back of his head hit the floor with an almighty thump. "That should knock some sense into him," she murmured unconcernedly but with a hint of satisfaction and with an indifferent shrug of her shoulders pulled him, brusquely, through the door of the flat. "Why do I get all the best jobs?"

Shannon kicked backwards at the apartment door, closing it with a bang and then quickly checked out each room, ascertaining that the unkempt property consisted of one main living room, a cupboard-size kitchen, bathroom, and a single bedroom. Dragging Fergal across the threadbare carpet of the living room, their progress scattered discarded newspapers and raised dirt from the carpet, shrieking in evidence that confirmed it had been some time since a vacuum cleaner had been run over it.

Passing the kitchen doorway Shannon observed a collection of empty bottles, a varied assortment of empty alcoholic drinks, accumulated both in the sink and randomly stacked on the floor against the refuse bin.

Callously dragging the limp Fergal through the open bedroom door, she heaved him on his back onto the bed and stared down with contempt at the foul, whisky smelling individual. The overpowering stench of repugnant body odour and whisky hit her nostrils like a gale force wind.

"Right; time to turn this place even more upside down." Turning away, brushing her hands together as if brushing away the unpleasant task of getting Fergal home, she adopted a business-like manner but instantly paused, turning back to look at Fergal. "I can't leave him like that. What if he's sick and chokes on his own vomit? Serves him right," responded her inner thoughts. "Yes, I know, but my duty is to find out what he's all about, not to help him in his obvious wished for demise, drinking himself to death like he is." "Oh, go on," replied her inner conscience, "You always were a soft touch."

Shannon removed Fergal's shoes, having to unknot the tightly knotted shoelace of one shoe. After taking off his jacket and, hesitating momentarily, she undid his belt, sliding his trousers off, revealing a dishevelled and not too clean pair of boxer shorts. Relieved that he was not naked, she muttered, "Oh well, at least you've got something on under your trousers. God, you really do stink of whisky!"

Holding her hand to her nose she began her search starting in Fergal's bedroom.

* *

The long dark hours of the night slipped gradually into the first light of dawn. Shannon absolutely shattered and desperately in need of sleep was startled and brought out of her reverie by a sudden high pitch sound that emanated from somewhere within the flat; Fergal's drunken snoring taking on a new tone, vigorous and unpleasant.

Obviously this new drill-like sound was disconcerting to his brain because a quick signal sent to Fergal's body told him to shuffle to a new position, the original dry, droning snore resuming its repetitive performance.

Shannon rubbed her head despairingly, "Jeez, that's a horrible sound. Why do men snore so loudly – especially drunken men? If I ever settle down and get married I'm going to invest in a lot of clothes pegs," she grinned to herself, "I'll fasten my man's nostrils together."

Everything had been emptied from drawers and cupboards in Shannon's search for information or clues to explain Fergal's reasons for being here.

In the bedroom Fergal was sleeping on top of the disarrayed

bed, his boxer shorts providing him with a modicum of respectability. The bedroom was a complete tip. Although the room had already been lacking in cleanliness, Shannon had added to the mayhem, displaying no respect for Fergal's possessions, mementoes or clothes, discarding them haphazardly during the throes of her thorough search. The bedroom floor was now covered with an assortment of bric-a-brac vying with the dust for a place to rest. However, Fergal's clothes had been incongruously folded and were lying across a chair, revealing Shannon's mothering instinct.

Shannon was now in the living room sitting on a worn and soiled armchair. In an attempt to protect her clothes and to keep a modicum of distance between herself and the dirt she had lined the armchair with sheets of paper towel torn from a previously unopened roll that she had found in the kitchen. The living room contained a second equally soiled armchair, the pair of the one in which she was gingerly sitting, plus a dining table accompanied by two rickety looking chairs, a badly stained and pock-marked coffee table, and an old television set which was placed in the corner of the room.

Having ransacked Fergal's apartment she was now spending her time scrutinising various papers and photographs that she had found and which were now in a pile on the floor by her armchair. Examining a photo frame, Shannon tore off the back support, but not finding anything, threw the photograph together with the torn back support and newly twisted frame onto the pile on the floor.

"Nothing; this is a waste of time, he's just a no-hope jerk," She muttered in exasperation glancing despairingly around the room. "And a dirty, foul smelling, drink soaked one at that."

Fergal groaned pathetically, "God, my head."

Shannon looked up inspecting the mess that she had created and nonchalantly shrugged her shoulders. Gingerly rising from the dirty chair she went into the kitchen where, opening the fridge, she took out a previously discovered carton of tomato juice. "Have to make this look authentic," Shannon muttered, quickly proceeding to smear her dress with tomato juice. Rinsing her hands under the hot water tap, but then espying a dirty looking tea towel she declined to make use of it, deciding instead to dry her hands by wiping them on her dress. Inspecting the large stain that had been created on her dress, she smiled in satisfaction and went to Fergal's bedroom, leaning expectantly against the doorframe.

Oblivious of Shannon standing in the doorway, Fergal massaged his forehead. "Bloody hell, my head; this is killing me, why do I do it? Got to get an aspirin!" Attempting to move only encouraged the pounding in his head, increasing to a crescendo like a hundred hammers all banging at the same gong, each hitting the metal in unison. Groaning and unable to withstand the pain he allowed his head to drop gently back onto the pillow, "Ah, shit." Holding his head in his hands he desperately tried to stop the intense pounding and also tried to keep his head from spinning, or was it the room that was spinning and not his head, he just didn't know. "Never again, *never* again!"

Shannon looked on with disgust.

Fergal continued to berate himself, "You always say that and then you'll start again...as soon as the memories come back; I wish I could erase the memories!" Groaning, he muttered, "Must have some tablets, and some water." Raising his torso he suddenly noticed Shannon and jolted upright in surprise. The sudden movement brought an even sharper pain to his head, which he immediately clutched with intense pressure as if desperately attempting to stop the head from falling off. "Oh bollocks!"

Staring fuzzy-eyed at Shannon, he demanded, "Who...what the...?" Realising that he was almost naked and becoming embarrassed, he modestly pulled the sheet over his body, "Get out! Who the hell are you?" He winced, "Ahhh, get out; get the fuck out! You're making my head even worse."

"Not until I get my money."

"Your money; what fucking money? Oh God, I didn't pick up some damn cheap prostitute last night, did I?"

"*Cheap Prostitute*! Hey buster be careful what you're saying!"

Despite the incessant hammering in his head Fergal sat up, "Look...ahh." He raised his hand to his head, frantically rubbing his brow, "Get me an aspirin, a bottle of aspirins, then I might pay you; god, my head."

Shannon smiled, "So, the head hurts does it? Want an aspirin, do we?"

Fergal pleaded in desperation, "Yes, yes please. I'm sure that I was in no state to get it up last night so if you want any money just get me some aspirin, please!"

"Take it easy or you'll bust a blood vessel."

"Please! The tablets are in the bathroom cabinet."

"I know," Shannon grinned broadly, "I know, I found some earlier. Okay, I'll get you your tablets and then we can have a nice chat."

Fergal frowned, and focusing his eyes, he gave Shannon a thorough eyeball examination, "Look, I'm not in the mood and even if you took all your clothes off, it wouldn't do anything for me. You're not my type. I like my women with larger breasts."

Indignant, she glanced down at her chest, resentfully retorting, "Cheeky little shit!" Turning petulantly on her heels she swooped out of the bedroom.

Fergal momentarily relieved, collapsed back onto his pillow. He could hear Shannon walking to his bathroom, opening the bathroom cabinet and a few seconds later closing it. Presumably she'd found the aspirins and he couldn't care less if she's found the KY Jelly or his condoms; the condoms had been a good deal, ten for the price of six. He wondered if he'd ever get round to using them, the alcohol intake over the last few weeks certainly reducing his opportunities of a little bit of slap and tickle with members of the fairer sex. Fleetingly he thought of Shannon and shuddered, "No, breasts too small; besides, I never pay for it."

Clutching the pack of aspirins, Shannon headed for the kitchen, pulling a glass from the cupboard; it was filthy. "Ugh, this is disgusting; he obviously recycles his glasses without washing them." Clearing a space within the debris of soiled dishes, pots, plates, glasses and bottles in the sink, she managed to position the glass under the cold water tap. A trickle of brownish coloured water quickly cleared to a cleaner colour. "Obviously doesn't use water very much," she complained contemptuously. Emptying the glass, she rinsed it a couple of times and then allowed cool clear water to flow inside. Task achieved, she turned off the tap, returning to Fergal with the water and packet of aspirins.

"Here we are then," she uttered cheerfully, "Aspirins as requested and some water; sit up."

Slowly and with very fragile movements, Fergal raised his torso, reaching for the aspirins. Shannon extracted two pills, placing them in Fergal's upturned palm. Without a second thought he scooped them into his mouth, swallowing the pills with great difficulty because of his extremely dry mouth. "Throat feels like sandpaper," he complained as he sunk back onto his pillows, closing his eyes very tightly.

"I've got water here, moron; you're supposed to swallow the pills with a glass of water."

Fergal reluctantly opened one eye, fixing Shannon with a beady stare. "Don't want it. Don't want to move again."

"You need the water; it'll help dissolve the aspirins for speedier absorption and help prevent acidity in your stomach."

Reluctantly Fergal reached for the water and gently sipped the contents whilst Shannon held the glass to his lips, her other hand behind Fergal's neck to prevent him sliding down. Fergal finishing the drink, wiped the drops from his chin, settled down and almost immediately fell back into a deep sleep.

"Terrific!" muttered Shannon. She returned to the kitchen and feeling very thirsty, she poured water into the kettle and switched it on. Finding the cleanest cup located from the pile of used cups residing in the sink, she ran the hot tap until she felt that the water was hot enough. Filling the cup with hot water, she rigorously scrubbed it with washing up liquid and a pan scourer until convinced that it was thoroughly clean. Inspecting the cup, she rinsed it twice more with hot water and then made herself a cup of hot black coffee. "Now, we have to wait until our drunken friend wakes up and is, hopefully, recovered from his hangover."

Regaining her armchair, ensuring once again that the seat and back were lined with protective paper towels, she settled down to wait, occasionally taking a sip of her repugnant and bitter tasting coffee.

When Fergal finally did resurface almost two hours had lapsed. Shannon ordered the confused and bewildered individual into the shower, giving him the companionship of a freshly made black coffee.

Still nursing a sore head, Fergal appreciatively accepted the coffee and gratefully escaped to the bathroom, firmly locking the door behind him. He didn't know who this woman was or what she wanted but at this moment in time he just didn't care. Whoever she was, at least she'd made him a coffee and given him the chance to freshen up under a warmish shower; he vaguely remembered her feeding him with aspirins in some earlier life. Dismissing Shannon from his thoughts, convinced that he could get rid of her later, he gingerly indulged himself with a couple of sips of the coffee, almost scalding his lips. "Bloody hell, that's hot." Placing the cup on a shelf, he took off his dressing gown and dropped his boxers, throwing both garments across the bathroom. Stepping onto the shower base, pulling the shower curtain across, he turned on the taps and instantaneously yelped as the cold water hit his body. "Shit; too fucking cold!"

Shannon chuckled, muttering, "Serves the bastard right!"

A few minutes later, unshaven but showered and wearing his dressing gown, Fergal emerged from the bathroom, immediately his eyes fixing on Shannon's back; he glared balefully at her shape silhouetted against the window. Frowning, he demanded, "Who are you? Can't you get laid somewhere else? I've got no money anyway."

Shannon, arms crossed over her chest, standing silently yet staring unseeingly out of the dirty window onto the street below, gracefully turned to face him, a neutral expression on her face.

Fergal persisted, "You can't stay here. I can't accommodate you or feed you."

Shannon replied with utter contempt, "You don't have to tell me that. Your cupboards are bare and the only thing in your fridge is a dried up meat pie and some tomato juice – unless you count the beers."

Fergal was irked, "Who the hell do you think you are, going through my things?" He suddenly became aware of the additional mess scattered on the floor, abruptly snapping, "And the mess! All my things chucked all over the floor. What have you been doing, trying to find something to steal?"

Shannon's unflinching eyes wrinkled at the corners; amused, she wryly replied, "The mess? *The mess*! I don't think you could notice the difference between the pigsty that I walked into last night and the current state of your place."

Beginning to get really pissed off, he took a pace in Shannon's direction, "Right, that's it, I've had enough." Reaching Shannon, he roughly grabbed hold of her, "Get out you... you slut!"

Shannon, ice cool, gripped Fergal's arm and pushing forward together on his arm and chest forced him backwards off balance. As he tried to regain his balance she pulled him against her hip, suddenly tilted back, and then tugging the off-balanced Fergal forward she used her leg to help throw him over her shoulder and above the arm of the armchair, all in one practised and seemingly effortless movement.

Flying through the air Fergal landed with a hefty wallop on the far side of the armchair. Dazed and with his hangover starting to kick back in, he clambered unsteadily to his feet, his right arm supporting him against the armchair. With querulous voice, bloodshot eyes staring balefully up at her, he almost wailed, "How the hell did you do that and who the bloody hell are you? What do you want?"

"Just my money, mister; just my money."

"Look, I didn't have sex with you..."

Shannon, tickled, laughed, "I know, I'm not your type."

"Then why? Surely I don't have to pay?" His eyes lit up, "Unless you want to give me a blow..."

"Take a hike!" she snorted with evident disgust.

"Okay, okay, I guess you have to make a living," he sighed with resignation and turning, he headed for the bedroom, demanding over his shoulder, "How much...for one night of non sex."

"*You* could never afford me."

Fergal totally dumbfounded, stopped in his tracks, reeling round, "Then what the fuck is this all about? What do you bloody want?"

"I told you, I want what you owe me. You ruined a very expensive dress yesterday and I want recompense."

Fergal perplexed, stared at her dress, "I did what? How, when?" He rubbed his head as if it would restore his memory, "And how did you get in here?"

"I brought us both back here, in a cab."

His head now beginning to pound like never before Fergal just wanted to get rid of this woman. He turned back towards his bedroom, resignedly mumbling, "Okay, I'll get you your dry cleaning money."

"The bar tab was fifty-three three dollars but that's the least of it; my dress is ruined. Dry cleaning won't sort this out," she glanced downwards at her heavily soiled dress. "You'll have to pay for a new dress, two hundred and fifty dollars!"

Fergal stunned, spun round to face Shannon, "What! I haven't got that much."

"I hope that you're joking," she answered as sternly as possible.

"Seriously, I lost my job a couple of weeks ago; some people I know had been supporting me but now the money's dried up. I'm virtually broke."

"Well, how do you pay for your drinking habit and how are you supposed to live?"

"I'm hoping the Northern Ireland aid," He stopped himself, annoyed at his indiscretion. "It's none of your damn business!"

"I'm afraid it is *my* business at the moment. You owe me money and I want it, *now.*"

"I'll get you the money but I need time. Tell me where to contact you and I'll send the cash."

"Sure, we've all heard that one before."

"Fine, I'll see how much I've got left." Bitterly he mumbled, "Don't you worry about me not being able to afford to eat."

Shannon cheerfully sniggered, "Okay, I won't."

Fergal bestowed a scathing look at the unabashed Shannon, but not obtaining any sympathy he scowled and stomped towards his bedroom, disappearing in a medley of oaths and profanities.

Shannon smiled happily, then calmly sat down on her paper towel protected armchair whilst she listened with amusement to the assortment of sounds that emanated from the bedroom; rustling, drawers opening and being slammed closed, and general noise of an intense search taking place, all the sounds interspersed with a stream of foul profanity.

Finally Fergal cried out, "Damn it, it's not here." He paused, demanding, "You sure that you haven't stolen my wallet?"

"If I had then I wouldn't be here, would I? Don't push your luck. Is this another one of your bullshit excuses?"

Worried and scratching his head, Fergal re-entered the living room. "Seriously, no kidding; my wallet's gone, all my cash; I'm stony broke."

"Yea, sure; just pay up; this is getting tedious. I've waited here all night."

Fergal annoyed and fed up, was extremely pissed off, "There's nothing else that I can do or say. I've got no money; I really am penniless. Shit!" His stomach rumbled, "And I'm starving." Kicking out in anger at the nearby armchair, he griped, "Sodding bloody country. This has been a disastrous mistake." Rather than kicking the chair cleanly he banged his leg against the chair leg, bruising his shin, "Ouch, oh bollocks."

Feeling hard done by and sorry for himself, Fergal massaged his tender shin; his face fell and he inadvertently adopted an expression of a petulant little boy who just could not do anything right. Shannon chuckled but noticing Fergal's baleful stare, put her hand across her mouth to hide her smile.

"It's not funny," he snapped balefully, massaging his shin, "I really am in a mess." Limping pathetically to the second armchair, he slumped down, visibly sad and forlorn.

Although not wishing to appear weak, Shannon was unable to prevent her attitude softening, contritely enquiring, "Look, I'm hungry too. How about we get some lunch? I'll loan you the cash; you can add it to your bill."

"I told you, I'm broke," his words spilling out in a very melancholic manner, "There is no money and no possibility of any money coming in."

Shannon did not say a word, merely fixing Fergal with an intense stare.

Fergal, disconcerted and unsettled under her harsh gaze, his negative attitude withering under her intense stare, wiped his brow with his hand and reluctantly muttered, "I've got people...back home, in Ireland...who could wire me some money, but that may take a few days."

Shannon bounced up from her chair and with cheerful efficiency proclaimed, "Well that's settled then. I'll buy you lunch and you can pay me back, everything you owe, in a day or two." She smiled sweetly.

Fergal scowled, resentfully moaning, "What did I do to get embroiled with someone like you?"

Shannon's smile broadened but she didn't reply.

Fergal shook his head despairingly, "I must give up the booze because the hangovers are turning into nightmares!"

Shannon laughed, "Don't push your luck, buster; I could really give you proper nightmares, believe me. Come on, get you're lazy ass out of the chair and let's find a 'Diner', I'm starving."

Fergal slowly and reluctantly got up, his face of picture of discontent.

Approaching the door Shannon paused and turned to face Fergal, extending her hand, "By the way, I'm Shannon."

Fergal grumpily and grudgingly offered, "Fergal."

"I know," she chuckled light heartedly, "And for God's sake, get dressed!"

Fergal's scowl deepened in contrast to Shannon's spreading grin as, gaily, she turned and opened the door ushering the unhappy newly, but not freshly, clothed Fergal out of his own apartment.

Chapter 24

Shannon was getting to the final morsels of her salad, delicately eating each mouthful whilst under the intense watchful gaze of Fergal. They were sitting opposite each other at a 'four-seater' in a Denny's Café in Boston. Although the food could not be described as haute cuisine Fergal loved coming here, that is, whenever he could afford it. The food was basic but always cooked well and his coffee cup seemed to be permanently replenished by one of the three very attentive waitresses who spent their time 'patrolling' the restaurant floor, taking orders, repeat orders, and filling cups on the merest whim.

Having taken full advantage of Shannon's benevolent generosity, Fergal had consumed a full 'Irish breakfast' of bacon, sausages, eggs, fried bread, mushrooms and tomatoes, and was now feeling replete. Having a satiated and satisfied stomach served to make most things better, the world beginning to take on a rosier hue. The stilted conversation between him and this strange woman had been sporadic, muted, hesitant and vague, with her tentative probing on various subjects; the woman continuously attempting to pry into his life but he had very firmly resisted her intrusive questions.

Shannon looked up and met Fergal's gaze. Embarrassed and feeling awkward, he turned away, staring out of the window.

"Exactly who *are* you?" enquired Shannon.

Fergal snorted and focused his attention back to Shannon, "I could ask the same question of you; in fact, I reckon that I have more of a right to ask, particularly as the first time that I can ever recall meeting you is in my own apartment."

Shannon grinned, scooped up the remaining salad with her fork, delicately raising the fork to her mouth, the food disappearing in one slow and extremely delicate purse of the lips.

Fergal was fascinated by the neat eating habits of this attractive woman and was enthralled, even though she had only got small breasts! However Fergal soon started to feel uneasy as Shannon slowly masticated her remaining food, never once removing her eyes from his. He forced his eyes free from her captive and hypnotic stare and turning his head away scanned an unseen object, starting to feel a desperate need to get away. This woman was beginning to spell danger. Ancient memories were being dredged up and not pleasant ones either. The memories were of unpleasant tasks and terrifying occasions, such as avoiding the security services in Northern Ireland, England, and Mainland Europe; intrigue, double-dealings, plots, counter plots, and betrayals.

Shannon delicately stirred the coffee in her almost drained coffee cup. She was deep in thought, wishing to push forward with her investigation but very wary because she realised that Fergal's hackles were now up and that he was beginning to fear her, beginning to feel trapped. She noticed the deep furrow forming on his brow.

Increasingly hot and flustered, Fergal turned his attention back to Shannon, "Thank you for brunch but I have to get going. Things to do, you know."

"Oh yes? I thought that you'd lost your job?"

"I have, I did," he frowned, "Besides, it's none of your business if I have or haven't."

Shannon making a quick decision decided that she had to be firm or else she would lose control of the situation and, God forbid, she didn't want to go through another night in Fergal's cesspit of an apartment trying to wheedle information from him. "I think it is very much part of my business; you made it so, at least until you've paid me up."

"Oh God, I hope I get my money quickly." He got up, "That's what I've got to do, contact my family In Ireland. The sooner I can get some money and get you off my back the better."

"What about security?"

"Security?" Fergal was taken aback, "There's no one after me!"

"I meant security for my reimbursement, not the authorities." Her eyes narrowed, "Why, are you in some kind of trouble with the security services?"

"No, no," he nervously wiped his sweating brow. "I just didn't understand what you meant. You mean you want some kind of security, guarantee that I won't do a runner and renege on my debt."

"Yes; how do I know that you won't do a runner? You could just disappear without paying me back? After all, I'm a hell of a lot out of pocket now."

Fergal remained standing behind his vacated seat, hands resting on the upright back of the seat, "You have my word."

Shannon smiled warmly, "That's okay then."

Fergal almost exhaled with relief, but his face dropped like a stone when Shannon continued with fierce venom, "Like hell! I can't let you disappear without some back up; after all, I don't know you from Adam, even though we did spend last night together!"

Two elderly ladies who were seated at the next table, enjoying the remnants of their mid-morning coffee, looked up startled, their faces a picture of shock and disapproval. They tutted in disgust, disapproval evident in their facial expressions. Fergal glanced from Shannon to the two elderly ladies, colouring with embarrassment.

"Shush; besides, we didn't *spend* the night together." He smiled bashfully at the two elderly ladies, then returned his attention to Shannon, "You just gate-crashed my living room."

Shannon smiled graciously, her eyebrow rising questioningly.

Fergal beaten, wearily sighed, "Oh, for goodness sake! Come back to my place and I'll give you something."

One of the elderly ladies could no longer resist and drawing herself to her most disgusted 'young people of today have no morals' demeanour, barked "Well!"

Fergal embarrassed by the two elderly ladies drawing attention to his plight hastily added, "I'll give you something as security." Adding as he smiled with awkward embarrassment at the two ladies, "Not something to do with sex."

"Well!" retorted one of the ladies in an even stronger stentorian voice, "Today's younger society, all they think about is sex and more sex. *Disgusting*!"

Fergal's voice dried up, his face colouring deeply crimson.

Shannon laughed and taking her handbag, gleefully announced, "So, *lover boy*, back to your place."

"Will you be quiet," hissed the mortified Fergal hastily following Shannon, who by now was making her way towards the exit, a waitress intercepting their progress with a bill in her hand. "I'll get this," smiled Shannon, "You can add it to your payment to me."

"Oh God," groaned Fergal, just wishing that the ground could swallow him up so that he could avoid the irked stares and disapproving comments from the fellow diners and, more importantly, wished that the ground would open up and swallow not only him but this overly cheerful bloody woman who was badgering him.

"She's only kidding," he vainly attempted to explain as a sickly, embarrassed smile spread across his crimson face.

Chapter 25

Shannon closed her front door and leaning with her back against it, felt shattered and exhausted, yet relief washed through her; she was home.

She let loose a heartfelt, weary sigh, the balm of being back home in her clean, domesticated, suburban house travelling through her body. It was such a relief to be back in her sanctuary, in the leafy suburbs of Boston, and at this moment the solitude of being alone was something that she was extremely grateful for. She had recently placed an advertisement in the local newspaper, and at the Bureau, for potential housemates to share her newly acquired three-bedroom domain but was now glad that she hadn't begun the interview process to determine suitable people to share with.

For now, she was immensely grateful for her privacy.

The purchase of the smart, modern house had been brought about as a result of years of frugal living coupled with the aid of a large contribution from her parents; obviously, to maintain the bank loan repayments she would require the additional income of at least one other rent-contributing person.

Shannon sniffed the air and was disgusted to realise that she was the cause of her own disdain. She smoothed down her dress as if trying to wipe off the contamination of Fergal's dirty apartment. "Ugh", she recollected, "What a disgusting place and what a loathsome man - if that is what you could call that foul smelling, dirty, drink soaked, repugnant Irishman!"

Tossing her head, she pushed herself away from the door, striding to her kitchen. In the kitchen, opening a drawer next to the store cupboard she removed a large plastic bag, placing it on the breakfast bar. Unzipping her dress she quickly slid out of the reeking garment, folding it carefully, placing it into the plastic bag and firmly folded over the end of the plastic bag. Taking a roll of sellotape from the open drawer she sellotaped the bag closed, sealing in the repugnant odour.

Inhaling the still unpleasant stench, she realised that her whole body was immersed with what she called the 'odour of Fergal'. "When I had dreams of mixing my body scent with the scent of a handsome man this definitely is *not* what I had I mind," she grumbled to herself.

Shannon placed the sealed plastic bag at the end of the

breakfast bar, closed the drawer and walked to her living/dining room area. Stepping smartly to the drapes, she hastily closed them having quickly taken in the sight of her neatly lawned garden with flower filled borders.

Mr Polenski, the retired neighbour on her right side, whilst nearly always pottering in his garden, constantly seemed to have his eyes fixed on her windows. Shannon figured that he was either a pervert or couldn't afford a television set. However she was not going to give him the chance of seeing her parade in her underwear. Mind you, there was very little of a sexual nature regarding the knickers she was currently wearing; they were more akin to old fashioned bloomers and looked a hideous sight – particularly with the bulge of Fergal's wallet still safely hidden in the prepared pocket in the knickers.

She glanced down, remembering the wallet, having long since become accustomed to it rubbing against her. Removing it, she carelessly tossed it into a drawer. When Fergal had been asleep she had removed the dollar bills from the wallet and in fact, with great satisfaction, had used Fergal's own money to pay for the brunch. She grinned at the memory.

There had been nothing else of note or value in Fergal's wallet and he didn't carry any credit cards.

Subsequent to their shared breakfast Shannon had accompanied Fergal back to his apartment, taken possession of his foreign driving licence and with Fergal's, albeit very reluctant consent, had also taken his passport as security for the debt. The passport was obviously a forgery, although an extremely clever forgery, but to her practised eye and with her recent experiences of investigating illegal aliens it did not fool her for long. Shannon had come to the conclusion that Fergal would have great difficulty in securing a duplicate or alternative passport because he was so obviously out of contact with his ex-terrorist colleagues and because he was separated from any support of the individual American-Irish organisations. Fergal appeared to be on a road of solitary self-destruction.

"Why, oh why, is that British security guy so keen to get hold of Fergal?" she mused, "Oh well, I'm going to have to delve deeper into this sad character." She sighed with resigned self-pity. Remembering Fergal's words, she looked down at her breasts, cupping them, examining herself in a mirror that hung above the fireplace. "They're not so bad, and not so small," she protested, "And despite that drunken Irishman's comments, I like them."

Turning away from her reflection she paused, glancing back at the mirror, adding as an afterthought, "But I must get myself some sexier bras."

Selecting a Macie Grey CD from her CD collection, Shannon inserted it into her stereo unit and humming contentedly, sauntered to the bathroom, where she quickly removed her underwear, gingerly dropping the bra and pants into the dirty laundry basket.

Stepping into the shower she turned on the water until it was as hot as she could bear and scrubbed the memory of Fergal and his apartment from every inch of her body. As she felt cleaner with each scrub her humming grew louder and a feeling of contentment spread across her body until, satisfied, she rinsed off with clean water.

Drying herself briskly with a bath towel, she yawned, the weariness of lack of sleep and the effects of the hot shower fast enveloping her body. With barely any remaining energy Shannon shuffled into her bedroom, collapsing exhausted, onto her double bed. Reflecting through her tiredness she was grateful that not only did she not have any house-mates, she also didn't have a boyfriend at this moment to share her bed. Actually, it had been a long 'moment' since she had finished with David, her partner of almost three years, but all she wanted to do now was to spread out onto clean linen sheets and have the whole bed for herself. Shannon wanted to sleep for a week and with tired, heavy eyelids quickly shutting, she drifted into a deep sleep almost interrupted by her first dream of Fergal, but soon fading into more pleasant scenes.

* * *

A fierce shrill noise screamed through Shannon's head, the sound accentuated by a heavy vibration as the very ground seemed to be shaking.

Unsure of what was happening she clung desperately to a cliff top as the loud pinging of a reversing truck's warning alarm was driving doggedly towards her, its wheels relentlessly seeking to run over her fingers with the intention of making her release her grip, making her drop to her death below.

She desperately sought a means of salvation and wondering why she hadn't spotted it earlier, she became aware of a rope ladder dangling over the side of the cliff and within reach of her left arm. Shannon desperately stretched out for the ladder as the reversing truck inched towards her fingertips; as she swung her body onto the rope ladder the truck reversed over the cliff, flew past her and smashed onto rocks below. Shannon quickly climbed up the rope ladder, pulling herself back onto the cliff top, leaping forward with relief as she did so.

But the ringing noise had not stopped and shaking her head Shannon opened her eyes; she was not on a cliff top but was on the floor by her bed, her sheet twisted around her in the shape of a rope. Quickly realising that she had merely been dreaming, Shannon blearily wakened, tottered to her feet and headed for the incessantly ringing telephone on the bedside table. "Ouch", she muttered, becoming aware of a large bruise on her thigh caused as a result of her falling out of her bed. She scooped the phone from its cradle.

"Shannon?" called out the voice through the telephone, "Where the hell have you been?"

"I've been here, at home, since I got in late this morning. What's the problem?" Shannon realised that it was Jim Nulty speaking to her.

"You didn't check in last night like you're supposed to. What happened?"

"I did Jim; I logged in with the duty officer and gave the correct codes."

"Oh no, you didn't. The last log entry we have for you is Tuesday night."

"So? It's only Wednesday." Jim Nulty was silent; Shannon impatiently demanded, "Hello, you still there Jim?"

"Shannon, its Thursday today," cautiously retorted Jim, the concern evident in his tone.

"Thursday, you're kidding?" She looked down at the alarm clock on the bedside table; it registered 11.15. Looking over at the drapes she was conscious of the strong light emanating from outside. "Shit! I've been asleep for nearly twenty-four hours; I've slept through the whole of Wednesday afternoon and Wednesday night!"

"You what? You're supposed to be on a mission; you can't spend your time sleeping on the Bureau's payroll." Jim reflected momentarily before adding in a conciliatory tone, "Shannon, are you overdoing it? Do you want time off, relief from this case?"

"Hell, no," She fiercely rejected his suggestion, "I finally made contact with Fergal on Tuesday night; spent the night at his place and didn't get back home until almost midday Wednesday."

"Oh yes? You *spent* the night with Fergal?" snapped Jim grumpily.

"Tutch, not in the way that your tone suggests, thank you very much. Give me more credit than *that*. I made contact with Fergal and tricked him into letting me into his apartment and while he was out cold in one of his usual drunken condition I completely searched his premises. There wasn't a trace of anything in the place, nothing at all to indicate why Willie Davidson would be searching for him. Also, in the days that I've been tracking Fergal no one has phoned, written, or attempted to contact him, or vice versa. In actual fact he's been too inebriated to contact anyone himself. He seems to be a total waste of space."

"So, it's all a red herring?"

"It does seem that way but I don't know yet; I'm just not sure. The positive aspect is that I think I've currently got a small hold over Fergal."

"What's that? What do you mean?"

"Oh, it's nothing heavy or anything like that. I managed to acquire his wallet, personally settled his large bar bill – the Bureau will get a receipt - and I managed to convince him that he owed me money. At the moment he doesn't seem to have anywhere to go or any idea of what to do, and I've taken possession of his passport. It's a forgery, of course."

"Good girl," purred Jim approvingly.

"I guess I overslept through sheer exhaustion. Now I feel recharged and raring to go. I'll keep tabs on Fergal, from a discreet distance, and let him stew for two or three days. Then I'll put the pressure on regarding repayment of my money."

"Okay, sounds good." With a lump in his throat, he gently advised, "But do take care, Shannon; remember, he was a part of an Irish terrorist cell, a cold blooded, ruthless organisation."

"Thank you Jim, I didn't know you cared," she chuckled, her voice light hearted.

"Don't get carried away," he gruffly snapped, "I take responsibility for all my Field Agents."

"Point taken, Boss."

Jim's tone softened once more, "Seriously Shannon, do be careful. You are a good operative and I don't want to lose you."

"Thank you and I do appreciate you saying that, but don't worry; I'm a big girl now." Smiling broadly she replaced the receiver.

Chapter 26

The instant that Feral had returned to his apartment, he kicked out in anger at the armchair, "Fucking woman, who does she think she is? I don't need this aggro; I've got enough problems of my own. I wish I'd never set foot in America! And now that that frigging woman has got hold of my passport, I really am stuck. And it cost me nearly all my reserves having to fork out five thousand US Dollars to the Irish-American contact in Amsterdam!"

Fergal ranting inanely, stomped across his living room, thumping out in frustration at any obstacle in his route; first the armchair, then a table, then the table lamp which went crashing to the floor and was promptly kicked across the room shattering against the far wall. "Damn, damn, fucking damn, I hate this life - especially that bloody woman!"

Fergal had utilised his previous experiences in the Provisional IRA and the extensive list of contacts to finally find the means to break free from the chains of his terrorist mentors. Some of the known contacts had been more of the commercial kind, with no loyalty to any side, their only consideration being the size of the gem stone or the colour and volume of money. These mercenary contacts had proved very useful in his subsequent lonely life of trying to build a new existence, a new life outside the clutches of the terrorist organisation. When he had finally broken free from the grip of the Provo's all he craved for then and now was peace, peace and quiet and the erasure of the painful and cruel memories continuously pounding round in his head.

The most useful contact and the one he had been most grateful for at the time was the 'Irish friendly' American Embassy employee in Amsterdam, who very kindly pointed him in the direction of a clandestine back street forger, working not far from the Central Railway Station in Amsterdam. This 'Forger', who officially ran a specialist bookshop, was a mastermind, particularly when it came to documents and whose services had been used by both sides in the 'Cold War'; he was now running a thriving concern providing false passports for third world and Eastern European refugees. In addition and usually at 'special cost' the Forger would produce one of his 'works of art' for the occasional miscreant who needed to keep out of the prisons of Europe or stay clear from the clutches of the various European Police and other security services.

Apparently, quite a few of Fergal's ex colleagues had visited this man, albeit most of them with the approval of the IRA Army Council, with the objective of keeping vulnerable men and woman, escaped Maze Prisoners and other motley personnel, out of hands of the British authorities. Subsequently, many of these criminals and terrorists, aided by friendly organisations, had made their way to the United States and were ultimately securely secreted within certain Irish-American organisations.

Most of those people changed their ways, settling down to lives of normality but a few did not and to this day actively promote a bloody uprising to solve the Irish problem.

His frustration boiling over, Fergal stormed into the kitchen, opened the cupboard under the sink and swept out all the unused cleaning apparatus from within. A collection of plastic bottles, tubs and packets tumbled onto the kitchen floor. Toilet cleanser mixed with scouring powder and a trickle of washing up liquid, spilling from the crushed plastic bottle which had rolled under Fergal's knee as he reached deeper into the cupboard, the washing-up bottle's contents being slowly squeezed out onto the floor. An unopened bottle of bleach rolled across the created mess but fortunately finished up against the fridge without spilling its contents.

Fergal reached to the back of the cupboard and with a gleam in his eye withdrew a full bottle of Bourbon. "Ah, my beauty, I didn't think I'd drunk you - my rainy day reserve. Well today it's raining, no it's bloody pouring and we need each other! Come to daddy." He hugged the bottle against his chest and went to the sink, grasping an unwashed glass. As he did so a cockroach quickly scuttled from inside the glass, disappearing under the plates in the sink.

"Bastard," muttered Fergal.

Without a second thought he merely rinsed the glass under the cold tap and with the lack of a clean tea towel wiped it dry on his shirttail. Hastily opening the Bourbon he poured a large measure into the glass. Placing the bottle down on the only available free spot on the kitchen draining board he raised the glass to his lips and immediately poured the liquid down his throat, almost choking as a blazing sensation spread down the back of his throat, burning into his lungs and onwards to his stomach. Spluttering and coughing, he wheezed, "God, throat's dry; I need a beer to wash this down."

Fergal extracted a bottle of Budweiser from the fridge, hurriedly removing the bottle cap by bringing the top of the bottle sharply down against the edge of the draining board. The beer instantly commenced to froth over the top, the bottle being brought smartly up to Fergal's lips before any of the liquid could escape. Greedily, he gulped the liquid, his Adam's apple moving up and down at an alarming rate as the liquor traversed its way down his throat. With a loud belch Fergal removed the empty bottle from his mouth, wiped a trickle from his chin before chucking the empty bottle onto the overflowing trashcan. Taking another beer from the fridge he opened it using the same method as the first bottle and with the bottle of Bourbon under his arm, the glass of Bourbon in one hand and bottle of Budweiser in the other hand, he sauntered back into the living room, slumping into one of the armchairs. "Ah, life is not so bad," he reflected as he gradually drunk himself into oblivion.

* * *

Unbeknown to each other the fates were beginning to parallel Fergal and Shannon's lives. He also woke at approximately eleven o'clock on Thursday morning but unlike Shannon he did not wake from a restful sleep but more from a head wrenching raging pain in his temples.

His throat felt like sandpaper, his guts ached and his head throbbed. As for his mouth it was so dry that he had difficulty separating his lips; desperately attempting to bring saliva to his mouth he feebly licked his parched lips. Bile began to rise from his stomach, upwards inside his chest and almost reached his mouth; he swallowed, frantically keen to keep the contents within. However with his head aching, his stomach churning, and his bowels beginning to realise that they would like to be included in his body's rebellious action he had no choice but to succumb to their demands.

Groaning, he gingerly raised himself up from his chair, then urgency prevailed as he rushed into the bathroom, not sure of which end of his body to place over the toilet bowl.

Fortunately Fergal lived alone for the sounds originating from his bathroom were not very pleasant. Stomach empty and bowels relieved, he staggered out from his bathroom, fumbling, and groggily groped his way to his bedroom, where he hastily undressed, ripping his shirt and tearing off two of the shirt buttons in the process. His unzipped trousers dropped down and being uncoordinated he was unable to fully remove the tangled trousers, almost falling to the floor in his pathetic attempt to separate trouser from leg. Giving up, he wearily and painfully crawled onto his bed, the trousers working their own way towards his feet, finally falling onto the floor.

The clothes were left in an untidy heap on the floor as he rolled groggily across the bed, his head finding the sanctuary of a pillow. The relief was only temporary, more of a micro-second, as the room began to spin, the incessant pounding in his head forming into a solid ball of pain, his head evidently being compressed ever tighter in a crushing grip by an industrial vice. "That's right you bloody Gods, have your fun, crush my skull into a tiny ball. God knows, I do deserve it!" he cried out but immediately regretted his ire, the anger and harshness of his words only serving to increase the ache in his temples. Desperately trying to prevent the bile rising from his empty stomach, his body decided to relieve his self-induced discomfort by allowing him to gradually drift off into a drunken but very necessary sleep.

Fergal spent the next few hours tossing and turning on the bed, sometimes under the sheet, sometimes on top. His body increasingly soaked in rancid beads of sweat that gave off pungent odours of alcohol together with a lack of hygiene.

As the afternoon set into evening and then fell into the darkness of early night his body was doing its best to repair the damage caused by months of misuse, its only aid being sleep.

Nevertheless, Fergal's brain remained tortured with memories of his previous life, the cruelty and fear and now the heavy regret of conscience. His mind wandered back to when he and Colm had 'disciplined' a small time drug dealer, Niall, the fearful, perspiring, spotty youth crying whilst slumped in a corner in the coal cellar of the local Town Councillor's house. It was a 'friendly' house, quite often used for 'discussions' and for the disciplining of individuals who broke the rules of the terrorist Council. The local Town Councillor, elected as an Independent Representative on the Council, was a well-respected figure, frequently 'wheeled' out by the press and television people, supposedly to put forward the voice of sensibility and reason. If only those people of the media had known the truth of it all!

Niall crying out in total fear, backed away, trying to melt into the corner.

"Did you think that you could trade drugs on my patch?" growled Colm, his tone deep and menacing, "You know that *I* am responsible for allocating drug dealers in this area and only we are allowed to control the sale and use of hard drugs."

"Please Colm," sobbed the youth, "It was only a few grams and it was only cocaine; I needed the money for me' sister. She needs an abortion in England."

"I don't care what you needed the money for," barked Colm, "You know the rules. If we let any piece of shit work our operation, then we lose control."

"Please Colm, please; I'm sorry," cried the youth, the colour draining from his face, making an horrific contrast between the bleached white pallor of his skin and the very dark blackness of the coal.

"I have to discipline you Niall. A lesson must be shown so that any other young prick who thinks he can make a few bob will think twice."

"Please have mercy Colm, I'm so sorry." The youth subsided into pitiful wailing.

"Quieten down Niall and take it like the man your supposed to be or I'll give you such a kicking that what Fergal and I did to you earlier will seem like an afternoon at the funfair. You obviously thought you were man enough to sell drugs on the side so you can be man enough to take your punishment."

"Oh God," sobbed the simpering Niall, desperately trying to control his abject fear and terror.

Colm looked to Fergal and tilted his head indicating that Fergal should do the deed.

"I can't," Fergal protested, "I grew up with Niall; I know him like a brother."

"You will Fergal or I'll put a bullet in *your* knee!" Colm's eyes narrowed to tiny slits as he glared with unquestioned authority at the confused and reluctant Fergal.

Fergal hesitantly stepped forward, and removing a revolver with attached silencer from his trouser belt, bent over the terrified Niall. "Niall I'm so sorry. I have to do this."

Fergal's sad eyes glanced at Colm then back to Niall.

Niall could discern the sorrow and fear evident in Fergal's eyes and in that instant was aware that Fergal had no choice but to follow through on the terrorist's code of discipline. Tightly closing his eyes, he clenched his fists into a taut ball, bracing himself as Fergal pressed the silencer against his kneecap. But when Fergal pressed the trigger Niall was unprepared for the acute pain and anguish that shot through him like a rusty nail tearing off his flesh. His flesh, blood and bone were splattered against the coal and the wall. In an almost dreamlike sequence, at one instant he was fascinated by the extent of the mess caused by one little bullet fired into his kneecap then by the plethora of different colours, a variety of shades of blood, flesh and bone adding assorted hues to the black coal. Finally and all too quickly, the fascination was quickly overtaken by the overriding pain racing through his body. As the initial shock subsided Niall screamed in pain, his howls being cut off by Colm's swift action, a prepared handkerchief forced into Niall's open mouth. With the ever-increasing intensity of pain racking his body, racing through nerve points that had lain dormant all his life up to this moment, Niall fainted.

Fergal, tears in his eyes, turned away and was violently sick, his eyes alternating between emptiness and focusing, as he desperately attempted to hang on to reality and to his sanity.

"You disgusting animal," Colm complained, "Can't you control yourself?"

Colm's comment brought Fergal to his senses; he didn't know whether to laugh or cry. "I'm a disgusting animal?" Straightening up, he turned to look at Niall's unconscious body and pointing, vehemently complained, "*That's* disgusting; what you made me do was disgusting. My being sick is only a bloody normal body function; what you do is *fucking* disgusting!"

Colm stared with surprise and unbridled malice at Fergal, who realising what he had said, quaked in fear, expecting to receive a bullet in his kneecap.

Both men glared at each other for what seemed an age.

"Look, what I said, well that was out of order Colm," Fergal hastily retracted, "I'm sorry but you know I don't like doing these jobs."

Colm continued to glare fixedly, Fergal's words appearing to fall on deaf ears. Slowly and without removing his eyes from Fergal he put his hand into his pocket.

Fergal wanted to scream, his stomach churning; it felt like a platoon of rats gnawing at his insides. "Jesus, I'm overstepped the mark," he thought, "Why couldn't I keep my big mouth shut."

Colm's icy stare slowly melted, he grimaced, "You know Fergal, you push your luck with me."

"I know and I'm sorry." Fergal had a desire to yell out with joy; the feeling of instant transition from utter fear into relief and joy was beyond description.

"I've trained you, looked after you, fed you in my home, taught you everything. In fact you've almost been like a son to me, so I'm going to overlook what you said." Placing his arm over Fergal's shoulder, he smiled warmly then paused, a serious frown spreading across his brow, and patting Fergal's cheek, he added, "But, as much as I like you, if you do mess up one day I will have to take action."

"Sure Colm, and I am sorry."

"Now clean up the mess and get rid of Niall."

*   *   *

Fergal's tossed in his bed, groaning, his eyes flickering as he almost woke from his disturbed sleep but rolling onto his side he quickly drifted off into another nightmare recollection.

Maureen was beautiful, an intelligent girl with a sharp sense of humour; she would make a remarkable catch for any of the young men from the locality. The Parish Priest had high hopes for her and was almost in love with her himself. With her dark hair and sparkling eyes, clear complexion and white gleaming smile, she could have the pick of most of the young Catholic boys. Francis had been courting her, on and off, for years, but Maureen knew that she could do a lot better and that there was a big welcoming world opening up to her. Although fond of Francis she had never led him on, always being keen to keep their relationship more akin to brother and sister.

Maureen's mother had frequently advised Maureen to get rid of Francis and that he would drag her down or become a bad influence on her but as kindly as Maureen tried to get her message across to Francis, the more tenaciously the besotted boy clung on to her. He wanted her and wasn't going to let her go. Maureen had toyed with the idea of moving to London – she had an Aunt who lived in a place called Putney – but Francis always seemed to find reasons for her not to go. Usually it was some family occasion that prevented her or someone who needed help or support, for

Maureen was always willing to help anyone in need.

When Maureen finally steeled herself to break free and had made the necessary arrangements to move to London, Francis said that he would go too. Maureen insisted that she wanted to go alone, and her intention was to stay with her Aunt and to have a complete break from Northern Ireland and the people that she had grown up with.

Francis, angry and upset, stormed out from Maureen's house, loudly slamming the door in unmitigated fury as he exited.

Disturbed and angry, he stomped home, his feelings of possessive love turning to hate. A plan quickly formulated itself in Francis' wicked mind and he determined that Maureen was not going to leave; if she couldn't be his then she wouldn't be anybody else's either.

Like certain unscrupulous people in his environment, Francis knew how to turn the difficult Catholic/Protestant troubles into something that would be to his own benefit.

Fergal's memories caused him to toss ever more violently, the sheets drenched with perspiration, holding liquid that would make a wet towel very proud. He drifted back into his nightmare.

With his plan simply formed and with evil intent permeating his being, Francis approached a known terrorist contact. Very soon a message was relayed to Colm and a meeting was arranged for the following morning at a safe house. Colm, Mick and Fergal were astonished to hear from a brooding Francis that there was an Irish girl in their midst who was not only having a clandestine relationship with a Corporal from the British Army – screwing him silly as Francis succinctly put it – but was also passing on information to the British forces at the same time. If any of them had thought the situation through with even a minor degree of thoroughness then they would have realised that there was no way that the young Maureen could have had any information to pass on, or indeed have access to any to the Provisional's information whatsoever. The whole thing was totally implausible.

However, leaks had been going on and the British Army and local Police *did* seem to be double guessing recent Republican operations in the North and on the British Mainland. Colm ever eager to please his paymasters, whilst also gaining additional hero status, decided to act immediately.

Francis was given the keys of a car and was despatched to the

Solicitor's premises were Maureen was employed as a receptionist. On a pretext that her Mother was ill and had been taken to a friend's house where a Doctor was now in attendance, Francis managed to persuade Maureen to leave with him.

Quickly obtaining approval from her superior, the very concerned and alarmed Maureen followed Francis from the Solicitor's premises and climbed into an old Ford Escort. In her concerned state Maureen did not bother to ask Francis where the car had come from or who it belonged to, her only though being concern for her Mother's well-being.

Actually, Fergal had had great joy in stealing the car from outside the Belfast home of an off duty RUC policeman, the memory providing momentary relief from his nightmare. The car's number plates had been changed and a few dents added. Not too much attention was taken in making the car unrecognisable as it had been planned to be used for one job only, an explosion outside a police station in Newry. However, Colm felt that loaning Francis the car to pick up Maureen would be of more value than the previous plan; the police station at Newry could wait.

Colm was going to enjoy interrogating this young girl.

When Francis arrived with the girl at the safe house her beguiling beauty almost took Fergal's breath away.

Pushing past Fergal in the hallway she called out, "Mammy? Mammy, where are you? I'm here now." Entering the living room she stopped in her tracks.

There to meet her were two stern looking men, sitting on the edge of the sofa. There was no welcome greeting evident in their faces and their aura spoke only of evil.

Maureen's internal organs performed a somersault and she turned to flee but the perplexed, doubtful, Fergal blocked her path. Beyond him, Maureen became aware of the evilly triumphant eyes and horribly smirking face of Francis. Alarmed and suddenly petrified, full of fear, she cried out, "Oh Franny, what are you doing? What are you getting me into; Mammy's not really hurt is she?"

"Traitorous slut," spat Francis, and brushing past Fergal he forced Maureen back into the living room.

"What are you talking about?" demanded Maureen, her voice quaking in terror.

"You know damn well! You been screwing with a British Soldier – and passing on information!"

Maureen glanced at the threatening faces that were intensely scrutinising her and then pleaded with her erstwhile friend, "Don't be stupid Francis, I don't even know any British soldiers."

"Liar!"

Desperately she turned to the more friendly looking face of Fergal. "Please," She begged, "I don't care what he's told you but I really don't know any British soldiers and I certainly haven't passed on any information to anyone."

Desperate, she grabbed hold of Fergal's shoulder, "I wouldn't know of anything to pass on."

Fergal's face furrowed and he looked into the terrified eyes of this young woman and believed her. But before he could think or have a chance to respond, Francis took hold of Maureen, pulling her from Fergal and threw her down onto the floor in front of Colm and Mick.

"Lying slut!" hissed Francis.

With tearful eyes, Maureen looked up at her hate filled besotted ex-friend and speaking softly asked, "Oh, Francis, how could you do this to me? What have I ever done to harm you?"

Fergal stepped forward. "I'm not convinced; we need to know a lot more."

"Shut up, Fergal," bellowed Colm, "You know sod all; don't let a pretty, scheming face give you the wrong idea. Just because the harlot's pretty, doesn't automatically mean that she is innocent."

"Yes, I know that, but...

"Shut it Fergal," interrupted Mick, his voice icy with menace, "Or I'll cut you instead." He removed a Stanley knife from his pocket and slowly pressed out the blade.

Maureen's eyes opened wide with fear and terror. "Oh dear God, no, don't cut me. Honest to God, I am totally innocent of anything." She looked up at Fergal, "Please help me!"

Fergal stepped closer towards the petrified woman but Mick leaped to his feet, knife poised at Fergal's throat.

"Okay Mick, take it easy," Colm calmly uttered as he slowly rose to his feet. "Fergal is young and impetuous and has a belief in the goodness of people."

"I'll give him fucking goodness," growled Mick as he pierced the skin on Fergal's neck, drawing out a small sliver of blood.

"Mick, I said leave it," ominously commanded Colm, "I'll decide who does what."

Reluctantly Mick withdrew the knife from Fergal's throat but continued to glower at the youthful Fergal.

"Fergal, go and keep watch. We'll sort it from here," Colm instructed firmly, his voice quietly authoritative. "Let me down or bugger off and I'll personally hunt you down. Clear?"

Fergal hesitated, looking disconsolately at the ashen, quietly sobbing Maureen and turned on his heel, exiting the room, Mick slamming the door closed behind him.

Walking with leaden feet to the front door of the house Fergal opened the door and exited. Pacing up and down on the pavement outside the house he was very aware of the whimpering sobs and howls emanating from within the house. If anyone else could hear what was happening then they were obviously too afraid to intervene, no one dared to get involved in a terrorist 'disciplinary' action or interrogation.

After what seemed like hours but in fact was only a few minutes a final blood curdling, piercing scream was heard and then total silence ensued. Very shortly thereafter, Colm, Mick, and a brutally ecstatic Francis all exited the house.

"As you're the soft bastard," instructed Colm to Fergal, "Use the car and get her dropped off near to where she can get some medical attention. You can leave her in the car or dump her and then lose the car; we'll have to steal a new car for the planned original job anyway."

"She...she's not dead then?" hesitantly asked Fergal.

"Of course she's not dead. We only taught her a lesson, a lesson for any shameless slut who betrays her own kind," replied Colm.

"Yes, that's right," beamed the vengeful Francis.

Without glancing back, Colm, Mick, and Francis sauntered off along the street. Mick, hands tucked in pockets, wondered why Francis was still walking with them and scowled disapprovingly at the young man but his disapproving stare went unnoticed by the vacuous liar.

"That was wicked," Francis chuckled, gleefully rubbing his hands together.

Colm stopped in his tracks, fixing Francis with an unfriendly stare, and coldly retorted, "Get lost son. You don't know us and we don't know you. Our mutual acquaintance is at an end."

"Oh, er, yes, okay." The cancerous youth had no option but to slope off in the opposite direction to that taken by Colm and Mick.

Fergal shaking his head in despondence and despair opened the door of the house, gingerly entering the living room. Seeing the unconscious, blood stained Maureen lying on the floor, he rushed to the young woman's side and hastily checked her pulse to make sure that she was still alive. Cupping her bloody chin in his hands, her turned her face towards him and gasped in mortified shock and horror. They had repeatedly cut and slashed at her beautiful face, the blood dripping from the deep, open wounds across Maureen's cheeks and forehead. Realising that his left foot was treading in a pool of blood, he looked down at his feet and discovered that Maureen had also been severely 'knee-capped'; there was no way that she would ever be able to walk properly again on both legs. Two bullets had been used to shatter the knee bone of her right leg.

"You poor girl," groaned Fergal, the tears rolling down his cheeks, "I'm so sorry that I couldn't help you."

Maureen emitted a very soft moan, a whimpering noise akin to the sound that a suffering puppy would make. Maureen's pathetic, heart rendering, soft whine assailed Fergal's ears; he just wanted to sit and cuddle the woman and take away all her pain if only he could.

Maureen's brain was desperately attempting to come to terms with recent events; it was not only the pain that was driving her mad, it was the total incomprehension that the innocent people of pure and good heart face when trying to comprehend the evil behaviour of people such as Francis, Colm, and Mick; she had never known that such people existed..

Controlling his abject feelings and nausea Fergal ran to the kitchen, picking up a clean tea towel and soaking it thoroughly. Returning to the young woman's side, he had done his best to stem the flow of blood. Once again running, in frantic panic, back to the kitchen, rinsing the blood-soaked tea towel and quickly returning to the whimpering Maureen, he had pressed the wet tea towel against her face as tightly as possible but not too tight so as to prevent her breathing.

Ripping off his shirt, he made a tourniquet, tying the shirt very tightly on her thigh to help prevent further loss of blood from her shattered knee.

With desperate haste, Fergal glanced around the room and rose quickly, virtually diving at the window. He ripped down a curtain, tearing it in the process, and wrapped the young woman up as tightly as he felt necessary. By the time he had finished she resembled an Egyptian Mummy, her face completely covered in the soaked tea towel bandage and her body and legs tightly wrapped within the curtain. Finally, he lifted her up as gently as he was able and took her outside, placing her gently on the pavement by the car. Quickly opening the car door, he tenderly laid Maureen on the rear seat, driving her to the nearest hospital casualty department.

Parking in an ambulance bay, he scrambled out of the car and stopped a teenage girl who was leaving the emergency department, her left arm in a sling. He slipped the teenager five pounds, telling her to make sure that Maureen was given emergency treatment. Then he retreated, hiding behind some bushes and watched from a safe distance, making sure that the teenager did as he had bid and only left the area when he saw a nurse and two porters rushing out with a stretcher. A Policeman closely followed behind them but by this time Fergal had safely disappeared.

A few weeks later Maureen, badly disfigured and marked as a traitor, hung herself from a beam at the local school's gymnasium. Her mother died of a broken heart shortly afterwards.

Months later Francis, in a drunken state and annoyed with a woman who was rejecting his advances in a bar in Belfast, had threatened the woman with a violent end. In this crowded bar Francis boasted of his 'connections' to the IRA and of how he had 'fixed' a woman who thought that she was better than him; if women didn't give him what he wanted then they would be very sorry.

The woman told Francis to piss off and quickly left the bar. It wasn't long after that incident that Francis disappeared and some say he ran away to the Mainland but the word was that he is buried in a peat bog in the south. Fergal knew which one of the tales was true because that was the only execution that he took part in that gave him any pleasure.

Body tossing restlessly in his bed, Fergal gradually began to climb from his recurring nightmare but the haunting vision of Maureen's face endured, staring back at him. She kept demanding,

"Why, why, why?"

Fergal had had no answer for her. He had been called in by the school caretaker who had been desperate to have Maureen's body removed before pupils arrived for the day's lessons. But the shock of seeing her hanging from the gymnasium beam, the transformation from beautiful woman to ravaged void was more than he could bear. His haunted eyes stared into the sad, hollow eyes of Maureen. The sparkle had gone from her persona and now all that was left was an empty shell of what had once been a bright star.

She was dangling from a thick rope, her facial skin shiny and white almost wax-like in appearance but intersected by ugly scars of faded brown. The rope was wound tightly around her neck with the other end tied over a ceiling beam. Next to her, now stationary feet, was a gymnasium vaulting horse, her walking stick discarded on the floor where it had been allowed to drop. Yesterday the schoolboys and schoolgirls had used the vaulting horse for fun activities during their physical education lessons but today it was a sad accessory to an untimely and so unnecessary death.

With tears in his eyes Fergal climbed on top of the horse and holding Maureen firmly around the waist, he cut the rope. He had not been prepared for the sudden increase in her dead weight, and they fell, tumbling to the floor, Fergal holding onto Maureen in a vain attempt of trying not to cause her any more pain. She landed on top of him, her face resting on his. Involuntarily, he had screamed and pushed her away.

Chapter 27

Disguised as an old tramp, Shannon had been patrolling Fergal's street for hours, surprised not to have seen him exiting for his usual excursion to some drinking hole. It was now seven o'clock on Friday evening and still Fergal hadn't surfaced. She was beginning to become alarmed. Was he all right, was he dead, or had he done a runner?

She sneaked into his building and using Fergal's spare that she had previously taken, entered Fergal's apartment. Cautiously creeping inside she discovered Fergal in a drunken, restless sleep; both the smell of Fergal and the odour from his apartment assailing her nostrils. The revolting stench almost made her nauseous but satisfied that Fergal was still in situ she quickly turned on her heels, exited, and made her way back down the street, heading for the nearest bus stop which would take her to the city centre. From there she would get a cab to her home and change into clean, fresh clothes and could then relax with a nice dinner and a romantic CD.

Walking along the pavement, lost in her thoughts of forthcoming relaxation, something disturbed her psyche. Unaware that Willie Davidson was passing her on the pavement, she felt something peculiar, the hair on the nape of her neck rising and she tingled nervously, shivering involuntarily.

Looking back to determine the possible cause of her internal body alarm all she could discern was a large, bearded, but harmless looking middle-aged man, walking as if burdened, the stoop of many years of heavy toil resting on the poor man's shoulders. This older man had a street map in his hand and he was evidently intent on locating a particular address, scrutinising the map with a deep intensity whilst glancing up at the buildings that surrounded him. Not knowing Willie - she was still waiting for a picture of him - and taken in by this man's very ordinariness, she shook her head, dismissing her feelings of misgiving and continued on her journey.

Willie walked forward a few paces, paused, turned, and watched her walk away, his face breaking into a contemptuous sneer; having watched her with Fergal he had nothing but contempt for the woman but he was curious regarding her surreptitious behaviour; bloody slag. Looking up at Fergal's building he shrugged nonchalantly then stood erect, his apparent stoop disappearing as if miraculously cured.

Checking the time indicated on his watch Willie cursed aloud and marched briskly off into the distance.

*   *   *

Waking fully from his nightmare slumber, Fergal opened his eyes but the image of Maureen's face remained. He squeezed his eyes tightly shut and then opened them again, the image finally beginning to fade as Maureen's face gradually receded into the distant recesses of his mind, her face getting smaller and smaller, her lips repeating the same question, "Why?" until she finally disappeared from view.

He shuddered, rising from his sweat stained disarranged bed. "Oh, Jesus, I need a drink." Rubbing his temples, he went to the kitchen in a desperate search for more alcohol that would help to deaden the haunting memories. Finding the fridge bare, he frantically searched his apartment seeking any money that might have been stashed, hidden in one of his rare sober moments. But he was penniless.

Defeated, dejected, he slumped down onto an armchair, holding his head in his hands, rocking backwards and forwards as if the motion would keep the ghosts at bay. A sudden thought hit him and he raced into the bedroom towards the chest of drawers, reaching underneath. Taped underneath the drawers was an old Rolex watch that Colm had given to him. Fergal had forgotten that he had hidden the watch not long after he had arrived at the apartment. Colm, being Colm, knew how to cream off certain percentages from drugs and protection rackets and when he brought himself a new Rolex, he gave his old watch to the very young and very grateful Fergal. It had become one of Fergal's proudest possessions and the only thing that he owned of any value. Now it was needed for an emergency and besides he no longer wanted to own anything that belonged to Colm or his past life.

Putting the watch in his pocket, taking his coat from a hook near the door, he exited the apartment.

Both Shannon and Willie, tired of their unsuccessful watching and waiting, had missed the opportunity of seeing Fergal as he left his apartment building, Rolex held in a tight fist within his trouser pocket.

Still not totally sober, unshaven and reeking of alcohol, Fergal made his way unsteadily in the direction of the local Pawnbrokers shop. It was a path that he was very familiar with and one that he had trodden many times previously. This would have to be his last journey because he was clutching his very last possession of any value but this item was of the greatest financial value. He had to maximise the money that that snivelling, snotty nosed Pawnbroker would give to him.

The light faded as the evening drew in, the streetlights beginning to flicker into life, some initially more hesitant than their companions, as if reluctantly giving up their bountiful light for the duration of another night. The contrast of dusk and the streetlights threw eerie shadows across the pavement and across Fergal, sometimes illuminating him, other times casting him into the dim darkness of the dusk.

He elicited curious stares from those whom he brushed past and one or two of those who scrutinised him did so as if summing up their opportunities of mugging this drunken oaf. One youth who was waiting further along the street, monitoring the progress of this potential mugging 'target', pulled a flick-knife from the pocket of his leather jacket and readied himself as Fergal approached.

Just before he prepared to lunge forward a shaft of light from one the streetlights traversed Fergal's face and the potential mugger recoiled, unsure of whether it was the look in Fergal's eyes or whether he had decided that this man was just another worthless, drunken bum with nothing of value. The mugger convinced himself that the reason for his withdrawal was not because of the fear, caused as a result of that indefinable anger in the man's eyes, but more as a result of a quick conclusion that the risk involved in mugging this drunk would not bring any reward.

The potential mugger slid his hand back into his pocket, under the intensity of Fergal fixing him with a contemptuous stare, and he quickly turned away whilst his potential intended victim continued on his path to the Pawnbroker's shop.

Entering the Pawnbrokers, Fergal approached the obnoxious owner standing behind a counter, protected from attack by heavy iron bars extending from the counter to the ceiling. The man's reptilian eyes gleamed in greedy expectation as Fergal neared.

"Hi Fergal, what have you got for me? What have you got left to pawn?" he drawled in a very oily voice, the eyes gleaming bright, but as Fergal slowly withdrew a clenched hand from his pocket, the Pawnbroker's eyes narrowed in fear. He didn't trust Fergal but was grateful for the drunk's business because he had made a tidy profit from the alcoholic's ex-possessions over the last few months. He almost yelped in delight as Fergal fully withdrew his hand, revealing its contents, the Pawnbrokers eyes widening with pleasure. But instantly aware that he had given Fergal a good selling signal he creased his forehead into a frown then scowled in apparent disappointment.

Fergal expecting such a response ignored the Pawnbroker's contemptuous demeanour and extending his arm, with his hand palm up, shoved the watch through the purposely designed small gap in the bars, holding the Rolex a few inches under the Pawnbroker's face.

Cautiously, the Pawnbroker took the watch from Fergal and checked it up against the light; he made an exaggerated show of examining the item, turning it in his hands, thoroughly checking the back of the watch and its strap. Finally, the Pawnbroker gave the watch a conclusive scrutiny under his magnifying eyeglass.

Whilst this show was taking place, Fergal waited patiently, leaning with his left arm on the shop counter, fingers drumming nonchalantly on the surface and eyes staring vacantly into the distance.

"It's a fake," declared the Pawnbroker.

"It isn't."

"Look, I'm sorry Fergal, but this watch is obviously a copy, a very good copy but, nevertheless it's a fake."

"Bullshit!"

"Genuinely...no, that's the wrong word...*genuinely*," he smirked at his own weak joke. "Seriously, this isn't a Rolex. It's not a bad watch – I can give you a few bucks – but it's not a genuine Rolex."

"Go fuck yourself. I know that it's genuine."

"If that's your attitude," he handed the watch back to Fergal, "Then you can take your business elsewhere."

Fergal regained the watch and turned on his heel.

His greed almost having got the better of him, he called out, "Um...Fergal...I could have been wrong. Can I have another look at the watch?" The Pawnbroker knew he was on to a god thing, his voice now reverting back to its usual oily contrite tone.

Expressionless, Fergal turned back to the Pawnbroker, dropping the watch into the man's grasping hands.

"Yes, you could be right," announced the Pawnbroker,

pretending to re-examine the watch. "It could be a genuine Rolex." His eyes flicked up at Fergal, "You do understand, I get many fakes and have to be careful."

"Yea, sure," retorted Fergal without sincerity.

The Pawnbroker swallowed, glanced slyly at Fergal, then muttered the lowest figure that he thought he could get away with "I'll give you fifty Dollars."

Fergal stood expressionless waiting for a proper response but his eyes registered a mixture of disgust and contempt.

"Seventy Dollars," exclaimed the Pawnbroker.

Fergal didn't move a muscle.

"You'll ruin me," complained the Pawnbroker now beginning to feel nervous, "One Hundred and Twenty-five Dollars?"

Fergal was tiring of the game; he needed a drink, the craving beginning to gnaw at him. "Come on, give me a serious offer and let's get this done. I need the money, you need the watch."

"I don't need the watch," protested the Pawnbroker.

Fergal raised his eyebrow, his eyes meeting those of the Pawnbroker.

The Pawnbroker sighed, reluctantly giving way. "Oh, all right! I suppose that I could re-sell the watch, as a favour to you."

"Just make me a serious offer," demanded Fergal now becoming quite weary of the entire process.

"Three hundred."

"Five hundred," snapped Fergal.

"Three-fifty."

"Four hundred."

"Okay, okay, four it is." The Pawnbroker exited the shop via a door behind the counter, reappearing almost as quickly, eight fifty-dollar bills clutched in his hand. He passed the money to Fergal who made a great show of counting the money, holding each dollar bill up to the light, checking for authenticity.

"Hey, there's no need for that," complained the Pawnbroker, "I'm honest."

"Yea right, an honest pawnbroker - I don't think so," snorted Fergal, satisfied that he would now be able to sate his body's thirst for alcohol. Folding the dollar bills, he tucked them into his pocket but quickly remembering the previous loss of his wallet, he separated the fifty-dollar bills, placing some of them in his socks, others in his trouser pockets and three in the torn lining of his jacket. Temporarily happy, he departed the Pawnbroker's shop without a backward glance.

The Pawnbroker was even more pleased than Fergal, running the Rolex through his hands, "Well my beauty, you'll fetch me a tidy profit." He returned to his side room behind the counter where he opened the Safe, happily placing the watch into the deep recesses of the secure metal box.

Having left the Pawnbroker's shop Fergal paused, scrutinising the area, looking up and down the street for anything that did not fit or blend in. Although he was not totally sober, years of intensive training and of being part of a terrorist hit squad - albeit usually only on an observation/'look out' basis – had made him a valued early warning system for people such as Colm and Mick. Fergal's experiences had made him very conscious of the unusual or unnatural and of being able to instantly notice anything out of the ordinary. Obviously, once his alcohol intake capacity levels had been breached – all too frequently these days – then Fergal's capability for observation and survival waned and decreased in direct proportion to the consumption of alcohol. For the moment he had money on his person, was reasonably sober, and wanted to make sure that he could safely make it back to his apartment but not before collecting a couple of bottles of comforting 'Jack Daniels' on the way back.

Deciding that the route was clear Fergal tucked his hands into his trouser pockets, hunched his shoulders and slouched off in the direction of the nearest liquor store. Although giving the appearance of a down and out bum, his eyes were sharp, peering out from under a mop of hair falling down over his forehead, the eyes continuously scrutinising his surroundings. A couple of youths observed Fergal but having tangled with him in the past, quietly crossed the street to avoid any possibility of a confrontation. Fergal entered the 'All Night' store, confidently selecting his drink and as an afterthought, begrudgingly snatching up a bar of chocolate, his body telling him that he ought to eat something!

With the minimum of pleasantries Fergal paid for his purchases, the shop assistant providing a large brown paper bag to house the booze. They exchanged grunts, neither the immigrant shop assistant nor the unfriendly Fergal being prepared to make use of the English language; Fergal made his way back to his apartment.

But there *were* eyes watching him and Fergal knew that but now he didn't care, he had his whisky and his food. He checked inside the paper bag to make sure that the bar of chocolate was safely within and hurried along. Reaching the street that housed his apartment building he stopped, pretending to tie his shoelace but then quickly reeled round looking up at the same instant.

Two youths instantly ducked back into the shadows of the preceding brownstone-block doorway.

Firmly holding his prized purchases, Fergal charged off in the direction of the two youths, bawling, "Right, you little fucking shit-bags, I've had enough of you following me; now I'm going to beat the crap out of you!"

For a second the two potential assailants were frozen to the spot, the younger one looking up at the older youth for guidance. The older boy squared his shoulders and taking a knuckle-duster from his pocket, spread and firmly planted his feet on the ground; grinning, he awaited the arrival of the hapless drunken bum. The younger of the two, suddenly feeling more courageous as a result of the apparently bold behaviour of his accomplice, followed suit, pulling a flick-knife from his back trouser pocket. They stood side by side, confidently waiting for the oncoming charging Fergal.

Fergal reached the over confident youths and just as the younger one jabbed forward, stabbing with his flick-knife, Fergal side-stepped and landed a crippling punch on the teenager's soft temple, making the boy crumble unconscious into a heap on the pavement. Before the older boy could blink in surprise Fergal raised his leg, bringing his knee with massive force into the juvenile's balls. At the same instant, he used his free hand to pull the yob's head forward, suddenly smashing his head sharply into the boy's forehead, head-butting the youngster with a practised force. His potential attacker's head split open, the eyes glazing over, the splitting pain of bruised and bleeding head, together with his aching groin make him collapse on to the ground. For good measure Fergal kicked him in the groin as the yob lay on the floor, doubly increasing the older teenager's pain and probably having a severe negative effect on the young man's future child-giving possibilities.

Crouching over the defeated miscreant Fergal grabbed a handful of hair and pulled the boy's head, whispering threateningly in his ear, "If I ever, *ever,* have any more trouble with you or any of your friends, then I'll slit your fucking throats. Is that clear?"

The youth, grovelling in pain, vigorously nodded his head, his hands desperately trying to cup and protect his throbbing manhood and testicles. Holding his testicles didn't seem to lessen the pain and he groaned in anguish.

In a voice demonstrating an aggressive meanness Fergal growled, "And, I don't want you guys following me or watching me in the future. Is *that* clear as well?"

The youth winced in anticipation of receiving a further blow and additional pain, his head bobbing up and down in acquiescence.

Checking his potential assailant's pockets, Fergal found a wallet and an outdated student identity card. He scrutinised the wallet's contents and checked the picture on the card. Satisfied that the youth matched the image as shown in the picture, he memorised the address. "Right, I also know where you live. So, if you or any of your scum friends try anything I'll come straight back for you."

The younger attacker, eyes beginning to focus, scrambled muzzily to his feet, and taking in the scene he immediately turned away, determined not to make unwanted contact with Fergal's eyes.

Fergal glared at the younger yob, his voice made more menacing by using a sotto tone, and warned, "I've just told your friend here," Gesticulating with contempt at the bleeding youth, "Of the dangers in bothering me in the future. If you do then you'll both be extremely sorry; you've both been hanging around too much for my liking. If I see either one of you, or smell you in the area, then I will come and hunt both of you. Now take your friend and *piss off*!"

The terrified teenager hurried to his accomplice and helped his bleeding and doubled-up companion as they staggered off hastily, their progress being as fast as they were able with the younger one supporting the heavier older boy as best he could.

Fergal remained stationary watching them depart. When the teenagers had disappeared round the corner Fergal remembered his drink. The brown bag was still clutched in his left hand; gingerly, he opened the bag and peered inside. Thankfully both bottles were intact and Fergal released a contented sigh, turned round and headed back towards his apartment. Initially the adrenaline of survival action had made him almost totally sober and with the haunting memories now taking a back seat in his brain he walked with a lighter step, returning in the direction of his apartment. At one stage he broke out into a rendition of 'Danny Boy', whistling tunelessly as he jovially continued his journey.

A passing old lady made a point of firmly planting a finger in each of her ears thus reminding Fergal that he was virtually tone deaf. He smiled broadly at the woman, who scowled in response, but taking her point he terminated his tuneless rendition.

At his apartment block Fergal bounded up the stairs to the first floor and entered his domain. The first thing that caught his eye was a picture on the wall depicting a fishing boat leaving a secluded harbour. A woman with sad eyes and forlorn expression was staring out to sea whilst waving her scarf in the direction of a man at the stern of the boat. The man was obviously calling out some kind of farewell with assurance of his ultimate safe return. Like the woman in the picture Fergal was convinced that the man would never return. He shuddered involuntarily, an aura of extreme sadness descending over him like a heavy fog; his previous jovial mood left him, his good spirits draining like a pulled plug. He shivered.

Fergal's memories drifted back to Ireland and particularly to a small cold, icy, wind-swept harbour in County Mayo on the North West tip. It was a daunting thought that nothing but thousands of miles of forbidding ocean separated the mouth of this tiny west coast harbour from the land of the Americas.

Though a very small community had established itself around the mouth of harbour they were pretty much cut off from the rest of civilisation. A small, winding road led down through miles of peat bog, which in turn was interspersed with pockets of woods and closed in by a mountainous terrain. The local inhabitants very rarely received visitors other than a routine visit from the Fish Merchant who arrived in a very old van and who paid a paltry amount for the fishermen's hard won catch. The village contained a very small store which only opened for two hours a day, excluding Sundays, and provided everything from fuel to flour. Life was frugal but the community was close knit; the very isolation of the place, together with various escape routes over the peat bogs, suited Fergal's terrorist paymasters.

Fergal's face softened as he recalled hugging the love of his life, Rosein, tears rolling down her cheeks as she pleaded with him not to go. Holding her close he enveloped her in an unyielding grip of eternal fervour, sure that even through the thickness of their heavy coats he could feel the beating of her heart.

Rosein had found out that Fergal had been 'working' with the Provisionals and she was very unhappy about the situation. A truly good woman, she had no truck with terrorists or with any issues that people felt could only be resolved by resorting to violence. She had begged Fergal to give up his unsavoury occupation and leave with her, making a new start together somewhere overseas. Fergal had tried to explain that it was very difficult for him just to withdraw from the situation and that it was virtually impossible to walk away from the path that he had chosen.

People like Colm would see to that.

Rosein had pleaded with him, at least not to go on the boat now waiting patiently in the harbour, and that they would go home together and talk about it. It was too late, Fergal explained, and added that he was committed and had no choice but to sail on Brendan's fishing boat. What he could not explain or divulge was that, offshore, a large cache of Arms were left floating just under the surface under a thick fishing net, which in turn was securely marked and held in place by buoys. The Authorities did not expect any Arms 'drops' to be made off this area of the coastline and thus it was relatively easy for the Libyan vessel, registered in Liberia, to lower a boat and deposit the Arms package, waterproofed and securely tied with a float. This was then fastened under the fishing net previously set out by Brendan, the fishing boat's Skipper, during his fishing trip of yesterday. The net itself was anchored to a reef and supported by four buoys at each end; only a severe storm would have torn it from its moorings. However this particular drop point could only be used for a couple more times before someone would get suspicious.

Rosein had been adamant and had insisted that if Fergal left on the boat then their relationship was over. Fergal was torn. This woman meant everything to him, his life, his love, his very future. But Colm, Colm represented fear and oppression. Fergal explained that he would break free, soon, but now was not the time.

She held tightly on Fergal, and I had looked up into his eyes.

Deeply in love and becoming uncertain, Fergal felt a tug on his sleeve. It was Mick demanding that they go, *now!* Reluctantly, Fergal, with Mick's grasp still on his coat sleeve, followed closely behind Mick towards the boat, continuously looking over his shoulder at the love of his life, Rosein standing silently, tears rolling down her cheeks.

Fergal had stood in the stern of the departing boat, staring forlornly back at the motionless Rosein, her body unflinching except for the tears still falling ever more heavily down her cheeks until she finally raised her hand, waving gently, bidding him a morose farewell.

A foreboding had descended over Fergal and he had desperately wanted to jump overboard and swim for the shore. Reaching to undo his coat buttons Mick's heavy hand on his shoulder precluded any possibility of jumping overboard. By the time that Mick had removed his hand the boat was too far out at sea for Fergal to have any chance of being able to swim to the shore. He could still see the stationary figure of Rosein, unflinchingly still but now no more than a speck on the landscape.

That was Fergal's last ever sighting of his only true love. True to her word she had packed her things, taken her savings out from her bank, and disappeared.

Despite Fergal's frantic searching he had never found Rosein; she had literally disappeared from the face of the earth. Inconsolable, he had immersed himself ever deeper into the nefarious workings of the Provisionals, taking a misguided refuge in causing pain and grief to others.

Fergal wiped a tear from his eye as he focused back to the present, to his life as it was now, and hopefully to a forthcoming death that would be so welcome. Despite his background, his early religious education had ingrained in him the abhorrence of committing suicide, thus he would endure his current existence until someone could put him out of this misery. Perhaps he should have let those two pathetic youths knife him when they had had the chance!

Placing the bag down by an armchair he ambled into the kitchen, selecting a dirty glass from the usual source and returned. With heavily shaking hand he managed to unscrew the whisky bottle and holding the shaking bottle firmly to the rim of the glass, he poured a large measure, spilling a portion of the drink as his other hand also began to shake. Replacing the bottle on the floor, he cupped the glass in both hands, bringing it invitingly to his lips. Briefly savouring the aroma, Fergal swallowed a large measure and could feel the warmth travelling through his body. With two more gulps he emptied the glass, he was now beginning to feel considerably better, the alcohol anaesthetising his sorrow, alleviating his fears, and subduing his memories. He poured himself another large drink, this time not spilling any of the whisky.

The night darkened, the sounds of the city abating in the distance as Fergal finished the contents of the first bottle and then unscrewed the second bottle of 'Jack Daniels.' Slowly and surely he worked his way through the contents of the second bottle. All the while the sounds of the city passed without recognition. The occasional sound of a car being heard, slowing to a stop, followed by the slamming of its doors, which was then accompanied by the clamour of drunken laughter emanating from late night revellers climbing unsteadily out of vehicles or making their way along the pavement.

For each car that slowed and stopped there always seemed to be another car that would accelerate, growling with increasing noise until it reached far enough into the distance for the sound to fade and die. People were having fun and laughter was rising up from the street. An occasional scream was heard from some over exuberant female but tonight it seemed that the muggers and drunks were in benevolent mood or were keeping their activities to a very low level. It was generally a good night in the city with one or two minor exceptions of individuals experiencing sorrow or the occasional bellow of anger breaking the harmony. There was also a young woman who was leaning against the outside wall of the apartment block, crying unashamedly on being told by her boyfriend that he was seeing another woman and that he didn't want to continue their relationship. The discarded woman continued to sob as the boyfriend shrugged and walked away, crossing the street, continuing onward into the arms of another female waiting patiently across the street.

The sounds, particularly the sudden shrill sound of a woman whose screeching laughter would have been enough to wake the dead, passed over Fergal. In his present state the outside world had no meaning or relevance and he progressively sunk into a comatose condition. Gradually the city quietened, the sound of silence gently soothing the environment, a softening balm in preparation for the dawn's frantic reawakening.

The silence only served to exacerbate the sonorous reverberation of Fergal's drunken snoring, his body having finally succumbed to the contents of almost two full bottles of 'Jack Daniels.'

Chapter 28

Alistair Glen, anxious, strolled up and down through a thick-pile patterned Wilton carpet in the Tsaoich's private rooms next to the Tsaoich's office in Dublin's City Centre.

Simon Harvey, furrowed brow, tightly gripped the arms of a mock Jacobean chair as they both wait for Eamon to speak.

"Come on Eamon, it's not that bad," Alistair spoke softly, unable to bear the tension any longer. "Your potential Prime Minister said...

"He's not my fucking potential Prime Minister," growled Eamon.

"Yes, I know, but he is the Prime Minister of Ireland."

"And here we don't call him Prime Minister either, he's called the Tsaioch," interrupted a very unhappy Eamon.

"Yes I know," sighed Alistair, "But will you please relax. The Prime Minister, sorry, Tsaioch, has supported us in most of our aims and we are working to bring peace and a united Ireland together, under one government and one Prime Minister, um, Tsaoich."

"That's the problem," complained Eamon, "Our Party is not strong enough yet for us to win elections all over Ireland and I'm buggered if I'm going to work so hard just so some arsehole Paddy can take the benefit. If anyone is going to be the first Tsaioch of all Ireland then it's going to be me, and my party."

"Not to mention all the scams, illegal gambling, collections and drugs operations that your people would lose out on if someone else had total control of all Ireland," commented Simon dryly.

"Go fuck yourself, you English prat," snarled Eamon as he took a menacing pace towards Simon. Simon didn't flinch, remaining in a state of total calm and defiantly stared back at Eamon but his hands did grip more tightly on the arms of the chair.

"Please Eamon," Alistair softly interjected, gingerly placing his hand on Eamon's arm. "Simon can be a fool but he knows on which side his bread is buttered. He's one of the best operatives we have in British Intelligence and MI5 were very unhappy when I seconded him to run my new intelligence operation."

"I still don't trust anyone from British Intelligence," snapped the partially mollified Eamon.

"Simon's background is a bit different. His father was a refugee, coming to Britain just after the Second World War; came from the Ukraine. Simon has always been ambitious and unlike most of his colleagues has never been totally convinced of his loyalties to the

British people. He works for money and is ambitious to climb to the very top." Alistair winked at Simon, "Aren't you, Simon? Money motivated, yet ambitious?"

Before Simon could respond, Eamon grumbled, "I don't trust Judases!"

"I'm not a Judas," retorted Simon, his voice firm and insistent, "My father was a Nazi, an SS Guard at a Jewish Concentration camp in Poland. Just before the American soldiers arrived to free the Jews most of the inmates were killed or shipped off, thus it was very easy for my father to switch identities. The soft-hearted British subsequently welcomed him into Britain, particularly because they believed that he was a displaced Jewish industrial engineer. My Father was given a lot of help and became successful. I received the best possible education that money could buy and subsequently the opportunity of reading languages, French and German, at Cambridge, gaining a first class honours degree in the process. From Cambridge, I was recruited into British Intelligence – or lack of Intelligence as my father used to call it!"

"I'm not interested in you, or your background," testily snapped Eamon, "All I want to know is if you can be trusted?"

"Simon can be trusted. He's immersed himself in our operations for the past couple of years," insisted Alistair keen to protect his protégé.

"Anyway, as I was trying to tell you," Simon determinedly continued, "I have no love for the British. I have never forgiven the cruel taunts of my school friends whenever my parents turned up for open days; they used to tease me mercilessly over my father's strong accent. I vowed that I would get the opportunity of payback, and here I am."

Eamon ignored Simon, treating him as if he was some recalcitrant child and turning to Alistair, spoke in a cold, measured tone, "I'm still not convinced. How did you know about him? How did you find each other? He could be a plant from British Intelligence".

"You're being paranoid and not rational, Eamon. You know that Simon has performed various tasks on our behalf; he has blood on his hands that could not be explained away. Anyway, I'm sure I've told you this before but it was an Intelligence Officer in Northern Ireland who caught Simon's hand 'in the till'. Simon was running non-existent Agents and pocketing the money. Simon became alerted to the other Intelligence Officer's discovery and despatched the man to a watery grave but not before a report had been sent to senior officers. This report reached the security services during one of my visits to Stormont Castle. Fortunately only two men had seen the report, one of whom met with a very unfortunate car accident the following day." Alistair cocked an eyebrow at Simon, "Didn't he, Simon?"

Simons nodded laconically.

"The other guy, Noel, was already known to us and was already sympathetic to our cause. Fortunately Noel managed to get the original report to me. From there, I arranged for my personal Security Detail to organise a private meeting with Simon on the pretext that I could obtain an 'on the ground' feel from people at the sharp end of terrorism. I told my security people that in order to avoid the possibility of the discussion with Simon not being frank and open, I insisted that the meeting took place behind closed doors, between Simon and myself, with no one else being present; reluctantly, my request was granted. At first Simon was extremely wary but on showing him a copy of the misdemeanour report he became quite fearful, convinced that I was part of a trap to finish his career. It all went swimmingly well from there. We discovered our mutual dislike for anything English and established a joint aim and mutual objective of causing widespread havoc in the British Intelligence and legal systems," Alistair gleefully concluded, joyfully rubbing his hands together.

"It wasn't quite that simple," interjected Simon dryly, "It took a long time for mutual trust and confidence to develop."

"Well that was a load of uninteresting balls," with disdain Eamon feigned total disinterest.

Alistair, expecting praise, was crestfallen, his exuberance fading.

"More importantly," continued Eamon, ignoring Alistair's discomfort, "Is the fact that I'm not happy with the situation in the North. My q2boys are gaining more and more control of the Province but that protestant arsehole, Jimmy Henderson, is causing havoc with some of our operations and interfering with our street traders. His renegade branch of the Ulster Unionist movement will have to be stopped."

"I could have him arrested under the prevention of terrorism act," said Alistair hopefully.

"It's not enough; he'd soon be free again," protested Eamon. Simon, inspiration hitting him, leapt up, "Suicide," he determinedly suggested, "Jimmy could commit suicide."

"He'd never do that," Eamon condescendingly shot a withering glance of contempt at Simon.

"He wouldn't have to; we'd do it," Simon stated, his tone remaining soft and neutral.

"His people would never let us get near to him," Eamon was becoming impatient, even more convinced that Simon was merely an opportunist and a moron.

"You wouldn't have to. As I said, we'd do it, British Intelligence will do it," Simon persisted.

Aware that Eamon was becoming extremely irritated by Simon's train of thought Alistair decided to intervene, his tone conciliatory, "It's impossible, Simon. Someone would smell a rat and it would ruin or jeopardise everything we've set up so far."

"There are ways. As you suggested, we could have him arrested and taken into custody under the Prevention of Terrorism Act; this would happen two or three times occurring at very short intervals." Simon became increasingly animated as he explained his idea, "Each time his lawyers will get him released after a few days. Then whilst under arrest and in custody for the third time we can put it about, leak out a story that he's become depressed by the continual internment. I can then arrange a nocturnal visit, either by myself or Willie..."

"I don't want that fucker involved in this one," snarled Eamon.

"Okay fine. I will personally arrange Jimmy's suicide, no witnesses, only me. I can arrange access to the Prison, in and out, with virtually no one being aware. Once inside, arrangements could be made for the Warders to be occupied elsewhere and I could visit Jimmy where he would be held in one of the solitary confinement cells. It would be easy to fake his suicide. No one would have any proof and my nocturnal visit to the Prison would be explained as an Intelligence gathering operation. A mock interrogation could be arranged with one of the Provisional IRA detainees and put forward as my reason for visiting the Prison."

"Brilliant," cried out Alistair, delighted, "That's just brilliant." He looked to Eamon for approval, "Isn't it?"

Eamon grudgingly nodded in affirmation but not wishing to lavish any praise on Simon responded in a mundane, matter of fact tone,

"I suppose it'll be okay. It may work."

"See to it Simon," cheerfully instructed Alistair.

Eamon checked his watch. "We'd better get back to the meeting with that arsehole Tsaioch. God, I'm looking forward to arranging something unpleasant for him in the not too distant future. This is my bloody Ireland not his!"

*   *   *

"Thank you for granting us this interview, Prime Minister," the sycophantic reporter from the BBC enthused, "The peace process seems to be going well. The Provisional IRA has agreed a cease-fire and the Unionists seemed to be subdued subsequent to the suicide of the firebrand, Jimmy Henderson."

"Yes," beamed Alistair, smiling into the camera, his customary warm smile reserved for the Public, spreading across his face. His face clouded, "Although it was sad that a man took his life in the Maze Prison – it is always sad to hear of an unnecessary death, but it does appear to have speeded up the peace process."

Alistair's visage instantly altered and an earnest expression and professorial countenance spread across his face and continued as if speaking to an ignorant child. "As you are aware, we as a Government have been working hard with all sides to try and bring a lasting peace to the Province. With the support and guidance of the Irish Government we are monitoring arms dumps and have brought an understanding and harmony to the region. The Catholics are taking a greater role in the Province's activities, from local government to industry, the judiciary and police. Even many of the die-hard Unionists are beginning to accept that things must change, and change is inevitable, especially if we all want to move forward; forward to a peace for our children and for their children."

Alistair smiled triumphantly into the camera.

"That's very gratifying to hear Prime Minister," commended the BBC reporter. "I'm sure you will be nominated for the Nobel Peace Prize."

"Do you think so?" inquired Alistair taken aback, conceit and vanity taking control for an instant. Quickly regaining control he belatedly laughed at the suggestion, effusively burbling, "Of course that's not why we are doing this; it's our mission. We really do want people to live in harmony in these Islands. With common goals and aims and respect for one another, whatever their creed, colour, or culture."

"You really are a great man, Prime Minister."

"I'm just doing what I believe in, really. We are only trying to fulfil the policies that the British people voted for."

"And what about your policies on devolution for the United Kingdom?"

"We're giving people at grass roots level the opportunity of running their own communities. By setting devolution in motion for Scotland and Wales and the eventual aim of Regional Assemblies, or Parliaments, throughout England, we will give the population in each part of Britain the right to have a direct say in how their communities are run."

"But isn't that already the case? The voters elect a Government to run the country and then Councillors to control issues relevant to local communities?"

"Tch!," Alistair, peeved, leant forward as if admonishing a recalcitrant child, "You don't seem to understand; you haven't grasped my point." Realising that he might lose the reporter's hero worship, Alistair paused, smiled and raised his hand as if blowing away a cloud of smoke. With obsequious charm he resumed, "But I'm obviously not putting the issues across as clearly as I should."

He paused once more whilst the reporter's prickly expression softened, the man subsiding into the previous hero worship mode. "Bill – may I call you Bill?"

The reporter agreed with enthusiasm. "Wow," he thought, "I'm on first name terms with the Prime Minister."

"Bill," Alistair spoke almost conspiratorially, smiling his trademark smile, knowing full well that the BBC's reporter was, once again, virtually eating out of his hand, "The idea of regional representation and devolution is to take away central government's control of the important regional issues and allow local decisions to take place on issues including industrial development, buildings, housing, schools, policing, churches, and all other issues relevant to building up a healthy and happy society. What may suit a person in one area of the Country would be anathema to a person in another area of the Country. On this principle, people could elect a local Representative Body on the basis of local issues that affect their respective communities."

"But what about taxation, paying for the roads, the army, and so on; wouldn't anarchy follow if one area decides to have a completely different policy to its adjacent area? Say, for example, Liverpool decided that it would be a Nuclear Free Zone – I think the City Council has already expressed that wish – but if they did formally vote accordingly and didn't allocate any monies for defence, wouldn't that cause the Nation to disintegrate, effectively ending up as tiny satellite states of Europe?"

Alistair laughed, apparently amused by the reporters comment. "Of course central government would still be responsible for the major picture, the big issues such as national taxation, defence budgets, the Health Service and so on."

"Ah, I see," uttered the enthused reporter, "Westminster would still decide the national issues and the Regional Assemblies would determine the local issues."

"*Exactly!*" beamed Alistair in triumph, the backward child finally having understood the teacher's point! "Now surely you understand that it would be better if central government took a backward step out of people's lives?"

"Of course, Prime Minister."

Alistair smiled benignly at his pupil. The interview continued in the same vein with fresh subjects of discussion, each one increasing Alistair's popularity and raising his profile in the eyes of the public.

The reporter, rather than cross-examining and questioning Alistair with searching or probing questions, or ascertaining the demarcation between national and local issues, merely acted as an accomplice, the straight man in a double act.

Unfortunately this was not a comedy.

Chapter 29

When Alistair entered his Office in Downing Street, Simon was sitting on a sofa reading through the Prime Minister's official papers, a red Despatch Box lying open next to Simon on the sofa.

Alistair went to his desk and reached for a box of Kleenex tissues. Pulling out a handful of tissues he wiped the make up from his face. "I hate all this make-up stuff; it's disgusting but so necessary when in front of the cameras." He chuckled. "That was too easy, that dick-head reporter was eating out of my hand. When I first took on this job I expected a much harder time from both the opposition parties and the Press; probing questions, serious disagreements, threats, strong opposition and vehement arguments. In actual fact the opposition has been so weak and the Press so compliant; on the rare occasions that one or two people try to raise strong issues I merely deflect the subject, cancel the opportunity of discussion or disagreement and make denials so successfully that even the media are usually sucked in more often than not and end up heightening my public popularity and praising my non-existent achievements. We live in a society of the 'King's Clothes' you know, that old tale where a tailor convinces a vain king that he has made a suit of such fine quality and taste but in fact it does not exist. If you tell the people what they want to hear and keep telling them with the same positive message then in spite of their eyes and senses they begin to believe in the non-existent scenarios and not in the reality."

He threw the used tissues in the waste paper basket and looking over at Simon became aware of Simon's reading material. "Hey, what are you doing? Those are private papers, for the Prime Minister's eyes only."

Simon glanced up disdainfully. "I don't think that we have any secrets from each other." Adding impertinently, "Do we?"

"Of course not, but those papers neither concern you nor your operations!" Alistair approached Simon, snatching the private papers from his hand.

"Hey, no need to snatch," protested Simon, "I thought that we were on the same side."

"We are." Alistair placed the papers back into the red Despatch Box, "But I am the boss, don't ever forget that!"

"Sorry Boss," mumbled Simon, feeling peeved and annoyed.

"Although we work together on certain issues there are other things going on in this Country that you should not be party to." Alistair carried the Box to his desk, sat down and placed the closed Box on top of the desk. "Some subjects are for my attention only and those of the relevant Minister and Civil Servants directly involved in the pertinent subjects. It wouldn't do for someone else to be fully involved in the entire Governmental process."

"Are you afraid of me?" Simon chuckled, amused, "Afraid that I'll know too much, take over from you?"

Alistair fixed Simon with a cold stare. "Simon, you must know that if you ever overstep the line your demise will be very quick. Whether by Eamon's people or by the British Intelligence Services, your life would end in severe unhappiness and distress. You should know that a file detailing your activities is constantly updated and none of it would tie in to me... we've made sure of that. I would act as surprised as anyone if it was ever revealed that one of our top security personnel was a traitor or a rogue agent. Copies of your file would end up on various desks at MI5 and MI6 as well as Scotland Yard. We have all possible angles covered."

Beads of sweat formed on Simon's brow, his face turned ashen, saliva forming on the corners of his lips, his eyes burning with incandescent rage. He wanted to scream in anger at Alistair, "How dare you speak to me like that, me, who has helped you nearly every inch of the way; you little bastard!" But he didn't; years of self-discipline, from the early days at boarding school to University and his early intelligence service career, had taught him when to bite his tongue, hold back and to wait for the moment to attack, to go for the opponent's jugular. With tremendous will-power he forced his self-control to kick in, pleasantly responding, "Come on Alistair, you don't really mean it. You're making me feel like the hired help rather than a major integral part of the destabilisation process of Britain."

Alistair's eyes remained cold. "That's all you are Simon, the hired help, and never forget it. Never overstep the mark again."

"Yes, sorry, I understand," meekly offered the deflated Simon but could not resist adding as an afterthought, in a wry tone, "Boss", making a final attempt at redeeming his pride.

The last word passed over Alistair's head and, ignoring Simon's attempt at brevity, he stated in a matter of fact tone, "Just make the arrangements for our trip to Washington and the meeting with the President. Eamon will be in the USA at the same time on a fund raising trip. After the meeting in the White House we need to have a separate meeting between Eamon and our contacts in the FBI. I want to be there as well."

"Won't that be risky? Having a clandestine meeting with an official of the Provisional IRA whilst you are in a high profile situation?"

"I need to be there! Our FBI colleagues can arrange it. No one will know; we can arrange something in the Sheraton or a similar Hotel in Washington."

"You're not staying at our Embassy in Washington?" asked Simon incredulously.

"No, not this time; as I said, I want to take part in the planned meeting and that just would not be feasible if I stayed at the Embassy."

"But..."

Alistair snapped, "Just arrange it Simon; just make sure that it happens!"

Simon's mouth froze in mid-sentence, his rage boiling inside him; he really did hate being spoken to in such a manner. Visibly annoyed at this second put down from Alistair he meekly replied, "Okay, if that's what you want. Be it on your own head."
Turning on his heels he marched to the door, opening it to exit.

Wanting to demonstrate some semblance of being in control he childishly left the door ajar as he departed.

The Prime Minister's devoted female Secretary Alice looked up as Simon walked past her desk, her expression one of utter disdain and contempt,- and firmly ordered, "The Prime Minister likes his office door closed when people exit."

Simon stopped in his tracks, his face white with anger, and he glared at the Secretary now cowering under his withering stare. "If he wants the door closed then *you* bloody well close it."

"Well!" protested the indignant Secretary as the sulking Simon departed, now beginning to feel a little more cheerful having made another individual pay for his recent belittlement.

"No one treats me like that," thought Simon, "One day I will get my own back on Alistair, I always do."

His mind drifted back, recalling his schooldays, and in particular the two boys from the year above who were both Prefects. They had made the obnoxious Simon's life hell, no matter that Simon fully deserved it, the way that he had been treating the boys in the younger school years. Simon was notoriously renowned for his bullying of the juniors.

The two Prefects had tried their best to stamp out Simon's excesses and had hoped to teach him a lesson in the vain hope that he would mend his ways.

Simon had vowed that he would get even and after a few years within the Intelligence Services he had seized his opportunities. One of the ex-Prefects, by now a City 'High Flyer', had inadvertently become embroiled in an 'insider share trading' scandal. Although not directly implicated, Simon had put together a file that falsely catalogued years of improper trading and ensured that the file reached the desk of the appropriate Detective Inspector at Scotland Yard. Faced with this supposedly incontrovertible evidence the poor chap had had no option but to resign and was subsequently imprisoned for twelve months. Simon regularly checked on the man's subsequent progress and was delighted that that the man was now merely eking out a passable living running a boarding house in a North Wales seaside resort.

The other ex-Prefect had risen up within the ranks of the then Government with a glittering career ahead of him. Given the man's predilection for the fairer sex it had been relatively easy to set him up with an attractive, high class, prostitute. Flattered by the attention the testosterone-fuelled individual was soon suckered into a clandestine liaison with the young lady. Photographs were taken wherein the man also appeared to be snorting cocaine; the prostitute had subsequently arranged for the junior Government Minister to make a threesome with her friend. The second girl, an expendable double agent linked to an Eastern Bloc country, had been the coup de grace that Simon needed. Simon's anonymous dossier, together with incriminating photographs, soon found their way to the news desk at the Guardian Newspaper. It was only a matter of days before the Minister resigned from the Government and from Politics; his wife refused to have anything more to do with him and would not allow him access to their children. Retiring to lick his wounds and consider his options the man had taken refuge on his father's farm. Within six months the misery of his circumstances hit home and he was found with his head blown apart, his father's shotgun rigged by his side.

Recalling those memories made Simon feel so very much better. "Oh yes, people who tried to belittle him always paid the ultimate price. It was amazing what he had been allowed to get away under the guise of national security." Smiling, he exited the building.

Chapter 30

It was just after midday on Sunday and Shannon glanced at her watch, sighing in frustration; she had spent the past thirty-six hours patrolling up and down Fergal's street. Her stomach was also full from the numerous cups of coffee that she had consumed whilst sitting in the filthy cafe further along the road, the café allowing her a view of Fergal's apartment entrance.

Having adopted various disguises during each foray into Fergal's domain she had tried her utmost to blend into the surroundings. Each disguise had warranted a brief visit back to her house, with the result that the most prolonged sleep that she had had in the last two days had been five hours. The disguises were necessary because she didn't want any of the locals to get suspicious of her or enquire regarding her intentions.

Her current attire was a floral patterned kaftan top hanging down over a pair of corduroy dungarees and an old pair of heavy-duty work boots on her feet. The whole ensemble was topped with a really threadbare overcoat which would have looked beyond redemption at the worst end of a Salvation Army hostel. Her hair was tucked under a drab woollen scarf, her face partly obscured with a pair of horn-rimmed spectacles.

Despite her watchfulness she had not seen hide or hair of Fergal and was now becoming increasingly concerned. Tired and reaching a point where her operational capability was being reduced she reached inside her coat pocket, pulling out the key to Fergal's apartment. Looking at the keys she muttered, "I guess I'm going to have to risk it." Removing the scarf and the glasses she tucked them into the left hand pocket of the coat.

Steeling herself, Shannon entered the now familiar building, climbing the stairs to his apartment, ignoring the wink of the woman descending who was still dressed in the clothes that she had worn the previous night, her evening make-up smeared and the alcohol still wafting from her breath. Shannon shuddered with revulsion and quickly reaching Fergal's door hesitated only momentarily while she considered her options. She listened with her ear against the door and heard only a droning noise emanating from within.

Knocking twice, she waited. Nothing happened. She listened patiently at the door but all she could hear was that very strange noise similar to the sound of some kind of industrial tool; she thought of the chain-saw that her father had used to chop up logs when she was a little girl.

Banging her fist against the door she called out, "Fergal, its Shannon, let me in." There was no response. "Oh, what the hell," she muttered and checking left and right and over her shoulder, ensuring that no one was watching, she came to a decision to enter the apartment using her copy key. "Be prepared," she thought patting her hip, feeling for the security of the gun hidden in her trouser waistband, happy that it was safely with her. Unlocking the door she eased it open a few inches.

Peering inside Shannon couldn't see very much due to the dim light, however that awful droning noise had increased to an intolerable level. "Whatever has he got in there to make such a dreadful sound?" she murmured. Opening the door wider, she crept into the room, once again listening intently as best she could over the sound of the industrial tool. Satisfied that she was not about to be challenged Shannon gently closed the door, re-pocketing her duplicate key.

The droning sound changed to a splutter, the machine running out of fuel? She heard Fergal snort and then the dreadful noise recommenced. "What the hell?" Shannon thought as she cautiously made her way to the bedroom. Peering round the doorframe she spied Fergal, fully dressed, lying on his back - those god awful noises were emanating from the drunken slob!

"Disgusting!" she snorted, "And what a racket! I would never have believed that such a repulsive, grating sound could emanate from a human." She approached the bed, peering at the snoring and occasionally spluttering sad wreck of a man. "But of course, I forgot, you're not human, are you?" She held her nose, "And my God, soap and water would have a field day with you."

Fergal's booming snores ceased. Shannon alarmed, took a pace back from the bedside unsure of how he was going to react to her presence in his apartment, but Fergal didn't move, he didn't even breathe.

"My God, he's dead; the bastard has died on me!" Doubly alarmed she hastily recalled her training, the various life saving techniques that the Bureau had taught her. "I am not going to give *that thing* the kiss of life without something between my lips and his."

Quickly looking round for something to help she snatched up a reasonably clean looking lace doily from under an unused flower vase on the dresser, vigorously shaking off the accumulated dust, and rushed to Fergal's side. "Ugh," she shuddered at the thought of the dust-covered doily against her lips and her impending action.

Lightly placing the linen doily over Fergal's mouth Shannon bent over Fergal, but just as her lips were about to press down on the doily gently resting on Fergal's lips, the tickling of the doily caused him to twitch and loudly snorting like a distressed pig, his body decided to emit a breath, exhaling a plume of foul drunken air in Shannon's face. She recoiled, revolted, the vile odour permeating her pores and rushing up her nose! The stream of her invective even surprised herself; her language was as foul as his breath!

Without thinking she wiped her mouth with the dirty doily, immediately spitting out the ingested dust in disgust. "Oh my God, that's filthy!" Angrily, she threw the doily to the floor. "That was revolting...disgusting. Ugh! Yuck, yuck, yuck, urghhhhh!" Vigorously shaking her head from side to side, wiping her mouth strenuously with the back of her hands, one after the other, she rushed in the direction of the kitchen intent in getting a glass of water to swill out her mouth.

Fergal's eyes flickered open just in time to see Shannon's back view as she hastened from the bedroom.

Reaching the kitchen Shannon baulked as she realised that there were no clean glasses or cups and cursed aloud. Having no other option, the cold tap was turned on and cupping her hands under the tap she scooped up handfuls of water repeatedly swilling out her mouth. Feeling slightly relieved, she used another handful and swallowed, clearing the remaining dust from her throat; it took a further three handfuls before she was reasonably satisfied. Raising her head, water dribbling down her chin, her hair in a mess from her attempts to shake out non-existent dust, she noticed something out of the corner of her eye, suddenly aware that she was being watched.

Fergal was leaning against the doorjamb, watching her with a mixture of amusement, curiosity and anger, his left eyebrow raised questioningly. His eyes were bloodshot, his face with three days growth of beard, his clothes could not even be described as crumpled, more wrinkled and furrowed, and the stench, the stench was indescribable, stronger than ever before.

Shannon was startled. "Um, er," She indicated the taps and the kitchen sink, "I just needed some water."

"I can see that." He took a step forward.

Shannon visibly recoiled, holding her nose. "My God, where have you *been*, you *stink*!"

Fergal stopped, sniffed and stupidly rather than displaying anger, he raised his arm inhaling the odour from under his armpit; but he did fix her with a pair of baleful eyes. "I may smell, stink as you so kindly put it, but it doesn't explain why you are back in my apartment?" Glancing over his shoulder at the front door he then focused back to Shannon, "Or how you got in here?"

"Um, I was worried about my money; I couldn't get an answer so I just came in. I thought that you were dead."

"No such luck lady, but that doesn't explain how you got in?"

"The door was unlocked."

"Oh no it wasn't, I always make sure that I lock it."

"It was unlocked," insisted Shannon still firmly squeezing her nostrils closed.

Fergal stared at her through his blood stained eyes, "It was locked."

Turning on his heels he went to the apartment entrance. His own key was hanging on a hook by the door and with a backward glance at Shannon he grasped the door handle, turned it, the door coming open. Puzzled, he squinted back at Shannon, "It was locked."

"It was open."

"I always lock it."

"Well you must have forgotten this time, or maybe you got up in the midst of your drunken stupor and unlocked the door, going out for some reason."

"How could you know that I've been drinking," he demanded, alarm bells beginning to ring in his head. "Who the hell are you?"

"It was easy, you nerd," she hissed back, "I can smell it from here." She swept past Fergal and going to the armchair bent down, swiftly picking up the two discarded bottles of 'Jack Daniels'. "And these of course just might have given me a small clue," she added with sarcasm.

"You have no right," he wearily protested.

"I have every Goddam right," she shot back, speaking loudly, sensing that she was gaining control of the situation. "You say that you can't afford to pay me yet you can spend money on this. She slung the bottles onto the armchair for effect, "Pathetic; you are a pathetic mess."

"My life is none of your fucking business!"

"You've told me that before but until you settle up what you owe me then your life is very much my business," she calmly retorted.

Fergal held his head in his hands, "Can you speak more softly? You're hurting my head; I need a drink."

"There's none left; you've successfully drunk this place dry!"

"No, stupid woman, I need some tea or coffee," he growled brushing past her and onward into the kitchen, where he switched on the kettle.

Shannon followed, it now being her turn to lean nonchalantly against the doorframe. "There's no water in the kettle," She said kindly but with authority.

"Oh, God, I hate you!" he hollered, immediately regretting it, his head pounding with sledgehammers.

"Go and sit down," Shannon ordered, exasperated, but then continued in a kinder tone, "I'll make you some coffee but I'm not taking you out for food this time."

"I don't want your bloody food; I just want you to leave me alone."

Shannon smiled sardonically and switching off the kettle, unplugged it, filling it with cold water. Serenely and calmly she looked at Fergal whilst smiling almost contemptuously, returned the kettle back to the electrical socket and flicked the on switch.

Fergal stared at her, desperate to scream out for her to go way but he knew it would be of no use and it would only increase the throbbing pain from his hangover. Besides, this woman seemed to be sticking to him like shit to a blanket but not for the right reasons that he would want a woman by his side. He beat a retreat, plonking himself down on one of the armchairs. "Oh, shit!" he yelled, having gone and sat on the two empty bottles. Carelessly, he picked up the bottles, slinging them off his seat, his tired body sinking down onto the dishevelled fabric. Unfortunately and unintentionally one of the bottles hit the wall, smashing in a crash of splintered glass.

Shannon rushed into the room, "What the hell is going on?" And noticing one bottle on the carpet and the second in a pile of broken glass against the wall, raised her eyebrow questioning at Fergal, "So, what the hell are you doing, isn't your place a disgusting mess already? You now want to make it disgusting *and* dangerous?"

"It's my place and I can make it how I want; if I want mess, I'll create mess," he retorted petulantly.

Shannon, dirty cup and crusty dishcloth in hands, stared at Fergal for a second, shaking her head in despair. "True, it is your place and you can do whatever you like." Turning, she headed back to the kitchen, muttering under her breath, "Child."

"I heard that," hollered Fergal but instantly regretted shouting.

Humming cheerfully Shannon busied herself in the kitchen whilst waiting for the kettle to boil. Her first task had been to empty the kitchen sink and draining board, but being short of space she piled the dirty crockery, cutlery, utensils and pots on the floor, then ran the hot water tap until the water was steaming hot; putting the plug in the sink, she found a virtually unused bottle of washing up liquid amidst the mess in the cupboard underneath, squeezing out a large measure of liquid. Her first priority being something that she could use to wash up, she immersed the dishcloth, stirring it with a large spoon.

Meanwhile the water boiled in the kettle but continued to boil because the automatic off-switch no longer worked. "Typical," snorted Shannon as she dropped the spoon in the hot water, rushing to switch off the kettle. Rinsing out a cup under the hot tap she then delicately tipped in a measure of coffee directly from the coffee jar; not wanting to risk any of the dirty spoons being inserted into the coffee jar and not wanting to put a damp spoon in the jar, she figured that her method was providing the immediate answer. Pouring the boiled water into the cup she gently rotated the cup but was not content that it had been mixed successfully. "Oh, what the hell," she muttered, and picking up a dirty spoon from the floor she briskly stirred the coffee.

Cheerfully, Shannon bounced back into the living room proffering the black coffee to Fergal. "Here, get this down you, it'll do you good." Holding the cup by the handle she passed the drink over.

Fergal scowled ungraciously but took the cup. "Ouch, it's hot."

Shannon grinned.

With fingers burning, he hastily rotated the cup until he could hold it by the handle, but looking at the contents, Fergal moaned, "Its black!"

"That's right."

"But I take milk."

"Well good for you buster, but, 'a', you haven't got any milk, and 'b', black will be better for you."

Begrudgingly Fergal sipped at the drink, instantly spluttering, "Ugh, that's horrible, there's no sugar."

Shannon sighed with exasperation and said with a mixture of innocence and sarcasm, "Would you like me to nip out to the store and buy you some fresh milk and sugar?"

Melancholy staring at his drink he affirmed, looking up with expectation, "Yes that would be nice, please."

Shannon's eyes opened wide, the expression on her face one of utter contempt. "Do you really believe that I'm going to get your milk and sugar? You moron! Just drink your coffee whilst I make an attempt at cleaning your kitchen." She retired to the kitchen, "Though God knows why I'm doing this."

"God must really hate me, and she's more like a she-devil anyway, sending you to harangue me," muttered Fergal.

"I heard that," Shannon gaily called out.

Feeling slightly sheepish, Fergal sipped his black coffee, each sip reluctantly making its passage down his throat. In spite of his reservations the coffee was making him feel slightly better; hearing the sounds of Shannon washing up in the kitchen whilst humming a tuneful little ditty added to his feeling of well-being. Relaxing, he was beginning to feel better than he had done for many days.

Having completed the washing up Shannon breezed back into the living room, "Well, that's a lot better; I couldn't find a clean tea-towel but that doesn't surprise me." She smiled, Fergal reluctantly grinning in response.

He looked questioningly at her, "Why are you doing this?"

"I figure it's the only way to rehabilitate you."

"Rehabilitate me?"

"It's the only way that I can ever hope to get you back on your feet and my money back in my pocket."

"I telephoned some people back home," he replied gruffly, "They are going to cable me some money."

"Back home?"

"None of your business," his tone was aggressive.

"Fine, be a misery." Shannon waved her hands in the air. "But

I'm not letting you out of my sight until I get the money in my hands."

Fergal leapt up, his face colouring with anger, "Look..."

Shannon stood her ground, hands on hip, "Don't start this again; we are going to get you back on your feet whether you like it or not."

"You have no right!"

Ignoring his protest she interrupted, "Right, first things first; go and have a shower and shave. If I'm going to be around for a little while I don't want to put up with your awful smell for too long."

"Smell...you cheeky bitch!" He looked her up and down, his expression scathing, "You can talk! What a sight you look; you obviously have the fashion sense of tramp, and a very poor one at that."

"Why you!"

He smiled, "I guess that's why you need to harass me for *my* money; you obviously need some proper clothes."

Flustered, Shannon glanced down at the clothes that she was wearing. "God, I'd forgotten that I had this lot on, I do look a sight," she thought but looking up at Fergal, sweetly retorted, "It's *my* money I'm after, not yours! You cheeky little bugger and besides I'm not going to wear anything decent if I'm visiting your place; you don't take a cream cake to eat at a sewage depot, do you?"

"Sewage depot, you call my place a sewage depot, that's out of order!"

"You're right." She paused, "I'm being unfair... on a sewage depot!"

"Okay, that's it, get out."

"Shower, now! Oh and you'd better tell me where your vacuum cleaner is; I'll clean up your place whilst you clean up yourself."

Fergal's mouth opened and closed. Although angry the thought of having his apartment cleaned was appealing. "It's in the cupboard," he muttered unaware that the words were emanating from his lips. "Damn," he thought, remaining motionless, staring at Shannon.

"Come on, chop, chop," she pleasantly commanded, brushing her hands together, "Lots to do and it won't get done with you standing there, opening and closing your mouth like a drunken goldfish."

Bemused, Fergal quietly skulked off in the direction of the bathroom.

Chapter 31

The night air was crisp and in spite of the numerous lights of Washington D.C., the sky was brilliantly illuminated by a myriad of gaily twinkling stars. For young lovers canoodling in their cars or lying on blankets in secluded parts of the city's parks whilst ignoring the coldness of the night air the clear star lit sky enhanced the more romantic souls within them. One or two unscrupulous males were taking advantage of the situations that they were in, their impressionable female companions being carried away by the emotion of romantic yearnings.

Although it was a night for lovers a heavy air of oppression hung over a penthouse suite in an exclusive five-star rated Washington hotel. Rather than thoughts of love and harmony this penthouse suite weighed heavily with feelings of cruelty and malice.

The expensively furnished room was complete with all the necessary trappings expected of a top company executive, visiting head of state, dignitary, pop star, or a crime boss. As long as the hotel guest paid their bill and behaved properly in accordance with the requirements of the hotel then the Management welcomed all equally. The Head Porter could even make arrangements for a lady or ladies to visit the hotel guest and provide for their *every* need – but of course this extra 'service' came at an additional 'special' cost. Privacy was also ensured and it was for this reason that the current incumbents were using this room for a clandestine meeting having ascended to the suite by means of a private lift from the underground car park, the room having being booked in the name of Daniel Hogan.

Jim stood in front of the large plate glass window looking down onto the sights of Washington below. Although not the tallest building, the penthouse suite provided a good view of the city. Alistair nervously paced the floor whilst Simon was the epitome of calmness, sitting at the executive desk, quiet and relaxed whilst perusing a sheaf of papers. A gentle whirring sound preceded the arrival of the elevator, the doors sliding open with a well-oiled smoothness, Daniel Hogan entering the room accompanied by an unknown woman.

Alistair stopped his restless pacing, demanding with nervous impatience, "Where the hell have you been? We've been waiting for almost an hour."

"I got held up," responded Daniel without a hint of apology, "And

I could sure do with a strong drink."

Still annoyed at being kept waiting Alistair scowled and turning to the cocktail cabinet opened the top section, revealing a vast selection of wines and spirits, mixers and beers, and a bucket of ice plugged into a cooler. "Scotch?" he asked without turning.

"Yup, ice, no water," Daniel answered without any courtesy.

Simon also requested the same and Jim followed their suggestion but was courteous when responding, actually using the word 'please'.

Oblivious to Daniel's curt response, Alistair poured five scotches, dropping a single ice cube into each tumbler. With ire, he snapped, "This is very risky. The Embassy's and my own security bodyguards didn't appreciate being ordered off duty even though I explained that the FBI would take care of my security."

"Calm down Alistair." Daniel straightened his tie. "This meeting was arranged at your instigation and we had to be discreet for how else could we get Eamon here?"

Alistair scanned the room beyond the two new entrants. "Well, where is he then?"

Daniel grinning inanely, his hand extended, indicated the woman at his side, "Here!"

With a pronounced flourish Eamon removed his coat and slipped out of his dress, revealing a pair of trousers pulled up to the knees and tied in place by shoelaces. "Ah, that's better," he announced to the astonished faces of Alistair, Simon, and Jim. As they stood agog, Eamon removed his wig and stepping to the enormous, carved oak coffee table he pulled out a handful of tissues from the box of tissues conveniently located next to a knife, plate and a bowl of exotic fruit.

They waited patiently as Eamon extracted a small bottle of make-up remover, Johnson & Johnson 'Clean and Clear', from his trouser pocket, proceeding to thoroughly remove the make up from his face. Satisfied, he smiled at the gawping faces.

Amused, Daniel pointed to Eamon's ears and in particular at the forgotten earrings.

Eamon chuckled, removing the clips on the large looped earrings, "That's a shame; I've become quite attached to these." Dropping the earrings on the coffee table he massaged his tender earlobes.

Daniel laughed, "Makes a damn fine woman, doesn't he; almost fancied him myself."

Simon replied laconically, "Can't say he did much for me."

Recovering from his surprise Alistair, the relief tangible on his face, almost tripped in his haste as he rushed forward to greet Eamon, "Thank God you're here, I was getting worried."

Alistair and Eamon exchanged handshakes, Eamon's hand being firmly gripped in a two handed hold, followed by a shared warm hug. After a moment of unbounded awe and admiration Alistair turned his attention to Daniel, exchanging a more formal handshake. Simon slowly and languidly got to his feet, disdain and disinterest bordering just under the surface as he forced a smile of greeting.

Glancing in Simon's direction Alistair introduced his security associate, "This is Simon Harvey, head of an anti-terrorism unit that I've established and which is made up of Scotland Yard and MI5 intelligence operatives."

Daniel scrutinised the languid Simon, both exchanging wary and unfriendly eye contact. Their mutual handshake was brief and peremptory, neither individual warming to the other. "We've heard a lot about you," Daniel uttered in a non-committal tone with the implication that the comment could be favourable or otherwise.

Oblivious to the mutual animosity between Simon and Daniel, Alistair continued blithely, "It was so easy to set up a new intelligence unit. Once I had convinced the British Cabinet that we needed to set up a new operation to try and resolve the Irish issue and which would be staffed by newer, fresher and untarnished faces without the baggage of previous policies in Northern Ireland, it was then a relatively easy task to handpick my personnel.

Almost unnoticed standing by the plate glass window, Jim quietly interceded, "What about Willie Davidson? Surely he wasn't a fresh face?"

"That was a masterstroke by Simon," Alistair gleefully boasted, patting Simon on the back. "Simon suggested that keeping a completely immoral, unintelligent and inept individual like Willie would on one hand convince the Protestant hard liners that nothing had changed despite our official statements to the contrary, yet on the other would continue to unsettle the peace loving people who would continue to suffer through Willie's excesses."

Eamon dryly entered the conversation, "It's certainly working well."

Alistair glowed in triumph, his chest swelling with pride.

Eamon made himself comfortable on the four-seat settee, stretching out his legs in relaxed and luxurious manner. "I have to say though Alistair that I'm not happy with the progress of your judicial enquiry into Bloody Sunday and the British Paratroopers shooting and murdering my people in Belfast."

Alistair's face dropped, sinking like a stone in a deep pool of water.

"I want the names of all those soldiers involved made public, every one; we need to get our vengeance," continued Eamon, aware that he was making Alistair feel deflated.

Alistair almost stuttered, his voice ringing with regret and apology, "But... but, I'm doing my best. I appointed Judge Jeffries who as you know, is quite anti-establishment and whose mother was a Catholic originally from Northern Ireland. She indoctrinated him from a very early age in the dream of the formation of a single Irish State and she was very pro for fighting the cause by whatever means." Alistair paused looking away from Eamon, staring out at the view of Washington in the hope of some inspiration. Softly he added, "But even Jeffries is having trouble in trying to override the law on anonymity and to have the blame apportioned on the soldiers and their officers."

Ignoring Alistair's difficulty Eamon growled menacingly, "I want those names, those 'Bloody Sunday' names! You're supposed to be the fucking Prime Minister of Britain, the top honcho, so make it happen; pass a law or do whatever it is the British bastards do to make things happen."

Simon placating, intervened, "I've tried getting the names through Intelligence contacts but the Army insist that the troops were merely following orders and no individual, unless convicted of a crime, is ever named."

Eamon not convinced, roared, "Well, get them bloody well convicted."

"I thought that the soldiers were only acting in self-defence?" queried Jim.

Eamon, his eyes adopting a reptilian, vindictive glaze, sharply snapped, "They should not have been in Ireland! If they hadn't been following Fascists orders, the orders of an occupying army, then no one would have been killed."

Now standing by the cocktail cabinet, Jim picked up the drink that had not been passed to him, and savouring the aroma of a good scotch, he took a small sip. Pleased with the favour of the malted whisky, he turned to Eamon and with an assertive voice, yet softly spoken, said "I don't think it was quite like that or quite that simple."

His eyes almost popping from his head, Eamon was about to go into a rant but Jim didn't give him the opportunity of interrupting, "Also didn't the soldiers go into Northern Ireland in the first place to defend the Catholic community; in fact, wasn't it one of the Catholic leaders who originally requested that the soldiers be used?"

Eamon eyes bulged and his face mottled red with anger as he growled, "Whose side are you on? I'm not used to having people disagree with me - especially some American who knows sod all about the real Ireland."

Jim remained unruffled taking a further sip from his glass. "I think I am fairly well informed. I've also carried out an awful lot of research and studied numerous files on the terrorist movements of Irish Paramilitaries, with their potential link ups and associations here in the States. A lot of bad things were carried out in the supposed name of freedom and it *was* the Catholic community that needed the early protection afforded by the British Soldiers."

"Files, fucking files! What do files tell you about the real situation, you prick! What we need from you is support not a half-arsed political lesson or stupid opinions. Your President and Daniel here," his arm waving angrily in the direction of Daniel, "Promised us unconditional support to solve the issues of Ireland and that's what I expect from you! Clear?" The veins in Eamon's neck rigidly bulged on the surface of the skin, the skin streaked with lines of purple and blue, his face red, his eyes almost popping out.

Jim remained unperturbed, unruffled, this was his territory; he knew his business and knew how to look after himself. "Please don't push me. I am an American and not one of your people, an American who is intent on fulfilling the obligations of his President, an obligation to assist in obtaining peace for your Country. I will support you in getting a united Ireland but I won't be brow beaten."

Apoplectic with incandescent rage, Eamon rose from the sofa and approached Jim, malice and menace written all over his being. As a bully he didn't like not getting his way, didn't comprehend being thwarted, people just didn't argue with him. For God's sake, he *ran* the bloody Provisionals!

Daniel placed a placating arm around Eamon's shoulders, "Okay, okay, guys, go easy both of you." But Eamon shrugged off Daniel's arm, looking set to hit the unflinching Jim.

Eamon and Jim stood toe to toe, Jim calm, Eamon barely in control. There was something in the extremely calm Jim's eyes that warned Eamon that he was not going to brow beat or bully this individual. Eamon remained clenching and unclenching his fists but with the thought surfacing that he needed the FBI support, he managed to prevent himself from striking the threatened blow.

Watching from the side-line, Simon smiled like a Cheshire cat, revelling in the discomfort and unease being experienced by these people who thought that they were his superiors.

Visibly close to tears, Alistair pleaded, "Please Jim, Eamon." Then tried to explain, "Jim you have to understand, Eamon has been there, been involved at the coal front, the sharp end of the conflict; he's toiled at the mill as it were."

Standing eyeball to eyeball with Eamon, Jim suddenly burst out laughing.

"Why you jumped up little!" Eamon raised his fist, ready to punch this laughing jackass.

Jim side-stepped as Eamon swung, continuing to chuckle as he retreated, stepping backwards from Eamon's advance, the Northern Irishman having completely lost his temper, his fists swingeing madly at fresh air. Barely managing to speak through his chortling, Jim chuckled, "I'm sorry Eamon, will you stop it; I'm not laughing at you."

Eamon controlled himself, a look of doubt and confusion sweeping over his contorted face.

Jim mirthfully explained, "For goodness sake; didn't you all hear Alistair? The rhetoric; it was as if he was at some damn political rally, the ridiculous words had me in stitches."

"Well!" snapped the peeved Alistair.

Eamon looked doubtfully from the grinning Jim to the now sulky Alistair and then at the smiling Simon. Eamon's lips slowly broke into a smile, the stupidity of the situation hitting home. "You're right; Alistair does get carried away with his silly words, but they love it at those party conferences."

"Well thank you all very much." Disgruntled, Alistair picked up his scotch and taking a large sip, coughed loudly as the contents burnt his throat.

Simon delighted at Alistair's double discomfort but disappointed that a full-scale fight had not ensued, belatedly elected himself as peace maker, his obsequious side to the fore, "Calm down gentlemen; we all have the same objective, a united Ireland and the destruction of Britain." He spoke in a caring, fatherly tone to Eamon, "And I know that you want every single British soldier killed but, sometimes, we should put the past behind us in order to achieve our objectives. We can get our revenge later when everything is in place, then we can pick and choose our targets, and by the time Alistair's Government has turned Britain upside down most of the revenge targets can be achieved by legal means. We will make the laws and it will be easy to lead their left leaning legal profession by the nose."

Jim not wanting to reopen the debate was never the less uneasy. "I'm afraid I'm not here for the destruction of Britain or the killing of innocent people, merely an end to the Irish problem." He put his unfinished drink down on the cocktail cabinet. "Excuse me Daniel, I have things to do and reports to check. I also need to follow up on Shannon's progress."

"Okay Jim, it's probably best that I fill you in later on the discussions and future plans. We obviously have too many conflicting personalities in this room." Daniel winked at Jim. "I'll speak to you tomorrow."

Jim nodded, but thoroughly disgruntled and unhappy, he bid his farewell, firmly announcing, "Gentlemen", as he departed in the direction of the elevator. There was an interminable delay which actually only lasted for a few seconds before the elevator arrived. All in the room remained static, silent, until Jim entered the plush elevator compartment, the internal mirrors reflecting his angry face; the doors closed behind him. The gentle whirring started, the elevator commencing its descent.

The hotel room seemed to breathe with relief, albeit for a very short time.

Eamon was the first to speak, his voice tetchy and irritable, "I don't like him; he's not to be trusted."

Daniel glanced over at the closed elevator access door, "Oh, he's okay. We need him and I can handle him anyway; he's shit-scared of my authority." With the subject of Jim cursorily dismissed he turned his attention to Alistair, "Any new details or revelations from the inquiry into the death of your Prince?"

Alistair startled by the question, responded in a measured and slow tone, "Er, no. The Dutch authorities are treating the Prince's death as a very unfortunate but reckless accident." He asked Simon for confirmation, "Aren't they Simon?"

Simon pleased to be involved, replied with ebullient confidence, "Yes, I'm pretty sure that that's the conclusion they are drawing towards." However he added a word of caution, "But their investigations have not concluded as yet. There are still a couple of witnesses who claim that another car was involved."

"Kill them, kill the witnesses!" demanded Eamon.

Simon was shocked at Eamon's peremptory instruction, "Oh sure, we can send in hit squads and start leaving a bloody mess all over Europe."

"I'm getting sick and tired of all you negative people," growled Eamon instantly fired up, his temper once more on the boil. "When I want things to happen I make sure that it's done. I expect the same from your organisation. If you are not capable of doing the job then Alistair can replace you." Picking up a pencil from the desk he snapped it in half, "Just like that!"

Simon visibly withered under Eamon's aggressive outburst.

Alistair dumbfounded, glanced helplessly at Daniel for some kind of intervention; initially flabbergasted at this fresh burst of temper tantrum, Daniel calmly intervened, "For goodness sake guys, will you all relax." He put his arm around Eamon's shoulder and led him towards the window. "Beautiful view, isn't it?"

Eamon, fire breathing out of his nostrils, wanted to shake Daniel free but merely nodded in agreement. "I often like to look out over the city when I am feeling moments of stress," purred Daniel, "And seeing life going on, with or without me, is a very sobering experience. It's also good to contemplate a whole world out there, a world that could be better with the decisions we make and with the actions we take." He met Eamon's eyes, "Doesn't that kind of thought make you feel better?"

Eamon just wanted to shake this guy off and sling him out of the penthouse suite windows onto the streets of the city that he apparently loved so well; fucking dump.

Daniel gripped Eamon a little tighter and in an almost inaudible voice whispered, "Look, if you want our support you must remember that what we're doing is already very difficult. We all have to work in the strictest of confidence, particularly from within our own security organisations. So let's please all work together." He stared meaningfully into Eamon's eyes, unflinchingly awaiting a response.

Grudgingly Eamon agreed, but wriggled free from Daniel's grip and turning to face Simon he smiled, a fixed but evil smile, then walked back to the others, Daniel on his heels.

"Besides," Daniel added, "Remember, I'm virtually acting on my own, a clandestine operation, as I expect is Alistair's guy Simon, with all the burden of responsibility that that entails."

"What!" exclaimed Simon, "I thought that President Morrison had set up your operation?"

"He did, but purely unofficially, and illegally. Morrison will always be able to deny any involvement unless it all pans out then he'll push for all the glory and for the Irish-American vote."

Eamon annoyed at having been previously been baulked, gruffly announced, "He's a good friend of Ireland."

Simon for some unknown reason couldn't resist putting his spoke in, caustically retorting, "A good friend of the Irish-American vote you mean." He instantly regretted his remark, Eamon taking a step in his direction.

Eamon bellowed, "I've had enough!"

Previously pleased at his earlier attempt to forestall a potential violent clash Daniel now had a sinking feeling, wondering what the hell he was doing getting involved with these temperamental people, these nutters. Forlornly, he once more attempted to intervene, "Guys, come on, we need to sit down and sort out our combined strategy for the next few months. We *have* to work together."

"Fuck you," snapped Eamon, "I'm going to punch this English prick's lights in."

"I'm not English," retorted Simon, backing away but making the mistake of grinning in what he perceived to be a friendly manner and which only served as a red rag to a bull, tipping Eamon over the edge. As Eamon advanced Simon kept backing off until the desk against the wall restricted his escape.

Eamon leapt forward, punching Simon hard in the solar plexus causing him to double up with pain; a second punch hit him in the face, splitting open his lip and a third punch grazed the desperately ducking Simon's eyebrow.

Quaking, Alistair dared not intervene but Daniel bounded forward, coming between Eamon's flailing fists and Simons crouching body. He managed to duck as Eamon's fist made a further swing, the blow catching Simon on the side of the head and sending him sprawling onto the carpeted floor.

Daniel raised his voice, almost shouting, "Also, more importantly, *beyond your stupid squabbling*, there's a countryman of yours Eamon, who seems to have settled here in Boston yet is attracting a lot of interest from Willie Davidson."

Eamon stood still, mystified, "Who the hell are you talking about? Which guy from Ireland is Willie Davidson interested in?"

Simon, blood dripping from his cut lip, scrambled warily from the floor, wiping his lip and examining the blood now on his hand. Frustrated and angry he realised that there was nothing that he could currently do, but his day would come, oh yes it would come, yet another entry to add to his little black book.

Relieved at the momentary calm, Daniel glanced at Eamon and still nervous regarding any additional flare up, softly stated, "He's one of your guys, or at least he was but may not be now; a guy by the name of Fergal Mulroney."

"Mulroney, Fergal Mulroney?" Eamon racked his brain. "Oh I remember Fergal; he got involved to a small degree in various operations but hasn't been active for a long time now. As I understand it the last we heard was that he's just a piss-head now."

"I've never heard of him?" ventured Alistair.

Eamon focused his attention on Alistair, nonchalantly stating, "Fergal was one of those who escaped from the Maze prison when we had to get Bobbie Flaherty out. Fergal used to be a good operative, mainly as a look out or get-away driver but he ended up hitting the bottle; became a liability so the boys didn't want to work with him. We thought he had moved to Cork because he had an aunt who lived in the town."

Simon absentmindedly holding his bloody lip, cautiously enquired, "Why wasn't he ever taken out?"

Eamon turned to face Simon and for a fleeting second adopted a rueful expression at the damage that he had inflicted on Simon. "Nobody thought that Fergal was worth the effort; he was just a 'follower', no ideas, no brains and knew very little. A foot soldier of no interest to anyone."

"Well, Willie thinks that he's worth the effort," said Daniel softly, "He's obviously got something or some knowledge that is of great interest to your Mr Davidson."

"Willie's just a prick," spat Eamon, his voice heavy with absolute contempt. "Anyway", he directed at Simon, "Willie is supposed to be in your Department, under your supervision. You must have known that he's here in America and what his mission is."

"Actually he's on leave," responded Simon warily, "Visiting retired old colleagues. We have a contact address for him; it's Intelligence policy to always be aware of where we can get hold of personnel involved in sensitive operations even if going away for one day and out of mobile phone contact, everyone has to leave full contact details with the Department."

Subject seemingly resolved, Eamon's attention returned to Daniel, "I shouldn't worry then, Willie's on leave and as I said before, he's just a stupid prick."

Daniel was astonished at Eamon's dismissive response and if it wasn't for the previous contretemps he would have given this Irishman a piece of his mind.

Fortunately Simon, whilst backing away to a safe distance, cautiously declared, "We should check it out."

"I'm on to it," Daniel replied, relieved that someone appeared to be sensible. "I've got one of my Agents undercover, ingratiating themselves with Fergal."

"We don't need too many people involved," nervously stated Alistair, "Can he be trusted?"

"'He' is actually a 'She' in this case, and yes she can be trusted, at least for the time being and until we get what we want out of Fergal and Willie, then she'll meet with an unfortunate accident."

Feeling the tension draining from him Alistair happily affirmed, "Good, that's settled that then but I don't think Fergal will have anything to offer Willie or have much to interest us or other parties."

Simon, colour waning from an already strained face, cupped his chin in his hand; with trepidation, words hastily spilled from his mouth, "Oh shit, I've just realised, Fergal was initially part of the 'Amsterdam' team!"

Alistair looked as if the ceiling and the sky had fallen onto him,

"*What*!"

Daniel was dumbfounded. "You're kidding!"

"No I'm afraid not," replied the ashen Simon, "Fergal was part of an assessment team to work out possible strategies, safe houses, escape routes, and so on."

Alistair flustered, afraid and almost in a panic, turned wide-eyed to Eamon, vehemently demanding, "I thought that your men from the 'Amsterdam' operation had either been killed or sent to South America to co-ordinate the drug activities and to train terrorists."

Racking his brains for an explanation Eamon bemusedly responded, "They were, or at least I thought so." With ice-cold fury and looking to deflect criticism he turned his baleful eye on Simon, "Why wasn't I told that Fergal was part of the operation?"

Wiping his brow, his nerves on tenterhooks, Simon cautiously croaked, "It wasn't up to me. It was a Provisional IRA operation with my Department acting only as logistics providers and some discreet support. The Provos personnel involved were down to Liam and I wouldn't have known what he had told you anyway. Besides, Fergal didn't seem to matter especially as he had dropped out before the target had been revealed."

Irked that the blame was back on his shoulders, Eamon ranted, "He's not completely stupid; Fergal could have put two and two together!"

"Besides," continued Simon, his voice barely audible, "He was one of your trusted personnel."

"No-one is fully trusted in our organisation. I'd kill my own 'mammy' if I thought that she was not one hundred percent behind our cause!"

Ignoring Eamon's comment, Simon announced in a matter of fact tone, "I think it's pretty obvious why Willie is chasing Fergal; Fergal must have let something slip whilst under interrogation at the Maze prison."

Alistair smashed his palm to his forehead as if punishing himself for being so stupid, "Of course! It all makes sense now. Willie has a suspicion that the Provisionals were involved in the murder of our Prince and he must think that Fergal has some proof!"

"You never explained why the Prince was killed? It could so easily have backfired on you," asked the curious Daniel.

Alistair glanced apprehensively at Eamon before explaining,

"That was an easy decision. I couldn't stand the do-good bastard; his family were also wary of him and his 'goody-goody' deeds but most importantly he was about to set up a peace movement for Northern Ireland. So we had no choice but to act quickly. As soon as the media had confirmed the Prince's death – I waited for the BBC television report - then it was relatively easy to fake my apparent shock and utmost concern; not only did I manage to increase my profile with the Public I also made the Prince's family appear to be a bunch of heartless cretins. My 'sincerity' had the TV people eating out of my hand."

Simon took up the story. "Intelligence sources had picked up the fact that the Prince was working with a group of Irish, Irish-American and British interests; they were going to be funded through numerous charities being set up. A new cross-border, cross-religious organisation was going to be put in operation and it would have become an unstoppable bandwagon. We had to nip it in the bud."

"I don't understand," queried Daniel, "Wouldn't that have brought peace; surely it would have added a fresh impetus to our aims?"

Eamon intervened with malevolence, "We want this resolved our way not via the Prince or through others! The Prince's potential peace organisation would ultimately have wrestled influence away from the Provisional's political arm; the Provo Council and our political associates must be in control!"

Thoroughly irked by the preceding occurrences, Daniel mimicked, "We want this resolved our way not via the Prince." His blood rising in anger, he reacted, "Christ, what we all should want is peace and a resolution to the situation!"

Eamon startled, heatedly retorted, "I've told you before, Ireland is *my* Country and this is *my* operation, you boneheaded piece of..."

Once again afraid of being stuck between a rock and hard place, Alistair pleaded for tranquillity, "Gentlemen, *please*!"

Daniel frowned at the stony faced Eamon until Eamon's face softened, the scowl gradually dissipating. "Okay, okay, I'm sorry," Eamon murmured but without any depth of sincerity, "So, what are we going to do about the Fergal and Willie situation?

Simon, mentally scheming up vile and painful ways of hurting Eamon, responded with cold and ruthless efficiency, "*I'll* take care of Fergal – and Willie. I'll personally see to it that they're both of no further trouble or concern."

Eamon partially mollified, reached for the pipe previously secreted in his trouser pocket and sitting down, the doubt evident in his voice, queried, "Daniel, what about your Operative, can we trust her?"

"She'll have to be removed as well. I'll arrange a private debriefing first, finding out what she's learnt, if anything, and if she has passed on any information gained. But Fergal and Willie should also be my responsibility, particularly because they are in America."

"I can take care of it," insisted Simon.

"Not here in the States, you can't," argued Daniel. "Alistair, if you want our continued assistance we will need to do things my way." Ignoring Simon, Daniel waited for Alistair's agreement.

Unhappy at being put in the spotlight as decision maker, Alistair looked over at Eamon, desperately seeking guidance or some kind of an answer. Eamon nodded imperceptibly and Alistair felt a weight lifting from his shoulders, gladly stating, "Okay, it's agreed, you take care of Fergal and Willie; it'll be a shame to loose Willie as his work was really alienating the Catholic community but I suppose that he's outlived his usefulness."

Simon attempted to change the decision, he didn't like his personal targets being given to other parties to terminate, but a malevolent glance from Eamon persuaded Simon to curtail his intended protest.

"Great, I'll see to it; it will all be over and resolved in a day or two," cheerfully declared Daniel, relieved that he could now depart from this room of madmen.

"Keep us advised," instructed Eamon.

"Sure will. I'll be off now." Fastening his coat, Daniel walked to the elevator. Looking beyond the three men he took a fleeting look out of the window, "Looks like a storm brewing."

The three men looked over their shoulders just as the elevator arrived, the doors opening, Daniel bidding his farewells. Alistair unperturbed by the few heavy clouds visible, commented, "Doesn't seem much of a storm."

"I think Daniel meant more than just the weather," Simon dryly countered.

Eamon with an air of menacing authority and in an ominous tone that made Simon inwardly quail, snapped, "I don't think that this is time or place for your pathetic humour. Contrary to what we agreed with Daniel, I want *you* to personally take care of Fergal and Willie. If not, I will take care of you instead and it will not be pleasant; be part of Daniel's team! *Understand?*"

Although quailing under Eamon's fierce stare and harsh words, Simon was secretly pleased at the opportunity of disposing of Willie. Killing Fergal would be a bonus. "I don't even know Fergal", he thought to himself but I will make it as painful as possible for both of them. God, if only it was Eamon that I was going to punish and kill. As Simon's thoughts drifted pleasantly to the disposal of Willie and Fergal his inner self-esteem began to reassert itself.

Oh yes, people were going to pay for him being humbled here today!

Chapter 32

Taking a circuitous journey which included quite a few wrong turns, Eamon safely arrived at the delegated apartment. Removing his coat, he threw it nonchalantly over the back of a chair. The apartment in New York had been loaned to him by an affiliate of 'Noraid', who unlike other contributors was a sympathiser who was very much in favour of a violent resolution to the Irish problems.

Eamon understood that the owner was on holiday in Florida but in actual fact the man was sleeping rough on the floor of a friend's room; he considered it an honour for his home to be utilised by such a great 'hero' as Eamon. The use of the apartment and more importantly its telephone was necessary for discretionary purposes.

Later tonight Eamon would be in a four-star hotel in the City, the hotel booked by Irish-American sympathisers, and would be guest of honour at a fund raising lunch the following day. But for now an important telephone call needed to be made.

Eamon opened his wallet and extracted a piece of paper, hastily scanning the sheet for the information he required. Quickly locating the telephone he picked up the receiver, scrutinising the paper thoroughly, and pressed the button for each digit, carefully dialling the chosen number.

*   *   *

The air hung humid and sticky, sweat oozing from every pour of Liam, some of it spilling onto the young Colombian woman beneath him. The woman with clear, creamy brown skin, dark hair and wide brown eyes, moaned and occasionally murmured, "Yes, yes", under the laborious and intense thrusting from Liam, her legs entwined over his hips. The large man increased his tempo and the wooden bed, covered by a very thin mattress, creaked and groaned under the strain of the couple making frantic love.

Although the Colombian woman was quite slight, Liam's heavy weight was in danger of making the bed collapse, his increasing tempo making the headboard bang against the timber walls of the hut, providing an irregular staccato beat that reverberated around the wooden walls.

The coffee plantation workers, previously merely farm workers but now part of the rebel cabal that Liam and his Provisional colleagues were currently training in the art of guerrilla warfare, grinned at each other, the sound of Liam and the woman's lovemaking providing a drumbeat of unmelodic rhythm that echoed off the walls and spread out over the fields of crops.

Two Conures, parrot type birds, predominantly green with blue primaries and with beautiful heads, coloured with a mix of blue, grey, yellow and red markings, lost and resting, perched contently on a branch of a nearby tree before continuing their journey, were startled by the noise. The birds screeched in alarm and flew squawking in protest up into the clear blue sky.

Relaxing during this break from their training and from their work toiling in the fields where they had sown a new heroin crop on land forced from the local coffee plantation owner, the plantation workers/guerrillas enjoyed both the sound from within the hut whilst also rejoicing in their new status of being 'big men'. Ribald comments were exchanged and one the men quietly separated from his companions and creeping behind the hut, watched through a peep hole; he dropped his trousers, then discreetly carried out his own and very private, personal lovemaking.

The old man who owned this plantation, south of Santander and off the proverbial beaten track, lived in fear of his ex-workers who were now part of a rebel group which was heavily supported by a few white skinned men who spoke with strange accents - surely not American - their accents making it extremely difficult for the old man to follow the white men's instructions. The light skinned men were cruel bullies, having taken control of his plantation by kidnapping his only remaining relative, his beloved daughter Juanita. His son Carlos had previously been put to a slow and painful death by the largest of the white men, a strong brutal man who had a strange name more like a woman's, the man called something like 'Leanne'; the old man could not pronounce the murdering bully's name.

Liam and his 'friends' had been brought into the area by a local drug baron with the intention of setting up a mutual operation where the Irishmen would provide weapons and training and in exchange would receive a portion of the drug crop for resale in America and Western Europe. It had worked beyond Eamon's expectations and was developing into extremely good business in increasing the terrorist's coffers. However, Liam had seen the opportunity of expanding the operation's profitability by taking control of this particular plantation.

The old man and his two offspring had been very reclusive and had had little on no contact with the nearest town, thus they had been an easy target for the interlopers who were well armed and well connected with local rebel groups. It had been a simple task to bend the old man to do Liam's bidding, and Liam and his comrades, for all intents and purposes, now owned the plantation. Once a month a local government employee would arrange a courtesy visit but the terrorists were always given ample warning by the posted look outs and would disappear, either hiding within the coffee or heroin crops or taking refuge in one of the local villager's homes. The old man dare not say anything to the government employee or to the police because he desperately wanted his daughter returned safe and sound; he knew that the girl was still alive because Liam regularly made her write letters, each one containing details that could be validated by current events provided by a very old, but useable, radio.

The plantation owner's daughter was kept chained in the wooden hut that Liam was currently using for his shagging, but she had her head turned away in disgust at the revolting performance from this large fair skinned man. Just looking at the man made her want to vomit.

The woman under Liam, sensing that the big oaf on top of her was close to climax, screamed out in faked ecstasy, her threshing and panting bringing him to the 'boil'. With the shaking of the walls a cockroach was dislodged from one of the ceiling timbers, falling into the small of Liam's back; quickly wriggling to its feet, the creature travelled across his bottom, over the woman's thigh, dropping onto the bed, scuttling over the dirty sheet and disappeared over the side of the mattress. Liam oblivious, thinking that the woman's fingers were working behind him, stroking his buttocks, didn't work out in the heat of the moment that to do so she would have needed three hands, the fingers of the other two hands digging gently into his back. With a final roar he released his juices, thrusting like a labourer with a jackhammer. Contented, he rolled off the woman and lay on his back, his breath desperately drawing new air into his lungs.

After a few minutes his breathing subsided into a more controlled and slower pattern, and turning his head he smiled at the woman. "That was good for you, yes?"

The woman smiled in response, relieved that the massive weight was no longer on top of her small body and aggrieved that the man's interminable thrusting had made her extremely sore. She ached internally and externally and was actually looking forward to the time of the month when her period would start and where this ox usually, but not always, gave her a break. Although still only fairly young, she recalled with macabre humour of the days when she was younger and really detested having her periods; she never thought that the day would come where she would desperately wish for that particular 'time of the month' to come about so quickly.

Having recovered after his exertions Liam rolled off the bed and proudly swaggered in front of the chained Juanita, the girl desperately attempting to avert her head. He crouched in front of the cowering girl, lifted up her chin, and gloated, "You'd like some of this," holding his penis, "You must be really jealous. But not yet my pretty little tart, I have to preserve you to keep control of your father." He looked into her eyes, "Unless you want some of this now?"

Juanita recoiled, her disgust and revulsion overtaking her fear, and spat into his face.

Calmly, Liam wiped the spittle from his face with the back of his hand, grinned and stood up. "You know you want me, but not yet my pretty tart."

Pulling on his trousers, he hastily did up the zip and exited the hut, smiling in response to the sea of grinning faces that welcomed his arrival in the bright sunshine.

Juanita shuddered with revulsion and gazed with contempt at the very stationery woman on the bed. "Why do you do it?" she asked in Spanish, "He's repugnant."

The woman on the bed raised her torso, her sad eyes full of haunted sorrow and desolately responded, "I have no choice; my father was killed and my mother has five children to feed. I am the oldest and the only thing I have is this body. Without this, we would starve." The woman sunk back onto the bed, tears forming in her eyes and trickling down her cheeks.

Juanita gaped in remorse, the woman's situation making her realise that her own circumstances could be a hundred times worse. The thought of that man on top of her...vile, vile; she shuddered uncontrollably.

* * *

Eamon stood with the receiver pressed against his ear, his

fingers drumming impatiently on the table surface. "Come on, come on, where the hell are you? I don't want to be connected for too long." With one hand he re-folded the piece of paper, replacing it in his wallet. "I bet that Colombian dickhead who answered the telephone has forgotten that I'm waiting on the line; Liam will have to get someone responsible to take phone calls."

Eventually a sound could be heard, "Hello?"

"Liam, is that you?"

"Of course it's me Eamon; how are you?"

"Where have you been? I've been hanging on here for ages; you should get fucking better people."

"Yes, I'm fine too, thank you Eamon," responded Liam with light hearted sarcasm, "Actually we were down in the fields, supervising the planting of a new crop. Luckily I was on my way back otherwise you would have had to wait for half an hour."

"Why don't you get a mobile or a two way radio?"

"We can't. The Colombian government and the CIA monitor the airwaves; they'd track this operation in next to no time."

"Well, we'll have to sort out a better system," snapped Eamon with aggressive authority. "Anyway, that's not relevant now. I need you here in America, immediately."

"I can't leave now; I've just started the training of a new batch of freedom fighters and the old man on our 'tame' plantation is becoming a bit tetchy. If I don't keep a close eye on him then there's no telling what he may do; I think he's coming to the conclusion that he'll never get his daughter back. He was checking with one of the plantation workers as to how long it would take to walk to the town."

"I need you here now Liam," barked Eamon, ignoring his subordinate's comments.

"Didn't you hear me - is it a bad line? I can't leave yet!"

"No, I heard you, but this is more important. I need you to fly to America, to Boston, *immediately*."

"Why, what the hell is going on?"

"It's Willie, Willie Davidson."

"Oh, don't worry about that prick."

"Liam! Will you shut the fuck up and just listen."

"Okay sure, but it can't be more important than..."

Eamon snarled, "Liam, Willie has found Fergal Mulroney - do you remember Fergal?"

"Yea, he was a nobody, part of Colm's operational cell, wasn't he?"

"That's the guy. Well it seems that Willie has found out that Fergal knows something about the Amsterdam operation."

Liam whistled in surprise, the sound piercing through the receiver and resonating into Eamon's ear. Eamon separated the phone and his ear, glaring at the instrument with malice as if it had been the phone itself that caused his ear shattering discomfort.

"Eamon? Eamon, are you there?"

"Of course I'm bloody here; you nearly deafened me, you stupid prat."

Liam chuckled, "Sorry Eamon, you took me by surprise."

Not amused, Eamon persisted, "So, I need you to have a little 'chat' with Willie and Fergal and then make sure that their conversation ceases. Do you get my point?"

"Yea sure, no problem, but can't Simon or Daniel Hogan with his FBI boys take care of it?"

"Simon has already been instructed, and our American friends are also on the case, but I don't trust anybody and I need to make sure that the termination happens; I also want to ensure that all the information stops here."

"I get your point." Liam paused for thought, his brain cells rapidly ticking over. "But I can't leave immediately."

"Liam!"

"Hold on Eamon, listen will ya; I need a couple of days and will shoot over then. In the meantime we have a couple of boys in Portland, Maine, who could take care of the necessary for us."

"I don't want any more people involved."

"Don't worry, these are ex activists, escaped from the Maze and smuggled over to the US; now retired but very keen to help in whatever way they can."

"Who?"

"Pat Creary and Seamus O'Connor."

"Good men," purred Eamon approvingly, "Give me their numbers."

"I'd better phone them. They've never spoken directly to you and would be very wary receiving a phone call from an unknown source and they probably wouldn't cooperate in case it's some kind of FBI trap."

219

"Don't they know who I am?" Eamon barked, half in query and partially indignant.

"Of course they know of you officially but not in your Provo role - you know...the 'need to know' basis. Some things were not revealed down the line; they know you as a political figure and not as our Chief of Staff."

"Grandmother and eggs come to mind," caustically retorted Eamon, "I know the reasons, but I just thought that those two guys knew who I was."

"Nope."

"Well, see to it *now*," ordered Eamon sharply, "And keep me fully advised. Here, get a pen and take a note of this number. I'll give you a time and place so you can keep me posted regarding your progress."

Chapter 33

Pat Creary and Seamus O'Connor were on their way to Boston, Pat having received a telephone call from Liam whilst on duty as a porter in the Accident and Emergency Department of a Maine Hospital. Feigning abdominal pain and following a routine check-up from the duty Doctor, he had declined any further medical analysis, merely requesting absence for the remainder of the day.

Pausing only to collect Seamus from the Irish Bakery, and a Smith and Wesson .45 calibre revolver that had been secreted under his floorboards at home, Pat was now happily munching on an oatmeal bar whilst driving in his pickup truck, both of them heading down the freeway in the direction of Boston.

Cheerfully exchanging smiles, Pat and Seamus enjoyed the 'country and western' music churning out from the radio. "Yahoo," hollered Pat, pleased to be 'back in the saddle' as it were.
Both men sang loudly, raucously joining in with the songs, Pat tapping the wheel in tune to the beat of the music. Their mood, to anyone observing was one of jollity, two 'boys' off to a party, not two murderous thugs on their way to a killing.

Chapter 34

Back at the Denny's Café close to Fergal's home, Shannon sat in a seat by one of the windows as she and Fergal chatted away like a pair of newly discovered lovers. Twilight was slowly succumbing to the dark of the early night and the café resonated with the bustle of evening diners. The cold evening air assisted in keeping the café full; no one seemed to be in haste to leave after completing their respective meals, one coffee following another.

A few days had passed following Shannon's extensive spring clean of Fergal's apartment; she had even taken his sheets to be washed in the local launderette, watching in amazement that even after the second wash the water was still grey, and it took a total of three washes before she was satisfied with the cleanliness of the bedding. She also supervised Fergal whilst he washed his clothes, underwear included, in an adjoining machine. Fergal's face had turned beetroot red as he extracted his underwear from the washing basket, desperately attempting to hide their soiled condition but dropping two pairs of underpants on the floor making the situation worse. In spite of her initial revulsion Shannon had had to grin at his awkward embarrassment.

They had passed the subsequent days in brief meetings, usually on some pretext instigated by Shannon, which took place either at Fergal's apartment or in this café. He was becoming more relaxed in her company and Shannon, surreptitiously eyeing Fergal, clean shaved, washed, smartened up, inadvertently began to feel that he looked quite attractive, sexy even. He was beginning to stir an interest within her, her mind drifting to the possibility of a relationship between the two of them. "God forbid, what am I thinking of," she thought, revolted, as she dragged her mind away from such a disastrous scenario.

"Shannon?" Fergal's voice appeared as if it was emanating from within her daydream.

Shannon hauled herself back to reality, back from her daydream, becoming aware that the waitress was standing by their table, having already taken Fergal's order; the waitress was gaping expectantly at Shannon.

Shannon stared blankly in response.

The waitress, unnerved and feeling awkward under Shannon's blank stare glanced from Shannon to Fergal.

"Shannon are you with us?" queried Fergal, "I suggested two cappuccinos but only if you agreed. The poor lady is waiting for your response."

Shannon's eyes focused on Fergal and she grimaced in apology. "Oh I'm sorry, I was miles away." Smiling up at the waitress, she finally confirmed her drink, "Yes please, I'll have a Cappuccino."

The waitress, busy with the evening rush, produced a spectre of a smile and departed with their order.

"Was it good?"

"What?"

"Wherever you were? You were miles away."

Shannon blushed, afraid that he could read her mind.

"It must have been good, you've gone red," he teased, cheekily demanding, "Boyfriend?"

Her colour deepened and she laughed nervously, "No of course not. I don't have a boyfriend at the moment. I was, er, actually thinking that I have to buy something."

"You don't have a boyfriend?" he asked incredulously, but also feeling elated that she was single.

"No, not at the moment, I haven't had time recently," she responded defensively.

"I can't believe that, not someone as attractive as you." Now it was his turn to be embarrassed and he changed tack, "And what do you mean, you haven't got time? You always seem to be on my doorstep, certainly for the last few days."

"I'm not always on your doorstep," Protested Shannon, her face reddening once more and becoming defensive, "And hey, what is this anyway; can't we change the subject? And all these questions, especially from someone like you."

"What do you mean by that...'someone like me?"

"You know very well what I mean; the minute that I try to ask you questions about yourself you either clam up or get all negative and reclusive."

Fergal's eyes broke free from Shannon's gaze and he turned away looking out across the café at nothing in particular, his vision becoming glazed and unfocused.

"I didn't mean to offend you," Her words apologetic, but then continued brightly, "Listen, how about if you tell me about yourself then I'll tell you a little about me."

He re-focused back to Shannon's face, looked into her eyes,

hesitated, and then with self-effacement, muttered, "You wouldn't want to know about me; I'm not that likeable."

"Let me be the judge of that."

"No. Anyway, I'm fine being a closed book."

"Closed books are sometimes opened, especially out of curiosity; even boring ones!" She grinned challenging him to respond.

He couldn't resist smiling at her, "So, I might be boring then?"

"You could be; you damn well are at the moment. Here we are having shared a meal and are sitting across from each other at a table and I know damn well nothing about you, other than your name, which may or may not be true."

"It is my proper name," he said softly, "And that you found out only by turning my apartment upside down."

"Upside down!" she retorted sharply but with humour, "Upside down; it couldn't have been more upside or way, way down before I arrived; cheeky devil!"

They exchanged wry smiles and in the ensuing awkward silence each pretended to take an interest in other activity occurring within the café.

After a brief pause Shannon returned her attention to Fergal and smiled affectionately, favouring him with one of her warmest, sexiest smiles.

Despite attempting to resist Fergal cautiously smiled in response, his eyes lighting up with new life inside him.

"How about a deal, a trade off?" She pleaded, her eyes crinkling with amusement, her feminine wiles being engaged, "I'll tell you a little about me and then you can tell me," putting her thumb and first forefinger almost together to emphasise her point, "A tiny, tiny bit about you."

"You don't give up do you," his eyes sparkling with vigour.

"No I don't."

"So tell me all about Shannon."

"Ah, so now it's '*all* about Shannon'." She laughed, her brain racing to make up a simple but plausible story. "Actually there's not a lot to tell; I work as a writer, nothing major, mostly freelance work and I don't have a boyfriend at the moment – as you already know," grinning ruefully, "And I live with my folks."

"What?" he asked incredulously, amazed, "You still live at home?"

Shannon pretended to be defensive, "Yes, I *still* live at home; I did have a place with a boyfriend but things didn't work out." She adopted a hang-dog, forlorn expression, "He walked out on me a week before the wedding." Pausing for effect, she forced a tear to run out from the corner of her eye and ferreted in her handbag for a tissue. With seemingly immense effort she continued, her voice close to sobbing, "I couldn't afford my own place so I had to move back in with my parents." Taking the tissue, Shannon made a concentrated effort of wiping her eyes and sniffing at the same time, glancing at Fergal to ensure that her words were evoking sympathetic feelings from him.

Fergal's face was a picture of sorrow and remorse, "I'm really sorry; I had no intention of making you recall sad events or to bring up old boyfriend memories."

"Fiancé," she almost sobbed, tissue against her nose.

"Sorry, fiancé," he stretched across to hold her hand, hesitated, then feeling awkward, smartly withdrew his hand, tucking it safely in his lap.

"Damn," thought Shannon, "Almost had him." Inwardly she was amazed at how quickly she had made up her story and how plausible it seemed; she almost began to feel sorry for herself as well. "Don't be stupid, lady," laughing internally at her silly emotion, "It's only a story you made up."

Fergal shuffled restlessly, feeling awkward and uneasy. He had enough of his own emotional problems, a wagon load of baggage in fact and undoubtedly didn't want to take on board any more emotional issues, certainly not from anybody else.

Shannon affected a real effort in composing herself whilst internally actually wanting to laugh out loud at her acting performance. "So Fergal, now you have to tell me a bit, a tiny bit about yourself." Making a huge pretence of forcing a smile, "How are things shaping up for you?"

"Not good actually; I've, er, I've decided to go home. I can't settle here."

Shannon was taken aback, firing off staccato style, "Why, is someone after you? Can't you get any work; is it the total lack of money? I could wait indefinitely for my money. Perhaps I could help?"

"No, but thank you; it's not just the lack of work or the financial hardship."

"Well what is it then? You can't just suddenly decide to up sticks."

"It's not the first time; I've done it before."

"Okay, I appreciate that you must have done it before otherwise you wouldn't be here in America, but you've got to settle somewhere; you can't keep running away from whatever it is you're running from. Tell me why, tell me what it is? I'm sure that I can help in some way."

"Who says I'm running from something?" His eyes squinted, scrutinising her face, the years of being on the run making him ultra-sensitive to certain remarks.

"Well obviously you must be because you haven't been in this Country for five minutes and already you've decided to chuck it in, to give it all up."

"*All.* That's a joke; there isn't anything to give up."

Shannon adopted the most concerned and caring expression that she was able to muster and sincerely asked, (partly from her job perspective but also from a personal inquisitive point of view. This man was beginning to interest her on a personal level), "Why did you come here to the States; you're not a criminal on the run are you? Please say no. Tell me what's upsetting you or making you scared?"

Fergal response was firm, for as far as he was concerned the subject was closed, "Its private and you can't help."

A passing figure paused outside the café window, the outside evening darkness, coupled with the reflection of the internal café lights reflecting off the internal glass made the person virtually unseen from those inside. The person outside, having identified Fergal and Shannon, took a pace closer to the glass, their face almost against the pane.

Mrs Symonds, sitting at an adjacent table to Fergal and Shannon, was on a special treat, her once a month's visit from her daughter and son-in-law. Although they only spent a few hours with her and always brought her to this same café, never following up with coffee at her home, she was always delighted to receive the treat and in particular was extremely grateful at the opportunity of seeing her daughter.

Mrs Symonds momentarily glanced up at the window and because of the angle of her vision she saw the face at the glass, the face unnoticed by Fergal and Shannon. She froze in fear, an icy hand gripping hold of her heart, squeezing for all its worth. The eyes that were staring in, boring into her soul, were so cold and yet the eyeballs appeared to be shimmering in a sea of molten red lava, with a tiny black pinprick in each iris almost depicting a black ace of spades. Mrs Symonds, a very sensitive and Godly soul who considered herself something of a spiritualist, had never before encountered a face of such evil and malevolence.

"What's the matter, ma?" demanded Mrs Symonds daughter, "You look as if you've seen a ghost."

Mrs Symonds, ashen and barely able to speak, the blood pounding like a river's rapids tumbling through her eardrums, the roar deafening any sound, remained motionless, staring at the window, hypnotised by the evil eyes.

"Ma? Can you hear me?" re-iterated the concerned daughter.

The daughter turned to look in the direction of her mother's fixation, "Ma, what is it? What are you looking at?"

The motion of the daughter turning to look at him alerted the face in the window. The face turned away from scrutinising Fergal and Shannon, its eyes boring directly into the eyes of Mrs Symonds; Mrs Symonds breathing ceased for a couple of seconds.

The face recoiled away from the glass, disappearing back into the evening darkness and Mrs Symonds shuddered from her toes to her head, but began to breathe again.

The daughter, having not noticed anything untoward, having missed the face at the window, looked deeply and with loving concern at her mother, "Ma, are you okay?"

"Oh just die, you old bat," thought the unpleasant and disinterested son-in-law who hated to be dragged out to visit his wife's mother, albeit on the basis of only once a month.

"Yes thank you dear," breathlessly replied the Mother, a forced sweet smile forming on her lips, "I just thought that I saw something bad, something of the devil."

"Oh ma, you do worry me," the daughter placed a loving and affectionate hand on her mother's arm.

"We'd better get you back; you must be worn out," the disagreeable son-in-law interjected with false sincerity, using the episode as an excuse to cut short their monthly visit.

Mrs Symonds' daughter glanced at her domineering husband and doing her best to be cheerful, sadly agreed, "We'll see you again soon ma."

Reluctantly Mrs Symonds acquiesced, her eyes filling up with sadness and weariness.

Her daughter's husband called for the bill.

Unfortunately this would be the last meeting between Mrs Symonds and her daughter, the shock of the face in the window having set up a chain of emotional reaction that would end with her suffering from a massive heart attack. Alone in her home later tonight, the elderly lady would reach for the telephone but the cold hand of death would beat her, squeezing all life from her before she could complete the dialling of her daughter's telephone number.

Collapsing, with her finger poised over the remaining digit to be pressed, her breath struggling before coming to one final, massive intake, a wheeze that would be quickly expelled from the frail body. With the receiver grasped firmly in her hand she would fall to the floor, banging her head, unfeeling, on the table as she made her descent.

Mrs Symonds would become another victim, this time an unknown victim, of the face in the window.

Fergal and Shannon, ignorant to the existence of Mrs Symonds and her family, were totally unaware of the face that peered in through the window. Shannon was still searching for some way to penetrate Fergal's armour, to get inside that very secretive head, determining that she was not her father's daughter if she couldn't succeed. "Ah go on, Mr Impenetrable," she suddenly asked, "Tell me something about yourself so that I can see if I can help."

Not weakening under her imploring gaze, Fergal remained firmly determined that he couldn't open up. "It's private, you can't help."

Shannon was not giving up. "You know what they say, two heads being better than one, a problem shared is a problem halved."

Fergal exasperated, aggressively snapped, "You can't help!"

"I was only trying to be nice," she responded with affected hurt, "There's no need to be rude."

"Sorry, I didn't mean to offend, it's just that...that you won't be able to help me, I'm beyond all that; too many memories, bad ones." Fergal took a large sip from his glass of water.

Shannon waited for a moment or two and then hesitantly soothed, "Oh gee I'm sorry to hear that; poor Fergal." She extended her hand across the table towards Fergal's hand but he didn't reciprocate the last couple of inches, his hand being just out of her reach. Short of leaping up and grabbing his hand she couldn't put on a more sympathetic act.

Fergal becoming tense and fidgety, nervously examined the other customers in the café.

Shannon followed his gaze. He returned his attention back to Shannon becoming increasing awkward under her intense, sympathetic stare.

Unable to withstand her scrutiny, Fergal bleated, "I need a drink."

"The coffee won't be long." Shannon smiled, her eyes full of feigned heart-warming sympathy and affection.

"No, I mean I need a drink, a real drink."

"Oh, you mean liquor; I thought that you were on the wagon?"

"I am, was, but now I need a drink; would you mind if we left?"

Shannon studied the uncomfortably sweating Fergal but finally nodded in agreement.

Quickly settling the bill, paying for the declined cappuccinos, they exited into the night, Shannon's eye briefly catching sight of a figure that instantly disappeared into the shadows. She frowned and thinking quickly, dropped her handbag, surreptitiously scanning the street as she bent down to pick it up.

Fergal walking ahead, stopped to turn back, "What's up?"

Shannon unable to spot anything out of ordinary thought, "You're becoming twitchy, girl, even shadows are making you edgy." She smiled at Fergal, "Oh nothing, I just dropped my handbag." Picking up her bag she hurried up to Fergal, inserting her arm under his arm.

Fergal glanced down at Shannon's arm, and confident that his features weren't visible in the gloom, he beamed with pleasure.

Shannon knowing full well that Fergal was grinning gratifyingly, felt a warm glow spreading through her.

The unseen figure, deep in the shadows, watched intently as they walked down the street; as the figure cautiously advanced in the shadows a streetlight momentarily reflected off the pair of eyes watching their every move, eyes that reflected pure evil. The night itself wanted to shudder and scream out.

Fergal and Shannon having gone a short distance and located a convenient bar were sitting at a table in a quieter section, a bay window area, of the fairly full bar. They engaged in a deep conversation of absolutely no significance and the kind of meaningless conversation that two people of latent mutual love or lust have when in the throes of a potential relationship, a courting ritual.

The establishment they were in was split into two floors, the lower floor mainly for the serious drinkers and the upper floor for the social or occasional imbibers or for those who wanted a meal. She toyed with her tonic water whilst Fergal drunk deeply from a beer; next to his beer sat a glass containing a large malt whisky. Contented in his company Shannon was never the less worried about his excessive drinking habits. So plucking up her courage, her voice echoing genuine concern, she stated, "You should go easy on the booze, Fergal; you know what it does to you."

"Yes I do know," he bitterly retorted, "But it wipes out the terrible memories, the nightmares!" As if to reinforce his statement, he took another large sip from the whisky glass.

"What do you mean 'nightmares'?"

"Um, I have constant terrifying nightmares, haunting memories of bad things from the past."

"What? Things done to you, childhood abuse or something like that?"

Fergal, whisky glass in hand, shook his head, looked into Shannon's eyes and then back at his drink, "I don't want to talk about it." He downed the remaining whisky in one large gulp.

"You know, talking can help."

"Not in this case."

"There's never a situation that can't be eased by talking it through."

Fergal's eyes adopted a hardened and steel-like stare; his voice firm and full of anger he petulantly snapped, "Not in this case!"

"But..."

Fergal jumped up. "Look, if you're going to keep on then I'm going to go; I just *don't* want to talk about it, get it?"

Shannon extended her palms flat out in front of Fergal, in a gesture of surrender, "Okay, okay, I get the point; please sit down."

Fergal regained his seat and stared morosely into space.

Shannon quietly sipped at her drink but as she replaced her glass on the table, mumbled affectionately, "Miserable bastard."

Fergal glanced at Shannon, at first scowling but then grinning in response to her awkward, shy smile.

Meanwhile Willie, disguised with false beard and wearing heavy framed glasses, sauntered to a vacated nearby table. He sat with his back to Fergal and Shannon but within earshot. Almost immediately a pair of jovial young men approached Willie's table, the first one enquiring, "Are these seats free?" Willie looked up with an expression of total malice but did not respond. The young man persisted, his tone now demanding, "Well, are they free?"

Willie's eyes closed to a squint, he slightly opened his jacket revealing a gun holster and with a nudge of his head indicated that the young men should move off, his cold, murderous eyes never leaving those of the young man. Aghast, the man hastily turned to his friend, "I guess those seats are taken, we'll find somewhere else." Both men moved quickly away to the far part of the bar as Willie tuned his ears back to Fergal's conversation with Shannon.

Fergal reached for his wallet in the inside pocket of his jacket which hung on the back of his chair, "I need another whisky."

"I'll get you one, it is my turn, and I think that I need something stronger this time."

"Stick to the tonic, it's safer," he grinned.

"You're a fine one to talk."

"In my case it's different but if you're not a drinker then there's no reason to get started."

"I do drink but I'm a social drinker; maybe a couple of glasses of wine or a Martini once or twice a week."

"Wow, a real hell raiser," he affectionately bantered.

Shannon screwed up her face in mock indignation. "Hah, hah; anyway I'm happy with my habits."

"So am I."

She searchingly scrutinised Fergal's eyes, "Does that mean happy with me or happy with you?"

He coloured in embarrassment, "Um, er, never mind. I need that drink."

Shannon, amused, saluted, "Yes, Sir! Coming right up." Grinning broadly she went towards the bar, but as she approached Willie's table, he stiffened and raised his glass to his lips but did not drink. He was merely watching Shannon's reflection in the glass, absorbing every detail of her as she walked towards and then past his table, putting every detail observed into his copious memory store.

On her return journey with the drinks he studied her in greater detail, not flinching or averting his eyes as she grimaced at him, pulling a face.

Shannon looked down, avoiding eye contact from the intense stare of this seemingly over familiar man; she made a face but neither of them exchanged a word as she passed his table. Carrying her drinks on a small tray, she placed the tray on her table. "Here we are, another beer and a large Malt," she was feeling quite cheerful.

Fergal staring morosely out of the window, smiled up at her.

Shannon passed his two drinks across, picking up her own glass from the tray, "And for me, a 'Bloody Mary."

Fergal shuddered, causing Shannon to frown, "What's the matter, you don't like tomatoes?" She added with amusement, "It can't be the vodka that you dislike."

Fergal, his eyes heavy, sorrowful, replied wearily, "No, it's just the colour of the drink, and the name."

Shannon stared at the glass in her hand, "I'll take it back, swap it for something else."

"No it's okay, it's just me being silly; please just sit down." Fergal forced a faint smile. Frowning, Shannon sat down, both remaining silent. After a short interlude they decided to speak simultaneously, Fergal saying, "What do you...?" As Shannon uttering, "How long have you...?"

Fergal laughed, "Sorry go on."

"No you first, you go on with what you were about to say."

"It wasn't important."

Shannon grinned, "Neither was mine."

They both picked up their drinks, Shannon running her finger down the frost on the outside of her glass and then looked searchingly at Fergal.

Fergal catching the look in her eye, sighed, wearily stating, "Oh, oh, I'm in trouble, you're going to ask me another question, aren't you?"

She shook her head innocently, "No, no, I wasn't."

Fergal fixed her with a questioning stare.

Shannon smiled warmly. "Oh all right then, I was just curious about what...but never mind it doesn't matter." She sipped her drink, the blood red reflecting onto her face.

Fergal catching the image, shuddered involuntarily before swallowing a large gulp from the glass of malt whiskey.

Shannon replaced her glass on the table, "I know that you said earlier about going away but have you made any definite plans yet about going," She hesitated, "Or staying?"

"I just don't know; it's difficult to stay here but I can't go home either."

"And you won't tell me why?"

Fergal focused into the distance.

Shannon afraid that she had over stepped the mark, hastily cut in, "It doesn't matter if you won't tell me." After a short pause she couldn't resist adding an aside, "But I hope that you stay."

Fergal met Shannon's eyes, reading what he hoped was affection; she coloured and shyly smiled.

Fergal, his mouth initially forming voiceless words then began speaking, slowly and earnestly, "If you knew about me, the truth, you wouldn't want me to stay."

"It can't be all that bad; you're not some mass murderer are you?"

Fergal blanched; Shannon could have kicked herself, realising that she'd erred, gone too fast. Hastily she corrected herself, rushing her words, garbling, "Or someone hiding from the 'IRS' or whatever the Irish equivalent of the Inland Revenue Service is? Is it a woman, perhaps you're married and running away?"

The last suggestion caused Fergal to snort with bitterness, "God, no! Who'd have me?"

"Well, I, er, like you." They exchanged a deep meaningful look. "And I want you to stay," she added softly, her voice quivering with emotion.

Fergal reached for Shannon's hand resting on the table, wrapping it tenderly within his palm. "I'm afraid I'm not a very nice guy, or at least I wasn't a very nice guy."

"What happened, what could you have possibly done?" She pleaded plaintively whilst her professional self thought, "I am so close to unravelling this mystery; he *has* to tell me."

Fergal searched deeply into Shannon's eyes, trying his best to fathom if this woman was genuine; convinced, he opened his heart, "I...I was a member of an Irish terrorist organisation, the Provisional Irish Republican Army."

"That's not so bad if you didn't kill anyone or do anything evil; quite a few people seem to have been involved in the Irish freedom movement and they do raise money here in the States to support Irish independence. There are a few organisations that believe in the non-violent course of uniting Ireland, legally raising monies to send to Ireland."

Fergal momentarily adopted a bitter tone, "Yes, I know they do. The Irish-Americans, or many of them, have a sanitised, or jaundiced, view of the situation. A free and united Ireland is one thing, a thing that we all want but the reality of the current Provisional IRA is not like the dream of a happy Emerald Isle. To be in the Provisionals you have to kill or maim without compunction, you bully or murder without a second though, men, women, or children, it makes no difference. Decent human emotions and values disappear in a sea of evil and depravity, with the end justifying the means, or so the Council would have us believe! And many of the so-called Council make a good living because of their positions, profiting with a superior lifestyle. The hypocrisy of it all makes me sick!"

Liking him more and more and desperately not wanting him to be evil or to have an evil past she hesitantly enquired, "Did you get involved with any of the bad things?"

Fergal raised his beer glass, draining the drink without pause, the brown liquid gushing down his throat in one continuous stream, whilst Shannon, genuinely concerned, waited patiently for his response. Misty eyed, he gazed at Shannon, his face full of remorse, "I'm afraid so."

Utterly dismayed, involuntarily raising her fist to her mouth, Shannon despairingly muttered, "Oh!"

"And now the memories won't go away," the acrimonious bitterness biting through his words.

Seeing a modicum of light through the darkness Shannon muttered more in hope than anything else, "You can't be all bad if the memories are haunting you."

Unbelievably pleased and relieved to find a partially sympathetic ear, Fergal just totally opened up, "When I first joined I was full of patriotic idealism, fuelled by an education that kept telling us of the atrocities committed by the British. Of course, like in so many countries, it was just history – a bad history – but of things done by different people, most often of events in the past, by men and women of different generations. However when you are young and impressionable you do stupid things, so, knowing an important, some would stupidly say 'heroic' Provo cell leader, I joined. It was okay at first, me a youngster, receiving respect from people old enough to my grandfather." He sipped at his whisky. "I realised later that much of that 'respect' was not respect but was in fact total bloody fear. Fear of me, an eighteen-year-old boy!

Unscrupulous bigots created various adaptations of the original Irish Republican Army in order to intimidate others, and to mock those of the original organisation whose intentions were aimed at independence, initially fighting, but then resolved through negotiation and the ballet box. I now believe that a united Ireland will happen one day and soon, but it must be through democracy not through the actions of murderous thugs."

Shannon caressed Fergal's hand. "But now you've obviously broken free and I'm sure that there are organisations that would help you."

"Yes, sure," The bitterness welling up inside, "I've got too much information," He tapped his head, "Up here, that would make people, on both sides, want to get rid of me."

"Is that why you quit, why you're running?"

"No, I'd had enough; the sickening reality got through my alcohol and drug-induced state. I decided to pull out, let myself get caught and locked up. Seven years for accessory to murder." He continued with rancour, "Then some arsehole arranged a jailbreak, and here I am."

"If you go back will you get locked up again, I thought the British government had agreed a parole?"

"They have but not for people like me. I'd have to have a new trial first and then they might let me go after serving a fresh prison term."

"Surely that's worth it? You can finally be released to start afresh."

"Sure, released straight into the hands of a death squad."

"Why for goodness sake?"

"After I was sentenced I was interrogated by an ex-Inspector of the RUC, a guy called Willie Davidson; he told me that he was seconded to British Intelligence. Anyway in a moment of anger I let something slip and I know that he will pursue me for his own ends.

He was a corrupt policeman and was even worse when given his freedom under his new job. My life in the Maze prison was a living hell from things arranged by Willie but at least I was safe from the man himself."

"What was it that made him so vindictive and you so scared?"

"I hope that you're ready for this, it'll shock you to the core; it's almost unbelievable but I can prove it." Slowly at first but hastening as he got into his tale Fergal revealed the details that Shannon has been so desperately trying to discover. Unfortunately Willie was also getting a verbatim account of Fergal's closely guarded secret as Fergal commenced to recount his story, his mind flashing back to an interview room in the Prison complex in Northern Ireland.

Chapter 35

The room was dark, depressing, with two seats bolted to the floor on either side of a small desk which was also bolted to the floor. Fergal's forearms were resting on the desk, a pair of handcuffs securing him from being able to strike out at his interrogator.

Drawing on a cigarette, Willie exhaled the smoke in Fergal's face causing Fergal to cough, the stale smoke adding to the prisoner's already dry throat and irritating down into his lungs.

"Right you piece of shit," demanded Willie, "What happened to Colm; I know that you were one of his squad so who actually killed him and why?"

Trying to keep his mind blank Fergal fixed his attention on the opposite wall, dismissively responding, "No idea."

Willie swiped Fergal's face with the back of his hand, the blow knocking Fergal's head back; a trickle of blood oozing from the newly created cut on the prisoner's lip. Willie's ruthless eyes were fixed menacingly on the defenceless man in front of him, "When I ask a question you piece of shit I want a positive and frank answer, is that clear?"

Fergal nodded in affirmation.

"Right I'll try again," His expression was grim, "Who killed Colm?"

Fergal thought he saw sorrow in Willie's eyes but quickly dismissed the thought as being ridiculous, whilst Willie grumbled, "He was one of the best in the business; I always thought that I would be the only person who would be good enough to get through his defences. He got the better of me on one or two occasions but I was looking forward to my retribution." His focus drifted to a distant place, a look of evil satisfaction forming on his face, "Still, I once had the satisfaction of knocking nine kettles of shit out of him and of course," grinning maliciously, "I enjoyed screwing his woman, to death! Boy, did she finally fuck with a bang." He couldn't resist a chuckle.

Fergal, fuming, leapt from his seat, "You *did* kill her, you fucking evil bastard! We thought that it was you but could never be sure. Some kids found her decomposing body."

Willie smirked with gloating satisfaction but his reptilian eyes did not match the lips, "Yes it was me. She was begging for a fuck, so pleased for a decent screw after years with that limp prick." He laughed at the words he had just uttered, pleased he had thought of them on the spur of the moment, "Limp prick, I like that, Colm the limp pricked Fenian bastard."

Eyes blazing, Fergal attempted to get round the desk, scrambling forward in fury to attack Willie.

Calmly and with an evil smile etched on his lips Willie sidestepped and punched Fergal solidly in the stomach. When the winded Fergal fell to the floor Willie kicked him, viciously, in the balls.

Fergal doubled up in pain, rolling across on the floor, his groans of agony reverberating around the interrogation room.

A prison warder waiting in the corridor called out "You all right in there Sir?"

Willie tranquilly and nonchalantly brushing a fleck of dust from his sleeve retorted, "Yes I'm fine, the prisoner just fell."

The prison warder put his key into the door lock, "I'll give you a hand to pick him up."

Willie hurriedly yelled, "No! Stay out, this is high security business. Get the hell away from the door!"

The prison official was doubtful, "Are you sure?"

" Yes; now sod off before I see you on a disciplinary charge!" thundered the angry Willie.

"Yes Sir!" Abashed, the warder removed his key from the lock, retreating a few yards further along the corridor.

At the sound of the retreating steps Willie stepped over to Fergal, kicking him forcefully in the guts. Fergal still holding his private regions and groaning, grunted at the fresh infliction of pain but this time he was not going to give Willie the satisfaction of crying out.

"Get up you cowardly shit," ordered Willie, "Get the fuck up or I'll put my foot right up your fucking yellow arse."

Fergal painfully scrambled to his feet and hunched over, his eyes watering from the pain, he slumped onto his seat.

"Shall we try one more time," Willie triumphantly sneered, "Or would you like me to fuck you like I did Colm's woman?"

He unzipped his trousers. "I don't mind which sex I screw and I especially like inflicting pain up the arse, so long as the arse is a Catholic one; I always win, no matter what."

Shocked and dismayed, forgetting his pain, Fergal quickly rose from his chair, attempting to back away from this perverted madman, but Willie casually reached over and grabbed him, forcing Fergal face down onto the desk. With his handcuffed arms pinioned in front of him Fergal was unable to affect much of a resistance, trying futilely to wriggle free. Annoyed by Fergal's resistance Willie repeatedly thumped the prisoner's head onto the desk, then holding his captive securely he forced Fergal's face downwards until it was pressed firmly against the table; with Fergal's shoulder immobilised on the desktop he then reached round to undo the captive's prison issue trousers.

Bloody, bruised, and hurting, Fergal fiercely proclaimed, "Whatever you do, how much degradation you make us go through, you know you'll never win; you can't stop the people's will."

Panting with the effort of forcing down Fergal's trousers, Willie guffawed, "I *always* win."

"So you think; it'll soon be our turn, even your own Prime Minister is one of us."

"Yes sure kid, now shut up and enjoy." Fergal's trousers were now around his ankles and Willie quickly pulled down his own trousers, pulling out his penis.

"I have the proof," desperately uttered Fergal, sick with apprehension but determined to beat this man somehow.

Poised over Fergal's naked and exposed bottom, annoyed at the interruption, the unwanted diversion, Willie had no choice but to demand, "What? What proof, what are you talking about?"

Fergal seizing his moment raised his torso and smashed the back of his head into Willie's face, an abrupt crunching sound resonating in the room. Willie cried out, a shrill howl of unexpected pain rushing from his lips, the crimson blood flowing from his broken nose. "Right you bloody little shite!" he howled, grabbing hold of Fergal who had almost succeeded in wriggling free, and together they rolled in a tangle on the floor, Willie punching the defenceless Fergal.

Fergal did try to fight back, doing his utmost to retaliate as best he could, biting and kicking out and fending off with his handcuffed arms.

With the noise of the scuffle the warder had no option but to return to investigate, shouting from just outside the interrogation room door. "What the hell is going on in there?"

Now on top of Fergal and raining blows on Fergal's unprotected face, Willie ignored the prison official's verbal intrusion. The interrogation room door was hastily unlocked and the warder, quickly supported by two colleagues who he had earlier summoned, rushed into the room.

Instantly sizing up the situation, they dragged Willie off the now unconscious Fergal.

Screaming and ranting in incandescent rage Willie yelled, "Get off me you bastards, I haven't finished with him yet."

The senior warder retorted, "I think you have Sir." He glanced with total disdain and disgust at Willie's exposed penis. "Now please pull up your pants and get out of here."

Fuming, following the warder's eyes and glancing downwards, Willie suddenly awakened to his state of undress. Caught in his inopportune moment, the horror hastening onto his malevolent face, he continued to follow the warder's gaze now focused on the naked lower half of Fergal, now lying comatose on his side.

The other warders rushed to Fergal's bruised and bleeding body, quickly checking the hapless, battered and groaning individual, ascertaining if the prison Doctor would be needed to attend to any serious injury or if a hospital visit would be necessary in order to fix any broken bones. Luckily it seemed that although Willie had fought in a rage he knew how to hurt people without leaving too much evidence behind in the shape of broken limbs.

"I can explain," barked Willie, his tone ringing with authority. But now the warder was not prepared to allow himself to be browbeaten; after all he was in the firing line if repercussions were to follow and he sarcastically snapped in response, "Yes sir, sure sir, absolutely sir."

No longer his confident self, the warder's tone and sharp words driving away his self-assuredness, Willie determined to persist, attempting to make his voice overbearing with authority, "No I really can explain." The disdainful expressions evident on the faces of all three warders not dissipating made the bully angry and ruffling up into his full sense of inflated self-importance, he almost barked, "Do you know who I am, the authority that I have?"

The senior warder glanced down at the trousers around Willie's feet before looking with total contempt at Willie, "Authority s*ir*? I don't think that you are in any position to make threats! And I would," He continued ironically "Respectfully suggest that you pull up your trousers, *with authority*, and leave."

Fergal gradually regaining consciousness, aware of the conversation taking place between Willie and the warders, would love to have laughed but his body just hurt too much.

The incensed Willie pulled up his trousers and headed for the door, where turning, he glared at the awakened Fergal, growling with threatening venom, "This is not finished yet Fergal but by God you'll wish it had!"

Willie departed the cell, his face a mirror image of vengeful malice.

"Fucking pervert!" The senior warden's voice echoed along the corridor.

Chapter 36

Gobsmacked, almost speechless, Shannon whistled in amazement. "You poor dear; what an evil bastard. Why wasn't Willie charged?"

"I guess that it was because it suited the Prime Minister to have such an evil unrelenting bastard causing chaos and harm; it was all good propaganda for the Republicans."

"But surely if Alistair Glen wanted a peaceful solution to the Ireland issue then people like Willie should have been locked away, and in a very deep, dark dungeon."

Fergal smiled at Shannon's ire at Willie, but instantly became serious. "I've already mentioned it; Glen is one of us, he's Irish, a sworn member of the Provisional IRA and the son of one of our so-called 'heroes'."

Amazed before, Shannon was now dumfounded, taking a few seconds before blurting, "You're kidding...that's not possible!"

"I'm afraid it's true. I found out too late, and too late to help Colm, although I suppose his death was deserved for the things that he had done."

"Colm? Who is Colm?"

"Colm was my cell leader; a vicious but efficient 'administrator' of terrorist 'discipline'. He started off as my hero but I soon learnt that he was no more than a brutal thug just like Willie; they were two of a kind."

"Then why did you stay?"

"Fear I guess. Initially I enjoyed the hero status but as I became more involved the whole thing made me sick to the pit of my stomach."

Her heart racing Shannon quietly asked, "Are you sure about Alistair?"

Fergal hesitated for a fraction of a second before exclaiming in a torrent of words, "Colm was Alistair's true father, his biological father. Alistair's biological mother was Bernadette Hanratty, Colm's mistress, who was eventually killed by Willie."

Her brain now racing at the sudden influx of improbable information, she gawped senselessly at Fergal. Slowly her mind re-engaged, her words reflecting total disbelief, incredulously demanding, "Then why not inform on them...reveal everything to the authorities?"

"Who do I talk to? Who could I trust on the British side? And if the Provos found out what I know then I'm dead; after all, they killed Colm."

Shannon involuntarily whistled once more, "They killed Colm, Alistair's father! Why for God's sake?"

"I didn't know why at the time but I guess that the stakes were too high, Colm could not be associated with Alistair."

"If they don't know about you knowing how *do* you know so much?"

Fergal stared out into the night, softly he replied, "I killed Colm."

"What!"

"I didn't actually murder him by myself but I was part of the execution squad; at the time I couldn't figure out why or what we were doing. I do know that I was shit scared, me against a master killer such as Colm on the one hand, or me against the Council on the other hand, not a pleasant choice. I did shoot Colm but someone else administered the final shot."

Shannon shivered with distaste, "It's all very horrible."

"Then as we were leaving," continued Fergal, "Other members of the Organisation blew up our car. It seemed that evidence of the killing was to be removed and that the Protestants would be blamed."

"Then how come they didn't pursue you?"

"No one knew who the second member of the team was. I was supposed to be in London scouting on potential bombing sites and a guy called Derrick was to be in the Colm assassination team. But he had a guaranteed screw with a woman in London so asked me to swap. Luckily for me, but not for him, he got blown up planting a bomb, so no one knows of my role in Colm's death; the Provos thought that I escaped from London because I told them that some unknown Londoner got killed by my unsafe bomb."

"My God you've led a dangerous life," Shannon gasped, attempting to feign amazement whilst racking her brains and searching her conscious about what action to take, but she was also genuinely concerned, "Can you ever prove the claims regarding Alistair and Colm?"

"Yes I can. Colm hid a few of his things in a trunk at my house; he didn't want his wife to find out about Bernadette and their son. Ironically his wife did know about Bernadette anyway. When I decided to retire I went home to clean out my things and going through Colm's trunk I found photographs of Colm together with Alistair, some signed on the back, plus some private correspondence, some of which outlined the Council's plans."

Shannon eagerly leant forward, "Wow, where is this stuff now?"

Willie's ears pricked up and he sat stiff and erect in his seat, the sound of a pin dropping would not escape his finely tuned hearing. A malevolent gleam lit up his eyes.

Suspicious and wary Fergal scoured her eyes quizzically and queried, "How come you want to know that?"

Shannon rushed her explanation, "I'm sorry, I was just curious. It's not important just so long as you keep it safe. That stuff has got to be your insurance; you could take it to the major Press."

"I guess so, that is, if I knew how to use it. You just don't know who to trust these days. I could take it to one of the main British newspapers but how would I know if the selected Journalist was not already close to Alistair. It would be like putting my head in the lion's mouth. Alistair has it covered all ways, he's popular with most of the Press and he's got connections with the terrorists and British Intelligence."

"Not all the British Press guys can be close to the British Prime Minister, surely there are some you can rely on?"

"I just wouldn't know who other than one possibility, but more importantly, wouldn't want to risk that person being killed."

"Talking about trust and without trying to be funny or for you to get the wrong idea of me," She looked deeply into Fergal's eyes, "I do know that your proof is not here at least not in your apartment," she grinned, "Because I tipped your place upside down that time I was looking for some money."

Fergal's wary expression softened into a smile. "It's safe; it's with a friend in London." Reflecting, he consumed another sip of his whisky.

Willie's ears strained desperately, afraid that he was missing something important; he almost stood up and shouted, "Pardon, speak up!"

Fergal continued with his revelation, "I didn't fully realise what I had, what I knew, but it all became clear."

"What made you finally quit the Republican movement?"

"It was the murder of the British Prince."

"The British Prince murdered? *Noooo*! The newspapers reported that he died as a result of a terrible but unfortunate car accident!" Shannon was mortified, "You weren't involved in that? Oh my God! Why have him killed?"

"I couldn't understand it either but I guess that it was because Alistair was afraid that the Prince was far too popular and in order to manipulate the people, he didn't want any competition in the popularity stakes. He was playing a much bigger game."

Taken aback and visibly upset, Shannon could not believe what she was hearing, "But how; surely security was too tight?"

"We had support from what we understood was an Irish sympathiser within the FBI plus someone in British Intelligence was feeding us information and making sure that any material we needed was always on hand. At the time none of the levels of support or co-operation made sense to me."

Shannon angry and disbelieving, loudly protested, "Bastards! FBI operative you say? That can't be possible, our remit..." Quickly correcting herself, "Our Country's remit for the FBI is that they operate domestically here in the States. Our..." she almost slipped up again, "...the operatives in Europe are usually based at the Embassies for intelligence gathering only and investigation only. If anybody from the USA was involved on an operational basis then it is usually falls to the CIA; that person you mention must have been a rogue CIA operative."

"It was definitely FBI, I saw the guy's I.D. badge."

"Impossible!"

"True I'm afraid."

Shannon was inclined to believe Fergal's earnest assertion. "This is terrible, not only may American Agents be involved but FBI to boot; FBI supporting terrorists, unbelievable!" Her eyes widening with anger of the betrayal she heatedly demanded, "Who was he, what was his name?"

One or two faces glanced over from nearby tables, the people distracted by Shannon's heated words.

Fergal twisted, looking over his shoulder and in an almost hushed voice, warned, "Calm down, you'll get us...me...into trouble." Although Shannon now appeared back in control of herself his suspicions had been raised and he had to ask with reluctant, nervous disquiet, "Who are you Shannon, why did you ask for a name?"

Regaining her composure she determined to be as blunt as

possible. "Because I want to report the guy ensuring that we can bring him to justice. It would help you, and I thought that the Prince was lovely and can't bear the thought that Americans had anything to do with his untimely death."

Fergal slightly mollified, his suspicion partially waning, replied sympathetically, "I guess that there are bad apples in every society."

"Oh Fergal you really weren't involved in killing the Prince, were you?"

"Even I'm not that bad. I was told that the object was to scare him, frighten him off from making public appearances and also to demonstrate that we could reach any target. When I realised what was happening I ran and have been running ever since. Luckily no one realised how deeply I had been involved in the preparation and planning so that's why I'm still alive."

"Thank God you are," she gushed with heartfelt sincerity.

An awkward silence ensued, neither knowing what to say next. Shannon's brain was racing with the information gained. If what Fergal had said was true then it was in fact her Department, her superiors, Daniel and Jim, who were breaking USA laws. If this were the case then she had to be extremely careful because her own life would now be in danger.

For his part Fergal was wondering if he had said too much; was this going to chase her off? "God, I really do like this woman but what the heck, if she goes, then I can disappear back to Europe. It's probably for the best anyway," he thought reluctantly, his feelings for her growing stronger.

"I feel really down tonight." He kept his eyes resolutely on Shannon's eyes, realising how beautiful her eyes were. "Um, I usually hit the bottle when I feel this low. I, er, don't suppose that you fancy coming back to my place for a coffee and chat?"

Shannon's face reflected true affection, "Fergal Mulroney, that's one of the worst chat up lines that I've ever heard."

"Seriously, I don't want to be on my own tonight."

"And I suppose that you want me to just sit up with you, talking the night away."

Fergal responded enthusiastically, "Yes that would be great."

Shannon chortled, "You men, you're all the same; any excuse to get a woman into your bed."

Fergal grinned shyly, the colour rising in his cheeks, "That would be nice but really I don't want to be alone. Not now, not tonight."

Shannon met Fergal's gaze, their eyes locked in mutual appreciation.

Fergal frowned, not reading Shannon correctly, his face becoming longer as he thought her silence was evidence of her apparent reluctance to accompany him.

When she did reply her words slow, thoughtful, the words like music to his ears, "Okay, I'll go back with you but only for conversation and coffee."

Fergal exuberant, ecstatic proclaimed, "Thanks Shannon, you don't know what this means to me."

"Don't forget I'm only going to keep you company nothing else." She smiled affectionately, getting to her feet.

Broad grin on his face, Fergal stood up, allowing Shannon to lead the way to the exit. When they passed Willie's table Willie raised his hand to his forehead, keeping his face hidden from Fergal, but Shannon couldn't resist an involuntarily shiver, someone having trampled over her grave.

Long dormant feelings being re-woken, Fergal concerned, caringly asked, "Are you cold, do you want my jacket?"

Shannon continued towards the exit, speaking over her shoulder, "No thanks, I just had an incredibly bad feeling, almost like a premonition of evil. Something incredibly bad seemed to touch me."

"It wasn't me, I didn't touch you."

"Ha, ha, very funny." She began to feel slightly better, the weight of evil being discarded somewhere behind her. Shannon did not look back as she and Fergal left the bar.

The moment they left the bar, a shadowy figure hastily receded into the dim recesses of a derelict shop entrance virtually across the road from them and in doing so almost sent his shadow accomplice flying into the doorway.

"What's the matter?" the accomplice Shadow demanded.

"It's the guy we're after, Fergal," responded the first Shadow, "He's just left the bar together with the FBI Agent we've been told about. She seems a little bit too friendly with him."

"Perhaps he's screwing her," cheerfully responded the second Shadow.

"Lucky bastard; she seems a bit tasty."

"We have to take her out too," grimly reminded the second

Shadow.

"Shame," chortled Shadow number one, "I wouldn't have minded taking over from Fergal. Shall we follow them?"

"No, not yet; looks like they're going to Fergal's place and we've got the address. Let's see what Willie is doing – it's a long time since we made his acquaintance. When he comes out, then we'll decide how and when we kill Fergal, Willie, and the woman."

"Okay, it's your call," cheerfully responded the first Shadow as he poked his head forward, trying his utmost to scan through the bar window and into the lit expanses inside the room.

Meanwhile inside the bar, Willie thumped the table, speaking joyously to himself, "I've been a bloody fool; I should have known. I could never figure out why Alistair Glen's face seemed to ring a distant bell! He was the young man with Colm all those years ago in the pub in Northern Ireland! What a fool I've been." He rubbed his hands in anticipation. "Colm's son, it's better than I'd ever hoped for! It's going to be a pleasure to get another one over on Colm - I hope his soul is rotting in hell!"

The bar customers standing in the vicinity of Willie's table, becoming alarmed, began edging away creating a visible space between themselves and this lunatic. Willie rose up, his drink discarded as he hastened towards the exit, the evil and brutal expression on his face ensuring a clear path to the door.

Chapter 37

Ensconced in bed in Fergal's apartment, Fergal was making love to Shannon, not merely 'shagging' as Fergal put it so succinctly, but actually 'making love' to one another. It had been a long time since he'd made 'love' to a woman, all the quick fumbles with drunken females or rare, desperate sessions with ladies of 'ill reputation' only serving to relieve his baser instincts rather than fulfil him. Shannon would have liked to know how many women but Fergal had quickly changed the subject.

Two hours had passed subsequent to their arrival at Fergal's apartment and the initial strained and awkward conversation had drifted to delicate flirting, then a kiss and a touch that had soon turned into a riot of exploration, finally exploding into passionate lovemaking. Shannon had surprised him with her ardour, but of course it had been many months since she had finished with her last man.

Frenetic, frantic, sated, they rested, the conversation meaningless but comforting, affection overflowing to each another. Fergal lay on his back, waffling on and on about the beauty of a village he had visited in Ireland, and Shannon, lying alongside, but not really listening, moved across and commenced to kiss her way down Fergal's body from his lips to his stomach.

Enjoying every second beyond his wildest dreams Fergal was filled with profound pleasure, "I do like this 'conversation' that we're having."

Shannon looked up and grinned, "It's good to 'talk'." And recommenced her lip exploration of Fergal's lower body causing him to moan and groan with unbounded delight and pleasure.

"Now I really know what they mean about the 'oral' bit of oral sex," joke Fergal, panting, his ecstasy increasing at the same level as a part of his body increased. His face erupted into a huge grin, interspaced with contented groans.

Shannon raised her head and smiled, "Right, I think I've got you excited enough; now you can do something for me." She slid up Fergal's body and they gently began to make love once more, this time more slowly than their previous frenetic lustful embrace, but gradually increasing in tempo, culminating in intense and heated passion, the noise of their joyful bonding echoing out into the dark night.

After they have spent their energy they lay exhausted in each other's arms and, entwined, both gradually fell into a deep, fatigued sleep.

Chapter 38

Overcoat collar turned up, Willie crept forward. Having gaining entry to Fergal's apartment block he was now on the first floor of the building, standing outside Fergal's door.

He had already decided earlier that he was going to pay Fergal a 'visit' later that night and it had been relatively easy to fix the building's front door access earlier in the day by partially filling the lock with a superglue resin, thus ensuring that the lock would not catch properly. It would not be reported and subsequently repaired, if the landlord could be bothered, until the Maintenance Man was called the following morning.

Delighted at the bonus of spotting Fergal out with Shannon and in obtaining the initial information he had been seeking without having to beat the shit out of Fergal, he had watched them both return to Fergal's apartment. Biding his time, he had waited patiently in the shadows whilst leaning against a set of metal railings on the opposite side of the road, observing Fergal's window until the light had been switched off. He remained motionless, akin to an immovable statue, the passing human traffic growing ever quieter. Willie had waited a further hour just to make sure that Fergal and his 'slut' would be asleep.

Satisfied that all was quiet and that the coast was clear, he had moved in. Now, taking a multi-function Swiss Army type penknife from his pocket he selected an appropriate tool from the penknife, proceeding to silently pick the door-lock of Fergal's apartment. After a few seconds, gained through years of practice, Willie succeeded in turning the lock into the open position, rotated the door handle, and slowly, gently, eased the door open. With a final glance over his shoulder he opened the door wider and entered.

Cautiously he checked his surroundings, ears tuned for any sound of movement or activity. Willie gently pushed the front door closed behind him and once again listened for any sounds, initially picking up the sound of Fergal gently snoring and Shannon breathing with a delicate softness, both obviously in deep sleep. Allowing his eyes to become accustomed to the gloom of the room he returned the penknife to his pocket, flexed and un-flexed his fingers, and satisfied that nothing appeared to be amiss, moved forward into the apartment, seeking out Fergal and Shannon for their denouement.

Approaching the bedroom door Willie slid his hand inside his coat, pulling out a Smith and Wesson .357 Magnum revolver. Also from his coat pocket he took a silencer for the gun and calmly proceeded to screw the silencer onto the weapon's barrel. Double-checking that the revolver was fully loaded he released the safety catch and went onward, briefly pausing before entering the bedroom, his frame filling most of the space in the bedroom doorway, a gun evident in hand, the resultant silhouette creating a macabre image. From his trouser pocket Willie pulled out a set of police issue handcuffs and with extreme caution edged slowly to the side of the bed where Fergal was laying, fast asleep, his right arm resting on Shannon, his other arm lying slightly behind him.

A beam of moonlight through the thin translucent curtains threw an ethereal light over the sleeping couple. If Willie had had a heart he would have paused and said, "Ah." But Willie was as cruel, heartless and ruthless as 'Old Nick' himself. If ever a vacancy occurred in hell then Willie, along with his arch nemesis Eamon, would be the men to apply.

Willie stealthily crept to the bedside, tucked his gun loosely in his coat pocket, hesitated, then leant over the bed, gently cuffing Fergal's left wrist. Subconsciously feeling what he considered to be Shannon's touch Fergal emitted a sound of contentment but did not move. Taking hold of Fergal's right arm Willie yanked the arm with a sudden jerk, bringing it level with the left wrist, almost breaking Fergal's arm in the process.

Fergal awoke with a jolt of excruciating pain, yelling out, "What the fuck!"

Shannon stirred but her fatigued body remained asleep.

Before Fergal had the chance to rationalise what was happening to him Willie had forced the man's right hand next to the left, securing the other half of the handcuffs on Fergal's right wrist, ensuring that Fergal's hands were now securely cuffed behind his back. He stepped clear of the bed just as Fergal moved his upper torso, attempting to lash out with his feet.

He withdrew his revolver.

Fergal yelped with a mixture of pain and surprised shock, the handcuffs biting into his flesh as he tried to pull his arms free. "What the fuck is going on!" Now fully awake, his bleary eyes saw a large man silhouetted in front of him and he drew in a breath of dismay, "Oh fucking hell, what the hell do you want? Are you immigration?" He stiffened, registering that a gun was aimed at him, a mere six inches from his face.

"Be quiet you Provo scumbag; I think it's time that you and I had a meaningful talk," Willie announced with gleeful menace.

Shannon jolted, her eyes opening in surprise and shock at the unexpected intruder, "What's going on, who the hell are you?" Her upper body rose from the bed, revealing her nakedness.

Willie smirked lewdly and in a cold voice heavily laden with oppressive intimidation ordered, "Be quiet tart and behave or I'll have to shoot you. And don't scream; I hate screaming women - I'd have to smash your mouth up before shooting you. I might even want to cut out your tongue. So, keep quiet and keep the fuck out of this!"

Shannon closed her mouth but realising that this intruder fiend was ogling her naked breasts she slowly reached for the sheet, pulling it up to her neck.

Willie licked his lips, his eyes full with lust, "Small boobs but not bad."

Shannon didn't know whether to cry out, "Cheeky Bastard" or "Fuck off pervert," but she held her tongue, wondering if she could reach her gun concealed in her handbag. She would need to be careful, biding her time, until she could find out who this prowler was.

Willie went to the light switch and switched it on just as Shannon was in the process of leaping out of the bed. Turning to look at her, he smiled leeringly and salivated as he ogled her nakedness.

Fergal and Shannon blinked in the harsh light, Shannon sheepishly crawling back under the sheets, Willie watching her every inch of the way.

Fergal sucked in his breath, feeling that his temples were going to implode. A mixture of total dismay and utter hopelessness swept through his body like an electric shock passing from his toes to his scalp. He wanted to run, to hide, to scream, to crawl in a hole and disappear. "Oh God! Dear God, *No!*" he muttered eventually finding his tongue, "It's fucking Willie Davidson, the mad, perverted Ulster policeman."

Shannon held her breath, her eyes seeking any weapon that they might be able to use to fend off this corrupt British policeman. She was angry with herself for having been careless.

"Dirty little murdering Provo scumbag, you can't talk to me like that." Willie marched forward and pistol whipped Fergal, causing him to flop back on to his pillow, a nasty gash opening on his forehead.

Furious and fired up in readiness to defend her man Shannon sprang to Fergal's defence but Willie retreated, her hands missing him, Shannon merely falling across Fergal,

Annoyed at the 'whore's' aggression, Willie slapped her hard across the face and grasping the back of her head, he forced her head downwards so that her face was pressing on Fergal's groin, separated only by the bed sheet. With Fergal's arms secured behind his back and she with her face pressed firmly against Fergal, Willie depressed his gun into the back of Shannon's neck, tightening his grip on the trigger.

His feelings of total contempt directed at the person who he considered to be Fergal's bit of skirt, his tart, his slag, he snarled, "Typical bloody whore; even in moments like this you can't resist being depraved, trying to give this terrorist shit a blow job. Well, if you behave, I might let you nibble on something of mine a little later."

Fury replacing fear, Fergal attempted to head-butt Willie but was unable to reach anywhere close to his target and cried out in frustration, "You really are depraved, you son of a bitch. Touch her and I swear I'll *kill* you!"

Willie used his left hand to jab at Fergal's face but because his other hand was occupied keeping his gun pressurised into the back of Shannon's neck the punch had minimum effect.

As Willie and Fergal exchanged a look of mutual contempt Shannon tried to raise her head but Willie's gun pressed down harder, forming a weal on her skin. "Keep down bitch," he ordered, "Or I *will* kill you."

"What do you want Willie," asked Fergal in a resigned and weary tone, belied by his glaring eyes full of hatred.

Willie permitted a smile to form on his lips, the smile across his face feeling uncomfortable and not at peace with the evil pervading from within; the smile appeared so out of place, a macabre jest, an insult to mirth, at odds to normality, the face having stolen the emotion in contrast to a grimace or sad snarl which would have been more appropriate, more at home, on his evil visage. "I want to know where the proof is regarding Alistair Glen and Colm," he demanded, the cold, heartless eyes unflinching in their evil menace.

Fergal was taken by surprise, "How the hell did you know?" Quickly attempting to regain his composure he feigned ignorance, "I don't know what you're talking about."

"Oh, I think you do. In fact I know you do." Willie smirked, "I also heard you and your whore discussing it in Macy's bar. I was there."

"I thought something evil and slimy had crawled its way in there; I had a bad feeling," Shannon muttered, her voice partially muffled by the bed sheet.

"Shut up whore." Willie pressed down on her neck.

"Ow, you're hurting," she wailed.

"Leave her alone arsehole," Fergal's voice registered a mix of compassion for Shannon and indignity for her treatment.

Willie fixed his eyes on Fergal. "Any more crap out of your whore and this time I'll pull the trigger adding another hole to the slut's body. Now, tell me about the proof, the proof of the relationship between Glen and Colm."

"Go screw yourself!" retorted Fergal.

"You will tell me," Willie eyes flickered to Shannon, "If you don't then your whore will get even more pleasure from me than she could ever had hoped for. Even more than Colm's whore got, and she screamed with pleasure right to the end."

Livid, Fergal spiralled forward, missing Willie who merely edged backwards, the net result being Shannon's nose receiving a nasty thump. With aggrieved venom and frustration at his inability to defend Shannon, Fergal yelled, "Touch her Willie and I swear you will never rest. I'll follow you to the ends of the earth. I'll feed your balls to the fish."

Revelling in his power and merely amused at Fergal's words, Willie responded in a voice heavy with mocking contempt, "Now I really *am* scared; nasty little scumbag is going to hurt me." Hastily taking two paces forward, he gripped hold of Shannon's hair, forcibly pulling her head up, the pain bringing tears to her eyes. Again Fergal pathetically and ineffectually lunged forward but this time Willie brought up his gun hand, smashing the weapon against Fergal's face.

Fergal's lips were split open, his mouth also cut, a tooth chip falling out. Dazed, he collapsed back onto the bed.

With her hair held in a vice like grip Shannon could not pull free or resist, her eyes filling with tears of pain. Pulling her by her hair Willie tugged her off the bed, dragging her stumbling body across the room. Shannon wished she could resist, do something, but with Willie's strength and the pain she was just unable to break free. Half stumbling, trying to keep her feet, half being pulled, she followed Willie.

Dazed from the blow from the gun and feeling angry at his inadequacy to protect Shannon, Fergal's eyes blazed with frustrated fury, his body tensing ready for the opportunity that might come his way. Come what may he was going to leap out of bed and jump at Willie, perhaps using his shoulder as a battering-ram to batter Willie against the wall or cupboard door.

Dragging Shannon across the room, Willie sensed that Fergal was about to move, to try his luck, and he glanced over his shoulder, mirthfully stating, "Go on, just try it. If you want to be stupid then I'll just blow her brains out and concentrate on you. Your whore doesn't have to take part in this but if you want her to, well then I will be only too happy to have fun with her; it's entirely up to you."

Fergal, impotent, beaten and frustrated, subsided onto his pillow, his sullen, crestfallen face indicating a thousand regrets. "Please leave her alone, I won't try anything."

"That's better." Willie turned his contemptuous and venomous attention on Shannon, "Now, young *Lady*," (only Willie could make the word 'Lady' so disgusting and degrading), "I'm going to tie you up. If you resist, I'll just pull the trigger, but before you're dead I'll still have some fun with your body. Please believe me that your death would mean nothing to me; your being alive doesn't do much for me either." He chuckled before harshly demanding, "*Understand?*"

Shannon, tears of pain in her eyes, replied almost inaudibly, "Yes."

Willie dragged the hapless Shannon to the bedroom chair and pulled the cord from a dressing gown that had previously been discarded over the chair.

Fergal pleaded, "Willie, let her get dressed, and let her go. I'll tell you everything."

Willie retaining his grip on Shannon's hair, jovially responded, "You'll tell me everything regardless."

Fergal desperately wanted to find a way of getting Shannon out of this situation; he didn't want any more blood on his hands and certainly not the blood of someone who he had recently come to care so much about. He decided to play for time. "You may think so but how do you know what I'll tell you would be the truth."

Willie's voice was full of heavy sarcasm, "And, of course, letting her go would ensure that truth?"

"Yes," Fergal's tone was eagerly naive.

"You really must think that I was born yesterday. Now shut up while I tie your whore up." He grinned at Fergal. "Perhaps we can indulge in a bit of bondage later."

Fergal's face was like thunder, the blood pounding inside his head like a raging torrent.

Chortling merrily, Willie pushed Shannon face down on the chair, ready to tie her up, caressing her naked buttock with the pistol and silencer.

Fergal angrily barked, "Show her some respect, damn you!"

"Respect? For a whore? And a whore who's slept with *you* - you've got to be kidding. Any woman who spends her time with scum like you doesn't deserve any respect." He tightened his grip on Shannon's hair, demanding, "Do you, darling?" He licked her face, his rough tongue leaving a smear of spittle on her cheek.

Almost gagging with revulsion, she faintly replied, "No."

Fergal very much afraid for Shannon's well-being decided that he had to tell Willie the information requested. Determining his plan of action, he hurriedly declared, "The proof you need, about Alistair and Colm, well it's in London."

"Where in London?"

"With a journalist friend; she doesn't know what she's holding."

"Who is she?"

"Let Shannon go."

"Who's the woman in London?"

"If I tell you any more then there will be no reason to let Shannon go, so I've got nothing to lose if I don't reveal the information until I know Shannon's going to be okay."

Shannon squealed as Willie exerted greater pressure on her, pulling her hair tighter, while forcing his knee into the small of her back. "So, the whore has name and an Irish name to boot; might have known you 'Micks' would find each other."

Aching with frustrated impotence, Fergal protested, "The more you do that, the less I'm going to co-operate. Stop hurting her and let her get dressed."

Willie stymied, swore at Fergal, "Damn you, you fucking shitbag!" He released his grip on her hair and grasping her by the arm, flung Shannon, hard, against the floor, her body crashing heavily downward, the beginnings of a large bruise instantly forming which grew, spreading in a light purplish hue, across her shoulder. "Get dressed whore, but crawl to your clothes; I don't trust you."

Willie backed-off a couple of steps from Shannon, his gun still pointed at her head. With one eye on the fuming Fergal and the second fixed on Shannon he enjoyed watching Shannon crawling on all fours towards her underwear, previously discarded at the base of the bed.

Shannon picked up the knickers that she had hastily and enthusiastically discarded only a few hours earlier under much more pleasant emotional circumstances and, with some belated attempt at modesty, turned her back, attempting to discreetly put on her underwear.

Willie was having none of it, barking out, "Face me whore."

Reluctantly and angrily, Shannon turned to face Willie, quickly slipping one leg into her knickers.

"Slowly, whore; I don't want you to make any sudden movements."

Sick to the pit of her stomach, Shannon slowly put on her knickers and then her bra, all under the salivating features of Willie.

Fergal twitched, instantly Willie's gun pointing in his direction. With steam almost rising from Fergal's overheated head he had no option but to let this depraved son of bitch enjoy his own personal peep show.

Shannon stood, her arms unnecessarily protective in front of her previously exposed body. "My skirt and blouse are in the other room."

Willie smirked, "Couldn't wait to strip off for the scumbag, eh?" He stepped between Shannon and the doorway, glanced out into the room, and spotted Shannon's dropped clothes. "Okay, we'll get them, together." He warned Fergal, "If you so much as move an inch I'll blow the whore's head off, okay?"

Fergal nodded in affirmation, his eyes brimming with hatred.

Willie gripped Shannon's arm with an intense force and forced the tip of his silencer into the side of her head. "Walk slowly with me whore, pick up your clothes and bring them back in here." Leaving the bedroom, Willie instantly alert to the movement from the direction of the bed, called out, "I can hear you moving; don't forget I'm in control of your whore." He pressed the Silencer hard into Shannon's head making her squeal and causing a small nick on her temple.

"Don't hurt her, damn you," yelled out Fergal, "I'm not moving; I had a touch of cramp and only shifted my leg."

Shannon scooped up her clothes, then under Willie's firm and painful grip they made their way back to Fergal's bedroom. As soon as they returned to the room Willie released his grip, pushing Shannon away with great force. She stumbled in the direction of the chair but managed to keep on her feet. An enormous weal had formed right round her arm, matching the pressure points of Willie's powerful grip.

Shannon quickly dressed, the anger welling up within her soul; she had not realised until this day, this moment, of the fury capable of rising within her bosom.

Willie stepped to Fergal's side of the bed. "Right, now tell me, who's the woman in London?"

Reluctantly, eyes on fire with hatred, Fergal spat out the woman's name, "Melanie Bright."

Willie whistled in surprise, "Not *the* Melanie Bright, the famous English reporter? That's a laugh, she's very anti-crime. I don't believe you. How would a shit like you know her?"

"It's true, I'm afraid. Melanie was working on an undercover report on rehabilitated ex-terrorists, especially those currently in prisons. However, something happened and the BBC pulled the plug on her assignment."

"But why would she keep your possessions at her house?"

"She doesn't."

Willie's eyes narrowed; he raised his gun, taking a step closer to Fergal, "Don't get smart with me."

Shannon spotting an opportunity, inched towards the bedroom door, but Willie alert to the movement turned his head sharply in her direction, "Don't even think about it. I'd put a bullet through your beautiful arse. You'd be dead before you even reached the door."

Shannon stopped in her tracks.

Willie waved his gun at Shannon and pointed the weapon in the direction of the chair, "You get back here and sit on that chair where you'll be fully in my vision."

Annoyed with herself and her helplessness, she meekly complied.

Stepping to the bed, Willie reached forward making Fergal flinch at the anticipated blow. But instead Willie, still keeping one eye on Shannon, grasped hold of the sheet and tugged it towards him. With the help of his gun barrel, he ripped the bed sheet apart, taking the torn bundle over to Shannon. "Tear that into long strips and tie his legs together."

Shannon gaped at the sheet and, doubtfully, at Fergal. "Now, whore, do it now," ordered Willie. "You really are becoming a pain in the arse." Taking a pace towards Shannon, his face illuminated absolute evil.

Reluctantly, Shannon complied, tearing the sheet into strips and then, smiling with reassuring bravado at Fergal, she reluctantly tied his legs together.

First ensuring that she stood clear from him, Willie checked the tightness and not satisfied, made her tie the strips even tighter to the extent that the blood circulation was almost cut off from Fergal's feet.

Shannon protested, "But if I do it this tightly his circulation will be cut."

"Just do it whore, just do it; like I care if his circulation is cut off anyway."

Chapter 39

A car drew into the kerb outside Fergal's apartment block, three men quietly exiting the vehicle, none of them firmly closing their doors, merely pushing them until they heard a click of contact. If the car were to be stolen, a proposition very likely in this neighbourhood, then that would be of little or no consequence to these men.

The men entered Fergal's Tenement Block and finding the front door unsecured, they exchanged glances, cautiously making their way inside the building. Silently climbing the steps to the first floor they paused as a door opened, people spilling out from a room, voices raised in argument. A sudden slap was heard, silence, more heated words, and then two doors were simultaneously slammed shut. The quiet stillness descended as quickly as it had been shattered only moments before, once again bringing back the silent calm of the deep of the night.

The three men waited with bated breath for movement or any more activity but all was now quiet. The first man indicated to the others that they should proceed and they followed him, quietly continuing their journey to Fergal's apartment.

*   *   *

Peering round the corner, Pat Creary recoiled and swore under his breath. He had just seen three men exit from a car with one of them withdrawing what was obviously a weapon, the street light glinting off the metal. To Pat, they looked like Feds.

"Oh shit," he muttered, "What the fuck are they doing here?" He quickly retraced his steps to the pick-up parked in this side street.

Seamus was picking at his nails, removing the dirt underneath and flicking it on the floor of the pick-up. "What's up?" he demanded, recognising the look on Pat's face, a look reminiscent from past experience of aborted operations.

"It's the fucking Feds; they've beaten us to it"

"But isn't Willie already inside? We watched him go in."

"I couldn't give a fuck about Willie," snapped Pat, "Fergal's our main target. Willie's only to be taken out if he gets in the way. We'll just have to wait and see what happens. But if the Feds do leave with Fergal and Willie, then we'll have a quick decision to make".

"I'm not shooting any American cops or anyone from the FBI," protested Seamus, "Me and Enya have a new life here and I don't want to fuck it up like before."

"You'll fucking do what I say if it's necessary", growled Pat, "I'm not screwing with Liam's instructions".

Chapter 40

Secure in the knowledge that Fergal was securely bound, hand and foot, and being unaware of Shannon's operational FBI background, Willie merely ordered her to sit quietly on the chair. Rather than considering her as a potential threat, he only classified her as a source of pleasure. He still hadn't made up his mind as to how he was going to enjoy this woman, but that would be later and he licked his lips in anticipation. Firstly, back to the more important business at hand.

He towered above Fergal, a large smirk spreading over his face, "Right, let's try again. Where's the proof?"

"I told you, with Melanie Bright."

"That's it, I've had enough and I've lost my patience." He bawled at Shannon, "Get undressed; your boyfriend obviously doesn't care about you. So, I'm going to show him how to love a woman."

Shannon fearfully aghast, gawped in horror at Fergal.

Emotions straining beyond anything he'd ever experienced, Fergal frantically babbled, "No, don't! Melanie's got a safety deposit box. All my stuff is kept in a locked box in her bank safety deposit."

"Then why," asked Willie suspiciously, "Particularly, because she's a reporter, why hasn't she used your information for her own benefit, for a scoop?"

Fergal afraid for Shannon, desperate to please Willie, to keep him from despoiling his new love, swiftly explained, "Melanie has no idea what my box contains. As far as she was concerned I had had a bad past, realised the errors of my ways and was, one day, hoping to make a new life. She believes that my box only contains all my worldly goods, which in fact, it actually does."

Willie's lips formed into a combination of a grimace and a smile and pointing his gun in Fergal's face he prepared to fire, "Right, I don't need you anymore."

Shannon tensed, ready for action; she was not prepared for either of them to die without some last desperate action on her part. For God's sake, she was a trained FBI Agent; she must be able to do something.

"Now hold on," pleaded Fergal, "You still need me...us. Y need a series of numbers to open the box, numbers tha' only to Melanie and me."

"What are the numbers?"

"Let Shannon go."

Willie glanced at Shannon. "Oh sure, I'm just going to let my bargaining piece go like that."

"Then you'll just have to kill me, but I'm not going to say any more until I know that Shannon is safe," Fergal spoke with a calmness that was not matched by his racing heart. "If I give you the numbers now, you'll just kill both of us anyway."

Irked at being thwarted once more, Willie grabbed Fergal by his hair and pulled his head back.

Seizing her moment, Shannon slipped off her chair, taking a step towards them both but Willie instantly pointed the gun in her direction; she froze.

Keeping one eye on Shannon, Willie stuck the silencer barrel into Fergal's mouth making Fergal gag and he slightly rotated his head, trying not to vomit.

"Now talk," demanded Willie, "Tell me the numbers!"

Fergal, eyes watering, close to choking, could not speak.

"Oh terrific, you stupid moron," protested Shannon, "How the hell do you think that he can talk with that gun in his mouth?"

Petulant at being spoken to in such a manner, Willie focused his evil eyes on Shannon, "Don't push your luck whore, nobody calls me a moron. It would cause me very little lost sleep to put a bullet through your head." But he glanced down at his gun realising that Shannon was correct, and removed it from Fergal's mouth, a confused frown spreading across his forehead. Then he hesitated, reflecting on his options for a moment. Looking intently at Shannon, he glanced down at his spittle covered barrel and then having decided what to do, he used the bed sheet to clean the barrel.

"Okay, I'll make a deal," Willie declared to Fergal, "Your whore can stand just inside the living room, in my view, with the front door of the flat left open. You give the numbers, with one hundred percent proof that they are correct, and then she can run. That's the best, and only deal, that I can offer."

Feeling that a weight was now dropping from him, Fergal's eyes softened as he gazed with a mixture of resignation, and yet relief, at Shannon; wearily he nodded his head in agreement. At least she now had a chance which was so much more than she had a moment ago. I hope that she makes it, he thought to himself.

Willie fixed Shannon with a malevolent glare, his voice full of threatening menace, "If you try anything, or call the police, not only will I make his death very painful but you can rest assured that I'll track you down, and when I do, you'll wish that you'd never been born. I never fail."

Shannon glanced dubiously at Fergal but he merely nodded back at her and smiled, a sad smile indicating fondness, regret and farewell.

Frowning with a fierce intensity, she exited the bedroom, closely followed by Willie, the gun barrel pressed tightly in her back.

Pleased with his decision, but not satisfied because he liked to make his victims suffer and had anticipated spending some self-indulgent time with this whore, Willie exclaimed, "Well, it seems that your whore can live without you, lover boy."

Shannon opened the apartment door.

* * *

When the door to Fergal's apartment opened, the leading man outside in the corridor hastily indicated to his two companions to be silent; unnecessarily, he also pointed to the floor, the other two already having hit the deck. All three individuals remained absolutely motionless.

* * *

Willie stuck his head out, peering into the gloom of the corridor and down the stairway, muttering, "I thought I heard something." Glancing back at Shannon, he shrugged, and once again peered into the darkened hallway.

A thud emanated from Fergal's bedroom.

Willie gripped Shannon's arm, whispering in her ear, "Come on, your little shit of a boyfriend is trying to be clever." She was forced back inside the room to a point where Willie could keep his eye on her whilst speaking to Fergal in the bedroom. "Move before I tell you and I will kill him and then I will get you before you can get half way down those stairs." With one eye fixed on her, he hastily shuffled sideways back into the bedroom.

Arms handcuffed behind him, Fergal was hopping towards the window figuring that if he could distract Willie, or open the window and call for help, or do anything to help Shannon to escape, then that was the least he owed her; he didn't care about his own life, only wanting Shannon to have maximum chance of survival.

Willie aimed his gun, his voice a mixture of amusement and threat, "And where do you think you're going? I thought we had come to an arrangement." He turned his weapon to point in

Shannon's direction, "Oh well, I might as well shoot her now."

Desperate, his face etched in horror, Fergal pleaded, "No, no, don't, I'm sorry. Do as we agreed and I'll give you the numbers."

Willie grimaced, "That's more like it. Now, get back on to the bed."

Not forgetting Shannon, he gave her a reminder of her situation, "Remember, don't move until I tell you that you can go; stay just over there, without flinching." With merriment, he added as an afterthought, "I hope that you're a good runner."

Shannon suddenly tensed, alerted to a movement in the shadows, a crouching figure cautiously entering through the open apartment door. She started in surprise and was on the verge of crying out when the person stepped closer into a beam of moonlight, with a finger raised to his lips. She almost wept with relief – it was Jim! Thank God, thank God, thank God, she thought.

The grin starting to spread across her face was immediately halted realising that Willie could see her and containing herself, she adopted her previous bewildered and scared expression.

Having discerned an imperceptible rustle, Willie glanced in Shannon's direction but satisfied that she hadn't moved, stepped a pace closer to Fergal, "Come on, no more prating about...the numbers, and proof that they are correct. I won't take any more of your crap."

Fergal closed his eyes, the sweat pouring down his brow. "Give her a proper chance to get out."

Willie's reply was almost a growl, "The numbers; I need the proof that you have on Colm being Alistair's father. I'll show that bloody renegade Prime Minister of ours who's top dog."

Simon, one of the three men who had surreptitiously entered Fergal's apartment, was shocked and stunned, and exchanged glances with Daniel. Silently he mouthed, "How? How does he know?"

Daniel shrugged, mouthing in return, "No idea."

Simon raised his hand and using his fingers, indicating one, two, paused, and then pointed to Shannon, three. With one and two he indicated the occupants of the bedroom, next with the third raised digit, he again pointed at Shannon, drawing his hand across his neck.

Daniel nodded in agreement, taking his gun from his holster.

Shannon, in the dim light, was unaware of the unspoken conversation between Simon and Daniel.

Meanwhile in the bedroom, Fergal pointed his head in the direction of a chest of drawers, "The numbers, and proof you need, are over there."

Willie glanced in the direction indicated by Fergal but remained stationery, staring quizzically at Fergal.

"It's in the top drawer; get my wallet."

Dubious, suspicious, Willie edged from Fergal, glancing occasionally in Shannon's direction, and quickly went to the chest of drawers. He yanked open the top drawer with such force that it came all the way out, crashing onto the floor. Startled by the sudden noise created by his actions, he cried out, "*Shit!*"

Shannon jumped and peering into Fergal's bedroom, called out in a voice full of panic and concern, "Fergal, you okay?"

Daniel, gun in hand, quietly dived behind the armchair positioned furthest from Shannon and crouched, ready for action. Shannon's leg, involuntarily, began to twitch with a nervous energy. Simon edged along the wall towards the bedroom door, Jim holding his position behind the armchair nearest to Shannon, his first thought being to protect one of his Agents. He was totally unaware of the previous exchange of signals between Simon and Daniel.

Picking up the fallen drawer, Willie shouted, "He's fine. I just dropped a drawer."

With his tense voice being as dry as the times when he'd consumed a bottle of Jack Daniels, Fergal called out in an almost croaking voice, "I'm fine Shannon. Get ready to run; he's a murdering bastard."

"I'll keep my word," bawled Willie, "I said that I would give you a chance, and I will." Finding Fergal's wallet, he took it over to the now prone Fergal and held the wallet in front of him, "Here you are; show me the numbers."

Fergal, twisting, managed to hold the wallet, opening it with great difficulty behind his back. He slipped out a piece of paper from one of the wallet's compartments, "The numbers are 6, 8, 0, and 1." He suddenly shouted, "Run Shannon, run, run like hell!"

Reaching for the wallet and paper, Willie growled "You piece of shit," and turned to pursue Shannon.

Fergal tried to intercept him, "Here, hold it. Take the paper, it's the proof you need...let her go."

Willie's hesitation should have given Shannon a fair start but as Fergal peered over towards the living room he was astounded that she had remained rooted to the same spot, her face appearing serene and calm in the gloom.

Willie grinned triumphantly at Fergal, "Your whore didn't move."

Fergal moaned, complaining in bitter despair, "For God's sake Shannon, why didn't you run?"

Confused at the turn of events, Willie contemplated for an instant, stared intently at Shannon, then back at the wallet and piece of paper; he assumed that Shannon had been too petrified to move and with that conclusion, he returned, victorious, to Fergal's side.

A sudden thump shattered the silence in the apartment, a small table being knocked over by Simon in the living room.

Willie rushed to the bedroom doorway, "What are you doing? You've left it too late to escape!" He aimed his gun at Shannon.

Staring at the gun, sentient to Willie's finger tightening on the trigger, Shannon plunged into the kitchen, her legs leaving the room at the same instant that Willie fired his gun, the bullet thudding harmlessly into the living room wall.

Jim's gun, aimed at the bedroom doorway, jammed, and he banged it on the floor in frustration, "Fuck it; it's jammed, quick, shoot the bastard!" he bellowed. Peering from behind the armchair, Daniel let loose a round of shots, firing in the general direction of the bedroom doorway but missed with all of them.

Willie had jumped back into the bedroom, pressing himself close against the bedroom wall.

"You pair of prats!" ranted Simon, "Another second and I would have had him point blank as he left the room."

Jim snarled with fury, "Don't you call me a prat. You weren't the one in his line of fire, Shannon was."

Still crouching behind the farthest armchair, Daniel whispered, "Guys, I can hear movement in the block. We need to get this over with."

Jim called out to Shannon, "You okay Shannon; are you hit?"

Before she could reply, Simon intervened, "Shut up will you; we can sort her well-being out in a minute."

Willie was spread-eagled against the bedroom wall, sweating, confused, afraid. He shouted through the wall, "Who's there? I've got a hostage."

Simon glanced over at Daniel, who responded, "We're FBI and the guy you've got there is no hostage."

"What do you mean 'no hostage'?" Willie peered dubiously at Fergal, "Try anything and I'll kill him."

Dismissively, Daniel nonchalantly retorted, "Kill him or don't kill him, it's of no interest to us. Just throw your gun out and come out with your hands up."

"*Fuck* off," yelled Willie.

Pressed against the other side of the wall from Willie, Simon called out cheerfully, "We can do this the hard way or the easy way Willie."

Willie was now unsure of his ground. Like all bullies he was fine when he had the upper hand but now he was becoming scared. Nervously he yelled, "Who is that? How do you know my name?"

"I know your name, I know who you are, what you are. I know all about you Willie Davidson," replied Simon, his voice partially muffled by the dividing wall.

Fergal, also sweating, remained motionless on the bed, his eyes frantically searching left to right. He didn't feel that he could win either way but would prefer to be in the clutches of the FBI rather than this mad, bent and corrupt policeman.

Willie sensed that the voice he heard was somehow familiar; it sounded like Simon but it couldn't be; Simon was in England.

Simon spoke again, convincing Willie, that voice, he couldn't mistake it; it had to be Simon's voice. Dubiously, he yelled, "Simon...Simon Harvey? Is that you?"

"Of course it's me, now drop the gun and come out."

"Who's that with you?"

"It's as the guy said, the FBI."

Willie mimicked, his voice mocking, "The FBI, balls. Aggressively, he added, "Cut the fucking crap and tell me what's going on." He glanced at Fergal, "I'll blow the fucking hostage's head off."

Simon laughed and with a voice full of wry amusement, countered, "We really don't care about him Willie. Fergal has long since been of little interest to the FBI or the British Government. As far as we are concerned he's dead...or soon will be."

Fergal's blood ran cold.

Alarmed and quickly becoming unnerved, Willie hastily shouted, "But I've got something that you guys would love to have. Fergal's proof of a connection between the Prime Minister and Colm O'Driscoll, and I've got the numbers of the safety box where the information is locked away. So, let's talk."

"Talk?" retorted Daniel, "We've got nothing to talk about. You ain't going nowhere."

Simon whispered loudly to Daniel, "Shush. We need to talk him out, not threaten him out."

Willie overheard, "That's right Simon; tell that blockhead that he's dealing with a professional."

"A professional!" riposted Daniel, "That's a joke."

Willie scanned the bedroom searching for possible vantage points or an escape route, his eyes settling on the window. He checked his .357 Magnum revolver. Quickly, he pulled another gun from his sock holster, a Smith and Wesson Model 19, a small lightweight revolver approximately six inches in length and which he had acquired for 'emergency' purposes. Cautiously edging towards the open doorway, he yelled, "Okay, I'm coming out. We can talk this through."

"That's being sensible," replied Simon, sneering.

As the gun slid out of the bedroom and along the floor, Daniel rose from behind his armchair and stepped towards the bedroom doorway but Willie's head and arm suddenly appeared in the door frame, his hand holding his .357 Magnum revolver.

Fergal, too late, cried out, "*No*! Look out! He's got another gun."

Willie fired indiscriminately, rapidly shooting off four rounds into the living room, hitting Daniel at short range, and creating a booming, deafening sound within the flat. As he released the fourth shot, he dropped to the floor, rolling past the open doorway, and towards the window.

Daniel collapsing, fired a couple of rounds from his gun, the shots just missing Simon as he was rushing forward ready to shoot Willie. Simon ducked, dropping to the floor, Daniel's bullets embedding themselves harmlessly into the wall.

Crouching, Jim rushed towards the kitchen to check on the very quiet Shannon who lay flat on the kitchen floor. He breathed an immense sigh of relief when she rose to her haunches, a small trickle of blood dribbling from a wound evident on her neck. "Did you get him?"

Jim answered in the negative.

Shannon alarmed, wanted to know about Fergal, "What about Fergal?" And being given Jim's indifferently reply, she attempted to push past him into the bedroom.

Jim restrained her, "We'll sort it. How about you, there's blood on your neck?"

Shannon touched her neck and then glanced dismissively at the trickle of blood on her hand, "He only grazed me; I'll be fine."

In the bedroom, Willie got to his feet, checking that no one was about to enter from the open door and quickly opened the window.

Fergal cried out, "He's getting away - the window!"

Willie stopped, turned to Fergal, aimed and pulled the trigger.

Summoning up a superhuman effort, Fergal desperately rolled across the bed, landing with a thump on the floor but was hit.

Seizing his opportunity, Simon determinedly rushed into the room but took a hit on the gun in his hand, the gun spinning spectacularly out of his grasp, sliding under the bed.

Shannon screamed, "Fergal! Oh no, you murdering bastard." And breaking free from Jim's restraint she rushed to the bedroom.

Concerned that Daniel hadn't moved or spoken, Jim rushed to his superior's side, "You all right Daniel?"

There was no response. "Daniel?" He rolled him over, instantly seeing a serrated bullet hole in his superior's forehead, a pool of blood forming under the body. "Oh shit, he's been shot, dead!" The gun firmly gripped in Daniel's lifeless hand.

Shannon dashing into the bedroom, rapidly ducked, crouching to the floor, as Willie aimed his weapon at her. Expecting to be killed this time for sure she was amazed that her only pain was when her knee hit the floor; by some miracle she was still alive. Fortunately for her, Willie's gun was empty, his finger clicking on empty cylinders, he hadn't thought to check how many bullets he had.

In a fit of pique he threw the weapon at the now advancing Simon who had been cowering on his knees, and with one leap, Willie rolled out of the window, hanging by his fingertips for a second before subsequently disappearing below.

Running into the bedroom Jim collided with Simon who was lunging after Willie, both tumbling in a heap on the floor.

Simon quickly picked himself up, raging at Jim, "You bloody idiot, you're letting him get away." He tried to snatch the gun from Jim, but Jim was not prepared to let this maverick British guy loose in his own territory.

"No, I can get him," he snapped.

Coming to terms that she was still alive, Shannon noticed the bloodstained bed and the empty space where Fergal had been. "Oh God Fergal, what has he done to you?"

Simon furiously tried to wrestle the gun away from Jim but Jim was not going to let go. Frustrated and angry, Simon punched Jim hard on the chin, catching him by surprise and knocking him to the floor. He snatched the gun from Jim's hands and leapt towards the window, firing repeatedly and indiscriminately at the base of the building and along the sidewalk, aiming at the fleeing Willie.

Groggily, Jim got to his feet, staggering towards Simon. "If you haven't hit him by now then leave it; you'll kill innocent people down there. Cease firing!"

Simon ignored him and taking a spare cartridge pack from his pocket, he reloaded Daniel's Colt .22 automatic pistol; fortunately, Daniel had previously ensured that all three of them had each been issued with the very reliable Colt .22 automatic plus spare cartridges. Ignoring Jim, Simon leant out of the window and continued shooting into the distance.

Jim was outraged and grappled Simon, twisting him round to face the room, in the process managing to successfully knock the gun from Simon's hand, the Colt .22 dropping to the floor.

Surprised and momentarily nonplussed, fury and venom on his face, Simon exploded, "Why, you little fucker! I'll fucking kill *you*!"

Jim backed off a couple of paces, calmly explaining, "You could have murdered innocent people."

Simon furious, screeched, "*You've* let Willie go - I can't believe you stopped *me*!"

Jim was disgusted with this ranting British Agent standing in front of him and quietly but firmly retorted, "You're crazy. As I said, you could have shot an innocent person, firing indiscriminately like that. There are people down there."

Simon was unrelenting in his fury, "Letting Willie go with what he now knows will jeopardise the whole operation!"

"I'm sick of this operation!" angrily retorted Jim.

Shannon knelt down besides Fergal's prone, blood stained body and with tears in her eyes lifted Fergal's head, cradling it in her lap. As the tears rolled down her cheeks, she lamented, "You poor misguided idiot, what has that corrupt murdering bastard done to you?"

Simon stared at her with disdain, "Don't waste your tears on him; he's a nobody...and he wasn't innocent."

Shannon, her cheeks stained with tears, glared up at Simon, "And I suppose you are?"

He picked up the fallen gun, approaching Shannon, "I haven't got time for this nonsense." He raised his gun.

Jim startled, intervened, "No! What are you doing?"

Stepping ominously towards Shannon, Simon coldly explained, "No one can be left to reveal this; Daniel agreed."

Physically shaken and furious at this sudden turn of events, Jim protested strongly, bawling out, "Well, *I* bloody well didn't agree!"

Outside, the sound of police sirens were growing closer, which together with the stirring movement of life within the building - a general bustle of movement growing within the tenement block - served to create a minor diversion. The tenants were cautiously opening their apartment doors, enquiring of their neighbours as to what the hell was going on, the non-law abiding people becoming nervous. Crack cocaine, heroin, and other forms of addictive drug dealers were hiding their stashes just in case a police raid was in progress. The more nervous criminals were disposing of the evidence within their apartments, a lot of 'good gear' being flushed down assorted toilets.

Momentarily distracted by the growing bustle, Simon hesitated, but then choosing to ignore the growing sound of peripheral noise, he turned his gun on Jim.

Dumbfounded by the current situation that they were now in Shannon's tears slowed to a few misty eyed drops; then she caught sight of something glinting under the bed - it was the gun originally used by Simon. Unaware of who owned the weapon, not minding whose gun it may have been, she just hoped to God that it was loaded. Gently lowering Fergal's head on to the floor, she surreptitiously reached with her right hand for the gun.

Simon's face contorted with ferocious, murderous intent as he advanced on Jim, who was backing off, edging away from the advancing madman until he could go no further, his body coming into contact with the bedroom wall.

With Simon's pent up fury focused elsewhere, Shannon picked up the gun, got to her feet and pointed the cocked weapon at Simon, screeching, "Hold it arsehole; leave him alone. Drop your gun."

Simon reeled round to face Shannon. There was a tense moment as both prepared to fire, Simon's eyes narrowing but he could see the determination born by grief etched on Shannon's face.

Jim waited breathless, ready to pounce if Simon's pressure increased on the trigger.

Simon attempted to kowtow her, taunting, "You haven't got the nerve to kill me in cold blood. Go on, pull the trigger."

"Don't tempt me, you piece of shit." Fierce and dogged determination etched on her features, she threatened, "I'm a bloody good shot and I'm in the mood to blow your fucking head off!"

Simon studied her for a moment then lowering his gun, he adopted a cool and controlled demeanour, and talking in a condescending tone, he muttered, "Stupid vacuous mad tart."

Jim relieved, moved off the wall, firmly demanding of Simon, "Give me back my gun."

Simon glanced at the gun in his hand and then looked at Jim.

Shannon tensed, ready to fire, her nerves taut, but Simon merely grinned wickedly, tossed the gun in the air so that he could hold it by the barrel and then flippantly passed the weapon to Jim.

Jim exhaled a huge sigh of relief, his tension draining away. With cold disdain he instructed Simon to disappear, "The police will be here any moment and one thing they shouldn't find is someone from British Intelligence involved in an internal States problem. I suggest you bugger off *now,* via the window."

Simon peered over his shoulder at the window and smiled, "That's okay by me; we can resolve this matter later."

"I don't think so." Jim's voice was cold and he continued with controlled anger, "As far as I am concerned, our mutual co-operation is over."

Simon protested, "But your President..."

"It's over!" snapped Jim, reiterating his point. "The President was liaising only through Daniel. Daniel is now dead."

Simon chuckled with arrogant contempt. "We'll see about that. Alistair will merely call your President on the hot line and have you removed and a new team set up."

Jim prodded his gun into Simon's chest, "I suggest you tell your Prime Minister that the FBI co-operation is over. I think that we've been duped long enough; you are all just cold-blooded killers, and

Pal," He added with irony, then switched back to cold aggression, "Tell your Prime Minister that Daniel's files on this operation will be circulated within the FBI, even if it costs me my job; your Prime Minister will no longer be able to indirectly influence the President in the misguided hope of a few Irish American votes. It's over, o.v.e.r., Get it?"

Simon remained motionless, sullenly staring into Jim's eyes. Eventually he nodded in confirmation but hating to lose, smirked cockily.

"Now get out," ordered Jim, "You really are a piece of shit. I can't believe we've had to work with garbage like you."

Climbing out of the window, Simon determined to have the last word, "You're bloody mad and I guarantee that you're going to regret this."

"Get out!" bellowed Jim.

Simon dropped out of the window and out of sight, Jim turning his attention to Shannon who was sitting by Fergal, once again cradling his limp body.

Holstering his gun, Jim shook his head in woe. "What a mess this has all turned out to be, and Daniel dead." He glanced at Fergal's lifeless form. "I'll call in a FBI sanitation unit; in the meantime we'll have some explaining to do to the local police." His eyes flicked to the hollow-eyed, tear stained Shannon. "Come on Shannon, put him down, there's nothing more that you can do."

Shannon vacantly caressing Fergal's head, ignored Jim and spoke to Fergal's body, "You stupid misguided idiot. Why did you have to die just as we were getting to know each other?"

Uncomfortable with the behaviour of his Agent, Jim ordered, "Come on Shannon, get a grip."

Shannon gaped at Jim, an expression of hopelessness on her face, "I really grew to like him Jim; he was a nice guy underneath all his personal issues."

One of Fergal's eyelids partially opened and he studied Shannon; the second eye opened and he smiled. Shannon looking back from Jim became aware that Fergal's eyes were open, watching her. After a fleeting second wherein shock passed through her, her expression of love instantly altered to one of annoyance.

Smiling and with a twinkle in his eye, Fergal announced, "It's nice to know you care."

Shannon was not pleased, her angry voice evidence of her

feelings, "You let me worry that you were dead!"

Fergal's smile broadened, "I thought that it was the safest thing, what with all those bullets flying around and with all those crazy people trying to kill me."

"Oooh, you bastard, you let me go through all those emotions!"

Fergal grinned but realising that she was still cradling Fergal's head, Shannon moved away from under him, letting his head fall to the floor with a bump.

"Ouch, that's not very nice," he protested.

"Neither are you," She pouted, pleased that he was alive but annoyed at being duped.

Fergal was aggrieved, "But I am wounded."

Shannon concern was re-awakened, "Is it bad?"

"We'd better get an ambulance," intervened Jim.

Struggling to his feet and groaning indulgently with the effort, Fergal was hurriedly aided and supported by Shannon, her sympathy instantly restored.

Gingerly exploring the wound in his side, Fergal was delighted to be alive after his very close call. "I don't think that it's too bad; the bullet went right through me." He looked to the far wall, at a spent bullet embedded within the plaster. "Luckily the second shot only grazed me and then embedded itself in the wall."

Shannon withdrew her hand from supporting Fergal, both she and Jim inspecting the bullet embedded in the wall. Then she checked Fergal's wound, his shirt now damp with blood. "You've been hit just below the rib cage; it looks as if the bullet only went through flesh, not hitting bone." Looking into Fergal's face, she smiled, "Luckily, you've got those love handles to protect you."

Although appreciating her humour, Fergal was slightly offended.

"You're one lucky son of a bitch," muttered Jim in amazement.

"I know," Fergal's voice was serious, the lucky escape making him feel vulnerable.

Jim concentrated his attention on Shannon, "When the sanitation unit gets here you can take Fergal to the hospital, have that wound treated and then you both better come in for a debriefing."

Fergal eyed Shannon suspiciously and with alarmed hurt, he berated, "You're one of them...FBI?" Bitterly disillusioned, he turned to exit, speaking acrimoniously over his shoulder. "I should have known; someone like you couldn't really have cared for a person like me. You were using me."

Shannon placed an affectionate hand on Fergal's arm, "Fergal, that's not true, and don't say you didn't enjoy it." She added with a gleam in her eye, "It needn't be over."

Fergal brushed off Shannon's hand, angrily snorting, "Get off me."

"Shannon, what are you doing?" demanded the perplexed Jim, "You know the rules about getting involved with case targets, and now Willie's got away probably because you became over familiar with your subject."

"Shut up Jim," She replied kindly, and implored to Fergal, "Fergal, yes, I was doing my job, but I really did get to like you. Well, actually, more than that."

Fergal upset, spitefully retorted, "You were just using me."

"It wasn't like that."

"I'm off."

Jim un-holstered his gun, pointing it at Fergal, "You're going nowhere."

The police car sirens having reached the building were soon followed by sounds of heavy footfalls running up the stairs, a voice calling out. "This is the Police. Throw down your weapons out and come out with your hands raised."

Jim yelled in response, "Okay, keep cool. This is an FBI operation; I'll explain everything to your senior officer. We'll come out with our hands up but we have one wounded colleague." He hissed at Fergal. "Co-operate, and you'll leave with my unit. Don't co-operate and you'll end up at the local police station, facing a possible murder charge."

"Murder? But I haven't killed anyone," protested Fergal.

"My colleague is dead in the other room."

"But that was nothing to do with me - you can't pin that on me."

Jim raised his finger to his lips indicating that Fergal should not argue any further; the choice was that he could either leave with them or leave in a police car and subsequently be locked up for murder.

Fergal grimaced, knowing that it was just not his day; he was sure that he'd had worse days but couldn't remember when. Reluctantly he agreed to go along with Jim's instruction and conscious that Shannon was watching him, scowled in a surly response.

Shannon felt wretched but slid her gun along the floor and out of the room and Jim followed her example as they exited the bedroom with hands raised behind their heads, permitting themselves to be temporary prisoners of the Boston Police Department.

Chapter 41

Pat Creary, having retaken his observation of Fergal's apartment, automatically dived for cover, the sound of a gun being discharged and bullets ricocheting off metal steps of a fire escape, making him decide that discretion was the better part of valour.

As he dived to the ground he barely noticed a figure, a shadow, flying past the junction, the man's feet pounding on the road, before stepping once again onto a pavement. But looking up, his breath almost stopped, the thought of vengeance making his heart skip a few beats; he recognised the figure, the running man's features suddenly illuminated by a street light before instantly disappearing once again into darkness.

"Fuck," he swore under his breath before racing back to Seamus "Quick Seamus," he yelled, "Its Willie, running as if the devil is on his tail; we need to find out if he killed Fergal before the Feds arrived. Get the fucking thing started and let's get the bastard."

Seamus fired up the pick-up, but all hell began to break loose as they exited the side street, the sounds of approaching sirens deafening the night air.

Despite Pat's angry protests, and a gun pointed at his temple, Seamus turned off in the opposite direction to the running Willie, the thought of not being with his beloved Enya overriding any thoughts of retribution or discipline to the cause. He was an American now and he wanted to stay that way.

Chapter 42

Fergal awoke gradually, totally confused as to his whereabouts, his nostrils being assailed by an unpleasant smell, the all-pervading odour that seems to be prevalent in most hospitals. As his eyes slowly focused he noticed a bedside table next to him adorned with a vase of fresh but weakly scented flowers, a combination of beautiful lilies and chrysanthemums (not that he would have known what kind of flowers they were), and there was a bowl of grapes.

His first ridiculous thought was that he hated grapes; they gave him the most abominable wind. His vision traversed the room and it gradually dawned on him that he must be in a hospital, then turning his head slightly to the right his eyes found Shannon sitting on a visitor's chair, leaning forward and smiling warmly but warily.

"Oh God, it's you," groaned Fergal turning his head away.

"Well, thank you, Mr misery-guts," she responded cheerfully, but her eyes clouded.

Without looking in her direction, he mumbled, "You used me; you work for the FBI!"

Shannon's smile disappeared; she was becoming a little peeved. "Oh grow up. Yes, I am an FBI agent and yes I was doing my job but I got to care for you – I don't know why – and I want to see you through this."

"Through this?" he childishly retorted, "It's finished, I lost. Willie's probably back in London as we speak, getting all my stuff and will be using the information to cause chaos. I'll have people from all sides after me now, that is, after I've been imprisoned and then deported from the USA."

"Have you finished?" Shannon asked affectionately, then grinned, "You'll be pleased to know that you're under FBI protection."

"Are you kidding?" he responded doubtfully, his eyes wandering past Shannon and staring blankly out of the window at a view of cloudy sky, a forlorn expression etched on his face. "How can this ever end?" Fergal sourly demanded, his eyes still staring ahead blankly.

"It seems that you were right about the FBI involvement in all this mess and Daniel was party to some of the machinations of Simon and his people. After Daniel was killed by Willie, Jim, my boss, gained access to Daniel's secret files. It took some unravelling and some deft work by one of our encryption specialists to deduce

Daniels's password, but his computer revealed a whole host of illegal activities, unfortunately none of which could prove a connection to President Morrison. Although Jim knew of President Morrison's support for Daniel's operation he never knew the depths that we were sinking to. Jim is a good man and purely wanted to work for the benefit of all sides."

"Surely there must be something that connects President Morrison to the operation?" demanded Fergal incredulously.

"I'm afraid not," her voice was full of undeniable regret. "Morrison was clever enough not to have put anything in writing. I'm sure Daniel must have had some cover, some protection, somewhere, but despite searching his office and ransacking his home we can't find anything. So, it seems that Morrison is off the hook."

"Bastard!"

"And the good news," she added mirthfully, "I will check on you from time to time."

"Oh, terrific," bitterly responded Fergal, his eyes wandering past Shannon. "Jesus, what a complicated mess!" Fergal focused his attention back to Shannon, thinking how attractive she looked.

Shannon was now dressed in her professional wardrobe of designer label, smart clothes, hair tied back and face fully made up. Although he had liked her before, in her streetwise dowdy disguises, currently she looked like a million dollars. Definitely out of his league, he thought with regret.

"So, what is going to happen; how is this going to work?" he asked plaintively.

Shannon cheerfully retorted, "Jim is going to arrange for a new identity for you, under a witness protection programme. Fergal, the ex-IRA man will disappear, and Fergal the good American citizen will be born."

"Wow, thank you." The years of being in fear of discovery dropped from his shoulders but Fergal's glee was instantly cut short, the thought of not seeing Shannon clouding his new found ebullience.

"And not only will I check on you from time to time, I will be your regular liaison, your contact!" Shannon concluded triumphantly, a broad smirk flying across her face.

Made in the USA
Charleston, SC
16 November 2016